Hunt

Kelsey's Burden Series: Book Eight

Crime Drama Series
KAYLIE HUNTER

This book is a work of fiction. All names, characters, places, businesses, incidents, etc., are the imagination of the author, and any resemblance to actual persons or otherwise is coincidental.

Copyright 2021 by Kaylie Hunter
All rights reserved.

Cover design by ebooklaunch.com

BOOKS BY KAYLIE

KELSEY'S BURDEN SERIES
LAYERED LIES
PAST HAUNTS
FRIENDS AND FOES
BLOOD AND TEARS
LOVE AND RAGE
DAY AND NIGHT
HEARTS AND ACES
HUNT AND PREY
HEROES AND HELLFIRE

STANDALONE NOVELS
SLIGHTLY OFF-BALANCE
DIAMOND'S EDGE

For an up-to-date book list, visit BooksByKaylie.com

Dedication

Happy 70th birthday, Mom!

Covid prevented me from throwing you a big surprise party, but at least I get to embarrass you here. Thank you for being my constant rock. You mean the world to me.

Love and kisses from your favorite child.

Chapter One

KELSEY
Sunday, 9:30 a.m.

The neck cramp I'd earned from staring through the scope for two hours with my head tilted wasn't half as miserable as the runny nose due to the rotting, soggy leaves piled beneath me. Cold, wet, and in desperate need of a tissue, I held my position and listened to Grady's familiar call, a squirrel's clucking, which alerted me that Team Alpha was getting closer.

Based on the fog-horn blasts that signaled when contestants were eliminated, Team Alpha was down to three players. Team Kelsey also had three players left.

At the start of the contest, we'd sent Trigger and Tech, guns blazing and thrashing loudly, into the woods ahead of us to take out as many rivals as they could while the rest of us advanced without concern of making noise. I knew we weren't as stealthy as the other team, so a solid strategy was our only chance to win. Somehow Tech and Trigger eliminated one of our rivals in the process, which was an unexpected bonus.

A half an hour later, the fog horn had sounded for Katie and Bridget who'd been our second line of offense. Both women were top-notch shooters and had eliminated three Alphas. And now here we were, even-Steven, with each team having three contestants still in the game.

I flinched as the silent woods erupted with the sound of gunfire. The shots came from the far left, where Jackson had set up a nest for himself. After he fired off three rounds, I heard both Grady and Donovan curse. Two more rounds were fired near Jackson's location.

"*Damn it*," Jackson yelled, followed by the rustling of leaves and branches. "How the hell did you sneak past me?"

Bones' deep chuckle sounded nearby. "I'm part Indian. It's in my blood."

Jackson muffled a few choice curses under his breath. "At least I got Donovan and Grady first."

"Like I need them." I could imagine him shrugging his indifference. "Kelsey's no threat in this setting."

"You always underestimate her," Jackson said before stomping loudly between the trees to catch up with Grady and Donovan.

Grady had the ability to sense when someone was watching him so I was careful not to watch them leave. Unfortunately, I was now facing in the *opposite direction* of where my target was. Bones being behind our line wasn't good. The woods had already lost their leaves and any movement would be easy to spot. Not to mention heard.

His statement that the woods were more his element than mine, while arrogant, was nonetheless true. He could win in a sneak attack against me all day long. My only hope of winning rested on the mere few seconds when the fog horn blasts went off, which would allow me to roll over and not be heard.

I rested my paintball rifle on the ground as silently as possible. Under the netting, I edged my right hand to my hip to grip my pistol. I waited as I listened to the noises behind me. Only a barely audible snap of a small twig alerted me that Bones was moving north, deeper into the woods.

As the fog horn sounded, I rolled to the right, sat up, and sighted my target. My movements caused Bones to turn, gun in hand. We both fired.

The paintball hit me square in the chest at the same time I heard Bones yell, "*Motherfucker*."

I laid myself back in the leaves, both groaning and laughing. I used my left hand to rub my bruised breast plate, not caring that I was smearing the neon green paint in the process.

Bones walked over and looked down at me. "Where the hell did you get camo netting?"

I laughed as I reached my green-coated hand out for him to pull me up. "Our girly pink t-shirts with glitter lettering are reversible. It's all camo and netting on this side. Itchy as hell, though."

"Bridget and Katie's idea?"

"Of course." I rotated my head in circles, trying to loosen the kinks in my neck. "How do you guys stay still for so long? It was unbearable."

"You get used to it." Bones gently shoved me toward the houses. "Donovan's going to be pissed when he sees us walk out together. At least we ended in a tie." He looked over his shoulder at me. "Team Alpha was three points ahead after the obstacle course this morning. We officially win the tournament."

I didn't say anything as we exited the woods. Team Kelsey saw both of us walk out and started cheering. Bones looked back at me again. I winked before turning toward Pops. "Two more blasts on the fog horn, please."

Pops signaled the horn that two more players were eliminated. Seconds later, Anne's gleeful shrieks were heard from the far end of the woods near the road.

"Son of a bitch!" Bones growled as he punched the air.

"Push-ups, Mr. Bones," Hattie said while hiding her giggle.

The look on Bones' face was murderous. Donovan's wasn't much happier. The rest of the men, including the men from other teams, grumbled their complaints or kicked at the grass.

Grady was the only one who seemed entertained, grinning at me. "You bet on our arrogance."

I shrugged. "You guys categorize people by threat level. And we all know Anne's shooting skills are lacking."

We'd left Anne in hiding to be our last man standing, covered under a layer of leaves and nets. Her only job was to count the fog horn blasts until they hit the number thirteen. Even if I wouldn't have eliminated Bones, the rules stated that once a player walked out of the woods, their participation in the competition was over. Our last hope of winning had been if team Alpha forgot about her or miscounted the fog horns and left the woods.

"Nicely done, cousin," Charlie said as she wrapped an arm around my shoulder.

As Team Alpha and the other teams cussed their way back toward Headquarters, Team Kelsey and family waited for Anne. When she emerged from the woods, she ran to Whiskey, jumped into his open arms, and wrapped her legs around him. She was laughing into the nook of his shoulder. He chuckled and started carrying her to the house as we all followed.

I was in desperate need of a shower and had already decided I was going to skip the singles competition for the

Circle of Hell, the fighting machine Carl had built. I was sore and tired from the long weekend. Besides, Donovan, Grady, and Bones had practiced for weeks. One of them deserved to win. Taking the team trophy was more than enough for me.

As we approached the house, Agent Kierson stepped out on the upper balcony.

"Shit," Charlie muttered beside me.

"Trouble in paradise?"

"I wasn't built for this relationship crap."

"Must be in our bloodline. I can't seem to figure it out either. Even before Grady cheated, the idea of marrying him freaked the crap out of me."

"You got further than I did. After living together for less than a week, I was contemplating setting him on fire while he slept."

"Damn." I laughed as we separated. I walked with everyone else through the basement slider entrance as Charlie turned off to meet Kierson at the bottom of the deck stairs.

"Everything okay?" Hattie asked me. "Agent Kierson looked upset."

"I don't think they're going to make it as a couple."

"That's too bad. I'd like to see Charlie settled with someone who makes her happy."

"Based on the violent thoughts she just shared, Kierson doesn't have what it takes to make her happy."

"Mom?" Nicholas interrupted as he slammed into my hip. "Can Sara and I go watch the fighting tournament?"

"Ah, Nick," I said, wiping the sweat off my forehead with my forearm. "I'm tired, muddy, and smelly. Can't we sit this one out?"

"Please, Aunt Kelsey?" Sara whined.

"I'll take them," Anne said, still grinning ear to ear. "I'll have Tyler drive us over."

"I'll go with them," Jackson offered. "Tyler can watch them long enough for me to take a shower, then I'll bodyguard the little monsters." He ruffled Nicholas' hair. "I'll bring them home after the tournament."

The second I agreed, the kids raced up the stairs in a loud commotion of giggles and laughter, with Anne hurrying after them. Hattie shook her head as she climbed the stairs at a slower pace. Pops walked up behind her, there to catch her if she slipped. She had been sick, but the new medicine she was taking was working its magic.

I looked over at Jackson who stood beside me, smiling. "You're not competing?"

"Nah. No point. Donovan or Bones will take the trophy, which is how it should be."

"What about Grady? You don't think he has a chance of winning?"

Jackson's face lit with mischief. "I'm still a little pissed at Grady for cheating on you." He wrapped an arm around my shoulder and steered me toward the stairs. "I shot that paintball straight at his bad shoulder. He'll be icing it the rest of the night."

While on a mission in Mexico to save his ex-wife Sebrina, Grady had been shot in the shoulder. The bullet went straight through and didn't cause any permanent damage. The aftermath of him and his ex-wife reuniting, though, murdered our relationship.

Grady claimed he was faking the relationship to protect the family. Stay close to the enemy and all that. Whether that was true or not, he took things too far when he chose to spend his nights with her in his dorm room.

I looked up at Jackson. "Thanks, brother," I said as I slugged him in the bicep.

"That's what family's for," he said as he shoved me ahead of him up the stairs.

Chapter Two

CHARLIE
Sunday, 10:02 a.m.

"Why are you here?" I asked as I approached Kierson.

"The better question is, why are *you* here? You were supposed to come back to Atlanta so we can make this relationship work." He carefully shifted his suit jacket away from his hips to place his fists there. The move rankled me. I mean, heaven forbid he'd chance being caught in wrinkled clothes, even while off-duty.

"You and me... we don't work." I glanced around to be sure everyone had cleared out.

"We just need more time."

I rubbed a hand on the back of my neck. "Jimmy, we are great in bed together. But the rest of the time—*is horrible*. We can't go five minutes without fighting. And not the good kind of fighting."

"Horrible is a pretty strong word. We've struggled, sure, but—"

"*We have nothing in common*! I like baseball. You like football. I like to cut loose on a dance floor. You like quiet evenings at home reading. I bend the law here and there, and you recite the rule book. We're just not compatible."

Kierson slid a hand around me, pulling me into his body as he cupped my face with the other hand. "I think we are."

"Then you're a fool," I whispered, pushing him away.

We both remained quiet for a long time. Kierson was an amazing man. I kept hoping that I could make it work with him, but it was like oil and water. And we both knew I was the oil.

"I'm sorry. But I'm done pretending," I said, finally looking back up at him. "I'm not the woman you're looking for."

I turned and climbed the hill to the front of the house, leaving him behind. In the front yard, I saw Katie reversing out the drive and waved to get her attention as I jogged over.

She stopped and rolled the window down. "You need to make a fast getaway?"

"Something like that. You going across the street?"

"Yup. Hop in. We've got room for one more."

"Where are the kids?" I asked Anne and Whiskey as I slid into the back seat with them.

"Already at Headquarters with Jackson and Tyler," Anne answered. "I needed a quick shower first. I stunk."

"Kelsey with them?"

Anne shook her head. "She wanted to soak in the tub until her skin wrinkled. She's ready for this weekend to be over."

"Between the tournament, the cartel, and all the shit with Grady and Sebrina, she deserves some down time."

"You forgot the part about Wild Card buying Nicholas a dog," Anne grumbled.

"Jager will be good for Nick." I fastened my seatbelt. "Is Wild Card on assignment for Aces?"

"He didn't say," Tech answered from the front passenger seat. "But I don't think so. He told Kelsey that a buddy of his called and needed help."

Katie stopped at the stop sign at the end of the private road, before looking over her shoulder at Anne. "Why are you so against Nicholas having a dog?"

"Nicholas isn't ready for a dog. He doesn't know the first thing about taking care of one."

"Which is why Wild Card asked Nightcrawler to teach him," Tech said. "And I agree with Charlie. Jager will be good for Nicholas. Besides, every boy should have a dog. Especially a boy who lost three years of his childhood and is now dealing with this Grady crap."

Whiskey chuckled as he wrapped an arm around Anne's shoulders. "She knows all that. She's just frustrated that Sara's now begging for a cat."

"I hate cats," Anne said as she shivered. "They act all passive, but you know they're plotting against you." She looked at me and held up two fingers, gesturing toward her eyes. "You have to watch their eyes. They're always planning. Preparing to pounce."

I laughed at the same time Katie gunned the gas pedal to turn onto the highway. I grabbed the door handle to brace myself as I looked at Anne. "You're scared of cats? Why?"

"They're predators," Anne said. "They hunt and kill while we sleep. One day, they'll turn against all of us. Just wait."

Katie stopped again in the center turn lane with her blinker on to turn left into Headquarters. She looked at Anne in the rearview mirror. "What the hell have you been smoking?"

"They're evil," Anne muttered as she crossed her arms over her chest.

"Just tell Sara no," Tech said, leaning around the seat to look at Anne.

"How am I supposed to tell her no after Nicholas got a dog?"

"Buy her a rabbit?" I asked as Katie made a sharp left turn, sliding both Anne and me toward Whiskey in the back seat. As I pulled myself erect and shuffled back to my side of the seat, I added, "Or fish?"

Whiskey leaned forward to look at me. "We've tried fish. They all died. And I'm not sure a rabbit would be a good idea with Jager around. Sara would be scarred for life if she watched Jager kill her pet rabbit."

Katie parked the SUV, and we all climbed out.

"What about a parrot?" Tech asked as he reached for Katie's hand. "I always wanted a parrot when I was a kid. Sara could teach it to talk."

"That's a good idea, actually," Katie said, looking up at Tech as we walked across the parking lot. "And when it starts to annoy all of us, we can throw a towel over the cage to shut it up."

Anne looked over at Whiskey. Whiskey shrugged as he threw an arm around her waist. "Might work. And changing the paper in the bottom of a cage beats the hell out of scooping poop from a litter box."

Tech held the door to Headquarters open as we all filed inside.

Anne waved and said over her shoulder, "I'll catch up with you guys. I'm heading to the War Room to shop for birds."

I followed beside Whiskey as we made our way across the gym. We stopped at the food table to pile up plates before we ventured to the basement where fifty men and women screamed for the contestant fighting in the *Circle of Hell*. I didn't know the guy competing, but Carl's manikins were beating the tar out of him.

This was the environment I belonged in: sweat, muscles, cursing... *and bloody knuckles.* Hell, this was the world I *thrived* in.

Chapter Three

KELSEY
Monday, 7:00 a.m.

After sneaking off to bed before anyone returned from the tournament, I clocked a solid ten hours of deep sleep. I woke to the sound of Jager whining loudly from another room. Feeling renewed, I slid into my robe, stuffed one of my Glocks into its oversized pocket, and walked down the hallway, dragging my fingers through my knotted hair.

"What is it, Jager?" I asked, spotting the dog by the kitchen door.

The German Shepard looked at me, then the door, then back at me as he whined again.

"You want outside?" I opened the door and followed him out into the cold.

He ran through the garage and into the side yard, pausing to squat over the patch of grass that had already been stripped of color. I heard a noise behind me and turned to see Tyler walk through the back door of the garage.

"Nick still sleeping?" he asked as he walked toward me.

"I imagine so," I said, wrapping my robe tighter around me to keep out the frosty air. "I just woke up myself."

"Jackson let the kids stay up for the full tournament. Didn't finish until near one in the morning." Tyler glanced over at me, checking my reaction.

"I'm okay with that." We walked further into the driveway to watch Jager as he ran around the yard, stretching his legs. "The kids needed the tournament just as much as the adults. A break from our everyday serious life. And staying up past bedtime on occasion is part of the fun of being a kid."

"Makes sense." Tyler offered me a cigarette from his pack.

I shook my head no. "Who won the tournament?"

"Bones." Tyler smiled broadly. "And Donovan took second place, but he's not a happy camper."

I inhaled Tyler's second-hand smoke, enjoying the familiarity of the toxins. "It ended the way it should've then. In a few short years, Bones and Donovan will be pushed out by the younger guys. I'm glad they got to show off while they're still in top shape." I shivered, pulling the robe's collar tighter against my neck.

"I suppose, but I'm not looking forward to listening to them brag for the next year." He tipped his head toward the house. "Head inside and get warm. Jager can make the rounds with me."

"Works for me. I'll have a pot of coffee ready when you're done making the circuit."

Tyler whistled for Jager as I turned back to the kitchen door. Stepping inside, I found Charlie sitting at the breakfast bar, sipping a cup of coffee. She patted the chair next to her where another cup sat waiting for me on the bar top. As I walked around the counter to sit, I spotted her duffle by the front door.

"You're leaving?"

Charlie set her cup down. "I have a flight out this morning. I'm heading back to Miami."

"Are you sure you don't want to stay a few more days? Thanksgiving is this Thursday."

"I promised Aunt Suzanne I'd spend Thanksgiving with them. Besides, it's time. I'm ready to go home."

"Is that where home is for you? Miami?"

"I think so," Charlie said. "I miss it. The heat. The sandy beaches. The dance clubs. Hell, I miss the odd smell of melted pavement and coconut oil."

"You must be homesick," I said, laughing. "You going back to the precinct? Going to wear the badge again?"

"I'm not sure. I'm officially still on leave for beating the snot out of my father—or rather my uncle, I guess." She shook her head at the complexity of our family tree. Neither one of us had wrapped our heads around the discovery that we were sisters, not cousins. "They want me to have a psych eval." She wrinkled her nose.

"Piece of cake. You only have to prove you're not a danger to yourself or others."

"Yeah, I know." She stared off toward the kitchen, not looking at anything in particular.

"Then what's the problem?"

She sighed, once again setting her coffee cup down. "You used to love Miami. We'd laugh... dance... go rollerblading... Or we'd sneak out to the beach in the middle of the night, lay in the sand, and talk for hours." She shrugged, looking away. "Even after you adopted Nicholas, we found plenty of things to do as a family." She glanced up at me, her eyes full of unshed tears. "It all changed after Nicholas was taken. I get why it had to, but I thought that when it was over, you'd come home."

I set my own cup down and wrapped my arms around her. "I did, too. I really did. But that was a lifetime ago, Kid." I rubbed circles on her back like I did when we were younger. "The thought of taking Nicholas back to that city... It scares the hell out of me."

Charlie nodded, but remained silent.

"We'll figure out a better way, okay? A better way for us to visit more often. And we can video chat each other. I don't want us to drift apart either."

She pulled away, sliding off her stool and standing. "Yeah. We'll figure it out," she said in a tight voice. She grabbed her bag and turned toward the door. Without looking back, she paused with her hand on the doorknob. "Kelsey?"

"Yes?"

"You're the best sister a girl could ask for."

My hand shook as I raised it to my chest, placing it over my heart. "Right back at ya, Kid."

She left, closing the door behind her.

I felt the warm tears on my cheeks as I sensed Hattie walking up behind me. She wrapped both arms around me, but didn't say anything. She didn't have to. Her presence alone gave me the strength I needed not to chase after Charlie and beg her to stay.

Chapter Four

CHARLIE
Two Weeks Later… Saturday, 11:25 p.m.

The lights flashed and spun in wild circles as the heavy base of the music thumped the floor beneath my feet. A middle-aged man wearing a suit, his tie still noosed around his neck, danced tight against my back. In front, a younger man—likely still in college—shimmied as he bunched his t-shirt, exposing his ripped abs. I smiled at the younger man as I lifted my arms to rest my wrists against the tops of his shoulders as we gyrated our bodies together. Working out on the dance floor beat the hell out of any elliptical bike or stair climber.

My skin, damp from hours of dancing, tingled as the air-conditioned current squeezed between the bodies to reach me. I didn't mind the heat, though. After years of being a cop and having to wear polyester pants during numerous heatwaves, I was used to it.

The young buck in front of me grazed his hand across my breast. I knocked it away and continued to dance. The man behind me skated his fingers up my left thigh. That was my cue to move on. Slipping away into the thick crowd, I relocated to the other side of the dance floor where a bridal party was whooping it up. The bride took an interest and started to dance with me. I didn't mind dancing with a woman—though it did nothing for me. I continued to dance with her for two more songs, before disappearing again, this time moving toward the VIP elevator. It was getting late and the crowd was reaching that handsy stage of intoxication.

As I approached the elevator, I smiled at the security guard. Without turning, he reached back and pushed the up button. His eyes, though, narrowed at something behind me. Glancing back, I saw that Mr. Suit and Tie had followed. I shook my head no to the guard. He squared off to block the guy as I stepped into the elevator. And although it was mean, I waved at Mr. Suit and Tie as the elevator doors closed.

"You've been dancing for three hours without pause. Bad day?" Baker's voice asked over the elevator intercom.

Baker was the manager and part owner of the club. Since I was one of his silent partners, he kept close tabs on me from the security cameras when I visited.

"Watching me again, Baker?" I answered, smiling up at the camera. "We talked about your stalker tendencies. They're creepy—even in a sex club."

"If you didn't want men watching you, you shouldn't wear a barely-there red dress."

I looked down at my dress and laughed. The halter top wrapped around my neck, leaving my entire back exposed. In the front, the fabric folded in vertical layers over my breasts, leaving the skin between exposed to my navel. The dress was short, but not so short I had to worry about sitting. And the heels that matched were flashy, but had arches that molded to my feet. "I do look hot."

Baker's laugh echoed off the elevator walls. "And you sound vain."

"It's not vanity. It's knowing how to dress to fit your body."

"And thankfully you have a body that's also good for business. Every man and most of the women couldn't take their eyes off you."

The elevator opened on level three, otherwise known as The Parlor, and I held my hand out to keep the doors open. "Are you coming down from your tower for a drink?"

"Give me ten minutes or so. I have some activity I'm monitoring in one of the rooms that might need my interference. In the meantime, check on Evie for me."

I looked across the room to the bar. Evie was one of the weekend bartenders and was currently serving a drink to a guy. "Why? She seems fine."

"She always seems fine. Just keep an eye on her."

"Whatever." I stepped through the doors.

The first and second floors of the building were open to the public, that was, if you arrived early to stand in line for an hour and security deemed you worthy of entering at all. The long line down the block allowed for them to be picky. The Parlor, an oversized bar with deep leather booths, fancy chandeliers, and five-star service, was for members only and took up most of the third floor. One entire wall was made of glass and overlooked a section of the dance floor two levels down.

The fourth and fifth floors, well... Those consisted of all kinds of naughty sexual play and would cost most people a small fortune to access. And because the laws changed so regularly as to what was legal and what could land our asses in prison, Baker had a lawyer who monitored all city and state regulations. Since I was a business partner who was also a cop, Baker always kept things clearly on the side of legal and didn't push the boundaries too hard. The legal boundaries at least. The moral boundaries were the reason I kept my ownership status private, especially when I was in uniform.

Since my first job delivering newspapers, I'd pooled my money with Kelsey in various investments. She had a knack for knowing which businesses would turn a profit. By the time we partnered with Baker, we were able to buy the entire building, renovating each floor as the club's success grew.

The Outer Layer, as the club was named, became one of Miami's hotspots for dancing and the upper floors became *the* place to go for the rich and perverted. And while I enjoyed being a cop, my financial freedom allowed me to take regular leaves from work to spend my time pursuing other interests as I saw fit.

"Good evening, Ms. Harrison," Evie greeted me as I approached the bar.

She placed a crystal glass filled with ice water on top of a coaster in front of the end stool where I typically sat. Even with two security guards in the room and numerous cameras, I still lacked the ability to sit with my back turned toward others. I had my father to thank for that paranoia—*the bastard*.

"Good evening, Evie," I said as I claimed my stool. "How's tricks?"

She flashed her blinding smile my way as she laughed. She'd told me once that she got a lot of crap for working at a sex club. People often mistook her employment as being a prostitute or a stripper. Being she worked on one of the member-only floors, the general population could only speculate as to what transgressed on the upper levels. If they could access the floor, they'd see her uniform consisted of a crisp white, button-up blouse and a simple black pencil skirt that ended just above the knee.

"It's slow tonight, but tips are up, so all is well," she said, leaning her elbows onto the bar. "How about you? Did you break all the men's hearts downstairs with your teasing?"

"Teasing? *Please*. If there was a man worth pursuing, I'd be all over it. I need to get laid." I tipped my head toward the all-glass wall. "The most tempting offer I saw down there was a wanna-be banker with a tan line around his ring finger."

She shuddered. "Yuck. Bankers are the worst."

A man who'd been eavesdropping from the other end of the bar, stood, preparing to walk our way. I held up a hand to stop his forward motion, and scanned him, not-so-discreetly, from head to toe. "Not even if I was desperate," I said loud enough for him to hear.

He sat down, disappointment dragging his face downward.

"Play nice, Kid," Evie said to me as she walked down the length of the bar. "Bobby here is going to make some lucky lady very happy someday soon. He's a catch." She reached over the bar and pinched his chubby cheek.

He blushed.

Oh, boy. He must be one hell of a tipper. I took another long drink of my water before moving it to the other side of the bar top. Evie would exchange it for a real drink when she returned. I scanned the room while I waited. Several of the booths had customers, varying in groups from two to eight. Only one of the center tables was occupied. And they had clearly been here for a while based on their glassy eyes and loud conversations.

"Are you staying for a while? I need to I cut them off." Evie said from the other side of the bar, nodding toward the center table.

"I'll jump in if needed, but this dress wasn't made for bar brawls. Best to give them a warning and have security on standby."

"One of them is a senator's son," Evie whispered. "I'm less worried about a fight than I am of getting sued."

I snorted. "Is his father a member?"

"Yeah. Doesn't come in often, but he's a VIP to this floor."

"Have Baker call *Daddy* and tell him it's past his son's bedtime."

Evie raised an eyebrow but reached for the six-line phone behind the bar, calling Baker. It was a short call, and we both waited to see what happened next. The young man at the end of the table lifted his phone when it started to ring. He must have hit the ignore button though, because he set it down without answering and continued telling a loud and offensive joke. Ten seconds later he picked up his phone again and as he read the screen, he stood, looking pale. He pulled a credit card from his wallet and flashed it at a nearby server. When the server disappeared with his card, he told his friends it was time to leave. Within five minutes, the entire group stepped into the elevator.

"Damn," Evie said, laughing as she set a glass of whiskey in front of me. "He's a grown ass man."

I lifted my glass, but paused before taking a drink. "A grown ass man who's likely living off Daddy's bank account."

I felt eyes watching me and glanced around.

The corner booth, the first booth along the glass wall, was occupied by a tall, muscular man with dark features. He sat alone, drinking a beer. When I spotted him watching us, he quickly turned to peer out the window.

"Who's that? I don't recognize him."

"He just started coming in this week," Evie said. "He might be a voyeur, but he must not be able to afford the membership fees for the upper floors. I keep catching him watching me. It's kind of spooky, but security's keeping tabs on him."

"Pull his name off his membership card. I'll run a background."

"No need," Baker said, sitting on the barstool next to me. He tossed a file on top of the bar. "My computer guy spent two days digging, and what little he found doesn't ring true."

I opened the file and rifled through the usual birth records, driver's license information, and employment history. The man claimed to be a wealthy real estate developer, but I spotted two red flags right away. One, I'd met plenty of real estate developers during my years working with my cousin to build our investments, and they typically spent a lot of energy looking and sounding like they were brimming with cash. This guy's suit was at least a decade old, and he was sitting alone instead of trying to chase the next deal. Two, I knew for a fact that he didn't own the small retail mall in Pompano Beach that was listed in the file as part of his portfolio, because it just so happened that it was owned by a shell company my cousin and I owned.

I closed the file and slid it back to Baker. "I'll handle it."

"He's been in here four nights this week."

"I said I'd handle it," I repeated, raising an eyebrow at Baker.

"If you do something stupid because of the club, Kelsey will kill me."

"Kid?" Evie laughed as she set a glass of bourbon in front of Baker. "Do something stupid?"

I narrowed my eyes in pretend scorn for the use of my childhood nickname. Kelsey had donned me the moniker of *Kid* during the years she'd raised me. Back when she was also a cop in Miami, enough people between work and our investment connections had heard the nickname that many weren't aware my legal name was Charlie. I was simply Kid, Kid Harrison, or Harrison. "If I paid you, would you call me Charlie?"

"Hell, no." Evie grinned as she wiped down the bar. "It's too much fun watching you squirm in discomfort every time I call you Kid."

"I need to go," Baker said, reading something on his phone. "Problem in playroom four." He stood, downed his drink, and walked briskly toward the elevators.

"And he's off again," Evie said, shaking her head. "I don't think I've ever seen him relax."

"We should snag his phone and hide it from him. See what happens."

"His head would spin," she said, laughing. "He probably sleeps with the damn thing."

I knew for a fact that he *did* sleep with his phone, though I wasn't about to tell her. It was obvious by the way her eyes kept wandering back to the elevator that she had a crush on Baker. And while he and I had shared an odd friendship that included the occasional mattress pounding, neither of us had ever entertained thoughts of romance. The physical history between us was a mutual itch scratching of sorts with the bonus of pissing off my overbearing cousin who believed it was inappropriate for me to sleep with our business partner. And our lawyer... and our real estate agent... and maybe a few others.

Instead of upsetting Evie with the truth, I replied '*probably*' as I pulled a twenty from my clutch purse, tossing it on the bar. "That's for you. Put my drink on my account."

"Are you leaving already?"

I glanced across the room at the man in the booth. He quickly looked away again. "Yeah. I have something to take care of." I waved goodbye to Evie as I walked toward the elevator.

CHAPTER FIVE

CHARLIE
Saturday, 11:55 p.m.

Sliding my membership card into the security slot of the elevator, I pushed the five on the panel for the fifth floor. All the keycards were programmed for the corresponding floors a member could access. Without the card, the elevator wouldn't let me past the second floor.

When Baker originally designed the access system, I had asked him to program my cousin and my keycards with *Extreme VIP* instead of our names. My reasoning was that it wasn't anyone's business who we were. And while most of the staff knew I was associated with the club in some way, they assumed I worked for Baker because I maintained a small private office next to his. The few who knew my name also knew I was a cop and understood my need for discretion. And even those small few didn't know I owned part of the club, though I suspected Evie had guessed.

I exited the elevator and turned down the hall. On my way, I looked through the one-way glass windows to the playrooms below on the fourth floor. One sex actor was earning his money the hard way. I chuckled as the female actor slapped his bare ass with a wooden paddle. I shook my head as I stopped to swipe my keycard to enter my office.

Though I kept an office, I didn't work at the club. Yes, I reviewed the quarterly financial statements before forwarding them to the accountant, but I normally did those bookkeeping activities from the comfort of my couch with my laptop balanced on my lap. This space was less of an office and more of an oversized closet, used for changing into either my evening slut-wear or one of my undercover outfits for nights like tonight.

I rolled my eyes, noticing that Baker had once again tasked someone with cleaning my room. The clothes I'd left scattered on the floor or draped over chairs were wrapped in dry-cleaning bags and hung in the closet. I flipped the halter neck of my dress over my head and shimmied out of it, grinning as I left the dress, along with the shoes, in a pile on the floor. I shuffled several hangers around until I found a pair of faded jeans, a well-worn dark-colored Miami Dolphin's t-shirt, and a scraggly pair of slip-on tennis shoes.

The best part of being on leave from work was not having to worry about my badge getting in the way when I was about to do something illegal. On the off chance I got caught, giving the police department the option of saying I was on leave when the crime occurred sat comfortably within my *I'm a good person* scale. That wasn't to say I hadn't broken a law or two while wearing the badge. I had just been more careful when doing so.

Unlocking the two-door steel cabinet with the key I kept hidden, I selected a waist-clip holster and a Glock 17, snapping the holster on before sliding the gun in place. Tugging my t-shirt over it, I moved to the vanity and selected a few makeup-remover pads. I wiped the eyeshadow and eyeliner off before pulling my hair into a ratty ponytail. Glancing in the mirror, I rubbed some leftover mascara under my eyes to leave dark smeared circles. I pulled a few sections of hair from the ponytail to have them wisp out in a crazy pattern. I looked strung out, which was perfect. Unless you were a cop, people tended to avoid eye contact with druggies, turning their eyes away as they hurried across the street to safety.

From the peg board on the wall, I selected the keys to the old, rusted-out Toyota short-bed truck which I stored in the city's parking ramp across the street. My everyday car was a drab cop-like dark sedan, bland on the outside but with all the electronic bells and whistles inside, including a souped-up engine under the hood. Then there was my baby: a metallic silver Mustang convertible I kept stored in the club's private parking ramp.

I glanced longingly at the keys to the Mustang before turning away with the short-bed's keys in hand. Exiting my office, I used my keycard to enter Baker's office.

"You look ridiculous," Baker said, barely glancing up from his stack of paperwork.

"Where did our guy from the Parlor park tonight?" I asked as I walked past the wall of security monitors toward Baker's mini-bar.

"He comes and goes from the city's parking ramp. That's all I know. The security team wasn't able to identify his car or plate." He looked up, setting his pen down. "Are you really going to do this?"

I shrugged, pouring a shot of whiskey into a glass. "He's obviously up to something. For Evie's sake, we need to figure out what he's doing."

"Evie is safe. I have a security guard watching her when she's here, and I can hire someone to watch her when she's not."

"Or I can do my thing and make the problem go away."

"You sound like a hitman."

I smirked at him as I sipped my drink.

He reached up and massaged his neck, likely trying to loosen the tension knots, as he leaned back in his executive chair. "Fine. Handle it your way. Are you coming back tonight?"

What he was really asking me was if I wanted to have sex tonight. Somehow knowing Evie had a crush on him made the invitation seem less appealing. "No. I better go home and water the plants. Maybe you should ask Evie to join you tonight." I smirked at him before turning away to look at the monitors. "For some crazy reason, she seems to like you. You should explore that avenue."

"You know I don't sleep with employees. Besides, Evie isn't the type of woman who'd agree to a no-strings relationship."

"Maybe it's time you try something new," I said, downing the rest of my drink. "Must get lonely up here in your tower."

"I have plenty of company." Baker lifted his phone. "Besides, Magenta texted me earlier to tell me she was bored."

I snorted. "Magenta? Do you even know her real name?"

"That is her real name," Baker said, not bothering to try to hide his smile. "She has a brother named Maroon."

"You're hopeless," I said, shaking my head and setting my empty glass on the mini-bar. "I'm out of here. Text me when our creepy guy leaves."

Before taking a single step, his phone vibrated from his blazer pocket. He pulled it out and read the display. "Your creeper is asking for his bill."

I started for the corner door which led to a private staircase and exit. "You should reconsider taking Evie for a spin. She might surprise you."

"Goodnight, Kid," Baker said dismissively.

I laughed as I entered the private staircase and started running down the five flights of stairs. By the last step, I was winded but happy to be wearing my tennis shoes and not the heels I'd worn earlier. I exited the door and stepped into the strangling humidity. I joined the small crowd at the street corner, crossing the street with them when the light changed.

One of the women glanced over her shoulder at me before tugging her man's arm to hurry into the parking ramp. I snorted as I took the stairs to the third level. Making quick work of getting to my truck and moving it to the first level, closer to the exit, I waited for my mark. Ten minutes later, the guy from the bar drove past me in a white truck. I let another car pass before I followed him from the parking ramp. When the car between us turned two streets later, I took a picture with my cellphone of his license plate.

If I was more like Kelsey, I'd go home now and run the plate, preparing for a confrontation in the future. But I wasn't my cousin. I was the impulsive one, thus why I continued to follow him, though I backed off enough for another car to change lanes and drive between us.

I continued to follow him for a dozen or more city blocks and then onto Highway 41 before changing lanes and following him onto North Highway 9 toward Brownsville. I kept my distance, keeping him several cars ahead of me at one point, but after we exited we drove into a residential area that left me nowhere to hide.

Not wanting to be spotted, I pulled into a random driveway, hoping the homeowner wouldn't wake at hearing a vehicle. I shut the truck off, including the lights, as I watched my target drive two more blocks before turning left. I restarted the truck at the same time the porch light came on for the house in front of me. I waved at the homeowner, a man in his late sixties wearing nothing more than a pair of boxers, as I reversed from his driveway.

Hurrying down the road, I made the left turn then drove slowly, looking at the vehicles parked in the narrow driveways. At the seventh house I spotted his white truck. I observed the house as I drove past. The lights were off and there was no blue glow from a television. All signs pointed to him calling it a night and going to bed. I turned at the next intersection and parked around the corner along the street.

Some of the residential blocks in Brownsville were decorated with accent lights, featured a plethora of white iron fences, and had yards decked out with rich landscaping. Some even sported the occasional two-story house. This guy's neighborhood wasn't one of those.

Every house was a rectangular one-story with the narrow end of the house closest to the road and only a small patch of spotty grass between the front door and a cheap metal fence. There were no sidewalks on his block, nor marked street parking. About every twenty feet was a posted sign, warning citizens not to dump their trash or they'd be subject to hefty fines. An old mattress leaned against one of those sign posts not twelve feet away from where I'd parked.

I checked my phone as I waited. My cousin Kelsey had texted twice, just asking if I was alive and well. I responded that I was fine, but busy working a case. She didn't need to know I only worked a few months a year these days. She'd worry. And the last thing I needed was my older cousin flying down to check on me, or worse, calling Uncle Hank so they could talk about me behind my back.

Uncle Hank wasn't really an uncle but a cop who'd taken us under his wing when we first moved to Florida. Since Kelsey had left, Uncle Hank and Aunt Suzanne had fully infiltrated my life. I both loved it and hated it. It's a nice feeling to have people care about you, but at the same time it feels invasive and smothering.

Headlights turned onto the road behind me and a black-and-white patrol car pulled up alongside my truck. I pulled my wallet from my bag, flashing my badge toward the officer driving. He drove onward without stopping to ask why I was dressed like a junkie and sitting in a rotting pickup at the edge of a subpar neighborhood. Guess he had better things to do.

Deciding I'd waited long enough, I tugged on a pair of nude-toned gloves, set my phone to silent, and grabbed my crossover handbag from the narrow space behind the passenger seat. Inside the bag were all the supplies I needed other than the gun which was already clipped on my waistband. The safer move would be to leave and return when he wasn't home, but playing it safe was boring.

I slid out from the truck and jogged past several houses before ducking behind my target's carport. Now taking my time, I walked the perimeter of the small rectangular house, keeping my distance from the windows. All the lights were off. I crept up the front porch, picking the lock with the tools from my bag. When I stepped inside, I was greeted by a low growl, only a few feet from where I stood in the pitch-black room.

I knew by the sound of the growling that the dog was large. I should've been scared. I suppose a normal person would be. But dogs liked me. Maybe because they sensed that I wouldn't hurt them. Maybe it was because they were curious as to why I wasn't afraid. Maybe it was because I carried treats. Moving cautiously, I sat cross legged on the floor and pulled a dog treat from my bag. I held the treat out, palm up, in front of me.

With my hand stretched out into the blackness, I waited for the low growling to stop and the snuffling sound to move closer. In less than a minute, the dog had taken the treat and continued to sniff me until his snout was snuffling my hair. I scratched his big block-shaped head and behind his ears. He laid a front paw on my lap, leaning his big body against my chest, nearly knocking me over as I patted him.

"Good boy," I whispered as I slid on night vision goggles and glanced around the room.

The front room was an unkept sitting area with an old couch along one wall, stacks of empty takeout on the table, dirty socks on the floor, and a thirty-inch TV in the far corner. The next room back was a small kitchen with a hallway on the far side. Based on the stacks of paperwork and files on the kitchen table, I wouldn't need to venture down the hallway.

I fed the large dog, a rottweiler by the looks of it through the night-vision goggles, another treat as I climbed up from the floor. He followed me over to the table where I sifted through the pictures of Evie and read the background information the man stalking her had. She grew up in Georgia which I already knew based on her faint Georgian accent. She'd moved to Miami about six months ago and took a job at the club shortly after settling. Evie lived alone in a small condo building in the better part of Little Havana. She was taking marketing classes at the community college, and based on the surveillance photos of her eating out and going to the local coffee shop, she didn't seem to have many friends. Her living such an isolated life seemed odd. Unlike me, Evie had a friendly, outgoing personality and was quick to make people feel at ease. So where were her friends?

I picked up an application from a private investigator's office, Spencer Investigations, which I found completely uninspiring for a PI company name. The application appeared to have been completed online using PDF field inputs. The next page was a printout of the receipt for a credit card payment. The amount paid was listed as a down payment with a hefty final payment due upon a missing person's whereabouts.

I flipped back to the application and read the description of the missing person which fit Evie to a T, but named the person as Genevieve Lawrence. *Shit*. Evie wasn't being stalked by this guy. Someone had hired him to find her. And by the looks of it, that someone had deep pockets and was very motivated, which in my book was worse.

Deep into reading the paperwork, I was startled by the ringing of a cellphone lying on the table in front of me. I glanced at the backlit screen which read: *Asshole* is calling.

Hearing footsteps hurrying down the hall, I jumped back and looked around the room. There was nowhere to hide. No closets. No partial walls. No fake Ficus trees. I scurried over to the kitchen counter, climbing on top of it and shrinking back as far as possible beside the refrigerator. I took off the night-vision goggles and pulled my gun. The man came rushing into the room and turned on the kitchen light.

"Hello?" he said, answering his phone.

I peeked around the refrigerator, but only got a quick glance of a naked body before I tucked my head back again. The dog, who was indeed a black and tan rottweiler, sat on the kitchen floor, watching both his owner and me. I gave the dog the evil eye, hoping he wouldn't give away my location, as I kept an ear to the one-sided conversation.

"No, I haven't confirmed it's her yet. I should know by tomorrow, the day after at the latest." There was a short pause before he spoke again. "No. You'll need to wait until I confirm it's her. It could be a lookalike. It happens a lot in this business." Another pause. "Yes, I'll call when I know."

He tossed the phone onto the table and then did something I wasn't expecting—he turned and opened the refrigerator. We stood staring at each other, neither of us moving. Of course, I had my gun pointed at him and he was not only unarmed, but *completely naked*.

"Don't believe in jammies?" I asked, sliding off the counter and keeping my gun pointed in his direction.

He glanced over his shoulder at his dog. "How the hell did you get in my house?"

"Lock pick set and doggy treats. Your dog really likes the peanut butter snacks."

He pulled two beers from the refrigerator. "I'm going to sit and drink a beer. My gun is in the bedroom so you can either join me or shoot me. I don't recommend shooting, though. Gunshots scare Beast. He'll pee all over the floor."

Without taking my eyes off him, I tossed him a dishtowel from the counter. "In case you want to cover up."

He tossed the towel back on the counter before moving to the table and sitting with his back against the wall. He uncapped both beers, setting one in front of the chair on the other side of the table.

I raised an eyebrow as I watched him. "You don't seem too concerned to find me here."

He shrugged. "I recognized you earlier at the club when you were talking to Evie. Kid Harrison. Half cop. Half criminal. You have one hell of a following, but as far as the stories go, you've never killed an unarmed man."

"Who are you?" I asked, though I was confident I'd already figured it out.

"Russell Spencer, private investigator." He took a casual drink of his beer.

"Why are you following Evie?"

"I was hired to find her."

"I saw the contract." I looked around the small house. "I know you could use the money so why are you stalling to tell your client about Evie?"

He sighed, rubbing a hand down his face. "Fucking conscience. One phone call and I could collect my money, but I get the feeling this guy is lying about why he's looking for her."

"What story did he give you?"

Russell motioned toward the file. "Didn't get that far in your reading?"

I laughed, holstering my gun as I walked over and sat. "If it weren't for the phone call, I could've been in and out with you none the wiser. Normal people take their phones with them to the bedroom."

"Hate the damn things. You know some say they cause brain cancer."

"And plenty of other studies have proven they don't."

"Why risk it?"

"I'm more likely to die from a bullet, so I'm not concerned. Tell me about your client, Mr. Spencer." I lifted my beer and took a drink.

"Call me Spence, and I don't know much. It was easier finding Genevieve than ID my client."

"Credit card search?"

He shook his head. "Prepaid card registered in Georgia."

"IP address from the online application?"

"Blocked."

"What about the phone number?" I asked, nodding toward his phone.

"Burner phone. From his voice, I'd guess he's in his forties or fifties, no accent but well spoken. Educated. Polished vocabulary."

"So... you narrowed it down to a middle-aged man who likely went to college? That's it?"

"Yup."

"You're not very good at your job, are you?" I hid my grin behind my beer bottle as I took another drink.

"Is that a challenge?" he asked.

"No. Only an observation."

He leaned slightly forward, a crooked grin lightening his facial features. "Honey, I've got skills that would wet your panties, but this guy is a ghost."

I leaned back in my chair, shaking my head in annoyance. "You call me *honey* again, and I'll break your fingers, one by one. Now what excuse did your client give you when he hired you to find Evie?"

He laughed before taking the last drink of his beer and setting the bottle in the middle of the table. "Said he was trying to find his cousin after a family fallout, but he's pushing a little too hard just to reconnect with a cousin." He waved a hand at the files. "I need sleep. Feel free to either join me or stay up reading my case notes." He stood, his semi-erect penis bouncing at eye level in front of me. "Though," he said leaning over with one hand braced on the back of my chair as he used the other hand to skate a finger down my neck, "I'm hoping you'll join me."

"Not happening," I said, knocking his hand away.

"Suit yourself," he said as he strutted his naked ass down the hall and into the dark bedroom.

Chapter Six

CHARLIE
Sunday, 3:46 a.m.

Spence offering to let me read his case notes was appreciated. Though, he never said I had to read everything at his house. I smiled to myself all the way home with the stack of folders and his phone sitting in my passenger seat.

Entering my apartment, I piled the files on my rickety dining room table before returning downstairs to empty my mailbox. Pauly, a homeless man from the neighborhood, was curled up under the stairs with a blanket draped over his head. Knowing he was harmless, I let him be and returned to my apartment. After a quick shower, I changed into yoga pants and a pink Nike t-shirt before settling at the table to read everything thoroughly.

Near sunup, I was about to go to bed when someone knocked on my apartment door. Looking through the peep hole, I saw Uncle Hank standing on the other side, grinning back at me. He was in full uniform. His trainee of the day stood beside him with a confused expression.

I unlocked and opened the door before turning toward the kitchen. "Give me a minute to start a pot of coffee."

"Let me guess, you haven't been to bed yet," Uncle Hank said as he walked in, followed by the rookie.

I dumped the last of the coffee grounds into the basket and poured the water into the reserve. "I went to the club last night and was asked to check into one of the new customers. Turns out, he's a private investigator—Russell Spencer. You heard of him?"

As the coffee pot started brewing, I joined Uncle Hank at the table. The rookie stood off to the side, nervously glancing back at the still open door.

"Yeah, I've run into Spence a few times. Seems like a straight shooter. Why? What's your beef with him?" Uncle Hank asked as he pulled some photos of Evie from one of the folders and started studying them.

"Now that I know he's working a case and not stalking Evie—I don't have a problem with him. Evie's a bartender at the club. Someone hired Spence to find her, but he's getting a bad vibe about his anonymous client. He's leery of telling him where she is."

"Anonymous, huh? That don't sound good."

"Agreed. I have a guy trying to trace the client's burner phone, but it's powered off at the moment."

"Spence always struck me as someone with good instincts. If he's got a bad vibe about this guy, you better warn this girl. And fast. Rumor has it, Spence is overextended. Eventually he'll cave for the payday."

"Gambling, drugs, or child support?" I asked as I walked back into the kitchen to fill coffee cups.

"None of the above. His sister had bone cancer and died last spring. He paid all her bills, including the funeral. He had to sell his house and move to a crappy rental from what I heard."

"It's an old house. Needs a lot of work. But I have to admit—" I looked around my apartment "—it's better than this place."

Uncle Hank scowled at me. "You went to his house?"

"I popped in for a visit." I shrugged, setting a cup of coffee in front of him.

"Were you invited? Or did you help yourself?"

I offered a cup to the rookie, but he shook his head and looked back at the apartment door. I sat with the cup, answering the question. "It was sort of a self-service kind of visit, but he caught me when he woke to answer his phone."

The fact that I was caught seemed to entertain Uncle Hank. His scowl was replaced with a smirk as he drank his coffee.

"So why the visit this morning? Bored?"

"There's a dead body downstairs. In the lobby. Looks like an overdose."

My head threw itself back involuntarily. "Pauly? Wearing a green coat?"

"Yeah. The guy's wearing a green coat. Was he there when you came home?"

"Yes, but I thought he was sleeping." I looked toward the apartment door, now understanding the rookie's behavior. "Pauly's a heroin addict, but non-violent so I don't throw him out. He sleeps in the lobby one or two nights a week."

"How well did you know him?" the rookie asked, getting out his pocket notebook. "Do you know his full name?"

Uncle Hank rolled his eyes.

I laughed and walked over to my filing cabinet, pulling a file. "Paul Leenstra, known on the streets as Pauly. Born in 1992. Repeat drug offender, but all misdemeanors. His parents live over in Coral Groves, but they haven't spoken to him in years. He has two older brothers, both successful." I handed the file to Uncle Hank, but he passed it to the rookie without looking at it.

"When was the last time you saw him alive?" Uncle Hank asked.

"With all due respect, sir," the rookie interrupted, "we should be positioned to monitor the body until the coroner's office arrives."

Uncle Hank ignored him and waved a hand at me to continue.

"I saw him two days ago," I said, thinking back. "Oh, *shit*! He gave me a gun. I can't believe I forgot." I walked over to my desk and pulled a paper bag from the bottom drawer.

The rookie pulled his service weapon. "Drop the bag and put your hands in the air!"

"Holster your weapon, Officer Regis," Uncle Hank ordered.

"She's armed, sir. I can't holster my weapon."

"She's a cop, idiot! Holster your damn weapon or I'll have your badge."

The rookie quickly holstered his weapon, but looked ready to pee his pants.

"Knock-knock," a female voice called from the doorway.

"Hey, Tasha," I said as I walked back across the room and handed the brown bag to Uncle Hank. "I have fresh coffee. You have time for a cup?"

"Sure. I've got a trainee with me this morning, so I'll let him do all the work."

"Sounds like a good idea," Uncle Hank said, glaring over at his rookie. "Officer Regis, go monitor the transfer of the body. And if you pull your weapon again, you and I," he pointed between them, "are going to have a serious problem. *Kapeesh*?"

"Yes, sir," Officer Regis said before scurrying out the door.

Tasha Gordon worked at the coroner's office, where we'd met on several cases. I liked her, which was odd because I didn't like a lot of people. I filled a cup of coffee in the kitchen and carried it out to her. She and Uncle Hank were inspecting the gun that Pauly had given me.

"This is a decent piece," Uncle Hank said. "Why'd he give it to you?"

"I'm pretty sure he stole it, but I didn't ask any questions. He told me he got it for protection but knew it'd be dumb to shoot up heroin while carrying a loaded weapon. He left it with me for safekeeping."

"For safekeeping? Didn't he know you're a cop?"

I shrugged. "Sometimes he'd forget. He's fried a few brain cells over the years."

"Why did he need protection?" Tasha asked.

"He wouldn't say, but he was acting odd. Real skittish, but his speech wasn't rushed, like it would get when he was high. Also..." I paused, concentrating my thoughts on Pauly.

"Also, what?" Uncle Hank asked.

"This isn't going to sound logical, but Pauly wasn't your typical addict. I mean, yes, he was hooked on heroin, but he was scared to death of overdosing. Are you sure he didn't fall down the stairs and crack his head?"

"Then dragged himself under the stairs?" Tasha asked.

I shrugged. "Maybe one of my neighbors moved him? Not realizing he was dead?"

"You know addicts only pretend to be in control, Kid," Uncle Hank said, reaching over the table to pat my hand.

[43]

"He had a needle buried in his arm. I'd bet a twenty that cause of death was an overdose."

I leaned back in my chair and released a slow breath. "Then you owe me twenty bucks. Pauly shot up between his fingers or his toes."

"You sure?" Uncle Hank asked.

"Positive. He worked irregular construction and carpentry jobs to pay for his habit. You can't get hired with track marks covering your arms, and you can't work construction in Florida wearing long sleeves. Thus, he shot up between his fingers and toes so it would be less noticeable."

Uncle Hank stood abruptly. "Shit."

Tasha's head whipped back toward the door. "Damn it. We left our trainees in charge of a murder case?"

They both rushed through the still open door.

I returned to the kitchen to dig out a new bag of coffee, starting another pot. I had a feeling more cops would be arriving soon.

Chapter Seven

KELSEY
Sunday, 7:02 a.m.

Showered, dressed, hair and make-up in place, I walked down the hall into a deserted dining room. "Where is everyone? It's Sunday," I asked Hattie.

"Oh, here and there," she answered as she set a cup of coffee down for me at the dining room table. "Alex and the girls are at the store, getting everything closed down for the winter break. They shouldn't be long since it was another sell out day yesterday. The graphic changes Nicholas made on the website were a hit. He's a natural." Hattie walked over and filled Pop's cup as he read his paper at the end of the breakfast bar.

"I saw the website," I said. "It looked great. I might need to put Nicholas in touch with Diego in Pittsburgh and start him on a career in marketing."

Pops chuckled from the other side of his paper. "As if you'd get that lucky. Nicholas is in the basement with Bones as we speak, working on his boxing skills."

"Figures," I said as I slid a stack of folders aside. "Where's Sara?"

Hattie sat at the table across from me, sliding another stack of files out of her way. "With Whiskey doing a walk-through of the new houses. Any chance you're going to move back to the War Room soon?" She motioned at the files on the table.

I looked down the long dining room table, cluttered with papers, pens, files, and laptops. It had been two weeks since I last ventured across the street to Headquarters. In that time, I'd turned our dining room into my personal office, all in the spirit of avoiding Grady. "I don't want to go back."

"Chicken," Pops mumbled, still looking at his paper.

Hattie giggled. "He's right. You're being a coward, dear."

"Are you kicking me out of my own house?"

Hattie tried to hide her grin. "Your files and the mess that comes with it, yes. I want my table back."

"Why do you care? You're flying back to Texas tomorrow."

"Because," Pops said as he folded the paper and placed it on the countertop, "she needs to know you'll be all right before she leaves, and the only way to know that for sure, is if you put on your big girl breeches and go face Grady."

I looked at Hattie and found her grinning down at the table as she sipped her coffee.

"Fine. I'll go hunt down some boxes and pack everything."

"I brought boxes," Bridget said as she juggled three empty boxes through the kitchen door. "Hattie texted me that it was moving day and I came prepared." She kicked the door closed with her heel before walking over and dropping the boxes at my feet. "Personally, I'm glad you're coming back to the War Room. It's too quiet and boring without you and Tech bickering all day."

Tech was entering through the balcony slider and had heard Bridget. "We still bicker. We just do it over the phone."

"But I don't get to hear both sides, so it's not as much fun for *me*," Bridget said as she piled a stack of files into a box.

"Maybe if you worked instead of filing your nails all day, you wouldn't be so bored," Tech teased as he grabbed a box and filled it with the laptops and other electronics.

Bridget threw a pen at him.

Tech caught the pen, tossing it in the box he'd just filled. "It's cold outside. I'll start your SUV."

He carried an overflowing box under one arm and left through the garage door. Bridget finished filling the last box, and the dining room table was once again clear.

I sipped my coffee.

"Aren't you coming?" Bridget asked.

I shrugged. "Maybe tomorrow."

"Kelsey Harrison," Hattie scolded, taking my cup of coffee from me, "get your butt out of that chair and over to Headquarters."

I sighed, stood, grabbed the third box, and followed a giggling Bridget out the door.

"There better be coffee in the War Room," I said before I slid into the back seat and let Tech drive me over.

~*~*~

I didn't make it to the War Room before Grady spotted me and jogged over to block my path. "Can we talk?"

"Maybe later," I said, holding the box up. "I'm busy at the moment."

"Hey, Kelsey," Wayne said as he walked over. "Let me get that for you."

Before I could protest, Wayne took the box I was using as an excuse and followed Tech and Bridget up the stairs to the War Room. I sighed, turned around, and started walking back toward the parking lot.

"Come on, Kelsey," Grady said, stopping me with a hand on my elbow. "It's been two weeks. Even Nicholas isn't mad at me anymore."

"Nicholas is better at getting over his anger than I am," I said, shrugging. "But there's one thing we're both alike in..." I leaned closer, smiling through my anger up at Grady. "We *never* forget." I jerked my arm away from him as I stepped away. "My son might not be mad at you, but he no longer trusts you. If he needs advice or comfort, he'll find someone else—Bones, Donovan, Whiskey—because he knows it's only a matter of time before you betray us again." I turned my back to him as I walked toward the exit. "We know who you are now, Grady," I said over my shoulder. "And there's no room for your brand of bullshit in our lives."

I threw the door open and stomped across the lot toward my SUV. My hands shook from the emotions coursing through me. This was why I didn't want to be here. It didn't matter what he said or did, he'd betrayed me. Betrayed my son. He could spew his nonsense of protecting us until the cows came home, I wasn't buying it. He cheated on me with his ex-wife. And worse, he threw away our relationship already knowing what an evil bitch she was.

"I take it that went well," Donovan said, jogging over from his vehicle to talk to me.

"I shouldn't have come over here. I'm still too angry."

"I'm thinking your anger isn't going to diminish anytime soon." Donovan playfully nudged my shoulder. "What now? You going to let him drive you away from the work you love? Leave Aces?"

I paced back and forth. "No." I glanced back at the building. "Maybe. I don't know." I ran a hand through my hair, tugging at it in frustration. "I just don't want to be around him right now."

Donovan shrugged. "We can work with that." He threw an arm over my shoulder and steered me back into the building.

Grady's eyes locked on me as we entered.

"New rule," Donovan said to him. "Stay the hell away from Kelsey so she can work in peace. Until I say otherwise, the second floor is off limits to you." Donovan shoved me ahead of him as we moved past Grady.

"Now, wait a—"

"*Shut up!*" Donovan said, spinning to the side and thrusting a finger at Grady's chest. "Don't think that because I'm still your friend that I've let you off the hook for the shit you pulled! You're forgetting that Kelsey is part of my family. And if she wants you to leave her alone, then damn it, that's what you'll do! Or else, I swear, Grady, I'll end our partnership. I'll tear Silver Aces to the ground and rebuild a new company without you."

Grady took a small step away, shocked by Donovan's words.

Donovan turned back and ushered me across the gym, stopping at the bottom of the stairs. "You go do your thing. I got this."

I stood on my tippy toes and kissed Donovan's cheek. "Thanks."

"No need to thank me. I meant what I said. You're family." He turned away, heading back toward the entrance.

I watched him a long moment as he walked away before I climbed the stairs and entered the War Room. "What are we working on today?"

Before anyone answered, an unmanned laptop started beeping from the end of the table. I walked over and saw it was flashing a code.

Tech pushed me aside and started performing his magic, maneuvering through screens at lightning speed. "Call Charlie for me. Put her on speaker."

I pulled my cellphone and called Charlie.

"Yo," she answered.

"Tech told me to call you." I set the phone on the table, already on speaker.

Tech glanced at the phone as he spoke. "I've got a rough location for the burner phone you wanted me to trace. It's bouncing off a tower in south Miami."

"Shit."

"What's wrong?" I asked Charlie.

"Nothing's wrong—yet. But I need to get a woman to a safe house. Tech, anything else you can tell me about the phone or its owner?"

"The phone was activated in Georgia, but that's all I've got. Sorry. Want me to keep monitoring the cell towers?"

"Yeah, if you don't mind. Thanks. I gotta run. Chat later."

"Hey—" I started to say, but Charlie had hung up. "Yeah, yeah," I mumbled to myself. "Good to hear from you too, sis."

"It's decided then?" Bridget asked. "You're calling each other sisters now?"

"I'm still test driving it," I said, shrugging. "Feels wrong, though."

Tech rolled his eyes.

Chapter Eight

CHARLIE
Sunday, 8:45 a.m.

Two hours later, the last batch of cops left my apartment. I carried the empty pastry box into the kitchen and jammed it into my trash can, using my foot to stomp it down. The sink was full of dirty coffee cups, but I'd wash them later. I turned off the coffee pot and walked out, finding Spence standing there with his hands perched on his hips and a pissed off look on his face.

"Your files and phone are over there," I said, pointing at my desk in the living room. "Thanks for letting me borrow them."

"We both know I didn't let you *borrow* them."

"Oh, I must've misunderstood."

He pursed his lips, but crossed the room to gather his stuff. "What's the deal with the herd of cops?" He shoved his phone in his back pocket and piled the folders under one arm. "They made me wait an hour before I could enter the building."

"A junkie was murdered."

"Damn. I thought my neighborhood was bad." He looked around my sparse living room and then down at my worn orange carpet. "Why the hell do you live in this dump? I ran your background this morning. I know you can afford one of those nice beachside condos."

"And be surrounded by snobby couples who name their poodles things like Muffy and Fluffy?"

He chuckled as he set the folders on the table and sat. "You could borrow Beast to scare the neighbors away. He hates poodles."

I slid back into my chair. "What's your plan with Evie's case?"

"Honestly? I don't have a plan. The truth is, I need the money."

"How good of a PI are you?"

He leaned back in his chair, looking defeated. "I'm better than the cases I'm getting. Hell, I'm a one-man act and I know I'm better than most of the big firms. But without a fancy office, I'll never attract decent clientele."

Having read his case files, I already knew he was thorough. He never would've found Evie if he wasn't attentive to small details and committed to his work. She made one mistake, calling her aunt from a pay phone at the bus depot. She thought it was safer than using her burner phone. Once Spence had an address he started digging into apartments and bars in the neighborhood and searched in an outward circle until he found her.

"Wait here," I said, standing and walking down the hall. In the bedroom, I opened the safe in the back of my closet, pulling out an envelope. I returned to the dining room and tossed the envelope to Spencer. "I'll pay your finder's fee in exchange for your silence."

He opened the envelope and flipped through the stack of hundreds. "If I fire him as a client, he'll know I found her. He'll just hire someone else."

"It might buy me some time. And he's already in town. His burner phone bounced off a tower in south Miami this morning."

"Shit."

"It's fine. I made a few calls and had Evie relocated. She'll be safe until I straighten this out. Just keep the information you found to yourself."

He glanced at the stack of files. "We both know my dog Beast is easily persuaded to allow strangers inside my house. You should keep the files." He moved the pile of folders to the center of the table. "I'll forward you my electronic records and then delete my copy. Since you're the client now, so it's only right that you'd get them."

"And if they come after you directly for the intel? Try to force the information from you?"

"I can handle myself," he said with a glimmer of excitement as if he'd welcome the confrontation. He held the envelope up. "You sure about this?"

"You solved the case. It's only right you get paid. And we both know I can afford it."

"When I ran your background, I saw the bank account balances, but I couldn't track the income source. The monthly wire deposits led me down an endless maze of shell companies."

I raised an eyebrow at him. "Is there a question?"

"Would you tell me where the money comes from if I asked, or should I keep digging?"

I smirked but didn't say anything.

"Fine. I've got better things to do with my time anyway," he said, pulling a few business cards from his wallet and dropping them on the table. "If you could pass my card to anyone interested, I'd appreciate it. I get the feeling you have a few contacts that could afford my services."

"I know some people—who know even more people. It's called networking."

He emptied all the cards from his wallet onto the table. "I'll bring a box of cards next time."

"Next time?"

"Positive thinking." He left, carrying only the cash envelope.

I picked up one of his business cards and took a picture of it before texting it to my business and investment contacts. After that, I forwarded it to all my police contacts before programming his name and number into my phone's contact list.

Gathering the pile of cards, I took them to the kitchen and dumped them into the overflowing junk drawer. I was about to head off to bed when my phone chirped. I spent the next hour fielding questions via text messages as people inquired about his services.

My coffee cold, my neck kinked, and my eyes starting to cross, I set the phone down and decided I'd finish the rest of the messages later. I stretched my arms over my head and yawned.

My phone rang. I sighed and picked it up, seeing Spence's name on the display. "Hello?"

"My phone is blowing up," Spence said. "Is this for real? Or am I being punked?"

"Don't make me regret recommending you. You can turn down any case you don't want, but the ones you take need to be professionally handled. And hire someone to answer the phone. Even if they have to work from your crappy house until you can afford a real office."

There was a long pause before he spoke. "I know someone who could use the work. Thanks. I won't forget this."

"It was nothing. Good luck." I hung up and tossed my phone onto the table.

Kelsey would've set him up in one of our buildings and offered him a partnership contract. I wrinkled my nose at the thought of having a contract with Spence. He was smart, sexy, and so far, unable to be intimidated. To be honest, I liked him. Which was exactly why I didn't want any contracts binding our lives together. It was best to keep my distance.

I needed sleep, but my thoughts started shifting back to Pauly. He didn't like violence, so why did he get a gun? *Where* did he get a gun? Who was he afraid of?

Most of my neighbors either ignored Pauly or complained to the landlord about him. Not that I blamed them. No one hopes for a homeless man to set up camp in their lobby. But there was *one* neighbor, Roseline Pageotte in apartment 3C, who, like me, occasionally left Pauly food or let him use her shower. Roseline might be able to shed some light on whatever had spooked him.

I should've told Uncle Hank about Roseline, but because she was an illegal, there was no way she would've confided to a man in blue. Besides, she worked the eleven-to-eleven nightshift at the truck stop. She wouldn't be home for a few more hours. I looked up at the clock and saw I had two hours. Plenty of time for a nap.

Chapter Nine

CHARLIE
Sunday, 10:30 a.m.

Startled from a deep sleep by my alarm going off, I shot out of bed, grabbing my gun. I staggered a bit, absorbing my surroundings as my brain cells started sparking to life. Once I processed where I was, at home in my shabby apartment, I tossed the gun on the bed and stumbled into the bathroom.

After taking my second shower of the day, I dressed in linen slacks, a lilac silk blouse, and comfortable cream flats and stood frowning at my reflection in the mirror. I looked ridiculous. But I had one of Aunt Suzanne's social events on the calendar today and there was no sense in changing outfits later.

In the kitchen I ignored the sink full of coffee cups and made a sandwich with the last of the sliced turkey and bread, both only a day or two away from morphing into something found on a compost pile. I was out of mayo and mustard so the first bite stuck to the roof of my mouth. I continued chewing, forcing myself to swallow the lackluster food.

I looked around the apartment thinking of all the crappy meals my cousin and I had eaten in this kitchen. This was our second apartment after moving to Miami. The first had been an attic-converted apartment above a bar. It had been impossible to fall asleep before three in the morning, and despite all the air fresheners, the apartment had always reeked of stale beer.

We moved to this apartment two years later. And after all these years, I still didn't care that there was only one bedroom or that the bathroom was the size of a coat closet. I didn't care that the neighborhood was sketchy. Nor did I care that some of my neighbors were assholes. This apartment was the place where, for the first time in my life, I felt like I didn't have to hide. I'd turned eighteen the day before we moved here. For the first time, I was able to sign the lease agreement, my name legally listed next to Kelsey's. After years of waiting for my parents to drag me back home, I finally felt free. Safe.

The night we moved in, we stayed up talking until the early morning hours. I told Kelsey I wanted to join the police academy, and after several hours of pestering, she agreed to take the training with me when I turned nineteen and qualified. Two years later, we could afford a nicer place to live, but I didn't want to leave. Kelsey moved into a nicer neighborhood, renting a two bedroom in case I changed my mind. I never did, though. This apartment was my home. With its ugly worn carpet, walls that hadn't been painted in two decades, and light fixtures that flickered when you flipped the switch, I felt safe here.

I finished eating the dry sandwich, and since I was still standing in the kitchen, eating over the sink, I brushed my hands together to knock off the crumbs. Back in the dining room, I gathered my purse and my keys and walked toward the door. Before I could open it, someone rapped their knuckles on the other side.

I opened it, startling Sergeant Quille. "Sir?" I asked, stepping back to open the door wider.

Sergeant Quille was a forty-something cop who lived the job. While he usually followed the rules to a T, this wasn't the first time he'd shown up at my apartment door.

I had a feeling he was here to guilt me into coming back to work.

"Is this a bad time?" he asked as he looked down to see my purse and keys in hand.

"It's fine. I was heading upstairs to talk to one of my neighbors before running a few errands."

He stepped back, waving a hand for me to walk out.

I stepped into the hallway and closed the door before locking my deadbolt. I decided to take it easy on Quille, getting right to the point of his visit. "How backed up are the cases?"

"We have six active homicides, including your homeless guy who honestly ranks low on the list. You coming back soon?"

"Can I work Pauly's case?"

"Who?"

"The homeless guy had a name—Paul Leenstra. Can I work his case if I come back?"

"Sure. As long as you clear at least three other cases at the same time."

"You know I'm not the only detective, right? What's the problem?"

"Henley's wife had her baby and he's on paternity leave. Jameson is home with the flu. Keller is on vacation. I have a handful of support staff and rookie detectives, but no one other than Ford to help me lead them. We need you back."

We walked down the hall toward the stairwell. An offensive aroma struck my nostrils, and I used my arm to cover my nose and mouth. "What the hell?"

"The smell from the dead homeless guy seems to be getting worse, not better," Sergeant Quille said, covering his face with his sleeve. "I'm surprised it hasn't cleared out yet. The landlord should prop the doors open."

"The landlord doesn't live in the building, but if the smell was from the DB in the lobby, I'd have heard about it. Most of the cops in our zone took their coffee breaks this morning in my apartment." I jogged up the stairs toward the third floor. The higher I climbed, the worse the smell was, choking me by the time I reached the upper landing.

Sergeant Quille had followed me and when we turned into the third-floor hall, we both had to backtrack to the landing as we coughed from the stench.

I set my purse on the floor, pulling out a pack of tissue. I stuffed pieces of tissue up my nose. "Call this in. We need the medical examiner." I pulled a pair of latex gloves from my purse.

"We haven't confirmed a body yet," he said as he grabbed the pack of tissues to bundle a wad under his nose.

"By the time they get a van here, we will have." I walked over to the stairwell window and looked down into the parking lot. "Todd Miller's car isn't here. I saw Felicia Rankin leave for work this morning, and the single guy who lives above my apartment went to Vegas for the weekend. Damn it. Roseline." I turned back, pulling my gloves on before grabbing my keys.

"Why damn? Is she a friend?"

"No. But Roseline was the neighbor I was on my way to talk to. She knew Pauly."

"I don't remember her name being mentioned in the report."

"That's because I didn't tell anyone about her. She's an illegal. She wouldn't have co-operated with a cop in uniform, but she would've talked to me. She works nights so I was waiting until she got home. I planned on getting the details and forwarding them to whichever detective was assigned the case."

Quille coughed into the wad of tissue. "In theory, sounds like a solid plan." He moved his arm over his nose and mouth. "But I'm thinking someone should've checked on her this morning." He glanced down the hall. "Which door is hers? It's been a decade since I've kicked in a door."

I held my keys up. "No need. I have the master for the building."

"Why would the landlord give you a master?" he asked with a raised eyebrow.

"He didn't. I borrowed an impression of his key when he came to fix my sink a few years ago."

"I didn't hear that." Sergeant Quille turned away to make the 911 call.

I approached the last apartment on the right. I was already coughing from the stench as I checked the door, finding it unlocked. I turned the knob and stepped inside, my stomach rolling when I saw what remained of Roseline. I'd been on plenty of gruesome calls before, but between what I saw and the realization that the body was someone I knew, I bolted from the apartment as I started gagging.

I ran past Sergeant Quille, down the three flights of stairs, and outside into the already scalding hot morning sun. Leaping forward, I grabbed hold of the front fender of my old pickup before doubling over and hurling my turkey sandwich. I was still spitting up the remnants when I heard sirens approaching. I stood, swayed, and felt Sergeant Quille's hand on my shoulder.

I looked back and saw he was sweaty and pale, close to losing his own lunch. He handed me my purse and I dug some gum out, offering him a piece which he waved off.

I glanced up at the building to the third floor. "One of us should go back up there and open the windows."

"Not happening," Sergeant Quille said. "Next person who enters needs a hazmat suit and a tank of oxygen." He coughed into his hand, followed by taking a deep breath. "As soon as you opened that door it was like breaking the seal on an old refrigerator and the stench just exploded."

"As bad as the smell is, the heat was worse. The A/C is off. The blinds are open. The apartments bake in the afternoon on the west side of the building which is why I have an east view."

"And the body? I didn't look inside."

I shrugged, spitting toward the curb. "Her body is lying in front of the windows." I didn't need to further explain. Quille had been a cop long enough to image the scene. The dried blood cemented to the body. The bloating. The rapid decay and liquifying of internal organs.

I walked to the other end of my truck and dropped the tailgate. I hopped up to sit and wait. Quille leaned against the back-quarter panel and directed the arriving cops, turning some away to return to other crime-stopping activities. Several of the officers who'd stayed on scene attempted to climb the stairs, most never making it past the second floor.

Tasha arrived half an hour later. "What? One body in your building today wasn't enough?"

"Upstairs neighbor—Roseline Pageotte. The apartment is well over a hundred degrees and rapid decomp has taken over."

"No air conditioning?"

"The A/C units here blow fuses all the time. Inside each apartment is a hallway closet where you'll find a fuse box and a stack of fuses on the shelf. Landlord doles them out like candy so tenants won't call him."

"Got it." Tasha started for the building.

"Tasha, you might want a mask."

"I'll be fine."

Two assistants followed her inside, carrying medical bags. One turned back as soon as he stepped into the building. We could see through the stairway windows Tasha and the other assistant climb the stairs. The second assistant made it as far as the third-floor landing before she ran down the stairs, out the door, and puked on the sidewalk. Tasha disappeared down the hall from sight as we waited. A few minutes later an officer standing at the far corner of the building gave a thumbs up signal. Tasha must've opened the living room window.

I wiped the sweat from my forehead with the back of my palm as Quille wiped the sweat on his neck.

He looked up at the building, then over at me. "We could wait in your apartment where the A/C is already cranked."

"I get enough *ode of death* at work. My apartment door is staying closed and locked until the building airs out."

"I was afraid you'd say that," he said, wiping the sweat from his neck again. "Are you going to stick around and work this case?"

"Assign one of the new guys, but I'll walk the scene. Officially, I'm not back yet."

"And unofficially?"

"I have an issue with two dead bodies in my building."

"And when are you officially back on the job? Before or after you catch the guy?"

"Depends on who did it," I answered before hopping off the tailgate and walking toward the building.

~*~*~

I was still in Roseline's apartment when Gibson, a first-year detective, arrived. He walked in, nodded to me, then turned to question Tasha. "Time and cause of death?"

"Not sure yet," Tasha answered as she bagged Roseline's hands.

"Was she sexually assaulted?"

"Not sure."

"Can you identify any weapon used against her?"

"Not yet."

"Is there anything you can tell me?"

Tasha shifted her weight away from the body and looked up at Gibson. "Your tie is butt ugly."

I snorted and walked over, pulling Gibson away from the body by his elbow. "You piss her off and you'll be ousted from the homicide unit. You can't work a body case if you don't play nice with the ME's office."

"I need the information for my report. I'm supposed to ask questions."

"Look at the body, Gibson. What's the cause of death?"

He looked back at the body and grimaced. "Why's she all puffy like that?"

"Bloating. The air conditioning was out and the oven was on. It was hot in here."

"That's why Tasha can't answer the questions? Because the body got too hot?"

"The heat impacts the body, yes. The organs start decaying at a rapid pace. Tasha will get you answers when she can, but you need to work the scene. What piece of information did you just miss?"

Gibson looked at me. I could see him back tracking in his mind, trying to find the missing clue. "The oven. Why was the oven on?"

"She was cooking a roast."

"Was it burnt?"

"More dehydrated than burnt. She was slow cooking it, so it shrank into a molted glob of blackness, barely recognizable as meat."

"Her attacker showed up sometime after she put the roast in the oven but before it was done cooking." He held up his notepad and looked at me. "How long does it take to cook a roast?"

"Do I look like Betty Crocker?"

He looked down at my outfit of linen pants, flats, and a satin shirt. "More like Martha Stewart."

I glared at him. "Call your mommy. Call your girlfriend, or boyfriend, or whoever cooks for you. I don't really care who you call."

"My mother knows how to cook roasts, but what if later she's asked to testify? I don't want to drag her into this."

"It's only information to narrow down the time of death until the ME's office gives us their report. You need to have a window of time to ask people their whereabouts."

"Right." He walked into the kitchen and studied the roast, before placing a call.

"Be sure to tell her the potatoes hadn't been added yet," I called out as I walked toward the door.

"What does that mean?" he asked.

I didn't answer. I jogged down one flight of stairs and unlocked my apartment. Uncle Hank sat in my living room, stretched out on my couch in plain clothes, watching TV.

"Did Aunt Suzanne kick you out?"

"Nah. But she told me you called about an overcooked roast. I figured you were working a case, so I called in and heard the hub-bub." He sat up, placing his sock covered feet on the floor. "Should I be worried? Two dead bodies in one day?"

"Technically we only found them today. They died yesterday." I tossed my handbag and keys on the table and retrieved a garbage bag from the kitchen. "I'm taking a shower. Gibson's been assigned the case. He's working to narrow down the timeline."

"You didn't share the information you got from your aunt?"

"What fun would that be?"

I disappeared down the hall and stepped into the bathroom. Stripping my clothes, I tossed them in the garbage bag, including my underwear, and pulled the tie tight. Careful not to be seen, I placed the bag in the hall before closing the door and taking my third shower of the day.

Chapter Ten

CHARLIE
Sunday, 12:35 p.m.

Once again clean, smelling less like a morgue, and wearing dress slacks and a blouse, I returned to the living room to find it empty. The trash bag of clothes in the hallway had disappeared along with Uncle Hank. An apple-cinnamon candle was lit and placed in the center of my dining room table.

I blew the candle out, grabbed my handbag and keys, and left.

Only five steps outside the building I noticed Garth, one of Baker's top security guys for the Outer Layer, standing on the sidewalk waiting for me. I walked over to him, tipping my head back to look up at him. Garth was big. Tall. Nearing the seven-foot mark. And as broad as a barn door.

He held out his hand, offering me a set of keys. "Baker asked me to exchange vehicles and remind you of your eight o'clock meeting."

I unclipped the keys for the old pickup and handed them to him. "Where did you park my car?"

"Half a block down," he said, pointing. "Sorry. Couldn't park closer with all the cop cars."

"That's fine. Be sure to park the truck in the city parking garage across the street."

"With pleasure." Garth partially bowed in mock respect before walking away. Though we both consider

Baker a friend, we also both enjoyed messing with him. And me parking cars in the city lot pissed Baker off.

I started down the block toward my car, spotting it immediately. It was a simple looking car, a dark blue Chevy Impala, only a few years old. But under the hood, I'd had a larger engine installed which kicked up the car's horsepower a few levels. I slid into the driver's seat, turning the engine over. Checking the display screen for the time, I noted I had ten minutes to cross town.

As I pulled into traffic, my phone rang and I pushed the button on the steering column to answer. "Yeah?"

"You're late," Aunt Suzanne said through the car's speakers.

"I'm not late. I have ten more minutes, and I'm in the car, heading your way."

"Pick me up at the car lot off tenth street. We can leave my car there."

I paused to think out her reasoning and realized she wasn't at home. She was running late and playing off that she was doing me a favor. Otherwise, she wouldn't miss an opportunity for me to drop her off later at her house, hoping to convince me to stay for dinner. "No. I'll meet you at your place. We have plenty of time."

"I insist, really. It will be quicker for you to pick me up at the car lot."

I smiled to myself as I turned onto the highway. "I went a different way. I'd have to backtrack."

"Charlie Harrison, *pick me up at the damn car lot!*"

I laughed out loud. "Are you sure you'll have enough time to get there before me? I'm guessing you're at the mall."

There was a long pause before she replied. "You're worse than your uncle," she grumbled before hanging up.

I cranked the radio and exited the highway. Stopping in the bumper-to-bumper traffic for a red light, I looked at the car next to me and laughed. Aunt Suzanne was trying to slide on sunglasses and duck out of view. I blasted my horn, which startled her and her sunglasses went flying. She looked over at me and gave me the finger. The *naughty* finger.

Five minutes later, I idled my car behind her parked car as she slid into the passenger seat with two large gift bags and her bulky purse. She inspected my outfit, which must've met her approval because she settled the bags at her feet before clicking her seat belt.

"Where to?" I asked, putting the car in drive.

"Coconut Grove. About a mile south of the sailing club."

"Fancy. Remind me... Is this a wedding shower, baby shower, or a lame selling party where I'm pressured into buying crap I don't want?"

Aunt Suzanne held up one of the bags that had a yellow elephant imprinted on the side.

"Boy or girl?"

"I'm not sure. The invitation didn't say, so I went gender neutral."

"And do I know the mother to be?"

"You went to the wedding."

"You've dragged me with you to at least four weddings this year, and in each case, I knew neither the bride nor the groom."

Aunt Suzanne, bless her heart, was an amazing woman, but she had an unusual addiction to attending social events: weddings, showers, charity auctions, candle parties, sex toy parties... It didn't matter what the event was, she wanted to attend. Uncle Hank and I took turns accompanying her. Occasionally we put our foot down and refused, but there were always consequences.

"The baby shower is for the bride from the spring wedding. The one at the big cathedral downtown."

"There's been a lot of big cathedral weddings. And she must've already been preggers at the wedding if it was in the spring."

"Whatever you do, don't ask if she was knocked up before they reached the alter. The last time you did that, I could've crawled under the couch. I was so embarrassed. And you should remember the cathedral. You swore and it echoed off the high ceiling for everyone to hear."

I remembered saying the swear word, but not the reason why. "It was only a little swear word."

"If you're counting letters, yes. If you're counting the look on the priest's face—*not so little*."

I smiled at the memory of the stricken look on the poor priest's face. Deciding to change the subject, I asked, "So what did I buy? And why were we invited?"

"I'm guessing we were invited because we give such great gifts. You bought a few outfits, some bibs, two rattles, a bottle warmer and those baby plates that suction cup to the table."

"I should've asked what I didn't buy," I said, shaking my head at her. "And why would they think we buy such great gifts? What did I buy them for their wedding?"

"A bread maker. She's one of those stay-at-home wives, so I'm sure she appreciated it."

"No one appreciates a bread maker."

"Oh, yeah? Then why'd she invite us to the baby shower?"

"I have no idea. But it wasn't because of a bread maker."

"We'll see. Turn left. Their house is the third on the right according to Google."

I turned onto the private community drive and parked a few houses down from where the pink, yellow, and blue balloons were strapped to the hostess's mailbox. I looked around the community as I climbed out of the car. The houses were grand. The yards thick with dark green landscaping. And you could almost smell the new-car smell from the shiny convertibles lining the street. "*Great*. Rich people."

Aunt Suzanne's smile was bright enough to blind someone as she handed me my offering—I mean gift bag. She hurried down the sidewalk toward the main event as if there was a door prize if you arrived on time. I shook my head, half jogging to catch up.

Five minutes later, Aunt Suzanne was in her element chatting away with women of all ages as I stood anti-social beside her and scanned the room. When I saw the very pregnant guest of honor walk into the room, I swear my heart stopped beating.

Tugging on Aunt Suzanne's arm, I got her attention and whispered, "We have to go."

"What? Why?" she asked with an eyebrow arched high.

"I remember the wedding." I tried steering her from the room, but when we got to the foyer she refused to move any further, planting her feet.

"Charlie, what the hell is going on. We can't leave. It would be rude."

I looked around to make sure no one was close enough to hear our whispered conversation. "We have to leave. I had sex with her husband."

"You slept with a married man?"

"No. Well, yes," I said, arguing more with myself for the right answer. "No! He wasn't married yet." I knew I needed to explain or she'd refuse to leave. "But he was married about fifteen minutes later."

Her face froze in a stunned expression when she realized I'd had sex with the groom before the wedding. She sharply inhaled a gallon of air as her eyes widened.

I wrung my hands as I explained. "I thought he was a *groomsman*! There was a big closet off the hall... Plenty of time to kill... He was cute... I was bored..."

"Charlie Harrison," she said leaning toward me and placing a death grip on my bicep. "You slept with the *groom*?"

"I didn't mean to! I mean— I intended to have sex—I just didn't mean for it to be the groom. You know I wouldn't have done that on purpose."

She stared at me, not saying anything.

"If it makes you feel any better, he fucks like a jackrabbit."

"Language!" she said, pointing a finger in my face.

I was relieved though to see her eyes start to dance with humor. The shock of the confession was wearing off. That is, until she looked over my shoulder and her eyes widened.

I didn't want to look. I wanted to run out the door straight to the car. But Aunt Suzanne was in heels and I couldn't leave her behind to clean up my mess. I slowly turned, finding a tall, primly-dressed woman in her mid-sixties smiling at me.

"Your f-bomb at the wedding when the groom and groomsmen took their places makes sense now." Her smile widened.

"I'm so sorry. I didn't know he was the groom. I'm not a homewrecker. I swear."

"I believe you."

"We should leave," I said, taking a step back.

"Nonsense," she said, chuckling.

Aunt Suzanne and I inhaled sharply, floored by her pleasantness.

"This is the third baby shower MaryBeth has had with Travis's flings. When my daughter first suggested doing this, I thought she was crazy. But she's raking in the best gifts. She'll want for nothing by the time the baby's born."

Aunt Suzanne elbowed me in the ribs. "Told you we were invited because we give great gifts."

"What was your gift for the wedding?" the woman asked as she steered Aunt Suzanne into the living room.

"A bread maker and..." Aunt Suzanne's voice drifted off as she walked away.

The Mother-To-Be waddled over to me, her nose wrinkling as she watched the women walk away. "I have to admit, I returned the bread maker."

"I don't blame you. They sell perfectly good bread at the store."

A smile lit her face. "You sticking around? Or making a run for it?"

"You're not angry? Pissed at seeing all these women?"

"Not even a little," she said, shaking her head. "And if I hadn't spent every dime in my savings to buy a small house for me and the baby, I wouldn't even be doing this. But I needed a strategy to leave Travis, and this was the best idea I could think of."

"Does he know? That you're leaving him?"

"Not a clue. He's too busy cheating to even notice I'm pregnant." She had been fake smiling toward the living room, occasionally waving, but glanced back at me and smiled for real. "He'll be surprised when he comes home from his," she paused to make air quotes, "*business* trip and finds half the furniture gone, though."

I couldn't help but like her. "If you weren't pregnant, I'd take you out for martinis."

"Stick around. These showers are a hell of a lot more fun. My grandma goes around whispering *slut* and then walking away. At the last shower, my aunt proposed to play a game of truth or dare, and three women bolted for the door. One of them stopped at the card box and dropped a pile of hundreds through the slot."

"I don't feel that guilty. Sorry."

She laughed, looping her arm through mine, leading me into the living room. "Did you bring a gift for the baby?"

"Yup."

"Then you're good."

Chapter Eleven

CHARLIE
Sunday, 2:25 p.m.

"Best baby shower, *ever!*" Aunt Suzanne said as I drove us back across town.

"Agreed."

Two women had run out the door crying. Another had emptied the cash from her wallet into MaryBeth's hands before leaving. And yet another blurted out that she'd gifted a thousand-dollar bond because she felt guilty about sleeping with Travis.

Within half an hour, most of the women had fled, but we stayed to watch MaryBeth open the gifts. Skipping the customary 'oohs' and 'ahhs', she ripped through the packages like an English terrier, tissue paper flying. Altogether, she'd swindled about three-thousand dollars in gifts, not including the cash and gift card donations. Well worth sitting in a room with your husband's flings in my opinion.

We'd left when grandma began searching online for a place to exchange the silver baby utensils for cash.

Aunt Suzanne turned in her seat to face me, bouncing with energy. "What's next? What should we do now?"

"I have a meeting to attend. *Alone*," I answered. "Then I need to follow up on a few things."

"Like the dead bodies that were found in your building?"

"That and someone hiring a PI to hunt down one of Baker's employees."

"Busy girl. I thought you were taking time off?"

"It's still time off if I don't have to sit at a desk writing reports."

"True. The paperwork was always Hank's least favorite part of the job."

I turned right onto Commerce Street and watched a silver Honda three cars back make the same turn. The car had been behind us since we left the baby shower. I didn't recall seeing it around this morning, or even earlier in the afternoon, but I was damn well aware of it now.

I pushed the hands-free button on the console and voice-commanded my phone to call Uncle Hank.

He answered on the second ring. "Shower over already?"

"We've picked up a tail," I said while dividing my attention between the car following me and the traffic ahead. "Who's hosting your Sunday poker game?"

"We're at Jack's place, over on Fisher Drive. How far away are you?"

"Give me five minutes. Can you be ready in the east parking lot? It's a silver Honda sedan with half tinted windows."

"We'll handle it. Reel him in, and we'll drop a net on him. But if anything jumps off before you get here, get your aunt somewhere safe."

"Roger."

"I can take care of myself!" Aunt Suzanne said, leaning forward to speak directly to the radio as I disconnected the call from the button on the steering wheel.

I'd seen Aunt Suzanne in action, and agreed that most of the time she could handle her own. But whoever was tailing us knew what they were doing.

Professional? I thought. *What if...?*

I commanded my phone to call Spence.

"Spencer Investigations," Spence answered.

"You wouldn't by chance be following me, would you?"

"No. I'm sitting in my truck outside a motel, waiting for a money shot. Why?"

I had watched the driver, now two cars back, in my rearview mirror while talking on the phone with Spence. The windshield on the Honda was only partially tinted. I couldn't see the driver's facial features from the nose upward, but unless Spence was a damn good ventriloquist, he wasn't the one driving.

"Okay. Later," I said before pressing the button to disconnect.

My phone rang seconds later and I pushed the button to answer. "Yeah?"

"Do you need me to meet you somewhere?" Spence asked, sounding concerned.

I chuckled. "No." I disconnected the call again.

"That was rude," Aunt Suzanne said as she window-shopped the stores passing by, perfectly relaxed about us having a tail. "Who was that?"

"Russell Spencer, goes by Spence. He's a P.I."

"Cute?"

"Yup. Looks good naked, too."

"Good in bed?"

"Don't know. Haven't slept with him. A private investigator isn't too far off from breaking my rule of not sleeping with the men in blue."

"But you had a relationship with Agent Kierson. And... that fellow in Texas. He was a deputy."

"Neither work in Miami. My rule only applies to within Miami-Dade County. And I wouldn't call the thing I did with the deputy in Texas a *relationship*," I said, sliding a smirk at Aunt Suzanne.

"How did you see Spence naked, if you haven't had sex?" my aunt asked out of curiosity, ignoring my relationship comment.

"He sleeps in the nude. I was sort-of in his kitchen when he woke to answer his cellphone."

"And?"

I glanced over at her, but couldn't read her expression. "And, what?"

"Was he, well, you know... big?"

I knew Uncle Hank was the only man she'd ever seen naked. Her curiosity of the unknown was the reason I shared some of my sexual exploits with her. Sometimes they made her blush. Sometimes, like now, I wondered if she'd run off to watch porn or buy a Playgirl magazine so she could figure out what "average" meant, and where Uncle Hank stacked up against the general male population.

I didn't want to know the answer to that question, but enjoyed watching Aunt Suzanne mentally stumble around it. "He wasn't fully inflated so I'm not sure what the end result looks like. I'd guess above average."

"Above average..." Aunt Suzanne whispered to herself.

I laughed out loud as I made the last left turn into the east parking lot behind Jack's condo building.

As soon as I stopped the car, Aunt Suzanne's door opened and Joe Jr., one of Uncle Hank's poker buddies, pulled her from the car and led her toward the back entrance of the building. I pulled my Glock from my purse and walked to the center of the lot as the Honda turned into the drive. Before he could change course, two cars pulled out, blocking his escape.

The driver watched me as he sat in his idling car. I couldn't see his eyes but felt them focused on me, waiting to see my next move. Unfortunately, old man Brody—known as Pimples to his poker buddies—walked out from behind a parked SUV and raised a rocket launcher, pointing it at the Honda.

The driver bolted from the car, knocking both Juan and Jack to the ground like a linebacker as he ran across the lot toward the street.

Being the only one under the age of fifty, it was up to me to give chase. I took off as fast as my ballet-style shoes would allow me to run, regretting my shoe choice for the day as my feet slammed against the sidewalk. The man jetted left once he reached the end of the parking lot, knocking people out of his way. I pushed myself to run faster, knowing that if he made it another two blocks I'd lose him in the crowd at the next public beach access.

A half a block later, I was only ten paces behind him when he turned into an alley. I was surprised by his change in direction but didn't think out the approach as I followed. Still running, I didn't have time to stop as he swung an arm out, clothes-lining it against my ribs. I doubled over, the wind knocked out of me, as I stumbled and tried to stay upright. Before I was able to correct my stance, a leg sweep to the back of my knees flung me backward to the ground, my gun bouncing from my grasp.

Lying on my back in the dirty alley, he pounced on top of me. His hands wrapped around my neck, cutting off my air.

Instinct. That internal switch that when flipped on, changes everything. The pain, the noise, the lack of oxygen... it all fades away. And instinct channels everything into one thought—*fight like hell*.

Releasing my hands from his wrists, I used my right fist to throat punch him while digging my keys from my pocket with my left hand. Weaponizing a key between my fingers, I knifed it between his ribs. He winced back, giving me a chance to stab him in the cheek with the next blow.

He growled a scream, jumping to a standing position. I rolled to the right, toward my gun, but as I reached for it, his boot crushed it into the asphalt.

I screamed out as I scrambled to tuck my legs under me, readying myself to stand. The last thing I saw was a boot coming at my face as I heard a nearby woman yell for the police.

Chapter Twelve

CHARLIE
Sunday, 3:15 p.m.

By the time my surroundings stopped spinning, I looked up to find a crowd of strangers and two young beat cops staring down at me as a familiar pair of paramedics pushed their way into the center of the crowd.

"Shit, girl. What'd you get yourself into this time?" Doug Robinson asked as he set his medical bag beside me and squatted to take my pulse.

"Oh, you know..." I sighed as I took a few deep breaths to clear my head. "Just a lazy Sunday spent window shopping."

The other paramedic, Ralph Stoggs, snorted as he placed a pressure cuff on my right arm. "Anything broken?"

"Aren't you supposed to tell me that?"

"I figure you've been injured enough times; you'd be the expert."

I jerked my wrist from Doug's grip and used my hand to push myself into a sitting position. They both shook their heads but knew better than to try to stop me.

For a brief moment the crowd swirled in my vision before everything settled again. I reached up and gingerly felt my nose. The cartilage seemed to be in the right place and blood had stopped gushing, but my eyes were watering from the throbbing pain. "Anyone see which direction the guy I was fighting ran?"

"We need to get a statement," one of the beat cops said, lowering himself to a squat.

I looked him square in the face. "No. You need to clear the crowd and find my gun."

"What gun?" the other cop asked.

"The gun that was somewhere in this area before I lost consciousness."

"She's a cop," Ralph told them.

"You heard her," Doug added. "Clear the crowd and find her gun."

"Show me your ID," the officer squatting in front of me ordered.

I raised my hand and uncurled my middle finger.

Ralph laughed. "We can vouch for her. This is Charlie Harrison, a detective out of the south-central precinct. I wouldn't mess with her, man."

The officers either knew my name or decided to believe Ralph because they jumped into action and started clearing the scene. When they said a few minutes later that they couldn't find my gun, I tossed the baby wipes I used to clean the blood from my face to the ground and reached a hand up to Doug, who pulled me upward. We all searched, but my gun was gone.

"Damn it." Frustrated, I walked to the far end of the alley. Just around the corner was a dumpster, baking in the Florida sun.

"I'm not going near that thing," one of the officers said.

"Me either," the other added.

"I could order both of you to search that dumpster."

They both grimaced as Ralph and Doug laughed. His hands still covered in protective medical gloves, Ralph walked over and opened the heavy plastic lid. Doug dragged a wooden pallet over and leaned it against the dumpster as a makeshift ladder. Both looked back at me, grinning.

"This day just keeps getting better and better," I mumbled to myself as I scaled the pallet to look inside the dumpster.

And then my luck changed. My gun, minus the clip, was lying on top of a garbage bag. I snagged the gun, climbed back down, and released a long breath—relieved that I didn't have to report my firearm missing. That was a pretty bad thing to happen to a cop.

Another patrol car pulled up, this time with officers I knew. They convinced the younger officers that typing up a report was a waste of time, then they gave me a lift back to Jack's condo building. Uncle Hank, Jack, and Pimples were still in the parking lot, waiting for me. I limped over to them.

Uncle Hank gave me a once over with his eyes. "He got away?"

I dipped my head in a yes.

"Your face is a mess. How bad is your leg?"

"Bruised knee. Anything in the car?"

"Not even a registration," Pimples said, shaking his head.

"Called the license plate and VIN into a buddy," Jack said. "It's a day rental. Paid cash."

"Video image at the car rental?"

Pimples' shoulders lifted proudly as he answered. "Already sent to your phone. He's got a hat on and wearing tinted sunglasses, though. Kept turned away from the camera for the most part."

"Doesn't surprise me."

"You sure you're okay?" Uncle Hank asked, placing a hand on my shoulder.

"Yeah. Nothing an ice pack can't fix. Just pissed he got away."

Uncle Hank's eyes narrowed as he silently processed his thoughts.

"What?" I asked him.

"I can't remember the last time you lost a fight."

"He surprised me. That's all."

Uncle Hank watched me, and I knew he saw it. I knew he saw that I was rattled. I'd trained routinely for years, never letting my guard down. It took a lot of skill for someone to beat me in a fight. And that guy had nearly been the death of me. I wasn't ready to process how close I'd come to the end, nor what that would've looked like for those left behind. Instead, I followed Jack into the building and into the elevator to the fourth floor.

In Jack's bathroom, I washed up the best I could and changed into one of Jack's t-shirts. My shoes and pants were filthy with streaks of bloodstains and tinted from other unknown substances, but they'd do until I got home and changed. Aunt Suzanne handed me an ice pack when I returned to the living room. I sat on the couch holding the pack to my nose as I blindly drank from a bottle of beer. The boys settled into their poker game again while Aunt Suzanne rummaged around in Jack's kitchen, making herself at home.

I'm not sure how long I sat there before drifting off to sleep. When I woke, I was lying on the couch covered with a blanket. I looked at the clock as I gained my bearings. I'd slept the afternoon away and into the early evening.

"I saved you a plate of food," Aunt Suzanne said, handing me a glass of water. "We didn't want to wake you. You've been burning the candle at both ends lately."

"Lately?" Uncle Hank laughed from the table. "You mean like she always does?"

"Catnaps," Jack said, snorting. "That's what she calls them. I don't know how she does it."

"Leave her be," Juan said. "That's one hell of a detective you boys are making fun of."

"Never said she wasn't," Uncle Hank said. "Doesn't mean I don't wish my girl would stop stalking Miami streets at night."

I tossed the blanket off, set the glass of water on the side stand, and ran my fingers through my hair. I started cataloging the day's events and wasn't surprised that I'd fallen asleep. Two dead bodies, Evie's case, a baby shower, and a street fight all accumulated into one hell of a day.

Then I remembered the rocket launcher. "Pimples, what's the deal with the rocket launcher?"

He chuckled and walked down the hall, returning with the launcher. "Pretty cool, aye?"

"I'm guessing you don't have a special permit for that."

"I might've bought the launcher from a guy I know who works in the gray area of the resale business. The rocket's not active, though. Would barely ding a car door." Pimples held the launcher out toward me.

"I used to shoot these in the military," Joe Jr. said as he reached out and took the launcher from Pimples.

Joe Jr. had been a senior citizen for at least a century. He was at that age where he no longer gave a shit what mischief he caused because he celebrated every day like it was a bucket list kind of day.

In one second, we all scrambled toward the launcher to take it away from Joe Jr. In the next, we all pivoted the other direction, trying to distance ourselves from the oncoming catastrophe.

With a bum knee, I was too slow. Pimples tackled me to the ground as the rocket zoomed through the space where I'd been standing and pierced through the living room wall.

A scream sounded, and we all scrambled for the condo door. In the building's hallway, we saw the perfectly round hole from our side which aligned with the perfectly round hole in the wall of the condo across from Jack's.

I ran over and pounded on the door, identifying myself as a police officer. An elder woman opened the door, looking shocked to the bone. I moved past her into the condo where I found the rocket embedded in her recliner. A TV tray lay on the floor next to the recliner. A plate of food had been flung to the center of the room. By the looks of the mess, the older woman had been sitting in the recliner when the rocket made its abrupt appearance.

I turned back and saw Jack was holding the older woman, offering her comfort. She'd went from shocked-scared to completely enthralled as she rested her face against his chest and rubbed her hands along his arms. Her blissful expression told me she was in the midst of inappropriate thoughts.

I limped toward the door. "I wasn't here. I don't want my name anywhere near this."

"That makes two of us," Uncle Hank said, following me out.

He towed Aunt Suzanne, her mouth still open in stunned disbelief, out with us.

Chapter Thirteen

CHARLIE
Sunday, 8:05 p.m.

"You're late," Baker complained when I walked through the door of the safe-house condo.

"You'll live," I snapped back, tossing my purse on the entranceway table as I moved into the kitchen for some ice.

The central-city condo was in a controlled-access building. It was used as a safe house, purchased under one of our many shell companies. It was seldom needed, but there was comfort in having it available when we did. Like now.

"Where's Evie?" I asked, joining him in the living room and throwing myself onto the couch. I placed the ice, wrapped in a towel, on my bruised knee.

"What the hell happened to you?" Baker said, taking in the damage to my face.

"Took a foot to the face. I'll heal. Where's Evie?"

"Here," she said from the bedroom doorway, staring at me. "Were you hurt because of me? Is this my fault?"

"Whether it's related to whoever is looking for you, is yet to be determined," I said, shrugging. "But the fault of my injuries rests purely on my own shoulders. I was caught off guard, and my opponent was bigger, stronger, and faster than me. It could've been a hell of a lot worse." I shook off the memory of his hands around my neck and motioned for Evie to join us.

She seemed hesitant, but then squared her shoulders as she walked over and sat in a side chair. "What's going on? Why did Garth bring me here and tell me to stay put?"

"The guy who's been watching you in the bar is a private eye hired by someone with deep pockets to find you. I've slowed them down, but it's only a matter of time." She went to say something, but I put up a hand to stop her. "And before you decide to run—they'll find you."

Her face scrunched in frustration, but after a minute of thinking out the situation, she bobbed her agreement.

"Tell me what's going on. I can help. If it's something over my head, I have the resources and connections to hire assistance."

"She's not exaggerating," Baker said, casually leaning back into the deep couch. "She's rich. She's connected. And she's street smart. If my ass was in trouble, I'd call either her or her cousin."

"Which of us would you call first?"

He turned his head to look at me. "Your cousin."

"Traitor," I mumbled to him before looking back at Evie. "Genevieve, come clean. What's this all about?"

She seemed startled by the use of her real name. "How much do you know about me?"

"I know your name, that you're from Georgia, and I have your prior employment and education information. What I don't know is why Genevieve Lawrence dropped off the face of the planet, only to emerge in Miami as Evie Lawry."

"This wasn't part of the plan," she said as she stood. "I came to Miami to figure out what he was up to and take the information to the police, but when I got here..." She wrung her hands. "What was I thinking? I'm an accountant from Georgia. What do I know about gathering evidence on a criminal?"

"Wait—" I held up a hand. "You came here with the *intention* of going after a bad guy?" I rubbed my hand across my forehead, frustrated with how naïve Evie had been. "Go back to the beginning. Who is this guy?"

"I only know the name he gave me: Xander Hall. I met him in a bar and hit it off. We dated whenever he was in Atlanta for business."

"How long did you date?"

"Almost a year," she said, sighing as she sat again.

"What went wrong?"

"Nothing really went wrong. The entire time we were dating, though, there were these little red flags that kept popping up, warning me to keep my distance."

"Give us an example," Baker said.

"Just shady behavior. Like sometimes he'd say he was one place, then later say he was somewhere else at the same time. Like he was lying and his cover story kept changing."

"What else?" I asked.

"Two phones. Late night calls. He'd leave the room to talk, saying it was business. Flashing cash. No regular work schedule, but he could afford expensive things."

"You just described me," Baker said with a smirk.

Evie shook her head. "Anyone who knows you, knows you work non-stop to afford your lifestyle. No, this was different. This was..."

"*Shady*," I said, nodding. "I get the picture. Then what happened?"

"I loved him. Or at least I tried to convince myself I did because he treated me like a queen. Designer clothes. Fancy restaurants. Chauffeured car services. And, I'm ashamed to say, I liked life on that side of the tracks. I didn't want to return to a life of budgeting my money and driving around for thirty minutes to find a parking spot. Eventually, though, self-preservation forced me to start looking into what kind of man he was. And the more I dug, the worse it looked."

She stood again and started to pace.

"He didn't have any friends or even any business contacts in Atlanta as far as I could tell. He always carried cash, so I didn't know his real name, other than the name he gave me of Xander Hall."

"But that's not his name?" I asked.

She shook her head. "I bribed someone from human resources at work to run a search on the name, nothing came up. *Nothing at all*. Wherever we went, though, his driver Colby Brown always traveled with us, so I had his name run. He had a criminal record. Assault. Robbery. Extortion. I should've broken things off then, but by then I was scared. I had to find out who he was."

"What did you do?" I asked, not sure if I wanted to hear the answer.

"I planted a recorder in the den where he took his private calls. And the next day when I listened to the one-sided conversation, I knew I had to run."

"What was the conversation about?"

"It was one sided, so it was just fractured pieces to a puzzle. Young girls. Prostitutes, I think. A dentist office. Cuba. Wire transfer. Miami."

Baker leaned his head back on the couch cushion and pinched the bridge of his nose. "None of that sounds good."

"Anything else?"

She thought for a moment, staring at the coffee table as she did. "Yeah, something. But I couldn't make sense of it. Something about hoping Mickey doesn't figure it out."

"Shit," Baker said as he stood. "We need to get her out of town."

The towel of ice I'd been holding against my knee started dripping so I walked to the kitchen and tossed the towel into the sink. "Stay here," I said to Evie when I returned. "Let me poke around."

"It's not safe to keep her in Miami," Baker argued. "Mickey owns this town."

"Mickey doesn't own me. And I'm not scared of him."

"That's the dumbest thing I've ever heard you say. Kelsey's even smart enough to keep him at a certain distance."

"Whether Mickey's involved or not, it's not safe to move Evie in a rush. If we need to get her out of town, arrangements need to be made. That takes time. For now, the three of us and Garth are the only ones who know about this place, so she's safe. Just give me a few days."

I walked over to my purse and dug out my phone. Returning to the living room, I showed Evie the still image Pimples had sent me of the guy renting a car. "Recognize him?"

Evie studied the picture. "I can't see the guy's face, but he doesn't seem familiar. Who is he?"

"He's the guy who attacked me earlier, but it's likely he's related to another case. I just wanted to make sure it wasn't your ex."

"It's not Xander or his driver Colby. But that doesn't mean it wasn't someone Xander hired. I only know Colby, but Xander was constantly on the phone ordering people around."

"Do you still have the voice recording?"

"Sort of." She looked guiltily at Baker. "I hid the mini recorder behind the brandy glasses at the bar. Figured it was safer there than in my apartment."

"I have a safe in my office, you know," Baker said, rolling his eyes.

"I'll head to the bar and make a copy. I'll move the original to my office." I walked toward the door and gathered my purse. "Don't go anywhere. If you need something, call Baker or Garth."

"Umm..." she said, looking between Baker and me. "I sort of need some feminine products."

"I'm not buying tampons," Baker said matter-of-factly. "No way. Not happening."

I raised an eyebrow at Baker. "How about I go buy the tampons and you go talk to Benny The Barber?"

His head swiveled my way. "Are you insane?"

"Which is it? Tampons or Benny? I can't do everything."

He grumbled a few curse words under his breath. "*I'll buy the damn tampons!*"

Chapter Fourteen

CHARLIE
Sunday, 9:18 p.m.

After stopping at The Outer Layer to copy and listen to Evie's audio file, I hid the original recorder in the safe in my office. I grabbed a pair of jeans and a baby-blue t-shirt from the closet, and carried them into my private bathroom to shower for the fourth time today.

Ten minutes later, I left feeling more myself, my bruises coated under several layers of make-up, my hair pulled into a loose pony-tail, and comfortable running shoes laced to my feet. I'd left the bloodstained linen pants and ballet shoes lying on the floor, imagining Baker's cleaning person flipping out the next time he sent someone in to clean. Maybe he'd learn his lesson. Then again, it was a sex club. Maybe the person cleaning wouldn't even notice.

I drove south to Benny's barbershop. Benny The Barber was well known for his skills. Not hair cutting skills, though I'd heard he was a decent barber, but his skills as a hitman were well known to law enforcement and criminals alike. Long range shots used to be his specialty, but word on the street was his eyesight wasn't what it used to be. Benny wasn't the type to take early retirement though. I was confident he'd been keeping busy with point-and-shoot, knifings, and the make-it-look-like-an-accident jobs.

Nailing Benny's ass and sending him to prison would make a lot of people happy, including me. But Benny was skilled enough that, even though everyone knew he was a hitman, the police couldn't pin a single crime on him. As far as the good guys could tell, Benny didn't take trophies. He didn't leave calling cards. He changed his MO regularly. He didn't leave witnesses. He didn't leave trace evidence—*ever*. And he'd been in the game for at least forty years.

It took a certain personality to be able to do that type of work. The type of personality that was often described using labels such as sociopath, anti-social personality disorder, or psychotic. And for that reason, I took a few extra minutes in my car, breathing in and out, to settle my pulse before I climbed out and walked toward the barbershop's front entrance.

I wasn't surprised to find the lights on in the barbershop, nor the doors unlocked. Benny kept odd hours, even on Sundays. I was surprised to be greeted just inside the door by Mickey McNabe's right- and left-hand bodyguards, and even more surprised to see Mickey himself getting a straight-razor shave from Benny.

"Let her through," Benny called out to Mickey's goons.

The bodyguards held their position, preventing me from moving further into the shop.

"It's fine," Mickey said as Benny handed him a warm towel and adjusted Mickey's chair to a sitting position. Mickey wiped the shaving cream off his face as he watched me approach.

I walked past them, choosing an empty swivel chair on the other side of the aisle, keeping the mirrors to my back and everyone within my line of sight.

A slight curve of Mickey's lips was the only change in his expression. His eyes remained cold, dark, distant.

Benny's eyes, on the other hand, held a level of curiosity. He scanned me with those eyes, looking for something. It wasn't a sexual look. It was... *something else*. Like how Uncle Hank had scanned me for bullet wounds earlier in the day, except unlike Uncle Hank, Benny didn't seem worried for my wellbeing. He seemed... *surprised*.

"I'm supposed to be dead, aren't I?" I asked Benny.

Mickey's eyes narrowed. He used his foot to swivel the chair a few degrees, shifting so Benny was no longer behind him.

Benny shrugged. "Makes no difference to me. The way you and your cousin stick your noses in everyone's business, doesn't surprise me to see someone got a piece of you."

"Is that a threat? Or are you trying to tell me something?"

Benny turned toward the counter and started cleaning the straight razor. "You should be holding a fresh steak to your eyes. Helps with the swelling and discoloration."

"Who is she?" Mickey asked Benny but kept his steely dark eyes pinned on me.

Benny dipped the straight blade razor into the alcohol solution a few more times before answering. "Kelsey Harrison's cousin, Charlie Harrison. A cop. Goes by the name Kid."

The crook of Mickey's lips curved into almost smirk level. "Kid Harrison?" Mickey asked, looking me up and down. His eyes lingered a little too long on the deep v-cut of my sleeveless blouse.

"You can call me Detective Harrison. Only my friends call me Kid."

"Maybe we should be friends then," Mickey said, raising his eyes to mine.

I held his stare as I responded with conviction. "I'd rather shoot you than be friends with you."

He displayed no outward change in his demeanor. He continued to study me until the bells on the barbershop doors rang. We all looked over to see Spence walk through. He stopped and lifted his hands to be frisked by the guards. Once he received the nod to proceed, he started walking our way. He stopped in his tracks when he saw me sitting in the chair.

"What the hell happened to your face? Did you get hit by a car?"

"I'm fine." I raised an eyebrow. "What are you doing here?"

Spence shook his head and pulled a familiar envelope from his back pocket, handing it to Mickey. "That's the rest of it. Appreciate the loan, man."

"I told you, I'm not worried about the cash. We can work out a trade," Mickey said, offering the envelope back.

"Nah. Thanks for the offer, but you know me. I don't like owing anyone."

Mickey inclined his head before sliding the envelope inside his jacket pocket unopened. "If you change your mind, you know how to find me."

Spence looked at Mickey, then Benny, then over his shoulder at me. "Everything cool here?" Spence asked me.

"Yes."

"You staying long?"

"No."

He seemed undecided on whether to stay or go. "I'll wait outside for you. I'd like to ask you a few questions about that odd phone call from earlier."

I tipped my head at Spence before turning my attention back to Benny who was leaning casually against the counter with his arms crossed over his chest.

I waited until I heard the bells on the door again, followed by the whoosh of the door swinging closed. "What do you know?"

Benny shrugged. "I know lots of stuff. Like how there was a ruckus in your building last night."

"Anything about that ruckus I should know?"

"Probably be good if you knew it wasn't me. Not that it matters much. If there was any evidence, it won't tie back to me. And if there wasn't any evidence—" he shrugged again "—still wasn't me. If that's why you're here, you're barking up the wrong tree."

Benny would never give up his clients' names, but him coming straight to the point about not being involved in the murders in my building told me someone had approached him.

Mickey stood and turned to face Benny. With a light hand on the old man's shoulder, he steered him toward the chair he had just vacated and nudged him to sit. Then Mickey moved two chairs away where his back would be in the corner and sat again. Everything about his movements screamed power, control, dominance.

When Mickey caught me watching him, I shifted my attention back to Benny. "Anything else I should know—*or not know*—about your involvement?"

Benny rubbed his chin, thinking out what he'd say next. "Maybe you should know not to look too close for the person who gave Pauly a gun. That person likely didn't know that one thing was connected to another, or he would've had his friend relocate until things settled."

For the first time in all the years I'd known Benny, he showed emotion. Not much, but a glimpse. He knew Pauly. He liked Pauly. They were friends. For people like Benny, friends were hard to come by.

"The gun is already in the evidence locker, but as long as the forensic examination doesn't come back with a match to another crime," I shrugged, delaying my agreement, "we could consider ending our inquiries."

"The gun will come back clean."

"And the reason Pauly wanted a gun?"

"Said someone was watching him. Wouldn't say who or where."

"Am I the reason Pauly's dead? Was I the target?"

Benny shook his head. "Got no bones about taking a good job for fair pay, but some work isn't worth the hassle. Combine you living in the building with a sketchy client, any halfway decent bastard would take a pass. But you weren't the target. Not for that job at least."

"But I'm the target for another job?"

Mickey leaned forward, placing his elbows on his knees as he silently listened.

Benny glanced sideways at Mickey, then back at me. "For Kelsey's sake—*not yours*," he pointed at me, "I'll admit the shit that happened in your building wasn't the only job I heard about."

The guy who was tailing me, I thought.

"A hornet's nest got kicked," Benny said, his eyes cold and dispassionate. "I don't know who did the kicking or the why behind it, but you'd be smart to get out of town for a spell."

His warning was clear. Whoever was behind having me tailed earlier meant business. And they were powerful enough that Benny was trying hard to stay out of it.

"I have a picture." I selected the grainy photo of the man who'd followed me earlier and turned the phone toward Benny as I stood and walked closer.

"Don't know him," Benny said without looking at the photo.

Mickey stood, pulled a gun, and held it to Benny's temple. "And now?"

Benny's eyes flickered in anger toward Mickey, but then he glanced at the photo. "Doesn't look familiar, but it's a shitty picture and the guy has his face turned away from the camera."

"It might be a shitty picture, but does it look like the guy you talked to? Same build? Anything?" I continued to hold the picture in front of him.

"No. The guy I talked to was scrawny. Nothing more than a middleman. As soon as the name Harrison was mentioned, I told him to leave." Benny's cold eyes let me know he was done talking.

I turned the phone toward Mickey. "How about you? Recognize him?"

He took the phone and studied the picture. "No. But it could be anyone. Do you have a better picture?"

"This is it for now."

Mickey motioned to his bodyguards to join us. He held the phone up for them to view and they shook their heads that they didn't recognize the man.

I took the phone back, tucking it into my back pocket. "One last question," I said looking directly at Benny. "Hear anything about a woman named Evie? Or a woman named Genevieve?"

Benny glared at me. "Doesn't ring a bell."

I stepped back to retrieve my purse before walking toward the door.

"Kelsey always leaves a tip for information," Benny snapped.

"I'm not Kelsey," I said, walking out.

~*~*~

I wasn't surprised to hear one of Mickey's bodyguards follow me outside. I was surprised that Mickey and his other guard also walked out.

"Does Kelsey know you're in danger?" Mickey called out.

I walked back toward Mickey, stopping only two feet away. "What I choose to share or not share with Kelsey is none of your business. The two of you might have some skewed alliance, but in my book, you're nothing more than a thug. Besides," I pulled my phone and opened the audio file I'd copied earlier, "you've got your own problems to sort out."

Playing the recording, the man known to Evie as Xander Hall threatened someone about a job involving prostitutes and warned to keep everything quiet so Mickey didn't find out about it. I wasn't sure how the reference to a dentist office fit in, but I did see the shift in Mickey's expression when he heard it. When the recording ended, I slid the phone into my pocket.

I waited, watching him. Watching as his eyes pinned me with rolling emotions that I couldn't read. Anger? Yes, but it was more than that. It was a challenge of some sort.

I was so focused on Mickey that I didn't notice Spence standing next to me until he wrapped an arm around my waist and gently pulled me back two steps away from Mickey.

Spence's presence startled Mickey. Mickey glanced around, taking his time to scan the area as his temper visibly settled. He glanced back at Spence, nodded ever so briefly, before looking back at me. Once again, he seemed hard, even cold, but now back in control.

"By everything I've gathered here tonight," Mickey looked down at me, "you have three problems. One, someone in your building was eliminated. Two, you are the target on another job and the person who's backing that contract is powerful enough to make Benny nervous. And three, you're sticking your nose into the dentist office which is already being managed by someone a lot smarter," he stepped forward, towering his height and broad body over me in an intimidating manner, "and definitely more in control than yourself." He walked toward his town car and without looking back, he said loud enough for me to hear, "Take Benny's advice. Get the hell out of Florida."

Spence stood beside me as we both watched the town car pull away from the curb and enter traffic.

I turned to face Spence. "Explain the loan. Why did you borrow money from someone like Mickey?"

Spence shrugged. "I know exactly who Mickey is, and what he's capable of if he's disrespected. But I grew up in the same neighborhood as Mickey. We ran together for years, only splitting apart when he started building his criminal business. We're not friends anymore, but that doesn't make him my enemy either."

"He's a thug."

"Half the politicians, lawyers, and cops in this city are dirty. The only difference between them and Mickey is that he doesn't hide who he is." Spence lightly pushed me toward my car. "Let's get out of here. I'll pick up a six pack and you can argue with me at your apartment. I can feel Benny's creeping eyes on us."

I turned toward the window of the barbershop, and sure enough, Benny stood at the window watching us. "I have an errand to run first. I'll meet you at my place in about an hour."

Chapter Fifteen

CHARLIE
Sunday, 9:43 p.m.

I slid into my car, taking a moment to release a long breath before turning the engine over and pulling away from the curb. I pressed the button to activate the Bluetooth for my phone. "Call Tasha."

Tasha answered on the second ring. "Medical Examiner's office, Tasha speaking."

"You know you don't have to answer your cellphone like that, right?"

"I've given the number out to too many colleagues. Everyone calls this number instead of the main office number."

"Fair enough. Speaking of work, got any details on the double homicides in my building?"

"You officially on the cases?"

"No. But Sergeant Quille green-lit my involvement. He's using the case to try and drag me back to work."

"Good enough for me. I've got time of death, but you're not going to like it."

"Hit me. I'm invincible when it comes to bad news today."

"Your friend Pauly put up a fight. Whoever killed him was stronger and faster. Likely choked him until he passed out, but then injected him with enough morphine to kill six people."

"Morphine? Not heroin?"

"Well, technically heroin is a synthetically altered drug made from morphine. I can go into the exact chemicals found in his blood work if you'd like, but I know you'd only yell at me for being nerdy. Therefore, simply put, it's my opinion based on the chemical analysis that Paul Leenstra had trace heroin amounts in his system, but the drug that caused heart failure was morphine. Another examiner might disagree, though."

"I trust your opinion, and thanks for keeping it simple. What's the time of death?"

"I couldn't get a precise time but calculated a window between one and four in the afternoon Saturday."

"Impossible."

"Science doesn't lie, my friend."

"I went home around seven that night. Pauly wasn't under the stairwell."

"That's the part you're not going to like. Roseline's time of death is the same window as Pauly's. And his DNA was found in her apartment, so Detective Gibson's theory is that Pauly killed Roseline, then got his hands on some morphine and overdosed."

"How does he explain the strangulation?"

"He had a couple of theories. Said it could be unrelated, happened earlier in the day. Or the more entertaining theory was that they had an erotic asphyxiation game going that got out of hand. Pauly passed out, and when he came to, he went berserk and killed Roseline."

"That jackass."

"Pauly?"

"No. Gibson."

"Oh, yes. That makes more sense." She giggled. "There's not enough science to prove Gibson right or wrong, though."

"Where in Roseline's apartment did they find Pauly's DNA?"

"Bathroom mostly. Looks like he showered. No blood trace in the drain."

"If you pulled DNA from my shower, you'd find Pauly's there, too. He was harmless, but when he'd gone too long without a shower, he'd stink up our lobby."

Tasha hesitated before speaking. "Pauly also had Roseline's blood on his left hand and on the lower left front of his shirt."

"Like he *leaned over* to check on her after she was *already* bleeding?"

"Can't say, but it's possible. Wasn't enough blood to convince me he'd done the deed. But Charlie," she paused, taking a deep breath before she continued, "Pauly could've done this. I can't prove he didn't."

"Just because your science can't prove Pauly innocent, doesn't make him guilty." I hung up by pressing the phone button on my steering column as I turned right into the parking lot at the police station. I slammed the car door shut as I stomped across the parking lot.

When I walked through the door, the front desk officer read the expression on my face and buzzed me into the inner offices without so much as a hello. I stormed past the patrol center and jogged up the stairs to the second floor, ignoring the pain in my knee as it threatened to buckle.

I found the detectives' room vacant, but heard voices coming from the breakroom. Upon entering, I ignored everyone else and zeroed in on Gibson.

"What are we so happy about, Gibson?" I said as I walked into the center of the room and silenced their laughter. "The fact that you're pinning a double murder on an innocent dead man who can't defend himself? Or the fact that you managed to break the world's record at doing the shittiest police work ever?"

Several of the younger officers cleared out in a hurry. A few senior cops stayed, but moved away from the center of the argument.

"The evidence lines up. Pauly did it," Gibson said, defending himself.

"There's not enough evidence to prove his guilt or innocence. You just don't want to work this case because it's not high profile enough for you. Admit it—you're nothing but a ladder climbing jackass!"

"I interviewed the neighbors. You said yourself that Roseline often fed Pauly. She let him in her apartment, and he killed her."

"I also said, repeatedly, *'Pauly was harmless!' Did you miss that part?*"

He stepped back half a step, before shrugging and saying, "We both know you can't predict what someone will do given the right circumstances."

I stepped forward, inches from Gibson's face. "But you can gauge what it would take to push someone over that edge. You think I didn't test him? A homeless man—*sleeping in my building*? You think I'd allow an unstable and violent man to roam around in my building? Shower in my apartment?"

I stepped back, kicking a chair across the room.

"*Pauly didn't do this!*" I pointed a finger at him. "You either pull your head from your ass and prove it—or I will. But I promise you, you're not going to like the consequences to your career if you don't take this seriously."

"Are you threatening me?" Gibson asked, squaring his shoulders as he tried looking less nervous than he was.

"You bet your ass I'm threatening you."

I turned to leave, but Quille was standing in the doorway. He stepped back into the hall and off to the side to let me pass before following me down the hall. "Thanks."

"For what?" I snapped, walking at a brisk pace back to the main room.

"Saving me from having to call Gibson into my office for a lecture."

I glanced over at him, seeing he was struggling to keep up. I slowed my steps. "You're not mad at me for threatening him?"

Quille chuckled. "You didn't threaten to harm him, only to tank his career as a detective. We both know he did a shit-show job on this case. Now," he tugged at my elbow to stop me, "when are you coming back to work?"

"Can't right now. I've got myself involved in something that needs to be sorted first." I pointed to my bruised face.

"I noticed." He sighed. "The gossip in the breakroom is you got into a fight in an alley near Sunset beach access. What happened?"

"I got my ass kicked is what happened. I'm not sure who the guy was or what he was after. I'd noticed him following me, and when I led him into a trap, he took off. I gave chase until he caught me off guard. That's all I know at the moment, but I'm working on figuring it out."

"Could be related to a case. We need to report it."

"It's more likely related to something I did or didn't do that I wouldn't want IA to know about. I'm handling it. Until I figure it out though, wearing a badge has to stay on hold." I turned and looked behind us to make sure no one had followed us. "Got a minute?"

He glanced at his watch. "I promised my wife I'd be home for dinner three hours ago. I'll be sleeping on the couch tonight, so yeah, I've got time."

I walked into Quille's office and over to the credenza, sitting on top of it like I always did. Quille's guest chairs were positioned so your back would face the full-glass wall. The seating arrangement wasn't to my taste, and Quille learned years ago not to press the issue. I liked to think he kept the top of the credenza on this side cleared of pictures and files just for me.

Skipping any idle chitchat, I said, "I had a chat with Benny The Barber."

Quille glanced at the bottom drawer of his desk where I knew he kept a bottle of rum. He glanced up at the clock before crossing his arms and leaning against the far wall. "Some days I can't tell if you're brave—or stupid."

I ignored the comment. "Pauly was collateral damage. The target was Roseline, but if I put those details in a report, IA will be all over my ass to investigate Benny instead of finding Roseline's killer."

"Not to mention he'd put you on his hit list if you documented the conversation," Quille said as he walked behind his desk and sat.

"Benny was offered the job, but turned it down. He either doesn't know who took the job or he's not willing to tell me."

"So... Someone wanted Roseline dead. This was planned."

"Planned to kill her, yes. But her brutal death suggests that a professional wasn't involved. Benny knew I lived in the building. That's why he wouldn't take the job. It's possible the person who wanted her dead, couldn't find someone willing to take the contract."

"It's possible. It's also possible there's an amateur trying to level up to pro on the hitman market. Then you have two other theories to consider. One, the hitman wanted Roseline's death to look like a rage killing, pointing it toward Pauly as the killer. Or two, the hitman enjoys the kill and lost control."

This was the reason I liked bouncing theories off Quille. He had the experience on the job to offer fresh perspectives. "In both scenarios, why move Pauly's body? Why take the extra risk of moving the body to the first floor and possibly getting caught in the act? What's the point?"

"How do you know the body was moved?"

"Time of death. I went home around seven and left again just before nine. Pauly wasn't in the lobby either time."

"You sure?"

"I always look under the stairwell for him. I checked in on him. He wasn't there until I came home again, around four in the morning."

"I'm going to send forensics back to Roseline's apartment and run a blacklight. If Pauly died in that apartment, maybe they missed some evidence that will prove it. Meanwhile, I'll have Gibson do a deep dive on Roseline's past. Any skeletons in her closet that you're aware of?"

"No. She was illegal, so she kept to herself mostly. Did Gibson interview her next of kin?"

"Not according to his notes. He notified Pauly's family, but I didn't see any family mentioned in the file for Roseline."

"All right. I'll track someone down tomorrow and give the death notification while I'm at it. Maybe someone out there knows her well enough to fill in a few blanks."

"What about the guy who followed you? Could he be linked to this case?"

I hunched my shoulders. "I doubt it. According to Benny, someone tried to hire him for another job. Me."

Quille's eyes narrowed and his face flushed bright red. *"Are you telling me there's a contract on your head?"*

I hunched my shoulders in another maybe. "I'll get it sorted. I'm pretty sure the guy in the alley was the person who ended up taking the job."

"You need to take this seriously! That guy in the alley could've killed you."

"I know. He's good." I leaned back against the wall, looking up at the drop ceiling tiles. "I'm not even sure how long he was following me before I spotted him. I wonder if he knows where I live. I'm guessing he does."

"Kid! Quit pretending this is a non-issue!"

"What do you want me to do about it? I'm not going to run and hide."

"Unbelievable. Bad enough you have a contract out on you. But to a guy who can beat you in a street fight? Shit... This is not good." Quille jerked the bottom drawer of his desk open, pulling out two glasses and the bottle of rum.

"I'm looking into it. In the meantime, I'll be ready if he tries to target me again."

"Yeah, you do that," he said, standing to lean over the desk and hand me a glass. "And you might even want to consider giving up this lone wolf act while you're at it. You don't have to take this on alone, you know."

I smirked as I took a drink of the rum, thinking of a wolf out on some country hilltop. Too country for me, I thought. "One last thing," I said, changing the subject. "You know anything about prostitutes and a dentist office?"

He shook his head before swallowing a shot worth of his drink. "Should I know something about prostitutes and a dentist office?"

"Guess not," I said as I slid off the credenza. "Go home to your wife and start sucking up. Might help if you stop by Sandcastle's diner and pick up a homemade pie."

"Kid Harrison," he said, pointing a finger at me. "It'll be a cold day in hell before I take relationship advice from *you.*"

As I walked toward the stairs, I could still hear Quille swearing to himself in his office.

Chapter Sixteen

CHARLIE
Sunday, 10:57 p.m.

When I left the precinct, I couldn't stop thinking about pie so I stopped at Sandcastle's and ordered four specials and a lemon cream pie. As I was leaving, Quille entered. I smirked; he scowled. Neither of us spoke as he moved past me toward the counter.

Ten minutes later, I opened my apartment door and found Spence sitting at my dining room table. Beast was lying at his feet.

"This is a no dog building," I said as I walked over and dumped the food bags.

Spence uncapped a beer and slid it my way. "Please tell me you bought enough food for both of us. I'm starving."

"I bought plenty, but you'll owe me. I planned on eating leftovers the next few days to avoid going grocery shopping."

Spence walked into the kitchen and grabbed silverware.

I opened two containers and snuck a noodle under the table for Beast.

"*I saw that!*"

I hid my grin by taking a drink of the cold beer.

"Fill me in while we eat," Spence said, sliding me a fork.

I waited until after the third mouthful of food went down before explaining my day. By the time I caught him up, my dinner was three-fourths gone. I opened the pie container and stabbed a forkful.

Spence smirked as he uncapped another beer. "I saw plates in the cupboard. Would you like me to get you one?"

"Don't play Mr. Etiquette with me. Your house has more takeout containers and beer cans lying around than a frat house."

"Until I hired Mrs. Allen to be my secretary." He stabbed a chunk of pie for himself. "She cleaned my house while she worked today. Even did my laundry."

"Sounds like a keeper. She single?"

"Widowed. But it would never work between us. Even if I was into women twice my age, she's scared of dogs." He set his fork down before leaning back in his chair and rubbing his non-existent belly. "Beast had to ride with me today, which isn't ideal. Hard to be discreet with a hundred-pound rottweiler's head hanging out the window of your truck. Which leads me to a question."

"No."

"You need a bodyguard. He needs somewhere to be during the day. It's a win-win."

"I'm not running a kennel. No."

Beast whined from under the table.

I looked down at him. "No offense, buddy. Just wouldn't work. We'd drive each other crazy."

He laid his head on his paws and whined again.

"Fine. *One day.* That's it." Beast's tailless backside started wiggling. I rolled my eyes and sat up. "Beast can hang out with me tomorrow, but only tomorrow. You'll need to sucker someone else into watching him after that."

"Deal," Spence said as he gathered empty food containers. "I brought my laptop. You want me to run some backgrounds?"

"Yeah, that would be great. Run Colby Brown's. Can you also see what you can dig up on Roseline? I don't trust Gibson to be thorough with this double-homicide case."

"Sure thing," Spence said, dumping the food containers into the trash can and smashing it down so the overflow didn't fall out. "I'll run the backgrounds while you do the dishes."

I spotted a three-foot by three-foot cloth-covered cube sitting in my living room. It had a handle on one end. "What's that?" I asked, pointing. "Beast's bed?"

"Nope." He walked over and pulled a Velcro strap, unfolding the contraption into a long floor mat. "My bed."

"Why is it here?"

"I planned on sleeping in front of the door. Unless of course you invite me to share your bed." His eyebrows danced up and down.

"And at what point did you decide we were having a sleepover?"

He flashed a wicked smile at me before answering. "I keep the mat and clothes in my car. Let's not forget that there's a contract out on your head. And this arrangement—" he pointed to the mat, "—is just for tonight. Tomorrow, you need to arrange some protection."

"I can take care of myself."

"Darlin," he said, shaking his head in disappointment. "Have you looked in a mirror lately? You look like a racoon."

I stuck my tongue out at him before walking down the hall to the bathroom. Looking at myself in the mirror, I saw Spence was right. The swelling in my nose had gone down, but no amount of makeup was going to hide the bruising which extended above my eyelids and went downward to mid-cheek. I did the best I could with another layer of foundation before I fixed my hair into a twist.

Returning to the dining room, I tossed my purse inside my oversized crossover bag and grabbed my keys.

Spence looked up from his laptop. "Where to now?"

"The truck stop where Roseline worked. I want to interview her coworkers. If nothing else, maybe I can get a name for next of kin."

"Beast and I will come with you."

"No. Stay and work the backgrounds."

Spence closed the laptop and tucked it under one arm, then held up his phone in the other hand. "I have hotspot internet on my phone. I can run the backgrounds while you drive. Besides, Beast isn't ready to call it a night yet."

I looked down at Beast who stood at my feet, his backside swaying in excitement as he stared at the keys in my hand. "Fine. But don't interfere. I don't need a partner." I looked down at Beast again. "That goes for you, too."

Beast barked twice. I opened the door and let him run ahead of us downstairs.

~*~*~

I sat in the car an extra ten minutes, just watching the customers and vehicles at the truck stop. I had parked in the shadows of the parking lot, just outside the circle of flood lights stationed closer to the store.

Spence didn't question my reasoning. He worked silently on his laptop from the passenger seat. Beast, with his head extended between our seats, panted in my ear.

I grabbed my bag.

"Here," Spence said, handing me something.

"What is it?" I asked, not being able to see the small plastic object in my palm.

"A screamer. Pull the cord if you run into trouble. Beast will come to your rescue."

"A screamer?" I laughed. "I'm not a teenager going to her first unsupervised concert. I'm a cop."

"A cop working without a partner on three different cases. Either clip the damn thing to your jeans, or I'm tagging along."

I rolled my eyes but clipped the screamer to my side as I got out. When I closed the door, I saw Beast jump into the driver's seat. "Pains in the ass," I muttered to myself as I walked toward the well-lit store entrance.

Inside, the abundance of fluorescent lights overwhelmed my eyes. I squinted until they adjusted, then walked over to the register.

"Is there a manager working tonight? I'm here on behalf of the Miami PD."

"Am I in danger?" the young kid asked, looking around the store at the handful of customers.

"Not that I'm aware of," I answered honestly.

He released a big breath. "Whew. You scared me. I gotta stop watching all those action movies."

Everything about the kid screamed pot-head. Including his short attention span. "A manager?"

"Oh, yeah, right." He jogged over to a side door behind the counter, popping his head in the other room. A minute later, a burly woman with a five o'clock shadow walked out.

"I'm Sue Dodd, the manager. What's this about?" she asked briskly.

"Can we talk in private, Sue?" I asked.

She led us past the slushy and coffee machines, over to a nook which held a handful of mini tables and chairs. "This will have to do. I'm not allowed to let anyone in the back office."

"This is fine." I took a seat and waited for her to sit. "I'm here about Roseline Pageotte. I understand she didn't work last night."

At the mention of Roseline's name, I had the manager's full attention. "Is Roseline all right? I've left about a dozen messages for her. In the five years she's worked here, she's never missed a shift. Never even been late as far as I can remember."

I didn't remember seeing Roseline's cellphone on the evidence log. I'd have to follow up with Gibson on the phone. "We found her body this morning. She was murdered. I'm one of her neighbors, but I also work for the Miami PD."

Sue's shoulders slumped as she dropped her head and closed her eyes.

I gave her a few minutes to grieve before I laid a hand on her forearm to get her attention. "Does Roseline have any family? We need to notify next of kin."

She shook her head. "I'm not aware of any family. I'll check her application to be sure, but she never mentioned her parents or any siblings."

"What about close friends? A boyfriend?"

She shook her head again. "Roseline kept to herself. I was probably her closest friend, but I knew better than to pry. She even told people she was an illegal immigrant as an excuse to avoid social outings."

My head snapped back as I realized Roseline had lied to me. She'd confided to me she was an illegal just after she moved into the building. I remember it was when I asked her to join me for a drink at Bailey's pub. I didn't recall any indication that she wasn't being truthful. "Are you sure she wasn't an illegal?"

"Positive. We run backgrounds on all employees, and the corporate office in New Jersey has to approve every application before we can hire anyone." A frown formed on her face as she stared at the floor.

"What? What did you remember?"

"I didn't hire her," Sue said as she looked at me. "The corporate office called and said she was a good employee, relocating from one of their other stores in Lauderdale. They transferred the file to me."

Red flags, I thought. "Can you get her file for me?"

"I need the corporate office's permission to show it to you."

"No, don't call anyone. I'll call in a search warrant instead." I pulled my phone from my handbag.

"Wait. Stop," she said, holding out her hand. "The last time I had black and whites sitting in the parking lot, the truckers stopped coming here for two days. They all know each other, at least by radio handles. And they're wary of cops." She stood and walked toward the counter. "I'll get the file."

A few minutes later, Sue returned with the file, leaving it with me as she helped the kid at the counter with a line of customers. I skimmed most of the information, taking pictures of a few pages, and then dropped the file at the counter on my way out.

Exiting the store, I looked around. Customers shuffled back and forth from the fuel pumps and store. I walked to the side of the building where three cars were parked in the far corner near the back. My guess was the vehicles belonged to employees.

I started walking in that direction but before I reached the cars, I was grabbed from behind. A gloved hand clamped over my mouth as another hand latched onto my left wrist, pulling my arm across my body in a vice grip.

I threw my right elbow back into my attacker's ribs, but it bounced off a bulletproof vest as he dragged me into the darkness. I could make out the shadow of a car, parked behind the building. I bit his hand, but the glove was too thick. I reached up and jabbed my thumb into what I hoped was his eye, and his grip loosened. I jabbed again and this time when he jerked away, I was able to spin myself to the right and duck under his arm to escape.

As I turned to run, his arm snared around my waist, and our forward momentum toppled us to the ground. My chin bounced off the asphalt, slamming my molars together. As my eyes watered, I tried to crawl out from under him, but he grabbed me by the back of my hair with one hand and by the waistband of my jeans with the other, dragging me upward as he stood.

And then, my luck changed.

As I jerked from his grip, he must've snagged the cord on the screamer. The little black box emitted its high-pitch siren at decibels loud enough to cause permanent hearing damage. As I turned to fight, my attacker's hold vanished. He was already running toward his car.

Out of breath, I didn't bother to chase him. Instead, I leaned over, my hands on my knees, panting. Blood dripped from my chin and splashed on my white sneaker.

A growling creature zoomed past me. I realized it was Beast as Spence ran past. The car was already peeling from the parking lot with its lights off. I leaned over and picked up the screamer, placing the pin in the hole to silence it.

"You okay?" Spence asked as he jogged back.

"You get a plate number?" I asked as I continued to suck in air.

"Plate was dark. No lights. Sorry." Placing a finger gently under my jaw, he lifted my head. "You might need stiches."

"I'll live."

"What happened?" Sue asked from the sidewalk near the front of the building. Several truckers and the kid from the counter stood beside her.

"I'm afraid I need to call in the calvary. Sorry."

Several truckers looked at each other before hightailing it toward their rigs. She sighed, watching them leave.

The kid bounced on his heels. "This is just like in the movies."

~*~*~

I sat on the ambulance's bumper as a paramedic taped the sides of my split chin together with Steri-strips. I watched Quille cross the parking lot, looking both pissed and tired.

"I'd just fallen asleep," Quille said as he walked toward me. "In my own bed—not the couch, I might add. And then you called."

"You didn't need to come," I told him.

"Hold still," the paramedic ordered.

I waited until he finished before turning to Quille. "I wouldn't have called it in, but I needed the forensic team to do their thing."

Quille reached forward and grabbed the zipper on my sweatshirt, pulling the material away from my body and zipping it closed. "Is there a reason you're not wearing a shirt?"

Sometimes Quille was Sergeant Quille, my boss. Sometimes he was my friend. And other times, like now, he acted like a father-figure, covering me up so no one would see my black bra.

"I bagged my shirt when the first officers arrived on scene. Mr. Tricky grabbed me from behind, so maybe we'll get lucky with hair or skin evidence."

"Mr. Tricky?" Quille asked as he watched the forensics team process the scene.

I laughed, hearing Quille repeat the nickname I'd labeled my bad guy. "He's gotten the jump on me twice now. I thought he'd earned a name."

"You could've been killed."

"I wasn't."

He was intentionally not looking at me, focusing his eyes on the rear parking lot where the team was bagging evidence and taking pictures. "You need a partner. Someone to watch your back."

I looked back toward my car and whistled. Beast barked twice as his paws pattered across the lot to stop by my side. "Meet Beast. He's my new partner until things settle." I reached down and patted Beast's head. He leaned into my leg, nearly knocking me over.

"Turner and Hooch, lovely," Quille mumbled shaking his head as he walked away.

"Hey, wait up," I said, following him. "Since you're here... And you're already in a bad mood..."

Quille stopped in his tracks and bowed his head. "Hit me with it. I'm ready."

"I have a new theory about Roseline. What if she was enrolled in WITSEC?"

"Witness protection? I thought she was an illegal?" Quille asked as his head snapped up to look at me. "How'd you jump from Roseline being an illegal immigrant to her being under federal protection?"

Spence walked over and joined us.

"I peeked at her employment file. It was too professional. Too detailed. And in some places, the handwriting changed, like someone else had filled in the blanks."

Spence sighed. "Shit. So that's who received an electronic notice."

I glanced over at Spence. "What are you talking about?"

"You asked me to run a background search on Roseline. When I'm online, I keep an operation screen open that shows me anything sent or received from my computer. I noticed a packet of data was copied, and before I could stop it, it had been sent to another I.P. address. I tried to trace it, but the I.P. address jumped several states until I lost it in a maze of data networks." Spence reached a hand out to Quille. "Sergeant."

"Spence," Quille said with a nod and a return handshake. "How'd you get sucked into this mess?"

"Just lucky, I guess," Spence said, grinning over at me. "The paramedic said you need stiches."

"I'm a fast healer."

Spence looked at Quille, but Quille only shrugged. "Don't waste your time. Short of gunshot wounds, I don't even argue with her anymore."

"How many times have you been shot?" Spence asked with a raised eyebrow.

I shrugged.

"Three times," Quille answered. "That I'm aware of at least. Wouldn't surprise me if there were times I didn't know about, though. This one's a handful. Consider yourself warned."

"About the Feds," I said, steering the conversation back to the case.

"Don't suppose you can call Kierson? Ask him to look into it?" Quille asked.

"Sorry." I scrunched my nose. "I sort-of burned that connection before I left Michigan."

"Burned it or scorched it into something unrecognizable?" Quille asked.

"I'd guess somewhere between the two. It's best if I stay off his radar for a while."

Quille shook his head as he laughed. "You're one of a kind, Kid." He pulled out his phone as he walked away. "One of a kind."

Greg, the lead forensic investigator, walked over. "We got what we could, but no promises. Tire tracks look standard. The trash and debris in the area could've been from anyone. Our best bet is your shirt, but like you told me, it was a brief encounter. I'll do what I can, but..."

"I know you will. Thanks, Greg. Text me if you find anything."

"Can do." He slid his wire rimmed glassed up. "Go home, Kid. Get some sleep. Even without the split chin and two black eyes, I can tell you're beat." He patted my shoulder before walking away.

"You two seem close," Spence commented.

"We've worked a lot of cases together. He's good. Thorough."

"That all?"

"I don't sleep with men connected to law enforcement. Sexism is alive and thriving in the blue brotherhood. It's not worth it."

"Plenty of women in law enforcement have relationships with their coworkers without it affecting their careers."

"And plenty of others are never treated as equals afterward. It's a line that once crossed, you can't uncross."

"Good thing I'm not a cop, huh?" Spence threw an arm over my shoulder, whistled for Beast, and led us back to the car.

"That's where you're wrong," I said, nudging his arm off my shoulder. "My rule extends to anyone working or associated with a case. You're on the wrong side of the line."

"I guess we better hurry up and solve the case then. Wouldn't want you to feel guilty when you break your rule," Spence said, taking my keys and pushing me toward the passenger side of the car.

I didn't argue. I was beat.

Chapter Seventeen

CHARLIE
Monday, 8:01 a.m.

I woke to the ringtone on my phone. Before I could focus on my surroundings, I felt the phone being placed in my hand and my hand lifted toward my ear. "Yeah?" I answered, looking beside me to find Spence leaned back in the driver's seat of my car.

"You awake?" Kelsey asked.

"Sort of," I said on a yawn. "Give me ten and I'll call you back."

I hung up and opened the car door. As soon as I stood, Beast leapt from the car, knocking me into the door panel. He ran over and lifted his leg on a bush before running around in circles in the parking lot.

"Well, he's wide awake."

"He's always full of energy in the mornings," Spence said, shutting the driver's door before walking over and dragging me toward my apartment building's entrance.

"Why did we sleep in the car?" I asked as I pulled my arm from his grip.

"I was afraid if I woke you, you'd start working again. I stayed awake and kept watch." He held the door open for Beast and me, and then followed us up the stairs. "Which is why I'm going to take a nap while you cook breakfast."

"I don't have to cook." I smiled as I unlocked the door and threw it open. Aunt Suzanne was in the kitchen. Heavenly scents of bacon and butter fried goodness wafted toward us.

"Food. Then bed," Spence said.

"You mean your floor mat? You're not sleeping in my bed."

"Wanna bet?" he said as he shut the door.

I sat at the table and was rewarded with a plate full of artery clogging deliciousness. Aunt Suzanne raised my jaw to inspect my chin, but only rolled her eyes before returning to the kitchen. She served Spence a plate, then delivered coffee and orange juice.

I took a picture of my plate with my phone, sending the image to Kelsey before forking some fried potatoes into my mouth. Thirty seconds later, I hit the answer button and held the phone up to my ear.

Kelsey started talking without greeting. "Tell Aunt Suzanne that I miss her and her cooking, but I need to talk to you about a case."

"Mickey called you," I mumbled through a mouthful of food.

"He did, but he wasn't tattling. That recording you played for him, about the dentist and prostitutes, that's a case I've been working. He only knows about it because I needed a special favor that I can't talk about over the phone."

"Okay. And?"

"I had planned on coming to Florida to finish the case, but I'm at a loss right now for someone to stay with Nicholas."

"You should stay in Michigan," I said, setting down my fork and leaning back in my chair. "Now's not a good time for a visit."

"Why?" I could hear her concentrating on my voice. She knew me well enough to read the change in my voice.

"I won't lie to you, but I'm not ready to share all the details either—especially over the phone."

"On a scale of one to ten..."

She didn't have to finish the sentence. It was a game we'd played during our rookie year in the police department. On a scale of one to ten, how worried were we that we might not survive.

"Seven," I answered, honestly.

"And how much of the problem ties back to the dentist office?"

"I've barely looked into it. I've had more pressing issues."

"You focus on your stuff; let me handle the dentist office. In the meantime, you need someone capable of watching your back. I can send someone from Aces."

"No need. I have a partner." I reached over and petted Beast's head.

Spence chuckled before carrying his empty plate into the kitchen. While his back was turned, I snuck Beast a chunk of bacon.

"I saw that," Spence said with his back still facing me.

I stuck my tongue out at him.

"Since when do you have a partner?" Kelsey asked. "Didn't the last one hand his badge over after working one day with you?"

"That wasn't my fault. He completely overreacted to the situation."

"Right." I could almost hear her eyes rolling. "Look, I need to go," Kelsey said, sounding distracted. "But promise me you'll stay safe and far away from the dentist case."

"I can't make either promise, and you know that. But I can give you a few days. I've got someone in a safe house, though, and that can't remain permanent."

"Now I'm intrigued, but I'll heed your warning about not saying much over the phone. We'll talk soon." She disconnected abruptly, knowing that the customary salutations were not necessary between us.

Aunt Suzanne walked over and refilled my coffee cup. "Was it smart not to tell her you got your ass kicked twice in less than twenty-four hours?"

"She's got a lot on her plate. Kelsey doesn't have anyone she trusts to watch Nicholas if she were to fly down here. Her relationship with Grady crashed and burned. Wild Card's out on a job. The only thing she can contribute right now is worry. And worrying helps no one."

"I could watch Nicholas. I'd love to, in fact. We could go to the beach like we used to."

"It would take an army of men guarding him to convince Kelsey it's safe enough to bring him back to Florida. She'll never forget walking into that apartment and finding him gone."

"She doesn't have to forget." Aunt Suzanne rested a gentle hand on my shoulder. "She just has to get over her fear."

"That's a big ask, Aunt Suzanne. It took her over three years to bring him home." I knew Spence was listening from the kitchen, but he stayed quiet as he washed the dishes. "I have work to do. Mind if I skip helping with the cleanup?"

"You know I don't mind. Scat." She walked into the kitchen. "You too," she said to Spence.

"Thank you for breakfast," Spence told her as he turned out of the kitchen and down the hall.

I followed him. In my bedroom, he threw himself on top of the bed, fully clothed. I didn't have the energy to argue with him. I pulled some clothes from the dresser and took them to the bathroom. Twenty minutes later, I could hear him snoring when I opened the bathroom door. Walking down the hall, I confirmed the kitchen was empty before I grabbed my bag, phone, and keys, and led Beast out of the apartment.

~*~*~

The precinct was my first stop. I wasn't going to leave Beast in a hot car so I took him inside with me. The desk officer raised an eyebrow but didn't say anything as he pressed the button to release the door to the inner offices.

On the second floor, Beast veered off and around a desk. He walked over to a bawling woman sitting in a guest chair and laid his head in her lap. She started absently petting him and he leaned his solid mass against her. Ford, a detective who'd been on the force long before I arrived, left the woman with Beast and walked toward me.

"What's that all about?" I asked him.

"Her son was shot in a drive by last night. Only four goddamn years old." Ford looked up at the ceiling, feeling the weight of the job on his shoulders.

"Let Beast keep her company for a bit. Go give yourself a minute to reset."

He bowed his head and walked off, slipping into the men's room.

I looked back at Beast. He had one of his paws across the woman's lap, and his head nuzzled against her shoulder. Her arms were wrapped around him as she unleashed a world full of grief into his fur.

"Got a minute?" Quille asked in a quiet tone from behind me.

I followed him into his office. "Any idea who the shooter was?" I asked, tipping my head toward the main room as I crossed over to the credenza to sit.

"Dark colored four-door car. That's it. That's all the information the officers at the scene were able to get people to admit."

"Where was the shooting?"

"Out in Crack Village, near the housing projects. Midnight last night."

I pulled my phone and called Chills, a gang leader with a God-fearing grandmother.

"I was expecting your call. Give me a minute." I could hear voices in the background, then a door close. "I'm working on finding the shooter. I've got boys living two doors down. Best I can figure, the shooters were gunning for my crew and hit the wrong house. I'll call you when I know more."

"Not so quick. Is this a turf war?"

"Naw. Just some young bloods trying to prove themselves. I'll take care of it."

"No, you won't. You'll get me a name and address."

"Can't do that. Bad for business."

"Don't screw with me, Chills. We're talking about a guy who killed a kid. That's front-page news."

"All right, all right. I'll see what I can arrange so the boys in blue look good."

"If you go rogue—"

"Yeah, yeah, yeah. Save your threats for someone who doesn't know how fucking crazy you are. Damn, I miss

Kelsey. At least she's somewhat sane." He disconnected the call.

"Anything?" Quille asked, nodding to my phone as I dropped it into my bag.

"Shooters hit the wrong house. My contact is looking into it. He'll ring back when he has something."

"I hope it's soon. The news stations are already running the story."

Cases like these were a powder keg. Either the community quietly mourned or outrage at the police overtook the city from every podium. In the chaos that always followed, there were never any good guys. Not on either side. How could there be. A little boy had lost his life.

"I got a confirmation from WITSEC that Roseline was one of theirs, but they aren't saying why. They're sending someone to talk to us."

"Great. Just what I need. Some uppity Fed telling me how to do my job."

"Ouch," Maggie said from the doorway. "That hurt my feelings."

I was about to exclaim my excitement at seeing Maggie when I remembered the grieving mother. I looked over, but both the woman and Beast were no longer at the desk.

Maggie followed my gaze. "You looking for the crying woman with the dog?"

"Yeah. Did you see where they went?"

"A detective moved them into the conference room at the end of the hall. What happened?"

"Drive by."

Maggie sighed. "It never ends."

"No, it doesn't." I waved a hand at the chairs. "Were you sent here to share intel? Or to tell us to back off?"

Maggie turned one of the guest chairs, angling it toward me, then sat before propping her feet up on the other chair. "I'm to tell you to back off. But I'd rather fast forward to the part where you refuse to drop the case and I'm forced to divulge details."

"I like her," Quille said.

"Yeah. Maggie's got style." I looked at Quille. "Sergeant Quille, meet FBI agent, Maggie O'Donnell. Truly, the best the FBI has ever had on their team."

"Ooh. Nice intro," Maggie said, leaning over to shake Quille's hand. "Call me Maggie. I like to keep a low profile."

"You can call me Quille or Patrick, but most people around here call me Quille."

"Like the pen. Got it. Now, as for Roseline Pageotte," she said, eyeing me sideways as she shook her head, "you really slammed into a mess this time. Heads are rolling in the DOJ."

"What the hell does the DOJ have to do with my homicide?"

"Roseline was the primary witness in an upcoming trial for a hillbilly heroin ring."

"What? How does a quiet woman like Roseline end up anywhere near Oxi dealers?"

Maggie's eyes lit with challenge as she watched me. "There was one detail in her background that wasn't fake. Can you guess which one?"

I looked down as my mind shifted through her background search and her employee file. "Shit. She worked at a truck stop."

"Ding-ding-ding," Maggie said as she rang an invisible bell. "I'm impressed." Maggie saw something out of the corner of her eye in the main room and her facial features morphed back to her all-business expression.

"The grieving mother?" I asked, not looking toward the window to see for myself.

When she looked back at me, it was her sad eyes that answered yes. "The Feds aren't releasing the details of their case yet, but I can share that Roseline documented trucks coming and going for over six months involving this drug ring. She was a sharp woman. Then one night something went wrong. One of the drivers shot a guy in the parking lot. Roseline hid until the cops got there. She's lucky to be alive. She asked the local police to call the Feds, then she turned everything over to us. She had collected video tape evidence along with detailed notes on over two dozen bad guys. These guys were never even on our radar."

Quille whistled.

I lowered my head, staring at the floor.

"She was your neighbor?" Maggie asked, though we both knew she already knew the answer. Maggie would've studied the details of the case before walking into the building.

I nodded anyway.

"Were you two close?"

I shook my head. I continued staring at the floor as I answered. "She kept her distance. She told people she was an illegal to explain why she was so reserved. I never guessed."

"But you respected her."

"Twelve apartments in our building, but Roseline was the only one who was willing to lend a helping hand to Pauly, a local homeless man."

"No," Quille said. "She wasn't the only one. You helped him, too. Don't forget that."

"I didn't do enough for either of them. They were murdered right under my nose. In my own damn building." I stood and walked over to face the glass, watching the uniforms move about in a hushed frenzy. "Where does the case stand?" I asked Maggie without turning around.

"The US Attorney's office will exhaust all efforts to keep the case alive, but unless we can prove the drug ring were behind killing her, the bad guys will likely walk."

"Did Greg find any DNA last night?" Quille asked.

"I don't know, but that case is about that contract I told you about," I said, looking over my shoulder to give Quille a pointed look. "Did the team go back to Roseline's with a black light?"

"Yeah," Quille said, digging out a file from under a ten-inch stack. "Haven't had a chance to read it yet." Something on the other side of the glass caught Quille's attention. "Gibson! Get your ass in here!"

"Yes, sir," Gibson said, hurrying to the doorway.

"What have you got on the double homicide?"

"Nothing new yet, sir. I just got in the office."

"I warned you," I mumbled loud enough for him to hear.

"You're off the case. Turn everything you have over to me and report to Riley. You're on desk duty doing research for him until I say otherwise."

"But sir, I—"

"*Get out before I fire your ass!*" Quille ordered.

"You better run, boy," Maggie said, flashing her pearly whites. "Poppa bear is pissed."

Gibson flushed but hurried away as if his life depended on it.

Quille opened the drawer of his desk and held up a badge. "I'm not going to ask you again." He tossed the badge at me. "Stop by the counselor's office and get your ass cleared for duty."

"Damn it," I grumbled, dropping the badge in my bag. "This isn't a good idea, and you know it."

"I need someone here who can help me control these idiots. And you're it."

"Fine." I stomped into the workroom. Walking over to the assignment board, I re-assigned a few names. When I turned around, everyone had stopped working and was looking at the board. "Chop. Chop. I want updates on every case we have going."

Each group brought over their files and filled me in. Most were on the right path, and I gave them the nod to continue. One had hit a dead end and I motioned to Maggie, handing her the file. "She's a profiler," I told the young detective to answer his unasked question. He followed Maggie over to a side table as she started reading the file.

Another detective had too many suspects and I reassigned Gibson to help with the background checks. When everyone had cleared out, I noticed the grieving mother standing near the conference room door, watching me with sad eyes. Beast sat her feet, leaning into her.

I walked across the room and faced her.

"Tell me someone's working just as hard to find the man who shot my son."

Detective Ford stood beside us, his head bending in defeat.

"We both know that witnesses don't talk in your neighborhood. That makes solving cases like your son's harder, but not impossible."

Ford's head flew up, a flicker of hope in his eyes.

"There are other methods... less conventional methods... that cops sometimes use to solve these types of crimes. I've made a call to someone who owes me a few favors. He's not someone I trust, not even someone I respect, but he's in a better position to find the person responsible."

Her chin quivered. Beast whined and rubbed his head against her thigh. "I'm okay, boy," she said, patting his head as she inhaled a shaky breath. "Thank you," she said to me. "For doing what you can to find them." She looked down at Beast. "And, for letting me borrow your dog. He's been a champ."

"I'm on my way downstairs to the counselor's office. Why don't you come with us? It will help."

I didn't wait for her to answer. I looped my arm through hers, leading her toward the elevator.

Chapter Eighteen

CHARLIE
Monday, 9:43 a.m.

Ford must've called downstairs and told them we were on our way. Marcie, the precinct's shrink, met us at the door, handed me a piece of paper, and led the grieving woman into her inner sanctum. I looked at the piece of paper. It was a signed release to return to active duty. A post-it was stuck on top of it: *We'll chat later. Go get the bastards.*

I dropped the release form off at the front desk and asked the officer to have someone run it up to HR before I had time to shoot anyone. He stood there confused, not sure how to react, just holding the form.

"She's not kidding," another officer laughed, taking the form. "I'll take it over myself, Kid."

"Thanks, Leland." I waved over my shoulder as Beast followed me outside.

"Trying to ditch me?" Maggie asked as she hurried out the door after me.

I turned toward her and watched her happy facial features morph into an expression I'd seen on my cousin's face more times than I could count. I didn't think—just dove toward her—taking us both down.

A mess of arms and legs tangled together as we tumbled down the concrete stairs—bullets ricocheting over our heads.

Landing hard on the sidewalk, unknown hands pulled us around the base of the stairs and out of the line of fire. The shooting stopped as police officers emerged from every direction, flooding the block. Maggie and I remained on our backs amidst some shrubbery, both panting.

We looked at each other at the same time, but she was the first to speak. "*Lucy... you've got some splainin to do...*" She bombed on the accent from the iconic tv show, but it was close enough for me to catch the reference.

"It's not my fault," I said as a laugh escaped. "I seriously have no idea why someone's trying to kill me."

"We best get to work at figuring that out then." She rolled to the side and pushed herself up. "I like a good mystery." She reached out a hand to help me up.

When I stood, my knee nearly buckled.

She caught my arm to help me stay upright. "Can you walk?"

"I can limp. That'll have to be good enough." I swatted off the worst of the dirt. "Shit! Where's Beast?"

"He's over here," Quille called out.

I hobbled around the corner to find Beast next to Quille who was helping an officer out of the bushes.

"That damn dog saved my life," the cop said, staring at me. "He tackled me into the bushes right as the bullets started flying."

"Good boy, Beast," I called out.

Beast barked three times and hopped around in excitement.

"Did anyone get a location on the shooter," Maggie asked.

"That open third floor window," Quille said pointing to a commercial building down the block. "Someone saw a rifle barrel. They're searching it now."

"Beast, stay with Quille," I ordered the dog, pointing at Quille.

Beast barked once, then sat.

"I want your dog," Maggie said as she jogged next to me down the block.

"Not my dog," I said as I tried to block out the pain in my knee. "Borrowed him for the day from a friend."

As we approached the building entrance, I tipped my head in greeting at the two-man team already stationed at the door. Maggie ran past them, flashing her badge.

I pulled my gun. "I need a radio," I said to one of the officers.

The closest cop unhooked his radio and handed it over. I walked through the door that Maggie held open. "This is Detective Harrison," I said into the radio. "Report status on building search."

"We've got nothing, Kid," Ford answered over the radio. "Shooter's nest is empty. He's gone."

"Search the place from rooftop to basement. I'll work the perimeter."

"Understood."

"What are you thinking?" Maggie asked.

"He would've left through a side or back door. Let's check out his options."

We returned outside and walked down the north side of the building. There were no exits on this side unless he exited through one of the closed windows, which was unlikely because of the busy street running parallel. On the west side, a main exit led into a parking lot.

I called out to a group of cops who were both guarding the rear exit and looking around for any suspicious activity. "Start searching those cars."

I walked around the building, peering down the narrow alley on the south side of the building. A service exit was partially open a few feet away, like someone hadn't shut it completely. I walked over and peered inside. The hallway was vacant.

"Detective Harrison," an officer called out. "Where do you want us?"

Two officers I recognized but couldn't place their names stood waiting for assignment. "Guard this exit until the building has been cleared. Radio Detective Ford and let him know we'll need this door dusted for prints.

"Yes, ma'am."

"Ugh. Sometimes I hate the South," Maggie grumbled. "Ma'am this, and ma'am that."

"Could be worse." I backstepped so I could peer down the alley. It was more of a walkway than anything, connecting the street and the rear parking lot. I looked back and forth, until out of nowhere, some instinct told me to look up. "Son of a bitch."

I started for the fire escape, but Maggie pulled me back and grabbed the ladder, starting up first.

"What the hell, Maggie?" I complained as I watched her climb.

"We both know your knee is trashed! Head to the end of the block!"

She was right. I yelled for the officers in the parking lot, sending half up the ladder with Maggie and the other half with me down the block. Five buildings down, there was another alley, with another fire escape. A door to a restaurant kitchen was propped open and I pulled my badge, holding it up as I called out to the staff filled kitchen. "Police. Anyone see or hear anything in the alley?"

"Like a guy coming down the fire escape in a hurry?" one of the women answered robotically, not looking up from stirring something in a large pot.

"Yeah, like that. What'd he look like?"

"Big. White. Dark hair."

"How long ago?"

"Two, maybe three minutes ago."

"Which direction?"

"Toward the street," she said pointing toward the southeast.

The officers who were with me took off running toward the street. I didn't follow. I knew my knee wouldn't take it. I radioed in that suspect was spotted leaving the vicinity and his last known location. If we were lucky, we'd find a picture of him on one of the street cameras, but even that felt like a long shot.

I walked out to the alley, and leaned against the other building, taking some of the pressure off my knee.

"Are you fucking kidding me?" Maggie called out from the rooftop above.

I shrugged. "I need a beer!" I yelled back at her.

She looked at her phone, before yelling down to me again, "It's only ten in the morning. I haven't even had breakfast yet!"

"Oh man, you missed out! Aunt Suzanne cooked this morning!"

Her reply was a single finger. The *naughty* one.

Chapter Nineteen

CHARLIE
Monday, High Noon

Two hours later, the employees of the detective's squad followed me into the patrol room, and Ford helped me climb on top of a desk. Protocol dictated that formal memos and announcements were made as necessary to the other officers. My way was faster.

I whistled, grabbing everyone's attention. "Listen up, this will be brief. Most of you know me, but for those who don't, I'm Detective Harrison."

"Go, Kid!" one of the officers yelled.

"Give us a lead, Kid!" another officer yelled.

"This morning was the third time in two days that some asshole tried to take me out. Detective Ford pulled nearby security footage, and, bless his heart, managed to get a photo of a guy fleeing the area in a silver Hyundai. Description and partial plate information will be sent shortly to your phones." I patted Ford on the top of his head before taking the picture from him and holding it up. "This photo is for only the eyes of the girls and boys in blue. Do *not* share with the media." I continued to hold it up as I spoke. "One more thing… He's a professional. He might've failed three attempts, but his first two attacks led to street fights and in both cases, *the only* reason I'm here today is because I got lucky."

The room went quiet except for one rookie whose laughter caused everyone to turn to him. He read the serious expressions and snapped his jaw closed.

"Give us the run down," Ford said.

"This guy is patient. Organized. He's strong. He's well trained in fighting, both offense and defense. And each time he's come at me, I never knew he was out there. If I had to guess, I'd say he has a military background. I'd also wager he's working for someone. This is the third vehicle he's had in two days. Someone's bankrolling his operation."

"You going to a safe house?" one of the officers asked.

"Yes," Quille answered.

"No," I said, smirking back at Quille. I turned back to the room. "If you see this car, call it in. Do not try any heroic crap. We've already had too many close calls."

"Protect and serve!" Leland bellowed.

"Protect and serve!" the men and women in blue responded.

I reached over and both Ford and Quille helped lower me to the floor.

"Your friend Maggie has taken over my unit," Quille said as we walked out.

I pointed toward the elevator. My knee was better, but not ready to climb a flight of stairs. "That's a good thing. Maggie likes to keep busy. She'll have the homicide unit caught up on cases, organized and polished, before she gets bored and leaves."

"She's making me look bad."

"She won't take credit for any of the work, and by the time she leaves you'll have the most effective unit in Miami. You might even make it home for dinner a few nights this week."

That made him smile.

My phone rang. I pulled it from my purse and saw it was Chills. "Yeah."

"My boys tried to make a delivery, but there was too much action for their comfort in your district."

"What kind of delivery?"

"The kind with three beating hearts. They dropped the packages off at the chapel on 10th. Better get there quick before someone unties them." Chills hung up.

"Ford!" I yelled toward the stairs where he was walking with some of the other guys back to the second floor. "Your shooter was just delivered to the church on 10th. You'll need three cars."

Ford ran down the stairs, stopped to kiss my cheek, then ran from the building with several officers following.

Sensing someone watching me, I looked over to see Marcie, the department shrink, watching me as she helped the grieving mother stay standing. The mother covered her face as she wept.

"Where's Beast?" I asked Quille.

"Well," Quille said, scratching the back of his head and trying to hide his smile. "Funny you should ask."

I followed him over to a sidelight window that ran alongside the front doors. Outside, Beast stood on the top of the landing doing his bark, happy dance, bark again routine as the reporters took his picture. I looked over at Quille and rolled my eyes. Without stepping outside, I ducked my head and opened the door, whistling for Beast. He ran inside and followed me to the back of the building and out the rear exit.

We walked down two buildings, cut through an alley, then another half dozen yards to my car. I let Beast in first, him leaping over the driver's seat and into the passenger seat, before I slid behind the wheel.

"What were we working on before everything went crazy?" I asked Beast as I pulled into traffic.

Beast barked once.

"Right. We need to find Roseline's killer."

I realized I never read the second forensic report from Roseline's apartment. Not wanting to turn around and drive back to the precinct, I called Greg instead.

"Perfect timing," he answered. "I was just about to call it a day. I've been working for twenty-hours straight."

"Want a beer? I can meet you at my place, and you can walk me through Roseline's apartment."

"Is the beer cold?"

"It will be," I answered.

He laughed. "Deal. See you in ten minutes."

I turned right into the parking lot of a corner gas station, running inside to buy beer. On the way to the checkout counter, I grabbed a jug of water.

"Is that your dog?" a woman asked from the doorway, pointing over her shoulder.

"Depends. What did he do?" I asked as I stacked the beer and water on the counter.

"You left him in the car," the woman said with her hands on her hips.

I pulled my wallet and handed cash to the young man behind the register as I responded to the woman. "I left the dog in the car with the car running, the air conditioner cranked, and the front windows completely down. Relax, lady."

"I'm calling the cops!"

I glanced over as she stepped back outside. I snorted as I took the offered change from the cashier. He was looking back and forth between us. "She's really calling."

I shrugged while gathering the beer and water. "With the air conditioner running, the dog is more comfortable than we are."

"Aren't you worried someone will steal it? Leaving the car running like that?"

"Would you steal a car with a rottweiler sitting in the front seat?"

He shook his head.

I walked out as a police cruiser pulled into the lot. The officers slid out of their car, and while ignoring the woman, they walked over to pet Beast.

I tilted my head toward the woman already raising holy hell from the sidewalk. "You going take care of the batshit crazy lady for me?"

They both sighed as they glanced over at the woman. "We got it. Get out of here."

I didn't wait around for them to change their minds.

Chapter Twenty

KELSEY
Monday, 12:15 p.m.

When my phone rang, I looked at the caller ID and smiled as I answered, "Hey, Aunt Suzanne."

"Do *not* tell Charlie I called," she said hurriedly into the phone.

I raised an eyebrow. "Okay."

"She's in trouble."

"Did she get arrested again?"

"Not that kind of trouble, but the day is young."

Laughing, I said, "What's going on?"

Aunt Suzanne remained quiet, likely thinking out her response.

"Just tell me. I'm sure it's not that bad."

"Someone tried to kill her." Even after several decades living as a cop's wife, Aunt Suzanne tended to overreact.

"Charlie's a cop," I said as I sighed. "Someone tries to shoot or stab her on the regular. It's part of the job."

"*Three times*. The same guy has attacked her *three times* in less than forty-eight hours. She has two black eyes, a split chin, and she's limping. Your uncle is worried. Her boss is worried. That guy Spence is worried."

"Who's Spence?"

"He's a private investigator. He's cute. He—" she made a noise which sounded like a growl "—*Spence isn't important*. Everyone's worried about Charlie. There's a

[147]

manhunt to find this guy before he makes another attempt to kill her."

She was right. This wasn't good. Charlie pissing people off was normal. Someone wanting to kill Charlie was normal. Someone making three attempts *and living*, that was a whole new ballgame. "Let me guess, Charlie's doing her *I-can-take-care-of-myself* routine." I looked over and watched Katie, Anne, and Alex move into the dining room and sit. They were listening to my side of the conversation.

Aunt Suzanne released a long breath. "She needs you, Kelsey. She'll hate your meddling, but I'd rather listen to her rant about you being bossy—than have her turn up dead."

"I need to make arrangements for Nicholas. I'll try to get to Florida by tonight."

"Kelsey," Aunt Suzanne said, her voice laced with concern. "I know you're worried about bringing Nicholas back to Miami. But we'll keep him safe. Just come home."

After Aunt Suzanne had disconnected, I stared at my phone screen for several minutes. *Home*. Miami. The city I lived in before everything changed. The city that stole my son and ripped us apart for years. Could I keep him safe? Maybe. But I wasn't alone anymore, either. I'd take an army.

"What do you need?" Alex asked.

I looked at Alex. He looked back with a concerned, but determined expression.

"I need a rental house in Miami. Something with a pool for Nicholas. And *big*. It needs to have a shitload of bedrooms. I'm taking every available security guard with us."

"On it." Alex walked over and grabbed one of the house laptops.

I turned to Katie. "Go talk to Donovan. Sort out who he can spare on short notice."

She didn't say anything, but hurried to the front door.

Anne started for the stairs, speaking over her shoulder. "I'll start packing. We'll go with you."

"Anne—" I said, stopping her. "I don't know what kind of danger Charlie is up against."

"We'll take an army if we need to," Anne said, unwavering. "But we *all* go. Together, we'll keep the kids safe." She ran up the stairs, ending the discussion.

I walked outside through the back sliding door, down the side stairs, and over to where Tyler and Bones were watching the kids play with Jager. "Tyler?"

"Yeah?" he answered, not looking away from the kids.

"We need to make a trip to Florida. Charlie's in trouble. Can you come too?"

"Where *they* go," he pointed at the kids, "I go. When do we leave?"

"Soon. Travel arrangements are being made."

I could feel Bones staring at me, but my eyes were locked on Nicholas. Taking him to Florida scared the shit out of me.

"I'll call Bridget," Bones whispered. "We'll be ready to leave when you are."

~*~*~

Within an hour, we were driving to the airport. Tyler drove my SUV. I rode shotgun. The kids bounced in the back seat, chattering with Alex who sat between them. The rest of the family and security were in similar SUVs in front of us or behind us. Only Lisa had stayed home, but she and Abigail were moved into one of the apartments at Aces. They'd be safe there. Donovan would make sure of it.

I called Aunt Suzanne, but before I could say anything, she said, "Please tell me you're coming to Florida."

"We're on our way. All of us."

"All?"

"I'm bringing an army."

"Oh," she said, pausing. "I better run to the grocery store."

"First, pack a bag. I'll send someone for you and Uncle Hank when we land. Both of you will stay with us until this gets sorted."

"Is that necessary?"

"It is if you want to spend time with the kids. I can't have you traveling back and forth to the safe house."

"I know how to spot a tail," she grumbled. "But fine. We'll be ready." She disconnected the call.

"Kelsey," Tyler said in a low tone.

"Yes?" I said as I dropped my phone into my shoulder bag which was sitting at my feet.

"Three cars back. Blue sedan."

I looked in my mirror and spotted the car. "And?"

Tyler turned on his blinker before turning right into a residential neighborhood. Bones was driving the SUV behind us. He followed Tyler. When the blue sedan also turned right, Bones slammed on his brakes, turning the wheel so the SUV spun sideways to block the road. Another one of our SUVs cut off the car's escape. Tyler hit the gas, speeding through the neighborhood to get us out of there.

I called Bridget, knowing Bones would've ordered her to stay in the car.

She skipped the greeting and got right to the point. "Don't know yet, but Bones, Katie, Trigger, and Jackson have it handled. Go! Get to the airport."

"Call me when the dust settles."

"You got it, boss."

I leaned over my seat to look at Alex and the kids. The kids seemed unconcerned and continued chattering about Florida. Alex raised an eyebrow but didn't seem worried either.

"What's our rental like?" I asked Alex.

"Fabulous, of course. Would you expect anything less of me?" His hands danced in the air as he detailed the rental. "Imagine... A luxurious seven-bedroom oceanside estate with enough couches and daybeds to sleep twenty-five people. Not one, but two three-stall garages, with additional housing above one of them that connects to the main house by way of the second floor. Eight full bathrooms and three half baths. A game room. Heated pool. Hot tub. Private dock with a speed boat. Outdoor tiki lounge. Multiple balconies and a veranda overlooking the ocean. A chef equipped kitchen with—"

"Got it!" I said, holding up a hand to stop his sales pitch. "You did good."

"We need to put Alex in charge of securing housing more often," Tyler said as he merged onto the interstate. "Sounds like my kind of safe house."

"How big is the pool?" Nicolas asked.

"What's a game room?" Sara asked.

"Dummy," Nicholas said. "It's where you play games."

"Like monopoly?" Sara asked.

"Sure," Nicholas said, shrugging. He glanced at Alex, not sure at all. "Isn't it?"

"More like a pool table and arcade games."

"Sweet. Do we need quarters?" Nicholas asked.

"If you do, we'll get you some," I assured him before turning back in my seat and pulling my phone from my bag. Bridget had texted me about the car that had been following us.

Bridget: *Only Nightcrawler. He was driving Beth home when they spotted us.*

Me: *Thanks for the update. We'll hold the plane for you.*

Bridget: *You'd better. I have a new bikini that will drive Bones crazy.*

Oh boy, I thought.

~*~*~

Four and a half hours later, the only thing I could think as I walked with the kids through the first floor of the rental house and out onto the open veranda overlooking the pool, and beyond that the ocean, was *holy shit*.

"Cool," Nicholas said from beside me. "We really are rich."

"So... This is how the upper-class vacations," Anne said, walking out behind us. "I love Miami."

"I love Kelsey's limitless corporate card," Alex said, joining us.

"Holy shit," I said aloud before I started laughing.

Sara giggled. "Pushups, Aunt Kelsey."

I didn't argue. I got down on the pristine veranda and counted out the ten pushups. After, I stood and started toward the door. "Tyler, you're in charge while I'm gone," I called over my shoulder.

"Consider it handled. I'll coordinate security measures with Bones and Jackson."

Bridget followed me outside to a row of rented SUVs, handing me a Glock and holster, before she jogged to the passenger side. I slid behind the wheel and turned over the engine. Jackson was already on his way to pick up my aunt and uncle. I was tasked with a much more difficult—*and dangerous*—assignment.

To confront Charlie and force her to relocate.

Chapter Twenty-One

CHARLIE
Monday, 5:55 p.m.

It took Greg three hours to walk me through the autopsy reports and the forensic evidence from Roseline's apartment and the truck stop's parking lot. Greg was thorough. A downright nerd when it came to evidence. But that's why I liked working with him. When we were done reviewing the reports—my overloaded brain now a pile of mush—I dumped our warm beers in the sink and uncapped fresh ones. We were still in the dining room talking when Spence showed. He sat to drink a beer with us as I gave him the short version of the day's events.

I was taking a drink of my beer when someone banged hard enough against my apartment door that I was somewhat surprised the flimsy thing was still hanging on its hinges.

Beast, who'd been sleeping across my feet, half-barked, rolled over, and then continued snoring.

I unholstered my gun and stood. Spence mirrored my movements from the other side of the table. Greg, the nerd that he was, backed himself into the corner to stay out of the way.

"Feel! Free! Fine! Fummm!" Bridget's voice yelled from the other side of the door, ending on a giggle.

"That's not how it goes!" Kelsey's voice snapped from the hallway.

"Yes, it is," Bridget said.

"No. It's Fe, Fi, Fo, Fum, I smell a—" Kelsey stopped midsentence when I opened the door. "Hey, Kid. What's shaking?" Kelsey pushed past me and walked into the apartment. Bridget followed her inside.

I checked the hallway, but it was clear. I closed and locked the door. "What are you doing here?"

"Charlie?" Spence asked as a question.

"She's my cousin. She lives in Michigan," I answered as I holstered my Glock.

"Got anything besides beer?" Bridget asked, gathering some of the empty bottles before she carried them into the kitchen.

"We'll drink later," Kelsey told Bridget before turning to me. "Pack a bag. We need to leave."

"Leave? Where? Why?" My head was spinning trying to catch up. "How the hell did you get here?"

"In a plane, then a car," Kelsey said as she started down my hallway. "I'll pack you a bag. Grab anything you need from the bathroom."

My cousin had been running the playbook for my life since we were kids. Something inside me snapped. I picked up an empty bottle and threw it across the room, shattering it against the wall.

Kelsey stopped, turned, and walked back to me. She stood inches away, gauging my anger. "You good now?"

"I'm not leaving."

"It's no longer your decision. Do you hear me?"

We stood glaring at each other, neither of us willing to back down.

"Hi," Greg said from the corner. "I'm Greg."

"Hi, Greg," Bridget said, returning from the kitchen to grab the rest of the bottles. "You should leave, Greg."

"Okay," he said as he scurried for the door.

"Thanks for the report," I told him, turning away from Kelsey.

"Umm, should I call someone?" he whispered loudly to me, watching Kelsey over my shoulder.

"No. I'm fine. She's my sister." I opened the door, checked the hallway to ensure it was still clear, then held it open for him.

"I thought you said she was your cousin."

"She's both. Our family tree has a few kinks. Drive safe."

He wandered down the hallway toward the stairs, scratching his chin.

Kelsey turned to Spence, who had returned to his chair and uncapped another beer. "You should leave, too."

"No," he said. He leaned back, stretching his legs under the table. He slowly drank his beer as he watched her.

Kelsey smirked, raised her phone, and took a picture of Spence. Spence didn't say anything, just continued to watch her as she texted someone. My guess was she was ordering Tech to run a background.

Spence glanced over at me and smirked. "Well, she's fun."

Kelsey threw a glare at him but turned down the hall toward my bedroom. Bridget returned again, this time with a wet rag to wash the table.

Spence lifted his beer so she could wipe the section in front of him before he looked back at me. "You going with her?"

"Depends. She needs to explain what she's doing here."

Bridget snorted. "She got a phone call that someone was trying to kill the second most important person in her life. How calm would you be?"

"I'm a cop. It's part of the job."

"That's what she said. Then she found out that whoever is after you isn't some everyday thug. The whole family flew down. We rented a private estate packed with every available bodyguard, and—" she paused to glance down the hall, "—she brought the kids. Do you know how scary that is for her?"

"I can't just leave, Bridget. This is my home. It's where I feel safe."

Bridget looked around at my apartment. "Here?"

"Are you snubbing on my apartment?"

"Yes," she said, nodding. "This place is a dump."

I looked around, shrugging. "It needs fresh paint. And new carpet. But other than a few cosmetic updates, there's nothing wrong with it."

Bridget raised an eyebrow before lifting her eyes to the dining room light above us. "There's duct tape holding your twenty-dollar fake-brass plastic chandelier together."

I focused on Bridget, refusing to look at—*or be embarrassed by*—the dining room light that I'd taped together after the chain had snapped.

"Okay." Bridget returned with the dishrag to the kitchen. "But you should really think about coming with us. Between the house and guesthouse, there's over eight-thousand square feet. There's also a pool, hot tub, and an outdoor tiki lounge. Not only would you be safe, but you could pretend it's a vacation."

"If I go, Kelsey wins. And she'll keep bossing me around."

Bridget shook her head. "Does your life mean so little to you that you'd turn down a safe place to stay just so you can make a point to Kelsey?"

"I have safe houses. I have other places I can go."

Bridget walked over and sat at the table. "Then tell me, why are you here? Why haven't you moved to one of those safe houses?"

I didn't have an answer for her.

"She can't," Kelsey said as she returned with an oversized duffle bag. "It feels too much like the bad guy wins if she leaves. And we Harrison girls don't like hiding." She dropped the bag near the door. "I have an idea that might soften the blow, though."

I eyed her sideways. To be honest, the pool and hot tub were good selling points, but she was right. It felt like I was running away. "I'm listening."

"You hate shopping, dealing with contractors, and all that other nonsense. Turn Bridget loose on your apartment. You stay at the mansion a few days while she has your apartment remodeled."

I looked down at my table and considered it. The six screws holding the table leg together stared back at me. "I have some things in the apartment that would need to be moved first."

"I already emptied the safe," Kelsey said, pointing toward the duffle. "And the hidden gun cubby."

"We should pack anything else you want to keep," Bridget said. "That way, the contractors won't have to decide what stays and goes."

"Waiting for movers and finding a storage unit will take too long. I want to get back to the kids." Kelsey said.

"Most of the furniture is junk," I said, kicking the table leg and watching the table wobble. "There's a vacant apartment next door. I can store what I want to keep there."

I walked into the bedroom and emptied a box of miscellaneous crap onto the floor. I set the box on the bed and started packing knickknacks and memorabilia. By the time I made my way through the bedroom and bathroom, returning to the dining room, Kelsey had sorted my desk and file cabinets. Where they'd found the boxes, now full and stacked by the door, I didn't know. Bridget had bagged the rest of my shoes and clothes in garbage bags. Spence remained sitting at the table, watching us, while he drank.

"You staying or coming with us?" I asked him.

Spence wiggled his eyebrows. "You're imagining me in that hot tub, aren't you?"

"I don't know him," Kelsey said, shaking her head. "I'm not willing to risk the kids' safety on a stranger."

I started to argue, but Spence held up a hand to stop me. "It's fine. Besides, someone sent a shitload of business referrals my way. I'll be running my ass off trying to keep up."

"What about Beast?"

Spence shrugged. "He's your partner until this is over. He goes where you go."

Beast barked twice when he heard his name, jumping up. He trotted over and half sat on my feet, leaning his head into my thigh. I gave him a good scratch behind his ear.

Spence slid his now empty beer to the center of the table and stood. "I'll help load the stuff you're taking with you, then after you're gone, I'll move the rest to the vacant apartment."

"I'll help him," Bridget said. "Then after I take some measurements, I'll drive your car back to the mansion."

"Not a good idea," I said, shaking my head. "I don't want you here alone."

"I'll stay until she leaves," Spence said. "I'll keep an eye out for Mr. Tricky."

"Mr. Tricky?" Kelsey asked.

I shrugged. "We needed a name to call the guy who's after me. The name seemed to sum up the guy pretty good. He's a slippery asshole."

Bridget rolled her eyes and walked toward the door, but Spence stopped her with a hand on her forearm before she opened it. After moving her to the side, he unholstered his gun and glanced into the hall before nodding toward me. I grabbed the duffle in one hand and held my gun in the other as I led everyone out to the parking lot.

With Spence's help, we were ready to roll after two trips. I cornered him before we left. "Don't stay in the apartment tonight by yourself. It's not safe."

He grinned down at me as he lifted a hand and rubbed the pad of his thumb along my jawline. "Worried about me?"

I knocked his hand away. "No. I'm worried about the ribbing I'll suffer from other cops if there's a third dead body found in my building."

His smile widened. "I have surveillance gear in my truck. I'll leave after the rest of your stuff is moved and the motion activated cameras are installed. Your crappy apartment isn't worth me losing my life. Hell, it's not even worth me losing a good night's sleep."

I slapped him in the gut, but it just made him laugh.

"You can keep your cameras," Bridget said, pulling a box from the SUV. "Tech sent some equipment with me."

Two black SUVs pulled into the parking lot. All four of us pulled our guns.

Bones got out of the first, ignoring our guns as his eyes focused on Bridget. It took him a minute to see Spence standing next to us, but when he did, he smiled.

Not a smirk. Not a half smile. *Bones. Smiled.* His lips parted to display his perfectly straight bright white teeth.

"Russell Spencer," Bones said, walking toward Spence. "I'll be damned."

Spence laughed, bear hugging Bones. "*Bone-crusher.* Good to see you, man."

"Is my boyfriend smiling?" Bridget asked Kelsey.

"It appears so," Kelsey answered, watching Bones and Spence.

The door on the second SUV opened and I saw the lightness of the moment fade from Kelsey's expression as Grady walked toward us. I ducked around Bones and Spence to stand beside Kelsey, offering her my support by proximity.

"Let's go," she said to me as her eyes shot lasers at Grady.

I opened the rear door of the SUV and whistled for Beast. He launched the ten-foot distance with enough energy to fuel a pack of toddlers for a week. I shook my head as I shut the door. "I'll drive." I took the keys from Kelsey's hand and slid behind the wheel before she could argue.

When Kelsey slid into the passenger seat a minute later, she asked, "What's the deal with the dog?"

"He's my new partner. Spence loaned him to me."

"We brought Nicholas' new dog Jager with us. Think the dogs will get along?"

"I hope so. But for now, where I go, Beast goes." I glanced at her, narrowing my eyes. "You got a problem with that?"

"You're in a mood."

"Wouldn't you be?" I shook my head at her innocent expression as I drove out of the parking lot. "What if I showed up at your house, ordering you around?"

"Maybe I wouldn't have been so *bossy* if you'd taken a few precautions *to protect yourself*."

"Why the hell do you think Beast and Spence were there?"

"Who the hell is that guy? You've never mentioned him before. How do you know him?"

I tried to hide my grin as I turned right on the highway. "I met Spence a few nights ago when I broke into his house. We got to chatting about a case."

"You know him *that* well, *huh*?" The sarcasm was so heated in her voice that I swear it raised the temperature in the vehicle.

"Since our initial meeting," I said, throwing her a warning glance, "I've talked to Uncle Hank. He knows Spence and vouched for him." I checked traffic before making a left on a one-way street. "I also know Spence is a good investigator. He tracked down Evie, one of the regular bartenders at the Outer Layer. She'd made one minor slip up, calling an old coworker, and Spence somehow tracked her from there. He's good. And thankfully for Evie's sake, he hesitated turning the information over to his client."

"Is his client the reason Tech's been cussing about an impossible phone trace?"

"Same case, yeah," I said as I stopped for a red light. I looked around at the nearby buildings and street signs. "Where the hell am I going?"

"I was wondering when you were going to ask." Kelsey laughed. "You kept driving in the right direction, so I decided not to say anything."

I gritted my teeth. "You're aware how annoying you are, right?"

She chuckled. "Our rental is south of the bay. Near the nature center."

The light turned green and as I started forward. I turned on my blinker to warn the other drivers I needed to cross to the outside lane. "Did you get ahold of Aunt Suzanne and Uncle Hank?"

"Jackson's picking them up. They'll stay with us until it's safe."

"It'd be safer for them—*and the kids*—if I find another roof to sleep under."

"Kind of defeats the purpose of us coming here to save your ass, though, don't you think?"

I hurried through the yellow light, not answering her.

Kelsey half turned in her seat to face me. "Does whatever trouble you walked into have anything to do with this Evie woman?"

"Not sure. Maybe. But there was also a double homicide in my building, and another long list of enemies that I haven't even considered yet. Evie's situation revolves around Spence's client, but I don't have a name on the guy yet. The only thing I know at this point is that Benny The Barber confirmed there's a job with my name on it."

"THERE'S A KILL CONTRACT OUT ON YOU?"

The little old lady driving next to us whipped her head our way, looking panicked by Kelsey's yelling. I waved a friendly wave. She swerved into the next lane, almost hitting another car. I raised the windows and cranked the air conditioner. Beast leaned his big head between the seats and panted in my ear as he inhaled the cool air.

Kelsey made a growling noise. "Were you even going to tell me?"

"I thought about it. For like a brief millisecond." I got stuck at another red light and sighed, glancing over at her. "I'm not sure what I walked into, okay? I decided it was better not to say anything until I knew more. You've had your hands full with Nicholas, your job, and that pain in the ass ex-boyfriend of yours." I reached over and shoved her shoulder playfully. "Besides, I *was* taking precautions. Beast and Spence were shadowing me." I reached my hand up and scratched Beast's head. "Isn't that right, Beast?"

Kelsey raised her arm to blockade Beast from climbing over the console. I lowered my hand, not wanting to test how well I could drive with a hundred-pound dog sitting on my lap.

Kelsey was quiet for several minutes while she rubbed her lower lip between her finger and thumb. "How does *any of this* tie into the dentist office case?"

"Evie recorded a guy who mentioned the dentist office. What's that all about, anyway?"

"Human trafficking case. Uncle Hank stumbled across missing prostitutes and asked me to look into it."

"He sent the case to you?" I slapped my palm against the steering wheel. "I'm right here! Why the hell would he send the case to you, all the way back in Michigan?"

"Maybe if you weren't so reckless, he'd have sent you the information."

"You always were his favorite," I mumbled.

"Like how you're Aunt Suzanne's favorite?"

"Am not."

"Are too."

We were both silent for a long moment.

Kelsey sighed as she ran her fingers through her hair. "We sound like Sara and Nicholas."

"I know. Sorry. I'm tired. And hungry. I haven't eaten since this morning."

"Take a left. At the end of the road, turn right."

I followed her directions and when I cleared the last turn, I hit the brakes. My jaw dropped as I stared at the spectacular house in front of me. Three layers of crisp white architecture were stacked on display with jetting balconies and verandas. To the right, a three-car garage and guest house were half submerged behind palm trees and lush greenery. To the left was another garage with an oversized water fountain sitting beside it.

"Unbelievable."

Kelsey chuckled as she climbed out. "Wait until you see the backyard."

Several men from Aces walked out and started unloading as I climbed out and stood gaping at the house. Kelsey was right when she'd called it a mansion. It was huge. I opened Beast's door and he jumped out and looked around. He seemed unimpressed and ran over to lift his leg on a flowering bush.

Jager ran out, and both dogs took a few minutes to sniff each other. They must've decided to be friends because they raced together around the side of the house.

"One obstacle down," Kelsey said, glaring over her shoulder as Grady parked next to us.

"Assign his ass to night shift security," I told her.

"Tempting. If he wasn't good at his job, I'd send him packing."

"Pops and Hattie here?" I asked as we walked toward the front door.

"No. They flew back to Texas earlier this week. Lisa also stayed behind with Abigail and Donovan."

Alex stood in the foyer in one of his more conservative outfits: linen ivory slacks, ballet-slipper dress shoes, and a lavender silk blouse. "*Darling.*" He stopped me to kiss both my cheeks. "I told the boys to take your bags up to the Green room. Kelsey, you're in the Blue room."

"And that's where, exactly?" Kelsey asked Alex as she looked around the house.

"Third floor with the kids," he answered her. "Charlie's on the second floor with most of the family. Everyone working security divvied up the rooms between the first floor of the main house and the guest house."

"What about—" she started to say.

"I wasn't finished," Alex said, cutting her off and shaking his head at her. "So impatient."

"You're going to get my impatient foot up your—"

He raised a hand to stop her. "Tech, Katie, Tyler, Trigger, and Carl are also on the third floor. And both Trigger and Tyler claimed beds in the bunkroom with Carl and the kids."

Kelsey chewed on her lower lip as she absorbed the mental layout. "I'm not sure if the third floor is the best place for the kids to be."

I nudged her toward the stairs. "Go look at the escape options first. Make sure you and the kids can get out if you need to. If you can't, we can shift some people around to get the kids on the second floor."

She moved toward the stairs.

"There's an elevator, luv," Alex said, chasing after her.

She looked back at me and rolled her eyes. "Of course, there is."

Chapter Twenty-Two

CHARLIE
Monday, 8:45 p.m.

Kelsey and I had very different styles when working a case. She gathered and grouped her team for efficiency, relying on them to work together until they achieved their goals. I, on the other hand, didn't like to explain my theories and kept clues on lockdown until I'd solved the puzzle.

I had to admit, though, her way made sense when there was a room full of people who could anticipate each other's questions, answers, and emotional responses, before anyone even spoke.

During dinner, everyone pretended for the kids' sake that our stay was a vacation. The kids and Carl inhaled their food before racing back to the pool. Aunt Suzanne and Anne settled in the chaise loungers to watch them. The rest of us moved over to the huge outdoor tiki lounge fitted with cushy outdoor couches and wicker tables. Tyler leaned against a support beam, close enough to listen to us, but turned toward the kids. The rest of us found a comfortable chair.

I'd just started explaining the events of the last few days when Wild Card waltzed into the group and dumped his duffle bag in a chair. "Everyone goes on vacation and forgets to invite me?" he asked, pretending to be upset.

"Did you get things sorted?" Jackson asked him, being intentionally vague.

"Not really, but it can wait," Wild Card answered, just as vague.

Wild Card strolled over and plopped down next to me, throwing an arm over my shoulders. "I hear you're stirring up trouble, sis."

Wild Card's easy-going personality could make anyone feel lighter. It was a shame he and Kelsey had divorced. "Just doing my part to keep you boys busy."

"I need details," Tech said, getting straight to the point.

I spent the next hour explaining the events as they'd unfolded. When I was done, everyone seemed stumped.

"Right," Tech said, looking up from his computer. "So how many cases are we working on?"

"The life of a homicide detective," I said, grinning. "You just keep rolling from one to the next. It's the only way to survive the case load."

My phone rang and I looked at the display. "Shit. I forgot about Maggie!"

"Maggie's in town?" Kelsey asked.

"Yeah. The Feds sent her to Miami when we triggered a WITSEC alert." I hit the green phone icon to take her call. "I'll send someone to get you. Where are you?"

"I'm at your place with Bridget and this hunk of a PI you left behind. I hear the party moved to nicer digs. Room for me? Or should I get a hotel?"

"Plenty of room. Bridget knows where we are."

"Splendid. I hear there's a pool."

"There's *everything*. You won't want to leave."

"I have to fly out tomorrow for a new case, but I'm sure I can squeeze in some downtime before then."

She hung up, and I called Quille.

"You were right," he said as a greeting. "That friend of yours helped clear several cases, reorganized the whole unit, then announced she was bored and abruptly strolled out the door."

"Yeah, she does that." I stood and walked to the outskirts of the tiki lounge, watching the kids swim in the distance. "Wanted to let you know I relocated. My cousin came to town for a visit."

"Kelsey doesn't just come to town for a visit. She blows in like a hurricane. But I'll sleep better knowing she's got your back." I heard a voice in the background and Quille told someone to give him five minutes, before he said to me, "Anything new on the double homicide?"

"Greg confirmed Pauly's body was moved. Pauly was killed in Roseline's apartment. Spence is working some background searches for me, and I have another team digging into the Oxi angle."

"Something keeps bugging me," Quille said. "If Pauly was a heroin addict, but killed by a group of script dealers, why was he murdered by a morphine injection?"

I was silent for a moment as the question stumped me. "Good question." I paced a few feet away then turned and paced the other direction. "I'll reach out and see if anyone on the streets has an answer."

Beast padded toward me across the concrete, stopping to look up at me. I pointed toward the pool. He barked twice, ran, and leapt into the water, accomplishing one hell of a cannonball splash. Jager raced in after him.

"Was Chills' package still at the church?"

Quille laughed. "How you convinced a gang leader to turn those punks over is beyond me. Ford said those boys were scared shitless by the time he picked them up. They confessed to every detail of the shooting."

"Shooting a toddler is bad for Chills' business. He knew 5-O would rip his streets apart until we found the boys." I didn't want to dwell on the shooting. There was nothing else that could be done so I changed the subject. "And the manhunt for Mr. Tricky? Any sightings?"

"Not yet. We found his car abandoned in a parking lot. No prints. No DNA."

"Damn. I can't catch a break with this guy."

"We'll get him. Just lay low until we do."

"Call me if anything new pops up."

"You do the same," he said before disconnecting.

I returned to the sitting area. "You can cross the search for Mr. Tricky's car off the list. It was ditched in a parking lot and wiped clean."

"Why does it matter if it was clean?" Alex asked as he lifted a glass of iced tea from a formal serving tray and offered it to me.

"Clean, as in, no evidence," Kelsey answered for me as she also accepted a glass from Alex.

I took a sip and grimaced. It was sweet tea. I'd never acquired a taste for it. Kelsey watched my expression and set hers on the side stand, not bothering to take a drink. Wild Card took my glass, drinking half of it down in two massive gulps.

"Good," Tech said, pulling my attention. "I need a few hours to dive into the prescription drug ring. If Sara and Carl weren't having so much fun, I'd pull them in to help with the other searches."

"When Maggie gets here, she can help with some of the research if you can distract her from the bar."

"What are the rest of us supposed to do?" Wild Card asked. "I'm bored."

"Do you have a car?" I asked him.

"A rental," Wild Card answered.

"I need a lift. Bridget has my wheels."

"Lead the way." Wild Card stood and waved his arm out in an overexaggerated gesture for me to lead him.

I whistled for Beast who ran over and shook his wet fur all over everyone. It must've looked like fun because Jager ran over and did the same.

"Should we change our clothes before we go?" Wild Card asked as we looked down at our pants.

"This is Miami. Your pants will be dry before we get to the car. Besides, Beast is coming with us. We are going to smell like wet dog no matter what."

"I'm driving a rental. I'll lose my deposit."

"You can afford it," I said, tapping his cheek before following the landscaped path of flat stones to the front of the house.

I waited in the driveway with Beast. Wild Card ran out of the house a few minutes later with an armful of beach towels. He laid them out along the back seat to cover the upholstery. When he stepped back, I tried to hide my grin. Motioning to Beast, I watched him do his flying-leap thing which resulted in all the towels bunched to the other side in a pile. Beast's wet butt sat on the upholstery as he shook his head, coating the inside with his wet dog aroma.

I laughed at Beast. He looked happy.

Wild Card on the other hand—not so much. "Not a word, Kid. Not a word," he said as he got in the SUV and turned over the engine.

I giggled as I ran to the passenger side, hurrying before he decided to leave me.

~*~*~

First stop, check on Evie.

"It's Charlie!" I called out when I entered the condo.

Wild Card followed me inside, locking the door behind us. Evie peeked around the corner of the bedroom door at us.

I tipped my head at Wild Card. "He's a friend. Ex-military. Used to be my brother-in-law."

Evie raised an eyebrow as she joined us. "You hang out with your ex-brother-in-law?"

"I'm hard to get rid of," Wild Card said. "Kelsey's been trying to shake me for years." He held out his hand to Evie. "I'm Cooper. But everyone calls me Wild Card."

"I'm Genevieve. But everyone in Miami thinks my name is Evie." She returned both his handshake and his smile.

"Which do you prefer?" Wild Card asked as he wandered about the condo, looking around.

"Evie, I think. I've gotten used to it."

"Evie it is then." He turned back to me. "This place secure?"

"*Duh*," I said, rolling my eyes. "I wouldn't have hidden her here if it wasn't."

Evie sank to the couch to sit. "I'm bored. I know this is for my safety and all, but after Baker left, I've been going stir crazy with nothing to do and no one to talk to."

Wild Card glanced at me. "We could move her to the mansion."

"Too much going on there already." I shook my head. "Besides, it could compromise the legal case down the road. A defense attorney would have a seizure upon hearing she was living with the people investigating the case."

Wild Card looked at Evie. "I guess you're stuck here. Sorry."

"Maybe not," I said, grinning at my own devious thoughts. "There's another option."

"What?" Evie asked, sitting forward.

"We could move you to the Outer Layer."

"You mean I'd sleep in one of the sex rooms?" she asked, scrunching her nose.

"No. We can make Baker sleep in one of the sex rooms. You can sleep in his room, behind his office."

She threw her hands up in exasperation. "Of course, he'd have a bedroom in his office. That man needs therapy. There's more to life than work."

I laughed.

"So?" Wild Card asked her. "Which location do you prefer? The stylish condo or the sex club where Baker's likely to make you work for your room and board?"

"The Outer Layer," Evie answered immediately. "Working will keep my mind off things."

"Just so you understand," I said. "You'll have to stay on the upper floors. You can't venture below the third floor without one of my personal security teams. The club security isn't trained for this type of work."

"I can live with that. At least I'll have customers to chat with in The Parlor."

"Go pack, then," I said. "I left Beast in the car, so we can't dawdle."

"Who's Beast?"

"My partner."

"*Her friend's dog!*" Wild Card said, correcting my statement. "And I'll warn you that he went swimming earlier and the whole car smells like wet dog."

"I'll live," Evie said, shaking her head at such a minor issue.

When Evie left to pack, I decided to ask Wild Card a few questions. "What was the secret conversation between you and Jackson earlier all about? What were you supposed to handle?"

"I sort of did something a few years back that Kelsey's not going to like when she finds out."

"What kind of something?"

He hesitated, rubbing the back of his neck. "You can't tell her. If I can't fix it, I'd rather she hears it from me."

"This sounds good," I said, sitting on the arm of the couch. I rubbed my hands together, excited to hear something juicy. "Spill."

Wild Card paced a few times, inhaled a deep breath, and confessed in rapid speech. "I never filed the divorce papers. We're still married."

I was speechless. I didn't know what I expected him to say, but him confessing that they were still married wasn't anywhere in the ballpark.

"Say something," Wild Card ordered.

"She's going to kill you." I looked up at him and started giggling.

"Damn it!" he said, punching the air. "I know. I know. She's going to be pissed."

"But..."

Wild Card looked over at me with a hopeful expression. "Please tell me there's a happy ending that follows that '*but*'."

I raised my hands to my sides in an I-don't-know gesture. "Kelsey's a control freak. How could she *not know* she's still married? She would've checked on the filing. For tax purposes, if for no other reason."

Wild Card shrugged. "I have no idea why she didn't check. But my lawyer confirmed we're still legally bound to each other until death do us part."

"So, let's back up. Kelsey told me you gave her the papers and she signed them. Where did they go?"

Wild Card paced a few more times.

"Did you throw them away?"

He looked away while answering. "When I gave her the papers, the look on her face..." He shook his head. "Something broke. I saw it. I wanted so badly to fix it, but at the same time, I knew she was leaving. I knew the longer we stayed together, the harder it would be when she left. I didn't know why she was leaving, just that she was getting ready."

"I can see that." I walked over and placed a supportive hand on his shoulder. "She needed to find Nicholas."

"I know that *now*. But back then—I don't know—I guess I thought I wasn't good enough for her."

Kelsey could seem very detached at times. Reading her thoughts, let alone her feelings, was challenging, even for me. "So? Then what happened? You asked her to sign the divorce papers?"

"Then she disappeared. She packed her bags and left. The divorce papers taunted me from the dining room table for over a week. Every day I'd see them sitting there and it made me so angry with myself..." His pained expression was focused on the floor. "Then one day, I got the bright idea that if I burned them, she'd have to come back to sign a new set. It was stupid, but I thought—"

"You thought you'd have a second chance," I said, answering for him.

Wild Card kept his head bowed. "But when I went searching for her, I couldn't find her. And by the time I did, we had other shit to deal with, and well, then I forgot."

"Forgot?" I asked, smirking at him. "Or you pretended to forget?"

"Will it matter?" he asked me. "Or is she going to hate me no matter what?"

"Kelsey will know you didn't forget," I answered, laughing. "And when you explain the situation to her, I want a front row seat. It's going to be a brilliant fireworks display when Kelsey lights into you."

He chuckled, throwing himself in a chair. "I'm doomed."

"Look on the bright side." I paused until he glanced up at me. "Grady's going to be royally pissed when he finds out Kelsey's still your wife."

Wild Card smiled. "That jealous bastard is going to lose his shit."

Chapter Twenty-Three

KELSEY
Monday, 11:30 p.m.

"Go away, Grady," I said without turning around. I had been unpacking my clothes, hanging them in the closet, when I'd heard him near the bedroom door. He'd been watching me for several minutes.

"I miss you."

"You shouldn't even be here." I zipped the suitcase closed, moving it to the corner of the room. "This trip is family business."

"Which involves Aces. I have every right to accompany my men."

"Does Donovan know you're here?"

"He agreed I should be here. I'm good at protecting people, and you might need me."

"How exactly are you protecting anyone when you're spending all your energy stalking me?" I slid past him to escape through the doorway and down the hallway. I fought the urge to run, walking down each step at a normal pace.

"Kelsey, when are you going to admit you miss me too?" Grady called after me loud enough for people throughout the house to appear from various locations.

"HOW DARE YOU!!" I yelled, turning to face him. "You left on a mission, and two days later you were practically renewing your vows with your bitch ex-wife!"

"How many times do I have to explain?" He walked over and cupped my face with his hand. "I was protecting the family. I was protecting you."

I focused on his face as I whispered back, "You did the same thing to her."

"What?"

"You cupped her face. You held her face in your hand and looked *at her—*" I knocked his hand away "—the *exact* same way you're looking at me now."

Grady frowned. "I love YOU!"

I stepped back to add distance between us. "But you love her, too."

My fears were confirmed when he flinched.

I turned and walked away. "Leave me be, Grady." I walked through the main seating room, out onto the veranda, and down the side stairs. I followed the path past the pool deck and around to the railing that overlooked the ocean below.

The waves beat against each other in the evening breeze, crashing onto the beach before retreating. Despite the warm air and mild breeze, those waves seemed angry—as if they were trying to fight against the sandy beach. Or maybe, I was simply projecting. Seeing what I felt manifest around me.

I gripped the railing tighter, trying to reel in my own rage.

Chapter Twenty-Four

CHARLIE
Monday, 11:59 p.m.

"Surprise! I brought you a present," I said to Baker as we entered his office from the private stairway.

"Whatever it is, I don't want it," Baker said from behind his desk, not looking up as he read through a legal document of some kind. "The last present you gave me was purple socks with Christmas trees on them."

"Cashmere socks. They were expensive. You like things that are expensive."

Baker grunted.

Wild Card tossed Evie's bags into a chair before wandering toward the security monitors.

"Evie's your present. She's going to keep you company for a few days and stay in your hidden suite. She promised to stay above the second floor, but she was going stir crazy in the condo."

Baker raised an eyebrow. He glanced at Evie who was nervously standing near the stairway door. He subtly inclined his head at her before turning a stern expression on me. "And where do you expect me to sleep?"

"Do you really want me to answer that?" I asked, walking past him to the other side of the room.

He sighed loudly before saying a simple, "No."

I opened the wall panel that led into his private suite. Evie and Beast followed me inside. A small sitting room with a couch and TV took up this side of the room. On the far side was a king size bed and private bathroom.

"You good?" I asked her.

"Is he mad?" she whispered.

"No. He's pretty easy to read when he's mad. He yells and his face puckers up like he bit a lemon."

She grinned. "Then I'm good."

"Splendid. I have more to do tonight, so I'm going to change my outfit and then split."

"Where to next?" Wild Card asked me.

I held a finger up for him to wait a moment. "Is Garth working tonight?" I asked Baker.

"Yes," he said as he signed a form.

"Can you send him upstairs?"

"Yes."

I curled my finger for Wild Card to follow. Beast padded along after us.

Unlocking my office, I dug around in the closet for some street clothes and changed in the little bathroom. I didn't have to do much to my face except remove some of the foundation. The bruises were a green-purple blend that worked in my favor. I let my hair down and used hairspray to tangle the mass in globs.

From the mirror, I saw Garth open the door and look at me.

Wild Card looked over at Garth, took a step back and looked further upward. He took another step back, unkinking his neck.

Garth ignored him, watching me. "Always a beauty, Kid," he joked.

"Why thank you, Garth," I said, winking at him. "Can you grab the keys to the Mustang and take Wild Card—" I pointed to Wild Card "—to the car. I'll want the convertible for tomorrow. We can leave his rental in the city ramp."

Garth looked down his nose at Wild Card but spoke to me. "You want your truck for tonight? I can bring it over on my way back."

"Yes, please. You're the best."

Garth pulled both sets of keys from the peg board. "Anything for you, doll."

"We're separating?" Wild Card asked me. "I don't think Kelsey will like that."

"I need to work the street and ask a few questions. Beast will be with me. But you and all your muscles," I gestured toward his body, "will scare everyone away."

"You're forgetting you're the target on a kill contract. Let someone else dress like a homeless person and ask questions."

"Someone else wouldn't know where to go or who to talk to." I shook my head. "I'll be fine. I'll have Beast, and I'll make sure I'm not followed."

"You heard her," Garth said, running out of patience. "Let's go, pretty boy."

Wild Card's head swiveled back to Garth, but he was already gone. Wild Card looked at me. "Pretty boy?" he asked in a low tone.

I smirked at him in the mirror. "Garth calls it like he sees it. That's what I love about him. Well... that and the fact he helps me juggle my cars. Speaking of which..." I turned and faced Wild Card, pointing my finger at him. "If you get even so much as a microscopic nick on my Mustang, I'll be serving your head on a platter."

"What kind of Mustang are we talking here?"

I turned back to my makeup bag to add junkie tracks on my arm. "A GT coupe convertible refitted with an inline six engine rocking 470 horsepower under its beautiful metallic-silver hood. Don't make me regret letting you drive her."

~*~*~

I drove my beater short-bed truck from block to block for forty minutes until I found the new camp location. I could've made a few phone calls and saved myself the time, but since I didn't know who the bad guys were, driving in circles was safer.

The homeless camps were always shifting, moving to new locations. I wasn't a fan of relocation days, where the police were ordered to force the homeless to pack up and move on, but I also understood why the higher ups in charge of the city didn't want the camps to become too large or too permanent in any one location. And orders were orders.

I parked the pickup along the curb a half a block away from the camp. After getting out, I patted my leg for Beast to follow. He stayed close to my side as we walked toward the alley, where thirty or more of this city's homeless were gathering for the night.

Entering with the same hopeless shuffle as those around me, I kept my head tipped downward as I swept my eyes back and forth, both looking for Pauly's friends and keeping my eyes peeled for danger. In the far back, next to a dumpster, Lydia was huddled with her back to the wall.

"Lydia, it's Kid. Pauly's friend," I whispered, squatting a few feet away. "Can we talk?"

"Pauly's not here," she mumbled to me, pulling her jacket tighter around her with one hand and gripping something else, probably a knife, under her arm with the other.

I moved closer, leaning against the filth-layered stucco wall. Beast moved with me, but turned to watch everyone else. I tossed a brown bag toward Lydia. She flinched, watching the bag.

"What is it?"

"Sandwiches," I whispered to her so no one else heard.

"For Pauly?" she asked.

"No. They're for you."

"Something happened to Pauly, didn't it? That's why you're here slumming it with us. I remember you. You live in that building Pauly goes to all the time. You're the cop."

"I've got bad news, Lydia. Pauly was killed. I'm trying to find out why."

She took the brown bag and stuffed it under her blanket. She was quiet as she watched the others.

"Will you help me, Lydia?"

"He was too good for us, you know. If he could've kicked the habit, he could've had a real life. He was smart. Smart enough to make it."

"I think he died protecting someone. But there's a piece that doesn't make sense."

She narrowed her eyes at me. "What's that?"

"Morphine." I watched her expression, and as expected, she twitched when I mentioned it. "Pauly overdosed on morphine."

"I don't know nothin'."

"He was your friend. Help me."

"Everybody's always asking for help," she muttered. "Nobody's ever offering it back."

"I'll rent you an apartment."

She looked over her shoulder at me, eyes squinted in distrust.

"You said it yourself, you know who I am. I'll rent you an apartment. I'll pay six months in advance and you can live there for free." I leaned forward, and gently touched her arm. "You'll have a chance. A chance to start over."

She jerked her arm away. "What do I need an apartment for? Got no furniture."

"What do you want then?"

She thought for a few minutes before answering. "A favor."

"What kind of favor?"

"My daughter. She lives with a man who beats on her real bad. She's scared of him. You help her, and I'll help you."

"What's her name?"

"Cassie. Cassie Rickers." She leaned forward to look around the dumpster to ensure no one was listening. "She lives in the yellow house over on Pearl Street. You get her out, and I'll tell you what I know."

"What if she won't leave?"

"*You make her leave!*" Lydia shouted. Her own volume spooked her as it drew unwanted attention to us. She looked around as multiple faces swiveled our direction. She looked back at me, speaking in a hushed tone. "You get her that apartment you offered me—and you *make him* stay away from her. I know you. I know the things you've done. *You make her leave.*"

I dipped my head in agreement. "Meet me mid-morning tomorrow by the precinct." I started walking back toward the street.

"*You make her leave*," Lydia muttered behind me.

Chapter Twenty-Five

KELSEY
Tuesday, 2:35 a.m.

I stared at my phone, shaking my head. On one hand, I was glad Charlie had called so I knew she was safe. On the other, I couldn't believe what she'd just asked me to do.

I walked outside and joined the guys who were still up and sitting around the pool. "I need volunteers."

Wild Card, Jackson, Grady, Trigger, Bridget, Bones, and Uncle Hank stood, ready for anything.

"I haven't said the *what for* yet."

"It's two-thirty in the morning," Trigger said. "Only the really fun shit happens at two-thirty in the morning."

Everyone laughed.

"Charlie made a deal with a homeless woman. If she gets the woman's daughter away from her abusive husband, then the homeless woman will share what she knows about Pauly's death."

"I'm out," Uncle Hank said, sitting on a chaise. "I've got two more years until retirement."

"Address?" Wild Card asked.

I handed him my phone. Charlie had texted me the address. Bones and Jackson looked over Wild Card's shoulder.

"I know how to get there," Jackson said, leading them out.

Wild Card handed my phone back. "Leave your phone turned on in case we need to be bailed out."

Grady shook his head.

"You don't approve?"

"I'm not in the mood to play games," Grady said. "If the homeless woman knows something, Charlie should've gotten it out of her."

"Charlie's a homicide detective," Uncle Hank said. "She relies on street relationships to help her solve cases. She'd lose half her resources if she forced the issue."

"So what? Her reputation on the street is worth risking my guys being arrested?"

Uncle Hank stood and calmly turned to face Grady, stepping a little too close. "I didn't see anyone's arm being twisted. Did you?"

"Enough," I said, raising my hand between them. "I'm going to bed. Tyler's on watch. Grady, you just volunteered to replace him and cover security until dawn."

Grady walked away without speaking.

"I hope that means he's covering third shift," I said to myself.

"He'll cover the security shift," Uncle Hank said as he steered me toward the house. "He's just flexing his muscles, trying to gain some control around here. He's used to being Alpha, and with him being in the doghouse, he's ranked somewhere near Zeta. It pisses him off."

"Not my fault. Not my problem."

"Isn't it, though?" Uncle Hank asked, raising an eyebrow.

I stepped into the kitchen and turned to face him. "You think I'm being too hard on him? That I should forgive and forget? Take him back?"

"Don't get carried away, doll," Uncle Hank said, chuckling. "Whether you take him back or not is up to you. But you ignoring the problem and stringing him along with the silent treatment isn't helping everyone else figure out the pecking order."

"I love him, but I'm mad. Super mad."

"I see that. But what I don't get is why you're more angry than hurt?" He started for the elevator and spoke over his shoulder. "Makes me wonder if you're angry at yourself for something. That's usually when you can't let it go."

I was too tired to figure out his riddle, so I grabbed a clean cup and filled it with coffee.

"Grab me a cup?" Tyler asked as he walked into the kitchen. "I know why I'm still up, but why are you?"

I shrugged, handing him a cup of coffee. "My brain is spinning. I'm still trying to sort the cases and figure out where to start."

"Maybe you should take a back seat on the other cases. Stay focused on the trafficking case at the dentist office."

I arched an eyebrow. "Why?"

Tyler slid onto a barstool, watching me, but not answering.

"I'm not in one of my pissy moods. It's safe to explain why you think I should butt out of the other cases."

He watched me a few more seconds but must've decided it was safe enough to speak. "All I'm saying is that when people take on too much, things slip through the cracks." He paused to take a drink of his coffee before continuing. "Take my duties around here as an example. Sure, I could've left with the boys to thump on some wife-beating asshole. I'd even enjoy it. But that's not where I'm needed. I'm good at keeping watch over the family. And that gives the rest of you time to focus on everything else. And I'm okay with that. I like doing what I do. It's important. Just like the trafficking cases are something you're uniquely good at. And Charlie's one hell of a homicide detective from what I've heard. Just stay out of her lane. Let her do her thing, and you do yours."

"Your advice is to simply ignore everything else? Including the fact someone's trying to kill Charlie?"

"Are you sure they're trying to kill her? Sounded to me like the contract might be to kidnap her. But, yeah, work your dentist case, which might also be connected to the guy hunting down that Evie chick. And while you're doing that, let the hometown homicide detective work her murder cases."

"Who focuses on the contract hanging over Kid's head then? Who works that angle?"

"The way Charlie explained it, if the other cases get solved, one of them might be linked to Mr. Tricky. If not, then at least everyone will be free to follow the next clue. Besides, every cop in the city, plus our security guys, are watching Charlie's back. There's a good chance we'll spot him following her, and then we can toss the net and trap him." Tyler smiled, imagining something. "If you do catch him, lock his ass in a room with Bones or Wild Card for five minutes. He'll sing."

Keeping the cases sorted made sense. We had enough help to divide and conquer. "When did you get so smart?"

Tyler chuckled. "The night shifts are quiet. Lots of time to think."

Quiet. That sounded nice. "Maybe I should swap shifts with you."

"You'd be bored. Now go to bed. You need some sleep."

I poured my cup into the sink. "You going to bed, too?"

"I'll wait until the rest of the guys return. I trust Grady, but I'll sleep better knowing Bones and Wild Card are ready to fight if the warning alarms go off."

"They probably wouldn't hear anyone yell for help. This place is huge."

"They'll hear. Bones sleeps with one eye open. And Wild Card always sleeps in the center of the action. He'll probably sleep on the couch in the front room tonight, so he'll be close if needed."

"Wasn't he assigned a room?"

"Sure. He's always offered a room, even in Michigan. But he never uses them when we're on red alert— which is most of the time these days."

I laughed. "I thought he liked the excuse of walking around with his shirt off after his naps."

"Ha. That too. He enjoys getting Grady all wound up. I think it's his way of dealing with Grady sleeping with his ex-wife."

"Wild Card and I were married less than a minute."

"Not the way I heard the story told. You two fell hard, and then—*poof*—it was over."

"I don't remember falling. I remember fighting, having sex, then splitting up, followed by a miscarriage and moving to Michigan to continue pretending to be normal as I searched for Nicholas."

"See," Tyler said, shaking his head. "I get the miscarriage part making everything fuzzy. That would be hard. But did you ever process how you would've felt about the divorce if you'd never been pregnant?"

"There was no point. I needed to find Nicholas. He was my priority."

"And you couldn't have stayed in Texas while you searched?"

"No." I shook my head, confident of my answer.

"Why?"

"I don't know. I just couldn't stay in Texas."

"Are you sure you don't know why?"

I sighed, throwing my hands up. "You sound like Uncle Hank. Trying to say something without saying anything. I'm too tired for games. I'm going to bed."

Tyler hid his grin behind his coffee cup.

As I started up the stairs, I shook my head, clearing my thoughts. The men in my life spent too much time pondering over my love life.

Chapter Twenty-Six

CHARLIE
Tuesday, 3:22 a.m.

"What's the plan?" Bones asked as we gathered near the corner of Lydia's daughter's yard.

The yellow house, sitting squarely on its allotted parcel of St Augustine Floridian grass, presented a challenging situation, even for a skilled team. The neighboring houses were too close. The entire blue-collar block was dark, lights off, except for the street light on the corner. One scream, one broken lamp, or hell—a car door being slammed shut—and the whole neighborhood would be awake and peeking out their windows.

"You take the front," I told Bones. "I'll take the back. Quick and quiet."

"Do you know the layout of the house?" Wild Card asked.

"No. But most of these houses are the same. Combo kitchen and dining room toward the front with the living room on the other side. One or two bedrooms off the back of the house."

"Pause after entering," Bones said as studied the house. "Wait for us to regroup before anyone enters the bedrooms."

"Agreed." I glanced around the quiet neighborhood again. "If this turns south, though, everyone aborts and hightails it out of here. Don't wait for me."

"I got no problem with that plan. You have a badge. You'd have a better chance of talking your way out of handcuffs than the rest of us." Bones turned to the others to dole out orders. Jackson was assigned as lookout. Two other men would breach the front door with Bones.

Wild Card was assigned to breach the backdoor with me. He grabbed my hand and led me between the houses. Midway past the house, we stopped, hearing a clattering to our right. Our feet froze in place as our heads swiveled toward the neighboring house. The partial moon cast enough light for us to see a woman in the house next door standing in front of the kitchen window. She stood motionless with big eyes, staring right at us.

Wild Card raised a finger to his lips, signaling for her to keep quiet. She shook her head.

"Shit," I whispered, starting to retreat.

Wild Card grabbed my hand to stop me. "Wait. She seems weirdly calm."

We waited as the woman slid the small kitchen window to the side. She leaned close to the screen to whisper across the twenty-foot gap between us. "Do what you want with that bastard Danny, but you harm one hair on Cassie's head and I'll hunt you down." She held up a steak knife.

Wild Card lifted a hand and gave her a thumbs up.

"Their bedroom is the one on *this side* of the house. He was drinking earlier, so likely he's out cold."

I giggled as Wild Card tugged me toward the backyard. On the back porch, we found the door already unlocked and stepped inside. The back door led into a hallway, lit by a nearby nightlight. Bones stood in the hall, just outside the closed bedroom door. On the other side of the door, we could hear obnoxious snoring. Glancing past Bones, enough moonlight glimmered through the front house windows for me to see the other two men stationed near the front door.

I stepped beside Bones, nodding toward the bedroom to let Bones know I was ready. But before we'd moved, the bedroom door swung open. Cassie Rickers stood directly in front of us, staring at us as if she'd expected us. She slowly raised her hand which held a phone. The text message on the display read: *Stay quiet. People coming after Danny. They don't want you. Just get out of their way. Come to my place.*

I stepped aside so she could pass. Without a sound, she slipped out the back door and disappeared.

Bones narrowed his eyes at me, disapproving. I looked at Wild Card. He flashed his smile as he strolled into the bedroom.

Bones rushed to the bed and pinned Danny down. Waking abruptly, he tried to jerk away, but he was no match for Bones' strength. By the time Danny's brain was alert enough to yell for help, Wild Card forced a pillow over his nose and mouth. Rickers' eyes danced in the semi-darkness as he screamed into the pillow.

I turned on the light. The pillow was low enough that I could see him look to Wild Card, then Bones, then settle on me.

"Your choice, asshole," Wild Card said to him. "Either I cut off your oxygen supply and end this here and now, or you stop yelling like a little girl."

Danny settled and kept his focus at Wild Card.

Wild Card lifted the pillow but kept it close to Danny's face. Bones glanced at me, letting me know it was my show. Thankful that I'd worn gloves, I picked up a sock from the floor. Reaching past Bones, I wadded the sock into Danny's mouth before passing a large zip tie from my fanny pack to Bones. He zipped the tie tight around Danny's head, holding the sock in place and ensuring silence.

"Kitchen," was all I said before turning from the room and walking down the hall.

Bones and Wild Card dragged a reluctant and wide-eyed Danny after me, stopping in the center of the kitchen. I looked around, and on the shelf next to the stove I found a cutting board stacked with a pile of cookie sheets. I moved the cutting board to the counter before rummaging through the drawers. Locating the knives, I selected the largest one. The large curved-blade knife was the style chefs used on TV to chop vegetables. Perfect for what I needed.

I grabbed his hand and forced it on top of the cutting board. He shook his head vigorously back and forth. I didn't feel sorry for him.

"You used *these* hands to beat your wife. More than once, from what I hear. Now it's my turn. Tonight, you pack your bags, get in your truck, and leave. Tomorrow, you will file for divorce. You're going to forfeit the house, the car, and anything else of value." I watched fear shift to anger as he listened to me. "You will *not* contact her. If you see her on the street or at your favorite restaurant, *you leave*. Understood?"

His temper was getting the best of him. He glared, challenging my authority.

I slammed the knife down, chopping off the ends of his two longest fingers. One of the fingertips flew to the right, ricocheting off the refrigerator. A slow smile formed on Bones' face as he looked down at the other fingertip resting near his boot. Wild Card seemed surprised, but didn't say anything as he held a towel covered hand over

Danny's mouth. The sock muffled most of the scream, but the towel helped.

I waited for Danny to stop his muffled screaming. When he'd calmed to an annoying whimper, I continued, "Move out—*tonight*. File for divorce tomorrow. And don't ever cross paths with her again. If you do, next time you'll lose the whole hand."

His head bounced up and down so fast, I thought his neck might snap. Bones took the knife from me and held it over the flame of the gas stove. Danny started crying again as he watched Bones turn the knife side to side as it heated. When the blade was hot, Wild Card forced Danny's bloody hand toward Bones. And with obvious experience, Bones used the side of the scalding knife to cauterize the ends of Danny's—now much shorter—fingers.

I watched Danny's eyes lose focus before his body slumped and he wilted like a ragdoll to the floor. He was out cold.

"I'm not cleaning this mess," Wild Card said, waving a hand to the bloody floor and Danny's body. "I'll go check on the women next door. Maybe they'll offer to help pack his things while you two clean."

"Are we sure the women didn't call the cops?" Bones asked.

"Neighbor seemed almost happy we were here," I said as I grabbed the roll of paper towel. Tearing off a sheet, I used it to pick up one of the fingertips, tossing it into the trash.

Normally I wouldn't bother to clean, but this house was Cassie's home. I didn't want to leave the mess for her. And though I'd planned on moving her to the condo, the neighbor was obviously a friend. I didn't want Cassie to lose that connection.

I grinned at my thoughtfulness as I searched for the other fingertip.

Bones chuckled. "Best vacation ever."

Chapter Twenty-Seven

KELSEY
Tuesday, 7:30 a.m.

I slept four hours before noise from the first floor reached a volume that prevented me from turning over and conquering another hour of sleep. I rolled out of bed, showered, dressed, and went downstairs.

"People are trying to sleep!" I called out to the packed room.

"Yeah!" Wild Card yelled from the couch where he was lying with his eyes closed, chest bare, and a sheet covering his mid-section. His bare legs stuck out the other end.

I glanced around, searching for Grady. Sure enough, he was at the table glaring at Wild Card. I ducked my head to hide my grin as I gravitated toward the coffee pot. "Aunt Suzanne and Uncle Hank, can you two play lifeguards for the kids today?"

"Happy to," Uncle Hank answered from his perch at the breakfast bar.

The kids and Carl shrieked their excitement and went running up the stairs, likely to change into their swimsuits. Both Jager and Beast chased after them, barking.

"I need to clean the kitchen first," Aunt Suzanne said.

We both glanced around. Every pot, pan, and serving platter was dirty. Bushels of food must've been consumed while I'd slept.

"You cooked. I'll clean."

"I'll help," Wild Card said, walking into the kitchen and snagging my coffee cup from me.

I looked down and saw he was wearing khaki shorts. I looked up and found him grinning at me.

"What's the schedule today?" Bones asked, drawing my attention.

"We need to split up into three teams. One to cover the mansion security and guard the kids. A second team to work with me on the human trafficking case. And a third team led by Charlie." I looked over and watched her head snap up. "She'll need security while she works her double-homicide and searches for Evie's mystery man."

"What about Bridget?" Bones asked. "I don't like her working alone in Charlie's apartment building."

"I'll be fine," Bridget said, dismissively.

"No," Charlie said, shaking her head. "He's right. Two dead bodies are enough bad juju for my building. And Mr. Tricky might pop in asking how to find me. You can't be at my apartment unless you take guards with you. Even I don't trust being in my building without backup right now."

Bridget pouted. "Fine. Katie and Alex are going with me, so we'll need two guards."

"Take Reggie, Jackson, and at least one other guard," I said.

"Wayne and Ryan are due here any minute," Tyler said. "Wait for them."

"Wayne can be their third," I said. "I'll take Ryan and Trigger on my team."

"I get Bones and Wild Card," Charlie said, claiming them for her team.

"I can live with that but you'll have to share Tech," I said, pointing a finger at her. "You can't steal him."

Charlie shrugged. "Whatever. Spence is running background searches for me. He's first on my to-do list today."

Aunt Suzanne and I both smiled.

"Not *that kind* of *to-do* list. There's nothing sexual between Spence and me."

"That's a shame," Maggie said, winking at Charlie. "I look at that man and just want to lick him."

I could admit Spence was a good-looking man, but after working with the men of Aces on a daily basis, I'd gotten used to seeing hot bodies everywhere.

"If I'm going with Charlie," Wild Card said, changing the subject, "who's helping you clean the kitchen?"

"Everyone on my team will clean up after breakfast and Charlie's team gets the next main meal. We'll rotate."

"Deal," Charlie agreed as captain of her team. "Wild Card, you might want to find a shirt. We're wasting daylight and I need to talk to Spence before my meeting with Lydia."

Wild Card shifted in different weightlifter poses, curling his arms and clenched his muscles. "What? Not scary enough?"

The man had a beautifully sculpted body, but unfortunately, he knew it.

Grady growled, watching me watch Wild Card. "Where am I assigned today?"

"Well," I said as I turned on the faucet to fill the sink with hot water. "You don't play well with Wild Card and I have no interest in being cooped up with you all day, so I guess that means you work for Tyler."

Tyler hid his grin as he drank his coffee. Uncle Hank coughed a laugh. Everyone else looked down or away.

"Is that right?" Grady asked.

"Either that, or get on a plane and go home." I turned my back to him and started loading dirty pans into the sink.

"Fine. At least one of us will put the safety of the kids first. I'll stay to protect them."

Several sharp inhales preceded the now deadly silent room. I took my time as I turned to face Grady. My fists were clenched so tight, blood flow was likely cut off. Grady stood, ready for war, his eyes piercing mine.

Charlie walked over and stepped between us, turning to face him. "I get you're pissed. Frustrated. And maybe even feeling a bit left out. But if you make another dig about Kelsey not putting the kids' safety first, you'll be leaving this house in an ambulance."

"You're good, Kid, but not that good."

"Look around, Grady. You're outnumbered on this issue."

Grady glanced around. Every face in the room was scowling at him, disappointed with the low blow. He left out the French doors to the patio without saying another word.

Everyone exhaled.

Charlie walked over and looked at me. "Don't."

"Don't what?" I asked, tossing the dishrag into the sink.

"Don't let him get into your head. Tyler and Uncle Hank will keep the kids safe. There's a team of security here watching them. Hell, there's two trained attack dogs that follow them everywhere they go. They're safe."

"I know..." I looked away, my eyes threatening to tear up. I blinked rapidly to clear them. "It's just, we're here... In Florida. And I—" I shook my head as I swallowed my tears.

"I know. We all know. But Nicholas is safe," she said, rubbing my arm. "Nola's dead. Nobody is after Nicholas. You made sure of it."

"But..."

"No, buts," Wild Card said, stepping behind me and wrapping his arms around me. "You have human traffickers to hunt. We have a murderer to find. And while a dozen guards ensure their safety, the kids have a giant-ass heated swimming pool to entertain them."

Maggie walked into the kitchen and opened the dishwasher. "The kids are in good hands. Tyler promised to teach Anne and Sara how to dive before his shift starts while I teach Nicholas the breast stroke."

Several chuckles broke out.

"Get your mind out of the gutter, boys. You know dog-gone well I was referring to swimming."

I laughed and looked toward Anne. "You don't know how to dive?"

Anne shook her head. "I'd never even been in a pool before yesterday. Swam in a lake a few times when I was young, but that's been the extent of my swimming experience."

"Tyler's not teaching you how to dive. No way. No how," Whiskey said, narrowing his eyes at the man who sat across from him. "I'll teach you myself."

Anne shrugged, not seeming too concerned with who taught her.

"And you?" I asked Haley.

"I'll be sunning by the pool until one of you comes back needing stitches." Haley sauntered out the French doors, stripping her t-shirt off as she went. Her bikini top was barely within the threshold of being allowable to wear in front of the kids.

Maggie shut the dishwasher door and pushed the start button. "Holler if anyone needs a Fed. I don't fly out of Miami until four." She walked out, stripping off her beach cover up.

Based on the looks Anne threw in their direction, I was guessing she was feeling self-conscious to be out in the pool area with them. I could see the straps to her conservative one-piece swimsuit under her tank top. She stopped looking toward the patio and glanced down at her own body.

"You're a knockout," Wild Card said to her. "If Whiskey ever screwed up the relationship, there'd be a line at the door waiting to replace him."

"And I'd beat them to a bloody pulp while I begged for you to take me back," Whiskey said, leaning over to kiss the top of her head on his way into the kitchen.

The kids, Carl, and both dogs came tearing down the stairs. The kids wore their swimsuits and dragged their beach towels across the floor behind them. Jager continued after them.

Beast stopped to look at Charlie, whining with his hind end swaying back and forth.

"No. Sorry, buddy, but I'm driving the Mustang today. Wet dog and expensive leather don't go together."

He whined again, flopping himself onto the floor by her feet as he pouted up at her.

"It's best if we take two vehicles," Wild Card said on his way out of the room. "I picked up my rental on our way back from the finger-chopping event last night."

Charlie looked over her shoulder at Wild Card as he walked away. "Are you saying he can swim and then ride in your SUV?"

"Might as well," Wild Card answered without turning around. "My deposit is already a lost cause after yesterday."

"Quick," Charlie said to Beast as she pointed toward the door. "You've got two minutes."

Beast barked twice, jumped to his feet, and ran outside.

"Ahh," Charlie said. "He's so happy."

I raised an eyebrow at Charlie. "You know he's a dog, right? That he doesn't really know what you said."

"Leave me alone. After all these years, I finally have a partner I like."

I shook my head at her as she walked out.

CHAPTER TWENTY-EIGHT

CHARLIE
Tuesday, 8:15 a.m.

With the top down on the Mustang, wearing my oversized sunglasses, and the speedometer about ten over the limit on the inner-city highway, I felt more relaxed than I had in days.

Bones wasn't quite as relaxed. His head swiveled in every direction. He'd finally stopped complaining about the top being down, but he wasn't happy. What could I say? This was Florida. Sunshine over safety was the state's slogan.

Wild Card drove behind us in his rental with Beast's oversized head sticking out the front passenger window. From the rearview mirror, I could see Wild Card using exaggerated hand gestures as he conversed with Beast. I wondered if their conversation had to do with girls or food.

I glanced over at Bones. "How does Wild Card stay in a good mood all the time? Even when he's mad, it's short lived."

"I wish I knew," Bones said, looking over his shoulder behind us. "The man's entertaining as shit until someone pushes him too far. Then he morphs into a scary mother-effer."

"Mother-*effer*?"

Bones sighed as he leaned forward and selected a pair of shades from the cup holder. "I'm sick of doing push-ups. Decided I'd try to quit swearing."

"And mother-effer passes as not being a swear word?"

"As long as Hattie's not around."

My phone rang as I slowed for a red light. I saw the display indicating Spence was calling and pressed the green phone button on the steering wheel. "Where are we meeting?"

"The diner on the corner of 9th and Paradise Avenue. I'm starving."

"We already ate. And I'm not leaving Beast in the car. Order takeout and meet us at the park on the south corner."

"That'll work." He disconnected.

I glanced over at Bones who was grinning. "What's so funny?"

"Just remembering how I met Spence."

"Was it in the military?"

"No. It was in a bar. Been friends ever since."

I'd had plenty of conversations with strangers in bars but not once did any of those conversations result in a relationship lasting past dawn. "You going to share the rest of the story?"

"Nope." Bones glanced over at me. I couldn't see his eyes because of his sunglasses. "Light's green."

I floored the accelerator at the same time the stream of cars behind us started blaring their horns. That's just how it was with Florida drivers. You had about one and a half seconds after a traffic light turned green to get through the intersection or you were the monster keeping everyone from moving forward. And if something unfortunate happened, like a flat tire, be prepared for a mega headache.

The aggressive horn pressing of Floridians probably had to do with the heat being unbearable when you were sitting still. Or maybe it was because no one wanted to waste their time driving when there were too many fun things to do. Either way, I'd adopted the habit without even meaning to after living in the state for less than a month.

I saw Wild Card shaking his head as he looked in his rearview mirror. A smile flashed as he pressed his brakes and stopped in the middle of the highway. Car horns blared. He laughed as he hit the gas to catch up with me.

I also laughed.

"Is he messing with the traffic?" Bones asked. He continued facing forward, watching the cars and nearby shops around us.

"Yeah. He must be bored."

I turned right at the next light. Two blocks down, I turned into a city lot and parked. A public park with a few tables and benches sat adjacent to the lot. I spotted Spence wolfing down a container of food at one of the tables and started strolling his way. Beast saw him and barked twice before running ahead to greet him.

"He's supposed to be on a leash, you know," Spence said as he stopped eating long enough to give Beast a two-handed body rub. "State law."

"He doesn't like it," I said as I sat across from him. "You got backgrounds for me?"

He slid two files toward me. "Colby Brown. Age fifty-two. Height six foot four. Weight two-hundred and fifty the last time he was arrested. And he's been arrested nine times. Two of those arrests landed him in prison. The first stint was for two years. The second for six. Assault. Robbery. Extortion. Probably a shitload more crimes the cops could never pin on him."

"What about employment records?"

"Both times he was on parole, he worked crap minimum-wage jobs to keep from going back to prison. And both times, the day after his parole period ended, he went off the grid."

The information on Colby wasn't all that helpful, but in police work most of the information gathered was just noise. The remaining nuggets were the reason a good detective kept digging. "What about Xander Hall?"

"Ghost. Doesn't exist."

"Damn. Back to square one."

"Don't be so quick to doubt my mad skills," Spence said, grinning at me. "I went back and took another look at Evie. I backtracked to where she lived and worked in Atlanta. Spoke to former coworkers and her old landlord, that type of thing."

"Quit talking yourself up and spill already," Bones ordered.

Spence laughed. "You're no fun," he said to Bones before turning back to me. "I suckered her old boss into digging through their security footage. He found us a picture of Evie's mystery man. It's not great, but it's better than nothing." He slid a picture from a folder and handed it to me.

I stared at the image of a middle-aged man walking into a building. He had dark hair, either brown or black but the picture was black and white so I couldn't tell. His skin tone was somewhere between cream and light brown, but I couldn't make out any ethnic identifiers because of the large rimmed driving sunglasses. His suit was expensive. That's it. A lean man, with dark hair, and expensive taste in clothes. "How does this help?"

"Hey!" Spence said, sounding offended. "It's a start. Maybe we'll get lucky and someone will recognize him."

Bones snorted, taking the picture. "Not likely. You couldn't get a photo without the sunglasses?"

"I was told he always wore them when he was there, which wasn't often."

"Makes me wonder," Wild Card said, taking the picture and studying it. "Kid, can you think of a reason why someone would wear sunglasses inside a building with security cameras?"

The lightbulb snapped on. I grinned over at Wild Card. "He's hiding from facial recognition software."

"That'd be my guess," Wild Card said as he used his phone to take a picture of the photo. He texted it to someone.

"I don't understand. What am I missing?" Spence asked.

"Feds," Bones said. "No one wears sunglasses indoors unless they're hiding from the Feds and don't want recognition software to ID them."

"That's a bit over the top. Most of that stuff is make believe TV crap." He looked at each of us. "Right?"

I shook my head. "It's out there. My niece programmed recognition software for a retail store. It's a real thing. You bet your backside the Feds are using it."

Wild Card's phone rang. He answered, replied a few words, then hung up. "Maggie says she needs the picture scanned. Then she'll have Genie run it through the Fed database, but she doubts it will work based on the quality of the photo."

"Who's Maggie?" Spence asked.

"Fed. But also a friend of the family," Bones answered.

"Mind blown," Spence said as he gathered up his Styrofoam container and plastic silverware. "Well, it's been fun, but I have two adultery cases and a corner store register that keeps coming up short. And when I clear those, I've got three new cases waiting."

"Don't forget to bill me," I told him as I stood. "And that includes your hours babysitting me yesterday."

"Don't worry about it."

"Spence, she's loaded," Bones said. "And she knows the difference between friendship and business. She doesn't expect you to do the work and not get paid, man. That's not how she rolls."

"Yeah. What he said." I smiled over at Spence as he threw his trash away.

"Okay. I'll bill you for the background work, but I'm not billing you for the night at the gas station. Beast and I volunteered to ride along because we were worried about you."

I pointed my thumb over my shoulder at Wild Card and Bones. "How's that any different than the security jobs these guys do?"

"It just is," Spence said as he walked away.

"Man," Bones said on a chuckle. "He's got it bad for you."

"Poor guy," Wild Card said.

I sucker punched him in the arm.

Chapter Twenty-Nine

KELSEY
Tuesday, 10:00 a.m.

Parked half a block away on the opposite side of the street, Ryan and I sat in the car observing the construction crew at the dentist office. We were only forty-five minutes into the surveillance and I was already bored. Trigger at least was able to walk around. He'd circled past the building twice already, meandering around the block.

I was beginning to wish Trigger had stayed in the car with me instead of Ryan. Ryan seldom spoke unless it was job specific or when his wife was around. He wasn't the most ideal partner on a stakeout. So far into my many attempts to initiate conversation, he'd answered *yes* twice and *no* once. Still... His short, clipped answers were better than the times he just glared at me without answering.

I was beginning to think he had two personalities: One for his wife Tweedle. And one for the rest of the human race.

"Did you see that?" Ryan asked, breaking the silence so suddenly that I jumped in my seat.

My barely warm coffee slopped, covering my hand. "Damn it. You made me spill my coffee."

I set the cup in the holder and took the napkin Ryan handed me, his attention still focused intensely on something across the street.

"What did you see? The guy carrying boxes inside?"

"No. I saw Trigger cut behind the building into the alley."

"He's fine."

"How are we supposed to know if he needs help?"

"When Trigger gets himself into a mess, you can see it a mile away."

Ryan glared sideways at me.

I rolled my eyes and pointed to my ear. "I'll know if he needs help."

"You have an earpiece?"

"Yes." I decided to answer him with a one-word answer to see how he liked it.

"Mind sharing?"

"No." I picked up my cup and took another drink. I waited until I saw anger overtaking his normal, annoyed expression. Laughing, I grabbed another earpiece from my bag. "You're going to regret asking for this."

Ryan secured the mic in his ear and then looked at me. "What's he doing?"

I smirked. "He likes to sing. But he's *really* bad at it."

"He sounds like a dying pig."

"Why do you think I've been trying to engage you in conversation?" I said, throwing my hands up. "Has anyone ever told you your social skills are horrendous?"

One corner of Ryan's lips curved up a fraction. *Just a fraction.* It quickly morphed into a scowl when he asked, "What's that clunking noise?"

"That's the sound of Trigger doing something stupid."

"Meaning?"

"He's climbing on top of something, probably a dumpster. He likely spotted a way to sneak inside."

"But it's *daytime*. And there's people—*everywhere*."

"Yup." I shrugged. "I know. But that's how Trigger rolls."

"Aren't you going to stop him? It's a two-way earpiece."

"Ordering him to stop wouldn't do any good. He'd say 'okay', but still do it."

Ryan's eyebrow shot upward. "And you haven't fired him yet?"

"I punish him in other ways. Like the last time he got arrested, I let him sit in jail for two days before I sent someone to fix it. He behaved for almost a week after that."

"Why do you keep him?"

"Wow. This is the most I've ever heard you talk."

He shook his head. "I'm completely baffled."

"Give it some time. It'll make sense, eventually. If not today, maybe by tomorrow. You'll be Team Trigger before you know it."

"Unnecessary risks are dangerous in our profession."

"Agreed. But what we would deem risky, doesn't register the same for Trigger. And his methods are effective."

"He's *breaking* and *entering*... into a building *full of people*... in the middle of *broad daylight*!"

I smiled over at Ryan. "But he'll have a good reason."

Ryan looked at me like I had two heads, but ten minutes later Trigger rounded the corner of the building, smiling to himself, and started singing again.

"Hey, Boss," Trigger whispered. "I'm going to hang around at the side of the building until two guys in suits come out. Let me know when the guy in the dark gray one exits. Then relay his distance until he reaches the sidewalk."

I switched the mic on for the earpiece. "Copy. Waiting on dark gray suit to exit."

"What's he planning?" Ryan asked.

"I have no idea."

"You don't make him run his plans past you?"

"What would be the point? If it's something stupid, he'd just lie."

Trigger snorted, hearing our conversation, then continued singing as he leaned against the cinder block building and fiddled with a cigarette. He usually kept a smoke handy so he could pretend to be looking for a lighter if anyone questioned what he was doing. He didn't even have a lighter. He didn't smoke.

I looked at Ryan. "You might want to slip out and make a loop around the block. Be ready if needed."

"Ready for what?"

I threw my hands upward. "How many times do I have to tell you? *I. Don't. Know!*"

Ryan mumbled curses as he slipped out of the car and ran the other direction to loop around the block. I pulled my gun and gauged the distance. I could make the shot if I had to, but it would require everyone standing perfectly still and me getting out of the car. Any future stakeouts would be dead in the water. I just hoped whatever Trigger was planning didn't get to *that* level of crazy. But it was Trigger. I wasn't overly hopeful.

"You know you love me, Boss," Trigger said as he smiled at the sidewalk. "I entertain the shit out of you."

I laughed. I was about to reply something sarcastic when two men in suits walked out of the building. "Two suits are shaking hands. Only three feet from door and still talking." I watched as the men continued to talk for a few more minutes. "Gray suit on the move. Twenty feet. Fifteen feet. Twelve. Ten. Eight. Six. Four. Two—"

Trigger collided with Mr. Gray Suit hard enough to knock them both to the ground with Trigger landing on top of him. They were a tangle of arms and legs before Trigger suddenly jumped up—*and ran away.*

"What the—" Ryan started to say over the earpiece as we both watched Trigger flee down the sidewalk at top speed.

The man in the suit started yelling and I heard him say *wallet*, before several construction workers took off after Trigger. And by several, I mean at least twenty. There was a full-on mob chasing my top field guy—*who'd just mugged someone*. And the mob was gaining speed.

I laughed.

"You're going to rescue my ass, right, Boss?" Trigger huffed over the earpiece.

"I haven't decided yet," I said, still laughing.

Ryan casually walked back to the car, trying not to hurry. He slid into his seat and leaned his head against the dash. I watched his shoulders shake as he silently laughed. I started the car and pulled away from the curb.

Three blocks later, we saw the mob had dwindled to three guys, but they were only ten feet behind Trigger as he dodged pedestrians, cars, and even a bicycle that nearly took him down.

"What's the plan?" Ryan asked. "We can't pull guns on unarmed civilians and I'd feel bad if I had to fight them. They're good Samaritans, trying to catch a mugger."

"I'm thinking." I pondered our options as I juggled watching Trigger and driving.

"Think faster, Boss," Trigger wheezed into the earpiece. "I could use a lift about now."

"We're in Charlie's car so if I pick you up and someone jots down her plate number, she could lose her job. Assisting a criminal to escape a crime is kind of a cop no-no." I kept driving, but Trigger and his pursuers were running faster than the traffic was moving. That would change another half block ahead where the street intersected with a five-lane highway. "Half a block up," I said to Trigger. "Main road. Get there and let's hope you can give them the slip. Just don't get hit by a car."

I watched Trigger pick up the pace. When his pursuers saw him gaining speed again, one of them stopped running and leaned over with his hands on his knees to catch his breath.

"Two bogies left," Ryan said so Trigger was aware. "But they look determined to kick your ass. They won't give up easy."

"Shit," Trigger said.

Trigger reached the intersection to the main road and disappeared around the corner. Seconds later, the two remaining contractors followed him around the corner. Ryan leaned over and laid on the horn. Other drivers joined the orchestra as we crept forward.

"Thanks," I said, sarcastically. "That helped so much."

Finally reaching the intersection, I accelerated into my turn and picked up speed as we searched ahead for Trigger.

"Boss..." Trigger said.

"I'm here, but I lost visual."

"I'm about to do something dumb. If it doesn't work out, send flowers to my mother."

Ryan pointed and I followed his finger a half a block ahead where Trigger was running. He was one good arm's reach from being caught.

"I see you. What's your plan?" I asked.

He didn't answer. I watched the scene unfold as if he was a younger Bruce Willis in one of the many *Die Hard* movies. Trigger jetted into the road, causing two cars to slam on their brakes to avoid hitting him. In the third lane, another driver hit his brakes as Trigger ran in front of the car, staying in that lane and turning to run with the flow of traffic. Ahead of him was a five-ton commercial truck still accelerating through the gears after the last traffic light.

The truck had a non-standard back with tall side rails but only heavy straps were netted along the back. Trigger ran faster, trying to catch up to the truck, as I changed lanes and moved into the center lane.

"You lost the bogies," Ryan said to Trigger. "They aren't as dumb as you."

Trigger leapt forward, securing his hands into the cargo net. The truck lurched forward as the driver made another gear change. The jarring motion caused one of Trigger's hands to lose its grip on the net and his body swung from side to side. He managed to grab hold again as he was thrown around, but he was hanging too low to secure his feet.

"*Trigger—*" I yelled. "*Left foot to bottom outside corner of the truck*! There's a foothold!"

Trigger stopped scrambling with both feet and swung only his left foot out, searching for the hold. I watched his hand start to slip on the netting. The speed limit was twenty-five, but based on my own speed, the truck was moving along with traffic at closer to thirty.

I cut off another car and moved behind the truck. Horns blasted around me but I ignored them. "You're missing the foothold by two inches. *Farther left*! *Higher*!"

His foot found the cutout and he lifted himself up. We heard him release his breath over the mic.

I looked around, trying to gauge our location. A sign indicated that the exit for the interstate was one mile ahead and that both outside lanes would exit. Since the truck was in the third lane, I was hopeful. Then the driver turned on his right blinker to get over.

"Shit," I said. "He's taking the interstate."

"I can't jump, Boss," Trigger said, glancing back at me as I followed the truck over one lane to the right.

Traffic was moving even faster than before. If he jumped now, his body would bounce into another lane and he'd be squashed.

"What's the plan, Boss?"

"I'm thinking."

"Think faster. He could drive for hours before he stops again."

I ignored him and followed the truck onto the interstate. As we merged, a cop sitting on the side of the road spotted Trigger. The cruiser's lights flashed on and the officer charged full speed ahead to get in front of the truck.

"Trigger. Before that truck stops completely, you need to jump, then run back toward the exit. Find a place to hide until we pick you up."

"Can't you just pick me up now?" he whined, looking over his shoulder at me.

"In front of the cop? You just mugged someone, dumbass! Dispatch would've broadcasted your description by now."

"Shit."

I slowed, creating a larger gap between my car and the truck which was edging off the side of the road. The cop was in front of the truck. They both coasted as the truck prepared to stop. "Remember, if you fall, tuck your shoulder and roll."

Trigger looked down at the asphalt. It was still passing at about ten miles an hour.

"Now, Trigger!" Ryan ordered.

Trigger jumped.

Unfortunately, his legs swept out from under him and he rolled toward the shoulder of the road. There was zero tucking involved. He slammed, bounced, and then slid across the road, skidding through the gravel shoulder before toppling over the edge into a ditch. His body disappeared from our view.

Ryan and I both inhaled sharply. We sat frozen, staring at the ditch. Trigger, covered in greenish-brown slime, sprang up and ran back toward the exit.

I looked ahead and saw the cop was walking toward the rear of the truck. I'd waited too long and he spotted me. He started running, looking first to see that Trigger was gone and then running to our car and looking inside.

"Why did you stop?" the officer asked.

"There was a man—" I pointed to the truck, stuttering my speech "—on the truck. I didn't know... what I was supposed to do."

"Did you see where he went?"

Ryan pointed to the other side of the truck. "He ran into that ditch."

The cop's face puckered in disgust. "That's a runoff. It's filled with sewage and trash." He sighed and looked back at us. "Did he look injured? Because if he wasn't injured, maybe I let this one slide."

"He looked like an idiot!" I said. "But not injured."

"Hey!" Trigger said through the earpiece. "I heard that."

"Good enough for me," the cop said, nodding as he thumped the top of our car with his palm. "You folks have a nice day."

Chapter Thirty

CHARLIE
Tuesday, 10:34 a.m.

Beast whined again. We'd waited for Lydia for an hour and a half. The patch of shade we'd claimed under the corner tree was shrinking fast as the sun rose toward late morning.

"Come on, boy," I said, slapping the side of my leg. "We'll track her down later."

Beast jumped up and bounced alongside me as I signaled to Bones and Wild Card that I was calling it. They'd positioned themselves so they could monitor me from afar. Far enough so they wouldn't spook Lydia, but close enough if Mr. Tricky got any ideas.

As Beast and I walked toward the precinct, I wondered why Lydia hadn't showed. She couldn't have spotted Bones or Wild Card. It had taken me forty-five minutes to find Bones, and I never did figure out where Wild Card was stationed. Knowing him, he'd wandered toward the beach, following bikinis.

So, no, Lydia couldn't have spotted them. She was either hiding from me or someone prevented her from meeting me. I had a bad feeling as I climbed the stairs to the precinct. I held the door open for Beast. The desk officer buzzed the inner door and hit the automatic door opener. I followed Beast into the main room, where he was greeted with ear scratches and good mornings by officers as he made his way to the stairs. I stopped at the last desk and asked one of the rookies to put out a BOLO on Lydia. Turning back to the stairs, Beast sat waiting for me. Grinning, I ran at the stairs, racing up them as fast as I could. Beast barked twice before chasing after me. He beat me by one stupid step.

Unlike Beast, I was winded and put my hand on the wall to catch my breath.

"That's her!" a man yelled. I looked up and saw Danny Rickers standing next to Detective Ford's desk. "That's the woman who cut off my fingers!"

All the detectives froze in their tracks, turning to look at me.

"What?" I asked, looking around before walking toward the back of the room.

Ford sighed. "Did you cut this man's fingers off?" he asked loud enough for everyone to hear.

I snorted. "No."

I continued toward the far end of the room, stopping at my desk. It was piled high with files. I grabbed a nearby empty box, set it on my chair, and skim read the contents of the files before dropping them inside the box. Ignoring the chaos on the other side of the room, I was halfway through the pile before Quille walked over.

"You've been back on the job one day. *One day*! And you're already facing an I.A. investigation. That has to be a record."

"Quit worrying," I said, dropping another file into the box. "It's not good for the old ticker."

"Are you telling me you're innocent? Because somehow I doubt that."

I turned to face Quille. "I did *not* cut that man's fingers off."

It was the truth. I had *chopped*, not cut, *the tips* of his fingers off. I had every confidence that I could pass a lie detector test using that logic. Quille knew me well enough to know he wasn't getting the whole truth. He also knew he didn't want to know the truth.

"What's the worst-case scenario on this?" Quille asked, thumbing over his shoulder at Danny.

I glanced across the room. "Internal Affairs will get all excited when they hear my name, but in the end, it will get filed away with their other fizzled attempts at taking my badge. Danny's a scumbag wife beater. No jury will ever buy his victim act."

"He could sue you."

"He could try," I said, laughing. "I keep a lawyer on retainer who'd jam him up for years."

"Someday you'll make a mistake and get caught," Quille said, placing fisted hands on his hips. "Then what?"

"I have no idea what you're talking about," I said, slapping a file against his chest. "That's the ME report on Roseline. Notice anything odd?"

While he read the file, I texted Bones and warned him that Danny Rickers was leaving the building via the stairs and to make sure he and Wild Card weren't spotted. Bones replied a thumbs up.

I slid the phone into my back pocket as Quille looked up from his reading. "The bruise on Roseline's neck?"

"Bingo. Pauly had the same bruise. The question is, why? What's the connection?"

"Hopefully you're about to enlighten me, because I got no damn idea."

"No such luck. I'm all out of enlightenment today. This case is nothing but a pile of questions."

I spotted Maggie stepping off the elevator and was about to wave when I saw two men in black suits follow behind her. Bones and Wild Card casually followed the suits. How they'd managed to pass Danny without being seen, I wasn't sure.

Maggie spotted me and led the group my way. She didn't look happy. Whatever was happening was big enough to disrupt her plans of lying poolside until her flight.

"Sorry, Quille."

"For what?" he asked, glancing over his shoulder.

"I don't know yet. Just thought I'd apologize now to save time later." I walked over and opened the conference room door. I asked for the two researchers and the detectives to clear the room. As they left, Quille, Maggie, the two black suits, Bones and Wild Card entered.

"Who are they?" Quille asked, pointing toward Bones and Wild Card.

"Bodyguards."

Quille looked down at Beast and frowned. "You're not getting rid of the dog, are you?"

"Eventually. But not today." I walked around the table but didn't sit. I leaned against the wall, crossing my arms over my chest. "What's going on?" I asked Maggie.

"Seems our friends in the DOJ have an issue with you investigating Roseline's murder."

"Tough shit," I said, turning a glare to the suits. "My town. My murder investigation."

The shorter of the suits reached out with a business card. "I'm Deputy Byron with the U.S. Marsh—"

"I don't care who you are," I said, interrupting him.

"Behave, Kid," Quille warned, taking the card and shaking the man's hand as they went through the formalities of introductions. I listened as I pretended to ignore them. The other Marshal introduced himself as Deputy Wright. I looked over at Wild Card and rolled my eyes.

He laughed as he pulled a chair out and sat, leaning back and stretching his legs. Bones stood stiff as a board, guarding the only exit.

"I'm afraid your investigation is interfering with our federal case," Deputy Byron said to Quille. "We'll need to take over from here."

"And I'm afraid that just doesn't work for me," I said, stepping forward and leaning my hands on the table. "One of the victims, Paul Leenstra, was a friend of mine. No way will I walk away from this case."

"We could arrest you," Deputy Wright threatened.

"*Time out!*" Maggie snapped. "I'd like to remind everyone, we're on the same team. The good guys, *remember*?"

Wild Card laughed out loud which earned himself a glare from both suits and Quille.

Maggie ignored him and turned to face the marshals. "Your case is sinking fast. The way I see it, if you share information with Detective Harrison, she might find a way to salvage your case." She turned to me and pointed. "*And you*! Did you ever consider they may have details that will help you solve Pauly's murder? Huh?"

"What crawled up your ass?" I asked her.

She crossed her arms over her chest. "I was perfectly relaxed in a poolside chaise when my phone rang. I decided to get dressed and come down here to mediate this shit-show before you—" she pointed at me "—got yourself arrested. *You're welcome.* And you owe me a margarita."

Knowing she was right, I pulled out a chair and sat. "I'm willing to work together if I have to, but I'll need full access in return. I'm running blind here."

The deputies looked at each other, debating their next move.

"Quit wasting our time," Bones barked.

Byron looked back at me. "What do you know?"

"Roseline and Pauly were both killed in her apartment late afternoon or early evening Saturday. Roseline's cause of death was massive blood loss. Her heart stopped when there was more blood on the outside than inside. Her death was violent. There was a clear indication of overkill. Pauly, on the other hand, was likely choked until he lost consciousness before he was injected with enough morphine to kill an elephant. Then, his body was moved to the first floor under the staircase. Only someone who knew his habits would know to place him there. Either someone close to him or someone who'd been watching the building."

"Roseline was likely killed by a hitman," Deputy Wright said, shaking his head. "Someone hired by the Jameson crew out of New Jersey."

"If it was a hitman—and I'm not saying it wasn't because the rumor on the street is that it was—then it's someone new. No way a seasoned killer would've lost control like that on Roseline."

Byron snorted as he arrogantly inspected his tie. "You're an expert on contract killers?"

Maggie leaned forward, toward Byron. "She has firsthand experience. How about you? Ever faced down a professional hitman? No? What about standing in the crosshairs of a rifle scope?" When he remained quiet, turning slightly pink along the cheekbones, she turned back to me. "What else you got, Kid?"

"I'm done sharing until I get some information in return." I looked at the suits. "Tell me about the drug ring—the Jameson crew."

"I'm afraid we can't share those details," Wright said, leaning back in his chair.

"Assholes," Bones grumbled under his breath.

I winked at him as I pulled my phone. I looked through my contact list, finding Phillip Bianchi who was not only Lisa's brother, but more importantly, he was the second in command of the New Jersey mafia. I pressed the call button before moving the phone to my ear.

"Good Morning, Charlie Harrison. Is everything okay with the family?" Phillip asked.

"I haven't heard otherwise. But I'm calling about a case I'm working."

"Why do you and your cousin keep assuming I'm one of the good guys?"

"I'm not asking you to register as an informant. I just need some background information."

"Ask your question, but I won't guarantee I'll answer."

"Need to know about an organization in your neighborhood. The Jameson crew."

"New Jersey is a state, not a neighborhood. You make it sound like we all live on the same block."

"And yet, I'm sure you've heard of them."

Phillip sighed. "I have. What's your interest?"

"Double homicide. The Feds think my murder cases are linked back to the Jameson crew's pending legal troubles."

"Doubtful. They're dangerous, but not smart enough, powerful enough, or big enough to reach out of state. But whoever they distribute for could've agreed to handle it."

"Who would that be?"

"I don't know. And if I did, I wouldn't tell you." There was a break in conversation as I waited for Phillip to say more. "Between us, and only us, I'll share that the Jameson crew dealt in everything from heroin to grass. Their pipeline was well established. I've heard rumors their supplier resides south of the border."

"Shit. I was told they were hillbilly heroin dealers."

"What the hell is hillbilly heroin?"

I imagined Phillip wearing an Armani suit and smoking a Cuban as he sat in his Italian leather chair, a confused look scrunching up his perfectly-sculpted facial features. "It's OxyContin mostly. Prescription highs. Pharmaceutical pill poppers."

"Then no. Before their arrests, they were the biggest coke dealers around, and from what I hear, the quality of their products was excellent."

"That's interesting. What about more difficult to acquire drugs? The kind usually only found in hospitals?"

"From what I heard, if there was a buyer, they could acquire the product."

"Morphine?"

"Are you shopping for morphine?"

"One of my victims died of a morphine overdose. Liquid morphine."

"I can't imagine there's a big market in liquid morphine, but then again, I have no interest in sticking needles in my arm for recreational purposes. I only know what I've been told, which is that the Jameson crew had a solid supply chain."

"Anything else you're willing to share?"

"Talk to Mickey. And don't tell him I said that." The phone went silent. He'd hung up on me.

I looked down at my phone. The last thing I wanted to do was talk to Mickey McNabe again. The man was... *unsettling*. Maybe Kelsey would talk to him for me.

"Well?" Maggie asked.

"Their case," I pointed to the suits, "is centered on the Jameson crew, right?"

"Yes," Maggie answered before they could stop her.

"Then they can't help me. The Jameson crew is too small and too stupid to be behind this." I stood and started for the exit, but before I reached the handle the door flew open.

Bones, startled by the door, reached out and grabbed Ford by the throat.

"*Let him go!*" I said, grabbing Bones' arm with both my hands and trying to pull his arm away. "*He's a cop!*"

Bones flung his fingers apart, releasing Ford, and stepped back.

I placed my hand over Ford's wrist, stopping him from pulling his gun. With the other hand, I pushed him on the shoulder until he walked backwards into the main room. "My fault. Bodyguards can be jumpy."

Ford stopped throwing dagger eyes at Bones and looked at me. "*Bodyguard. Shit.* Sorry. I forgot. I was in a rush because I knew you'd want this." He handed me a note with an address as he continued glancing over my shoulder at Bones. "DB just came in over the radio. Homeless woman. Matches the description of the BOLO you put out."

Lydia, I thought. *Damn.* "What do we know?"

"Boys on the scene relayed that it looks like an overdose, but since everyone knows a homeless person was murdered in your building and staged as an OD, they sat on the scene. Nothing's been touched."

"Ford and I will go with you," Quille said to me. "Lose your bodyguards."

"Not your call," Wild Card told him.

"But it is mine," I said. "Head back to the mansion. Between Ford, Quille, and Beast, I'm almost confident that I can stay alive for a few hours."

Bones snorted. Wild Card held out his rental keys.

I took them as I asked, "Why are you giving me these?"

"I wouldn't want Beast's claws to tear up the leather in the Mustang. Best to swap vehicles." He smiled as he held his palm out.

I dug my keys out of my bag. "You get one scratch—"

"I won't," he said, cutting me off as he snagged the keys from my hand.

I muttered curses as I jogged to catch up with Quille and Ford. Beast happily barked, running beside me. "Yeah," I said to Beast. "You better be happy. I just picked you over my Mustang. That's just *wrong*."

Chapter Thirty-One

KELSEY
Tuesday, 11:15 a.m.

We caught up with Trigger three blocks from the interstate exit, sitting curbside, tipping back a bottle of vodka. As we walked toward him, I looked around the neighborhood. The curbs were caked with shards of glass, cigarette butts, and other trash. Rundown cars were scattered down the block, parked in front of decaying buildings. Kids played on the sidewalk down the street, eyeing us with bad intentions. Two prostitutes leaned against a nearby building.

Ryan took the vodka from Trigger, setting the bottle aside.

I caught a whiff of Trigger and backtracked a few steps. "You smell horrid. Did you consider cleaning up before buying a bottle of booze?"

"Owner wouldn't let me inside. The ladies," he gestured to the prostitutes, "ran inside to buy the bottle. It was helping to dull my senses, so I didn't choke on my own stench."

I entered the dingy, dark bar. Two well-weathered customers sat on barstools at the far end. The bartender, an older man with hard lines etched into his face, was drying glasses behind the bar. A booth off to the side held a pair of shady-looking characters talking in low whispers. Ignoring the customers, I pulled cash from my bag and slapped it on the bar-top in front of the bartender.

"You must be a friend of the sewer rat," the bartender said, nodding toward the front entrance. "He can't come inside. I'd never get the smell out."

"Not asking for you to let him in. But he could use a sidewalk shower. Sell us few buckets of soapy water?"

He used his finger to separate the twenty-dollar bills stacked in front of him. He restacked the cash and slid it into his pocket before nodding for me to follow him. At the other end of the bar, he led me into the kitchen where he grabbed two five-gallon buckets, lifting one to the slop sink and turning on the water. I grabbed a nearby bottle of dish soap, pouring in a third of the bottle.

The bartender returned to the main bar while I waited for the bucket to fill. When my phone rang, the display flashed a picture of Wild Card posing shirtless as he flexed his muscles. I wondered who he'd roped into helping steal my phone to take the picture. Probably one of the kids.

I shook my head, laughing, as I answered, "I thought you were with Charlie?"

"She made alternate arrangements. She doesn't need us for a few hours. You have anything for us?"

"Nope. Maybe later tonight."

"You still at the dentist office?"

"Nope. We're at a bar." I watched a cockroach the size of my hand scurry across the floor.

Wild Card chuckled. "Babe. It's not even noon yet. Are things really that bad?"

"It's been an interesting morning, but, no, things aren't that bad. The only one drinking already is Trigger." I turned off the water, but couldn't lift the bucket with one hand. "I'll explain later. We'll be at the mansion in about an hour."

I pushed the phone into my back pocket before using both hands to lift the bucket from the sink. After starting the next bucket, I grabbed a handful of trash bags and the dish soap, tucking them under my arm. I lifted the full bucket and shuffled mini steps toward the door with it between my feet. Before I reached the other side of the room, Ryan walked inside, rolled his eyes, took the bucket in one hand, and carried it out.

"Show off," I muttered as I followed him. Passing the bar, I hollered over my shoulder. "Bring the other bucket out when it's done filling."

"You paid for water. Not all the rest of that stuff," he said, waving a hand to the trash bags and soap.

"I paid you plenty. And I'll pay another twenty if you find us some clean towels."

"Forty."

"Fine," I said as I stepped outside into the bright sun. I took the bottle of vodka from Trigger again before handing him a garbage bag. "Strip. Put your clothes in a garbage bag."

"Out here? On the sidewalk?" Trigger asked, looking around.

Ryan crossed his arms over his chest. "Now. Or we'll leave your ass here."

Trigger's shoulders deflated. He stood and took off his shoes.

A light breeze floated by and Ryan and I stepped back as the smell of rotting food and sewage assaulted us. Trigger used his thumb and index finger to pull two wallets from his back pockets, tossing them both on the sidewalk. I retrieved sandwich baggies from my shoulder bag, securing a wallet in each.

When Trigger had stripped down to his tighty whities, I raised my hand up to stop him. "Really, Trigger?" I asked, motioning to his underwear.

"What?" A sly grin slid onto his face. "They're comfortable."

I rolled my eyes as I took a step away. Ryan, standing behind Trigger, dumped the bucket of soapy water over Trigger's head. The underwear, now wet, forced me to see more of him than I'd ever wanted. I walked away, joining the prostitutes who were still leaning against the building.

Physically, the women were opposites. One was tall, bony, with big blonde hair, and wearing a shredded black t-shirt with a missing sleeve, and a short black jean skirt. The other prostitute was short, plump but not fat, had darker features, short clipped hair, and dressed flashier in a sequin green tank top and a yellow spandex skirt.

"The only men who wear dos ugly-ass drawers is either old, or ex-cons," the tall prostitute told me.

The short prostitute giggled before calling over to Trigger, "Hey, *little boy*! Did yer momma buy you those big-boy undies?"

Trigger glanced over but continued smearing the dish soap over his body.

"That water cold?" the shorter prostitute called out again. "Or are you one of those turtle types?"

Ryan chuckled as he took the second bucket and poured it over Trigger's head. Blackish-green water raced toward the curb. The white underwear—not so white anymore.

The tall prostitute flashed angry eyes at me. She was a foot taller and, based on the track marks, a whole lot *higher* than me. "Your man is stinking up our block."

"Sorry about that. But while we're all here, have either of you heard anything about prostitutes disappearing?"

"What kind of ho?" the shorter prostitute asked.

"Not sure, actually," I answered.

"Well, you gotta narrow it down, honey," she scoffed as she tugged at her skirt, tugging it up, not down. "You got your hotel girls, your motel girls, your drunk bar girls, your sober bar girls, your corner girls, your alley girls, your delivery girls—"

"If'n you ask me," the tall prostitute interrupted. "Those delivery girls got it bad."

The shorter one bounced her head up and down in agreement. "I like me a little street action, but those delivery girls never know what the hell they be walking into."

"Or if'n they be walking out."

"Damn straight." They bumped fists before the shorter one continued, "But I could be one of those hotel girls if'n I had the clothes and shoes and stuff."

"Bitch," the taller prostitute said, placing a hand on her hip as she looked down at her coworker, "ya don't speak or look anything like those girls. New clothes ain't gonna to hide da fact you got *no business* being in one a those hotels."

"Based on the information I have," I said, cutting off their brewing argument, "I believe I'm referring to street or motel girls."

"The morgue, baby. This life is *hard*," the taller prostitute said. "And some johns are meaner than others."

I shook my head. "No bodies ever turn up. Here today, gone tomorrow, disappearances."

"You a cop?" the shorter prostitute asked.

"Nope. Used to be." I pulled a business card for Silver Aces from my bag, handing it to her. "I was hired to find out what's happening to the girls."

"Who da hell gonna front money to track down a couple of missing hos?"

"I took the case pro-bono," I answered honestly. "But it was a cop who asked me to look into it."

The taller prostitute squinted at me. "What kind a cop?"

"The kind who'd buy you a lemonade on a hot day and never look lower than your face."

"Not many of those around anymore," she said as she looked around the block. After taking a beat, she sighed, answering some internal question. "I might've heard of a few girls taking off, but don't know no details."

"Ferrari?" the shorter prostitute asked her.

"I thought she moved?"

"Nah. Remember that gash of a roommate swiped all her shit? Said Ferrari didn't come home, so she figured her stuff was fair game."

"Yeah-yeah... You knocked that skank on her ass, then took the purse," she said, laughing. "Shit. Forgot bout dat."

"Ferrari's purse?" I asked, trying to pull a few details.

"Not her regular *everyday* purse," the shorter prostitute said. "Her *ho* purse." She swung her oversized hot-pink purse out for me to see. "Flashy. But big. And got some weight to it. That's a *ho purse*. Best weapon a girl can have on the street."

The tall prostitute held her purse out. "I got a ten-foot chain in mine. Used to have a can of pepper spray. But you use them once, and they're done. A chain lasts forever. It's hell on your shoulder, but worth it when you get in the back seat with the wrong john. You just slam the purse upside his head a few times—" she held the purse up and demonstrated "—then get the hell out a there before his eyes come back inta focus."

It took me half a minute to shake off the image of half-naked bodies swinging purses, but finally I was able to return my focus to the issue at hand. "Was there anything inside Ferrari's purse?"

"Nah. Just the usual. Gum. Booze. A few business cards. Not even any change. But that skank roommate might've already taken any money."

"Was Ferrari a friend?"

The women laughed. The tall one scanned the street, but no customers had appeared while we chatted. "Street girls either get along—*or they don't*. Ain't nobody friends, though."

"Not even the two of you?"

"Let's just say we have common business habits, kay?" the shorter one said. "Like how neither of us work for pimps. And how we both like working this block cuz it's slower. Less cops. And da johns round here are into normal shit. Not the jam a bottle up your ass or cut off your titties shit."

I looked around the neighborhood again. It was a low-traffic, poverty-stricken neighborhood. They likely made ten bucks per blowjob at best, but they were safer here than the busier locations. And teaming up, whether they liked each other or not, kept them safer yet.

"By any chance, did you keep the business cards from Ferrari's purse?" I asked the shorter one.

"She keeps everything," the taller one scoffed. "She's a packrat."

The shorter one dug around in the neon pink bag and pulled out three business cards. I took them, flipping through them. The first was for a strip club. I'd have one of the guys check it out. The second one was for the dental clinic. My shoulders dropped. I barely glanced at the third—a hair salon offering a discount for new customers.

"When did Ferrari disappear?" I asked.

Both women were watching me, eyes narrowed.

"Bout three weeks back," the tall one said, dragging the shoulder of her ripped t-shirt back onto her shoulder. "She's gone for good, ain't she?"

I sighed, not wanting to tell them, but knowing they needed to be warned. "Looks that way. Just stick together, and you both should be fine. Don't go anywhere alone. Especially when you're not working." I glanced over my shoulder at Trigger and Ryan.

Trigger was using a hand towel to dry off as Ryan tore the corners out of a trash bag. Next thing I knew, Trigger took the bag, turned his back to Ryan which meant he was facing us, and dropped his underwear to the sidewalk.

I closed my eyes as I turned away, but it was too late. The image was burned into my brain.

"Guess he *ain't* one of those turtle types after all," the short one said, laughing.

"Where was he hiding dat thing?" the taller one said, chuckling. "We got ourselves a winner, folks!"

"Now what's he doin?"

Curious, I peeked. Trigger had stepped into the garbage bag which had holes in the bottom corners for his legs. He knotted the excess plastic around his waist and cinched it tight. He now stood in the middle of the sidewalk, grinning like an idiot, wearing a trash bag diaper.

He swung his head to the side to smile back at Ryan. Ryan's return grin held a tad too much sinister in it as he picked up the bottle of vodka and poured it on Trigger's road rash.

Trigger tried twisting away as he howled, but Ryan held him firmly in place with a hand wrapped around Trigger's bicep. Several people stepped outside to see what was happening.

"Damn," the shorter one cursed. "That looks painful."

"Looks like they're about ready to leave," I said, turning back to the women. I pulled some cash from my pocket. "Take the day off. My treat."

The tall one grabbed the cash and hurried off in the other direction. Likely worried I'd change my mind.

The shorter one scurried to catch up.

Chapter Thirty-Two

KELSEY
Tuesday, 11:55 a.m.

I tried paying a cabbie three-hundred dollars to drive Trigger back to the mansion, but the driver refused. Instead, we tossed Trigger's clothes in a nearby dumpster and now Trigger, in his garbage bag diaper, sat grinning from the back seat. Ryan was driving. I was in the passenger seat, flipping through the wallet Trigger had lifted, pulling out high-limit credit cards and fancy business cards for a Mr. Owen Flint. It appeared Mr. Flint was a real estate investment guru. But it was the membership card I'd found in the wallet which had me ordering Ryan to turn west, back toward the center of Miami.

"Where we heading?" Ryan asked as he followed the U-turn lane at the next intersection.

"The Outer Layer. Our guy at the dentist office is a member."

"So?"

"So... Baker keeps files on all the members, with full background checks."

"Will anyone be there? It isn't even noon yet."

"Baker has a residential suite next to his office. He usually stays there. But if he's not, I can get us inside."

"Umm..." Trigger said from the back seat. "I was sort of hoping to find some clothes."

"Charlie has clothes and a shower in her office."

"I got no issue wearing woman's clothes, but I don't think they'll fit."

"You can borrow something of Baker's then." I pointed for Ryan to make a turn at the next street.

We weren't that far from the club, and ten minutes later we walked up to the private entrance and I swiped my VIP card to enter. Trigger and I took the elevator while Ryan volunteered to take the stairs to ensure they were clear. This was a secure building, but Ryan wasn't used to sitting around, so I didn't argue. As I entered Baker's private office on the fifth floor, Ryan followed Trigger and me through the door.

"In this business," Baker said, sitting behind his desk in a full three-piece charcoal suit, "I've grown accustomed to seeing men in diapers. But trash bags?"

I walked over and greeted him with a hug. "He needs clothes and another shower. And I need some information."

Baker glanced over at a woman sitting in the guest chair. "Evie, can you show this," he pointed toward Trigger, "*person*, into my suite and find clothes for him?"

Evie smiled, but her nose was scrunched. Despite the sidewalk shower, Trigger still omitted a pungent odor. Evie led Trigger into the private suite, his garbage bag making rustling noises as he walked. A bark of a laugh escaped Ryan, before he turned away, walking toward the security monitors.

"Do you need the financial reports? Because I gave Charlie the third-quarter statements weeks ago."

"Nope. I need client details," I said, tossing Mr. Flint's membership card onto Baker's desk.

"Those files are confidential," Baker said as he picked up the card and read the name.

"Are we really going to play this game? You say I can't have the information, I say hand them over or else. And it goes in circles for ten minutes until you finally cave." I sighed as I flopped into a guest chair. "It's all so tedious. Can we just skip to the end where you give me the file?"

Baker snorted. "You used to like playing games."

"I've grown up."

"That's not growing up," Baker said as he walked over to the filing cabinet. "That's boredom. Something I never expected from you." He used his keys to open the third drawer on the cabinet. "Remember when you tied that guy with his own leather straps and stuffed the gag ball in his mouth? You left the poor bastard on the street and told him to find his own way home. I'll never forget him waddling away with the leather strap covering his ass crack."

Ryan walked back and looked down at me with one eyebrow raised.

I shrugged, trying to hide my grin. "He deserved it. He broke the rules and needed to face the consequences."

Baker tossed a file in front of me. He pointed to the file. "Owen Flint. Not one of our better clients. He's been scolded a few times. Getting handsy with the female staff, grabbing their arm, slapping their backsides, that sort of thing. Garth keeps an eye on him."

"How often is he here?" I asked.

"Every Tuesday night. He should be here tonight around ten."

Ryan crossed his arms, turning to face Baker. "You and me going to have a problem if this is the last night Mr. Flint ever shows his face here?"

"That's Kelsey's call," Baker said, waving a hand to show his indifference. "But I won't miss him. You'd also make Garth very happy if you included him in your plans. He's been bored."

"Says here," I said, interrupting their manly moment, "that Owen Flint spends most of his time in The Parlor before using one of the private rooms."

"Depends if he brings a date or business associate with him." Baker sat in the guest chair next to me. I knew his doing so was intentional. Sitting beside me, instead of behind the desk, was a sign of respect.

"Do you ever know which he'll bring? A business associate or a date?"

"No. But he's easily distracted by a beautiful woman. I'm sure you could lure him away."

Evie had returned and stood over Baker's shoulder, looking at the file. "I can do it. He has a thing for me."

"*Absolutely not!*" Baker said, jumping straight out of the chair.

"What's the big deal?" Evie said. "I'll bring him upstairs and then they can do whatever they want with him."

He shook his head. "Not happening."

"He'd be less suspicious of her," I said, looking over at Evie. "Someone new could spook him."

Baker glared at me. "Forget it. She's a bartender, not a cop—or whatever it is you do these days."

"Is she scheduled to work tonight?"

"Did you hear me say *no*? *She's not doing it!*"

Evie placed her hands on her hips, looking like she wanted to flip Baker the bird. Instead, she turned back to me. "No, I'm not scheduled to work tonight. But no one would be surprised to see me in the Parlor having a drink off shift."

I handed her my VIP card. "I'm thinking one of Charlie's getups would seal the deal. Steal an outfit from her closet."

Evie held the card like a winning lottery ticket, before sauntering toward the door.

"Does anyone listen to me anymore?" Baker complained.

"Relax. You know damn well that we'll keep her safe."

"I want Garth involved. You either include him—or I swear, Kelsey—I'll burn the club to the ground to prevent this from happening."

I raised an eyebrow. Baker loved this club. He ate here. Slept here. Even had dates meet him here. I had never seen or heard Baker put anything—or anyone—before the club. Evie had her hooks into him. Deep.

"It's not like that. *She's* not like that."

"What's it like then?" I tried to hide my smile. "Are you smitten, Baker? Has Cupid finally tagged you with an arrow?"

He walked behind his desk and sat as he picked up his cellphone. "Drop it, Kelsey."

I looked up at Ryan. He was also trying not to smile as he looked around the room. I looked back at Baker as his brief call with Garth ended. "Who are the business associates that sometimes accompany Mr. Flint? Anyone interesting?"

"Your everyday banker, lawyer, doctor, sort of crowd. No one stands out in my memory except—" he paused as he opened the side drawer on his desk and pulled another file. Flipping through it, he found a picture and slid it across the desk to me. "This guy didn't stay long, but seemed sketchy enough to land on my watchlist."

I looked at the picture, then back at Baker as I slowly stood. Every hair on my body also stood upright. "You're sure? This—" I pointed to the guy in the picture "—was the guy talking with Owen Flint?"

He handed me another photo showing the two of them in The Parlor sharing a table.

"Kelsey? Is that—" Ryan started to ask, looking over my shoulder.

"Yes," I said, cutting him off. I flipped the photo over to read the notes Baker had written on the back. The photo was six months old. "Was there a woman with them?"

Baker raised an eyebrow before sliding another photo, much slower, across the desk to me. "I assumed she was an escort."

"She's a professional, but not an escort," Ryan said, picking up the picture. "How is this even possible?" he asked me.

"I have no idea."

"What am I missing?" Baker asked.

I set the photo down, placing my fingertip on the image of the man sitting next to Owen Flint. "This is Santiago Remirez."

"And this," Ryan said, tossing the picture he was holding onto the desk, "is his diabolical girlfriend, DEA agent Sebrina Tanner."

I cringed at hearing Sebrina's last name. It still made me angry to know Grady had kept his ex-wife a secret.

Baker looked down at the photo. "Is she working undercover?"

"No," I said, shaking my head. "She's dirty. We recently busted her and turned evidence over to the agency. But we never heard what happened to her after we did."

"If you busted her, she'd be in prison, right?"

"Not necessarily," Ryan said, scratching the back of his head. "If they felt the case was too weak to force a plea deal, they'd fire her and allow her to disappear. It doesn't look good to have a media storm following a controversial case involving a dirty agent. The DOJ would keep tabs on her, hoping that after some time passed, they could arrest her as a civilian."

Baker looked back and forth between us. "What are the chances that they released her?"

"Likely," I said as I ran a hand through my hair. "I had enough to get her fired. To prove she had a relationship with the cartel. I didn't have enough to prove she *worked* for the cartel, though."

"What about her trying to kill you?" Ryan asked me.

"She can counter she acted in self-defense. That she feared for her life." I looked at Ryan. "I did kick her ass and threaten to slit her throat."

"That was to keep her away from the kids."

"It doesn't matter. It's still something she can use. So far, Donovan hasn't been able to find out what happened to Sebrina or her cohort Shipwreck. As for Santiago," I looked back at his photo, "he should be in a prison somewhere, but I can follow-up."

Ryan sat in one of the guest chairs. "If Sebrina and Santiago were financing the dentist office, and if they're now out of the business, then who's paying for the reconstruction work?"

"Good question. We'll need to talk to Tech."

The door to the suite opened and Trigger walked out looking like a gangster. His wet hair was combed back straight, and he was wearing one of Baker's designer suits.

I glanced at Baker. His lips were once again pursed.

"Send me a bill for the suit. Trigger handles a lot of undercover work for me. It could prove handy for us if he has an expensive suit in his disguise box."

"It's not the price of the suit that has me pissed," Baker said between clenched teeth. "Evie hates that suit. That's why she picked it. There's plenty of other clothes in my closet."

"You look better in grays and tans," Evie said, walking through the door.

The anger fell from his face as he looked at Evie. I looked over my shoulder and scanned her outfit. She was wearing a deep aqua dress that left little to the imagination. The matching pumps screamed sexual thoughts. Ryan grinned. Trigger drooled. Baker gawked.

"You look great," I told her. "But I won't know what the plan is until I do a little research. If we don't come back tonight, then *do not* engage this guy."

"Can I still keep the dress?" she asked, winking at Baker.

"Absolutely. That color is all wrong for Charlie anyway."

"Then I'm good," she said before departing into Baker's private suite.

Baker's head swiveled, following her backside as she disappeared. "She cannot dress like that! It gives the wrong impression."

I laughed at Baker. "If you don't get your head out of your ass, that beautiful, intelligent woman is going to find someone else."

"She's an employee. I don't have relationships with employees."

"They make legal disclosures that cover inner-office relationships. Look into it. Then take that woman on a proper date."

"If you're done playing matchmaker, we've got work to do," Ryan said, moving toward the private stairway.

Trigger walked over and with perfect poise, held his elbow out for me. "My lady?"

I hooked my arm through his, grabbing the files and pictures with my other hand before letting him escort me into the stairwell.

Chapter Thirty-Three

CHARLIE
Tuesday, High Noon

Walking into the morgue, I spotted Cassie Rickers, Lydia's daughter, weeping in one of the hallway chairs. Beast whined as he followed me over to where she was sitting. As I sat next to her, she looked up.

"Did he do this? Did Danny kill my mother?" she asked.

"No," I told her, resting a hand on her shoulder. "Your husband is an asshole, but he didn't do this."

"Why then? Why would someone want to kill a drunk homeless woman?"

"Cassie, your mother agreed to help me with some information I needed. I'm a homicide detective." I waited until the look of confusion was replaced with understanding.

She wiped the tears from her face. "She was going to snitch on someone?"

"I don't know what she was going to tell me. She was supposed to meet me this morning, but never showed."

"My mother was weak. I loved her, but there was never anything brave about her. So why now? Why would she help the police?"

"For you. She knew you were in danger."

Cassie gasped as she raised a trembling hand to her lips. "She sent you."

"Yes. That was our deal. I save you, and she'd tell me what she knew."

"It's my fault, then. That she's dead. It's my fault."

"No," I said as I lowered my hand to my lap. "And it's not your mother's fault. Or even *my* fault. Only one person is responsible and that's the person who killed her."

She dragged the back of her hand across her cheek, wiping away the tears. "Why does that sound so wrong? Too simple?"

I leaned back in my chair, shaking my head. "I don't know. Guilt. Grief. Maybe regrets. Our negative thinking takes over in situations like this and it's a natural shift to blame ourselves. But the truth is, the evildoers are the ones to blame."

Beast had been sitting next to me, but moved to sit between us, leaning his heavy body against our legs.

Cassie looked down at him as she spoke to me. "If Mom wouldn't have made the deal with you to help me, she'd still be alive."

"You're overthinking it. You never deserved for Danny to beat on you, that was on him. That was his choice. It's the same thing with killers. They're the ones to blame. No one else."

"I hear what you're saying, but—"

I placed my hand on top of hers. "Yesterday, a little boy was killed in a drive-by shooting. Was *his* mother to blame?"

"No! Of course not."

"But she let the boy play in the front yard—"

"It wasn't her fault."

I stood, pulling her gently up by the arm as I did. "I know. Just like Lydia's death is not *your* fault." I released my grip on her as I took a step away. "I'll find whoever did this. I'll make him pay."

Cassie released a slow breath. "I don't know what I'm supposed to do now. I don't know where I'm supposed to be, or..." She looked lost. Frail.

"There's nothing for you to do here. Your mother's body won't be released for at least a few days, if not longer. Go home. Rest. Remember the good days."

"There weren't many good days."

I reached into my back pocket and pulled out a photo, handing it to her. Lydia's belongings had been sent for evidence processing, but I had snuck this photo into my pocket.

Cassie looked at the worn photo of mother and daughter. "Where? How?"

"She kept it all these years. She watched over you. She loved you. Don't forget that." I walked away.

At the end of the hall, I pushed the door open to walk into the reception room. I jumped in surprise, my hand covering my heart as it slammed against my ribs. Tasha was standing on the other side of the door.

"You did good, Kid," Tasha said, pointing toward the hallway. "Now, come with me," she ordered before turning away. "I've got preliminary on your victim. Leave the dog with Huey."

Huey was the fifty-something receptionist who looked like a biker. Tattoos covered half his body and he had three nose piercings. Despite his rough appearance, he was highly skilled, transitioning between grief counselor and office bouncer.

I glanced over at Huey. "You okay if I leave Beast out here with you?"

Huey looked down at Beast. "He looks mean."

"As do you."

A devilish grin appeared. I took the expression as a yes, and hand signaled for Beast to stay. Beast looked around before wandering over to the wall and throwing himself onto the cool tile. I dug a treat from my bag and tossed it to him before walking through the next set of doors and down the hall to Tasha's office.

Tasha was waiting impatiently and shoved a tablet into my hands as soon as I entered.

I looked at the tablet, swiping the screen to flip through the notes and pictures. "You started the autopsy already?"

"Only the external exam. I knew you'd be anxious for answers. I also confirmed the substance inside the syringe was morphine, though I'll have to wait for the official lab report on the victim's blood work before I enter official cause of death."

"The morphine doesn't surprise me. Lydia knew something about Pauly's killer. She was supposed to meet me this morning." I threw myself into the guest chair which was placed along the wall by the door. Tasha had stopped moving the chair back to her desk years ago, adjusting to my need to see through the glass door while we talked.

"But this—" Tasha took the tablet and swiped until she found what she was looking for. She handed the tablet back, pointing toward a photo "—might surprise you."

I studied the photo. At first, I thought it was a picture from Pauly's autopsy. The bruise across the back of the neck was the same. Then I realized that the victim had dirty blond hair. "This is Lydia?"

"Bingo. Identical bruising as Pauly and Roseline on the back of the neck."

"Walk me through this. How does this type of injury happen?"

She waved for me to follow her and led me into the next room. She lifted the bean-bag manikin from its hook. They made computer modules for this type of thing, but bean-bag Bert, as he was named years ago, was a more user-friendly tool.

"The victims were all on their stomachs," Tasha said, throwing Bert to the floor. "Then the killer uses his own body to apply pressure on the neck until the victim passes out."

Tasha partially stood on Bert's neck. She scrunched her nose, as she stepped off, shifted her stance, and placed her other foot on Bert's neck.

I split my focus between her facial expressions and her demonstration. "You think it was a foot?"

Tasha shifted her weight again. "In theory, it could be a foot, but it's hard to imagine applying the right force while maintaining control of the victim. The victim would be struggling. Grabbing at the attacker to throw him off balance."

What she said made sense. The victims weren't likely to stay stationary once they realized they couldn't breathe. "A knee hold?"

Tasha got down on the floor and repositioned her knee directly on Bert's neck. "Maybe... But there wasn't any bruising on the back or shoulders. With only the knee to the neck, the victim could still unbalance the attacker."

She moved to lie on top of Bert, placing her forearm against the back of his neck. She shifted between straddling him mid-back level to lying flat on top of him. She slowly shifted upward again, with her upper body centered over Bert's neck. Her lower body remained over Bert's back and hips, pinning him down.

Nodding to herself, she finally spoke. "If I had to guess, this position seems reasonable. I'd need to run the computer module to be sure, but with the attacker lying on top of the body, the victim's movements would be limited. Also, the pressure is distributed over a large section of the body which accounts for the lack of bruising on the victims' backs and shoulders." She studied her position. "And the killer still has a significant share of his body weight centered behind his forearm to choke the victim."

I circled around Tasha and Bert. "But why? If the attacker is strong enough to take his victims down—*and* weighs enough to keep him there—why doesn't he choke them the old-fashioned way with his hands? Why this way?" I snapped a picture of Tasha and Bert with my phone.

Tasha glanced at my phone, then flipped me the bird as she stood. "Your attacker could lack the hand strength to strangle someone. Nerve damage or even arthritis could make using his forearm preferable." She leaned over and grabbed Bean-Bag Bert by the hand, dragging him back to his hook.

"You said a knee or boot wasn't feasible because of balancing while the victim struggled. Couldn't enough force be applied to the neck with a quick kick or punch to cut off oxygen?"

Tasha shook her head. "If you were to stomp on someone's neck that hard, you'd expect to see damage to the vertebrae. No such damage has appeared on any of the victims' x-rays. No. For whatever reason, the killer doesn't want to break their necks. He prefers to control their airway until they pass out."

I looked down at my phone and studied the picture. "Tasha?"

"Yes, Charlie?" she said, mimicking me.

My stomach did a summersault. "Did you scan the victims' clothes for semen?"

"I assigned lab techs to examine the clothes. They didn't report finding anything other than hair and fibers." She walked over, studying my face the same way I'd studied hers earlier. "Why? None of the victims were sexually assaulted."

"Just because their clothes were still intact, doesn't mean they weren't sexually assaulted. Look at your position on top of Bert," I said, turning my phone toward her to show her the picture. "Now imagine the killer was taller. Bigger. What if he rubs his body against the victims' while they lose consciousness? What if it excites him? That would explain why he chooses not to break their necks."

Tasha was silent a moment as she studied the photo. "You're going to delete that picture, right?"

"Nope. But because it depicts the killer's method of killing, I won't post it on Twitter." I closed the photo gallery app on the phone. "Can you rerun the clothes for trace? It's unlikely that there's anything there, but if the killer ejaculated enough to wet his own clothes, there could be transfer on the victims' clothes."

"I'll have all the clothes rechecked. It's a valid theory. In the meantime, I need a favor."

"I'm not deleting the photo," I said, sliding my phone into my pocket.

"Whatever," she said, waving a hand that she didn't care. "I've been photographed doing worse than molesting Bean-Bag Bert." She moved over to her filing cabinet and pulled a file. "Two years ago, a victim came through this office. I wasn't allowed to work the case because the victim was someone I knew."

I took the folder from her and flipped it open. Victim's Name: *Terri Weston*. Cause of death: *Severed artery on upper right thigh*. Details: *African-American Female, 26 years old, 125 pounds, five-foot three-inches tall. Her body was found in Hibiscus park near the jogging path.*

"Do you have the police file?"

"No. I'm not even supposed to have the autopsy. After Dr. Brighton retired, I used his login to print myself a copy."

"Naughty-naughty," I said, shaking a finger at her. "Who is she to you? How do you know her?"

"She was my college roommate. We went to medical school together, but she had to drop out because her mother fell ill. She switched to a nursing program and later was hired at the county hospital. We lost track of each other for a few years but reconnected when I moved to Miami."

"And it's a cold case? I thought I knew all the unsolved homicides."

"Her file isn't classified as unsolved. They arrested her boyfriend, Terrance Haines. He was sentenced to twenty years in prison."

I studied her face, but she kept her emotions hidden. "He didn't do it, did he?"

"I can't prove he's innocent."

"But you know him. Personally?"

"Yes. I knew him well enough to help him shop for a wedding ring the day before."

I closed the folder and leaned against the wall. "Maybe she said no. Maybe she laughed at him, and he snapped."

Tasha pressed her lips together in annoyance before responding. "That's the theory the DA used as motive, but I swear to you, Kid, she would've said yes. I know it. She loved him. Her face lit up every time he entered the room. He made her laugh, didn't put her down for her odd quirks, and gave her the space to become her own person. She adored him."

I glanced back at the folder in my hand. Whether the case was closed or not, Tasha was my friend. She needed closure. "I'll look into it. I swear. But Tasha," I said, shaking my head. "Why didn't you tell me about this? Why didn't you ask for my help before now?"

"You've had a lot going on the last few years. Between finding your nephew and then your cousin disappearing, I didn't want to bother you with it until I knew for sure the police had the wrong man."

"And now you're sure? That this—" I looked back at the notes to check the name "—Terrance Haines, didn't kill your friend?"

"Positive," she said, taking the file. She pulled photos from the folder, lining them out along the table top. "I think it's the same guy."

She took a step back as I took a step forward. My eyes absorbed the details of each autopsy photo. "*Son of a bitch.*"

"That's what I said!" She turned away from the photos. "When I got my hands on the report, I read the notes, but couldn't look at the pictures. It was too hard. I didn't want to see my friend like that. But this morning I remembered the description of the neck bruise in her autopsy report, and I had to look."

"I'll pull the police case files," I said, tucking the photos back inside the folder.

"I'm sorry to drag you into this. I know cops who stick their noses in other cop's cases aren't treated well. I don't want to cause you problems."

"You think I give a damn?"

She laughed. "No. But you should."

"Probably. But every cop who knows me, knows I'm a pain in the ass." I walked toward the door, tucking the folder under my arm. "I'll let you know what I find. Until then, don't mention this to anyone else. The last thing we need is the killer figuring out you were snooping into this case."

"Can I tell Terrance?"

I pushed the door open but stopped to answer her. "No. Not until we know something."

Her head bowed as her shoulders slumped. I slipped out the door, walking back to reception.

Entering the main room, I paused when I saw Huey sitting next to an elderly gentleman who was weeping. Beast had his head rested on the man's knee. The man absently stroked Beast's head.

Huey walked over to me. "Can I keep your dog for a little longer? The man's wife died in a car crash. They were married fifty-seven years."

"Of course. I'll come back in a few hours. I have some errands to run anyway."

Huey returned to the grieving husband.

I motioned for Beast to stay as I slipped out. It wasn't until I exited the building that I remembered I was supposed to text Ford or Quille for an escort.

I looked around but didn't see anyone. I hurried to Wild Card's rental, hitting the unlock button and climbing inside. Even though I knew the back seat was empty, I checked it again to be sure. Then I climbed over the seat and checked the cargo area. Returning to the driver's seat, I stared at the keys in my hand.

Paranoia was setting in. My brain argued with itself over the potential of a car bomb. After much consideration, I finally decided that Mr. Tricky had tried to kidnap me, not kill me.

I started the car, relaxing when nothing exploded.

Then I belatedly remembered Mr. Tricky also tried to shoot me outside the precinct.

I laughed at myself as I pulled out into traffic.

Chapter Thirty-Four

CHARLIE
Tuesday, 12:35 p.m.

The county hospital was only a few blocks over, and since it was lunchtime, odds were good I'd catch some of the nurses in the breakroom. My odds improved if I fed them, so I stopped and bought five pizzas on the way.

Most of the staff in the emergency room knew me, either from prior investigations I'd worked or from my multiple visits for stitches and x-rays.

Security waved me through the front doors. The charge nurse licked her lips, staring at the pizza boxes as she buzzed me past the waiting area and into the inner sanctum. And Sharon Johnson—an administrator and numbers pusher for the ER—held the breakroom door open as she shook her head at me.

"I don't know how you get away with it." Sharon followed me into the breakroom and helped me open the pizza boxes. "With anyone else, security wouldn't let them through the front door. But the entire staff lights up like a kid on Christmas when they see you coming."

I plated a slice of pizza for myself. "Security lets me in because they know if they didn't, I'd just find another way. The medical staff talks to me because, unlike some of my brothers and sisters in blue, I don't drag out the questions. I know the staff is busy. I'm happy to feed them in exchange for them sharing what little downtime they have between patients."

Sharon swallowed her second bite of pizza before asking, "What information are you digging for today?"

"Today's a doozie," I said, setting my plate aside as I grabbed my notepad. "I have so many questions, I can't keep them straight. But before everyone gets here, I have a question about a nurse who was killed about two years ago while jogging."

Sharon glanced over her shoulder to make sure we were still alone. "That's a tough one for this group. I wouldn't mention it casually over pizza. Terri was well liked and some are still grieving."

"Anyone in particular I should ask to meet with privately?"

"Yeah," she dropped into a chair, "me." She focused on the floor but shook her head. "But I can't talk about it here. Not during a shift."

"Can I ask just one question?" I said, holding up one finger.

Sharon's shoulders dropped, but she didn't say no.

"Do you think her boyfriend killed her?"

Her facial features were set with a determined look. "No. I don't. But I also couldn't stomach following the case, so I don't know what the evidence was against him."

"I get that. I've watched plenty of families make the mistake of hearing the gory details in court."

"I'm off shift at four today. I can meet to talk then."

Debbie, the charge nurse, came barreling through the door. "Kid, you made my day. I'm starving." She piled three slices of pizza onto a plate. "What's with all the makeup though? Do we need to have a counselor talk to you about those bruises you're trying to hide?"

Dr. Adams and nurse Erica entered, zeroing in on the food.

"The shrink at work would love to get me on her couch, but no, I'm good," I said, answering Debbie. "I took a boot to the face while on the job."

"And the bruises around your neck?" Sharon asked.

"That happened a few minutes earlier. Same bad guy."

"The cut on your chin should've been stitched," Dr. Adams said. "You're going to have a scar."

"Scars build character," I said as more staff entered. "I've got some quick-hit questions today, folks. First on the list, I'm looking for information on liquid morphine. Who has access? And where can someone get it?"

"You can get it," Sharon said. "But it's not easy. We already heard about the overdoses."

"Perfect," I said, rubbing my hands together and grinning. "If everyone knows about the ODs, then everyone already has a theory. Hit me with your ideas."

Erica leaned against the far wall next to the door, standing while she ate. "It seems unlikely that someone with legal access to narcotics would steal liquid morphine. If you're dumb enough to raid the medicine cabinet, there are better drugs to choose. I mean, it'll do the job if you're looking to feel no pain. But there's a tricky line between feeling high and falling asleep. It wouldn't be *my* first choice."

Debbie's eyes narrowed at Erica. "Maybe you should share with the group what your first choice *would be*."

Erica grinned at Debbie, but took a bite of her pizza, not answering.

Debbie shook her head. "Erica's right about the dosage being tricky. That's why we usually use the drip machines to pace the distribution. It's not as common to inject a patient directly unless they've been in a major trauma."

"Can you break into a drip machine? I've never paid much attention to them. I'm usually the one connected to the other end."

Sharon snorted as she grabbed another slice of pizza. "A couple years back, a teenager snuck into the hospital and stole one. He was still wheeling the machine across the asphalt when security caught up with him. Far as I know, he never got it open."

"Do ambulances stock morphine?"

"Sure. But the good stuff is locked in a cabinet," Erica said, winking at Debbie.

"And the paramedics have to report any missing narcotics."

I bit my lower lip, thinking. "What about hospice?"

Everyone looked at Dr. Adams. He shrugged. "It's administered by either the patient's doctor or a hospice doctor," he explained. "Same rules apply as in a hospital, but if the patient can still eat and drink, they'll be prescribed pills, not the liquid form."

"Any other loopholes?"

"There's a black market for everything," Erica said.

Sharon bobbed her head in agreement. "But with prescription drugs, we see more issues with pill popping. Usually by the time they start looking for a needle, they're into heroin, which is made from morphine." Dr. Adams tossed his crust into the trash before turning back to face me. "Are you sure the blood tests pointed to liquid morphine? Heroin is more common and hard to confirm in test results."

I leaned back in my chair. "Both Tasha and Greg confirmed the results. They explained their findings too, in long-winded detail. But I honestly didn't retain all the medical mumbo jumbo."

"Damn," Sharon said, standing and tossing an empty pizza box into the trash can. "Don't know what to tell you, honey. But if an addict wants something bad enough, they'll find a way."

Staff in a busy county hospital tend to eat on the go, and they were almost done eating. If I didn't move the conversation along, I'd risk losing them. I pulled out a photo from Lydia's autopsy and handed it off to be passed around. "Anyone see bruising like this on the back of a patient's neck?"

Everyone took their turn studying the bruise before shaking their head. More staff shuffled into the room as the first group shuffled out. Thirty minutes later, I'd talked to everyone on shift, including the security guards and the janitor. I was cleaning up the breakroom when Erica popped her head back through the door.

"Still hungry? There's two slices left," I said as I washed the table.

"Goodness no," she said, laughing. "I ate three, and that was after eating a sandwich an hour earlier."

"My kind of girl." I rinsed the dishrag in the sink. "What can I do for you?"

"That bruise in the autopsy photo," she said, taking another step into the room. "I think I *have* seen it before."

"Any details you can share?" I asked. Privacy laws would prevent her from giving me the full details, but the nurses were good at navigating the line and asking me to get a warrant if the line was too far into federal lawbreaking territory.

"I don't remember all the details. The patient was a heart attack victim. After he was pronounced, I was prepping the body when we moved him and I saw the mark. It wasn't a bruise, though. It looked more like a red welt."

"Like a wound that hadn't bruised yet?"

Erica shrugged. "Maybe. I just remember it was about three inches tall but ran straight across the back of his neck. It was an unusual marking. I noted it in the file."

"Do you remember how long ago this was?"

She placed her hands on her hips and looked up at the ceiling, thinking. "Maybe a year ago? Gosh—I'm not sure. It's been a while. If it helps, he died before he got here. Paramedics tried to revive him, but he'd been down a while before he was wheeled in here."

"Okay. I can work with that."

Erica smiled. "Really?"

"I'll task a grunt with searching death certificate records for heart attack victims."

"Now there's a horrible job. There'll be thousands of death certificates. Talk about a needle in a haystack."

"But if we find that one needle, it could hold all the answers." Throwing my handbag over my shoulder, I tucked Lydia's autopsy file under my arm. "And now, I'm off to see a man about sexual asphyxiation."

"Ewe."

"Agreed. Stay safe. And thanks for the info," I said before leaving.

~*~*~

On the way to the Outer Layer, I called Quille and asked for a researcher. He assigned me the young and incompetent Detective Gibson. I knew Quille had assigned me Gibson as punishment for Danny Rickers' missing fingertips which I.A. was now investigating. And the reason I knew was because Quille spent ten minutes screeching at me, telling me that was why I was getting stuck with Gibson. As much as I wanted to argue, I decided it was best to roll with it.

Next, I called Gibson, tasking him with three jobs: Find the heart attack victim, pull the files on Terri Weston's murder, and pull any crime files in the last five years that involved morphine. The last one was triggered by the story of the kid trying to steal a morphine drip machine from the hospital. I wondered if the kid was just stupid or if he had other reasons for his failed adventure. It seemed an odd enough story that broadening the search seemed reasonable.

Then I told Gibson to bring everything he could gather on all three requests to Hibiscus park. He started choking when I told him he had forty-five minutes to meet me there. I disconnected before he could whine any complaints.

Entering the Outer Layer via the private entrance, I took the elevator to the third floor. Stepping into The Parlor, I spotted Evie sitting at the bar talking to Eddy, another bartender.

I looked next to the elevator, then upward. "Garth," I said, nodding to him.

"Good afternoon, Ms. Harrison," Garth replied with a slight grin. "Will you need any transportation changes today?"

"Do I still have any vehicles here?"

"Only the truck."

I imagined the beat-up, rusty, short-bed truck parked outside the mansion, and my mood lightened. "I'll have someone take the truck on the next visit. It might come in handy."

Garth inclined his head but didn't say anything.

"If I watch Evie, do you mind running upstairs and asking Baker to compile a list of sexual chokers?"

Garth flashed his teeth in his version of a smile. "You don't want him to explain the intricate details of sexual asphyxiation?"

I scrunched my nose in disgust, but my nose was still bruised and I quickly regretted it as my eyes watered. "I was hoping to skip the educational speech. I just need names and phone numbers."

"I understand. He can sometimes get carried away explaining the details. Stay with Evie until I return so Baker doesn't have a meltdown."

Garth left in the elevator as I walked across the room and sat next to Evie.

"Anything new?" she asked as Eddy set a mojito on a coaster in front of me.

"I need more details. That's why I'm here. Anything you can share about your ex? Any scars, tattoos, names, dates, places?"

"No scars or tattoos. He was too secretive to mention any names, and he liked to stay inside."

"Tell me about that. Where did you guys live? Your place? His place?"

"He owned a condo near downtown. It was swanky. I kept my apartment, but I practically lived at his place."

I handed her a piece of paper and asked her to write down the address. "I have a photo, but it's black and white and he's wearing sunglasses. Is this him? Xander?"

"Yeah." She took the phone, studying it. "Did you get this from my old job?"

"Spence did. We can't make out his features, though. Does he have any ethnic traits?"

"He does have light brown skin, but I couldn't tell you anything about his family's origin. He doesn't speak with an accent."

"Does he speak any foreign languages?"

Evie took a long moment to think. When she remembered something, her face lit up and she started bouncing in her chair. "Yes! He yelled at a parking valet once in Spanish!"

I didn't tell her that I could also swear at someone in Spanish. "How often did he come to Georgia? Was there a pattern to his visits?"

"Once or twice a month, but I never knew when. And he'd only stay for a few days, then take off again. I seldom heard from him when he was away, but if I wasn't at either work or the condo when he came to town, he'd get mad."

"Mad, like how?" I asked, raising an eyebrow.

"Not violent. Xander was more strategic than that. He'd somehow make me feel bad for disappointing him."

"That's helpful," I said, leaning back in my chair.

"How does that help?"

"When I find him, knowing he's controlling, manipulative even, will help me figure out how to handle him."

Garth returned and handed me a folded piece of paper. We exchanged smiles and I slid the paper into my handbag without reading. He wordlessly returned to his post next to the elevator as a waiter walked over and set plates in front of Evie and me. Baker must've ordered us lunch. Since I had only consumed two bites of my pizza earlier, throwing the rest away after it had gone cold, I didn't complain.

Evie waited until the waiter left before speaking. "Since we don't know Xander's real name, how are you going to find him?"

"The condo address. It's not easy hiding real estate. I should've asked you for the details long before now, but I've been busy. Sorry."

She unfolded the cloth napkin, placing it gracefully across her lap. "And when you find him? Will he be arrested?"

I glanced at my napkin but decided it wasn't worth it as I picked up half of my sandwich. "For what? Even the recording of him talking about the dentist office doesn't prove he's involved in a crime."

"But he's talking about prostitutes," she said as she used her fork to pick at her vegetables.

"I talked several times today about prostitutes. We are *now* talking about prostitutes. What does that prove?"

I took a huge bite of my sandwich and moaned. Double-decker BLT with cheese on thin-cut toast and dripping with real mayo. *Mmm*. It wasn't on the menu, but the chef enjoyed spoiling me with all my favorites. As I swallowed, I looked back at Evie and saw she was grinning at me.

"I know you're jealous," I mumbled between bites.

Chapter Thirty-Five

CHARLIE
Tuesday, 1:26 p.m.

I devoured my lunch in record time before excusing myself and leaving. After picking Beast up from the morgue, I raced across town to Hibiscus park to meet Gibson. En route to the park, I called Tech and asked if he could spare time to run the condo address. He said he could probably get to it in a couple hours. He sounded frazzled. I called Spence instead. He took the address down and said he'd make it a priority. With any luck, we'd have Xander's real name soon.

Forced to park near a hotdog vendor, I held my breath after getting a whiff of sauerkraut. I hurried to let Beast out of the back before we jogged into the park, me trying to distance myself from the vendor. The scent of sauerkraut on a steamy ninety-degree day was not something that appealed to me.

Once out of whiffing distance, I slowed and Beast trotted beside me. My knee was protesting the brief stint of exercise, warning me not to push my luck. We followed the jogging trail until I spotted Gibson. Stacked next to him were three archive boxes with a laptop sitting on the top box.

"I'm supposed to report back if your bodyguards aren't with you," Gibson said, looking behind me.

"Beast is with me," I said, pointing to the dog. "He's my security detail."

"I'm not sure that's what Sergeant Quille meant."

"Let me explain how this works. If you tattle on me, then I tattle on you. Which one of us do you think will get fired first? The rookie detective already on the shit list? Or the detective who's always on the shit list but closed the highest number of homicide cases for three years running?"

"Well, when you consider all the data," Gibson said, looking down at Beast. "He does look like a trained bodyguard."

"That's what I thought. Now, what's all this?" I asked, waving a hand at the boxes.

"They're not all full, but I wanted to keep the information separate," he said, pointing from top to bottom as he explained each box. "The top box has information on any crime that contained the word morphine. Natalie in the research unit ran that request. I can't take the credit, and I didn't have time to read anything."

"So far I approve. Doling out tasks to get me the information within a limited time window and giving credit to others when deserved... Very good, Gibson. Maybe you're not a jackass after all."

"Uh, thanks?" He loosened his tie as he continued, "I worked on the second box, pulling the files on the murder case. The boyfriend is currently serving twenty years. The theory presented in court was that he proposed to her, she said no, and then he attacked her in the park, stabbing her in the leg."

"Any explanation for the bruise on the back of her neck?"

"You already know the details?"

"Only the highlights and the autopsy report."

"I saw the comment on the bruise and figured that was your angle," he said nodding. "Told the other detective as much. He said—"

"Wait—" I said, holding up a hand to stop him. "What? You talked to the detectives assigned to the case?"

"Don't worry. I gave you the credit. Said you were following a lead," he said, proud of himself.

Newbies. They frustrated the crap out of me. "Who exactly did you speak with?"

"Just Detective Chambers. His partner transferred to another unit."

I heard footsteps approaching and pivoted, pulling my weapon as I blocked Gibson with my body. A man in a worn suit, bags under his eyes, and a lopsided grin, raised his hands as he continued forward.

"That's him," Gibson said.

My irritation was escalating at a very fast pace. "That's who, Gibson?"

"Detective Chambers. Why are you aiming a gun at him?"

"A sniper tried to kill her yesterday, Gibson," Detective Chambers said, slowly pulling his suit jacket back to show me his badge. "Next time, warn her when you invite someone else to your meeting in a desolate park."

"I was getting to that part."

"Talk faster next time," I said as I holstered my weapon. I looked over at Chambers. "Wanna take him off our hands? I'm sure my boss wouldn't miss him if he were transferred."

"No thanks. We've got one of our own already. But Gibson's got potential. He somehow convinced me to drop what I was working on, help him gather copies of everything I had on the case, and meet you here."

"And how did a newbie manage all that?"

"It helped that this case never settled right with me. I walked into the middle of it when I came back from vacation. My partner had already worked the scene, questioned the boyfriend, and was talking to the DA's office. I only met the boyfriend once, but he seemed solid. I don't know. Takes all kinds I guess."

"What's the story on your partner?"

"Took a bullet to the leg six months ago. He's pushing paper until he hits the early retirement target. Still works in our unit, just works research."

"Good detective?"

"Solid, honest guy. I consider him a friend. We were partnered together for eight years."

"But?"

He glanced at Gibson. I glanced at Gibson. Gibson's head swiveled back and forth. He was eagerly observing every word.

"Take a walk, Gibson," I said.

"Now?"

"Yes, and take Beast with you," I said, digging out a plastic bag and handing it to him. "He hasn't had a bathroom break in a while."

Gibson took the bag and started down the path to the main grass area. I looked at Beast, then pointed at Gibson. "Go with the newbie." Beast trotted off in that direction.

I looked back at Chambers and waited.

"Off the record?" he asked.

I tipped my head in a slight nod.

"Pete Watkins is a good cop. I just want to make that clear first. But as a detective, he cut corners, moved too fast. He missed a lot of details."

"Better follower, than leader."

"Exactly. He'd work a case beside me with the energy of an English terrier, but he always needed someone pointing him in the right direction."

While thinking, I glanced down the path and saw Beast hunched over, already doing his business. Gibson's face was scrunched in disgust. I felt just as squeamish at the thought of picking up dog poo with one of those plastic bags, so I turned my attention back to Chambers. What he was saying made sense. Gibson had also tried closing a double homicide case using a rushed theory. That didn't mean he was a bad person. It just meant he wasn't ready to run a case solo. "Okay, if Watkins had been overenthusiastic when he arrested the boyfriend, why didn't the DA toss the case back to PD?"

"The murder hit the media. The DA's office was in a hurry to pin a face to the crime. It was an election year."

"Isn't it always an election year?" I looked skyward, trying to let my emotions settle. Most cops had felt the pressure to close a case too early because of the media. "You weren't on the case directly then, but you went through the files?"

"I reviewed a very thin file, but yes, when I returned from my trip I went through the report."

Gibson and Beast returned, Gibson carrying the plastic bag out in front of him.

"It's not evidence, Gibson. You don't have to keep it," I said, pointing to the trash bin.

"Right," he said, jogging over to throw the bag away. "Did I miss anything?"

"No," I said before turning back to Chambers.

Chambers walked to the edge of the path, near the park bench. "She was found over here," he said as he pointed to a section of grass about ten feet away. "There were signs of a struggle. She had bruising on her hands and neck, but the deep gash on her leg is what killed her."

"He cut an artery. The injury itself is weird, though." I opened the file I'd brought with me and flipped to the autopsy photos. "See here," I said, showing him the photo with the notations. "The wound angle indicates she was facing away from her attacker and was somehow stabbed upward into her thigh?"

"I never noticed that," he said, taking the file and reading the details. "How does that even work?"

"We need bean-bag Bert," I mumbled.

"I love that guy," Chambers said, chuckling. "Tasha's not too bad either."

"Gibson, I need you to play the role of Terri Weston."

"You want me to walk down the path, then jog toward you?" Gibson asked.

"No, just come over here," I said, having him follow me into the grass. "Now turn your back to me."

I held an invisible knife in my hands, but as I tested out several fake stabbings, they didn't add up to the injury in the victim.

"Gibson," Chambers said. "Lie on your stomach with your arms and legs slightly separated as if you were knocked down, and you're trying to climb up that incline."

Gibson flattened himself on the grass and in slow motion, inched his way up the small hill.

"Terri was small," I said, starting to understand. "Her attacker was likely a man. They fought while still on the path." I walked over to the path. "He grabs her, trying to pull her toward the brush."

"But she had taken self-defense classes," Chambers said, walking over to stand beside me. "She knew the rules. Strike—then run. If her attacker had managed to move between her and the running path, when she ran, she would've moved toward the trees. Away from him."

I remembered my fight in the truck stop. "Say that's true. That she struck him, then started to run toward the trees. If he grabbed hold of her while she was in forward motion, she could've fallen, taking him with her. But the knife is still in his hand."

I pointed for Gibson to move back to the original landing spot. When he was in place, I fell forward, low on his body, with the invisible knife driving upward into the back of his thigh.

"Now according to the autopsy," Chambers moved to stand next to us, "when the knife was removed it was dragged with the handle upward."

I forced the invisible handle toward Gibson's head as I scrambled on top of him and shifted so my forearm was braced against the back of his neck."

"Okay, that's not comfortable," Gibson mumbled from beneath me.

"Shit, sorry!" I shifted my feet out to both sides of him, stood and stepped over him, into the grass. When Gibson rolled over, I offered him a hand, pulling him up. "Thanks for playing."

"I'm not sure I caught everything with my face in the dirt," he said, wiping the dirt off him, "but happy to help."

"What was that last part?" Chambers asked, facing me with a confused expression. "How did you know that's what the killer did?"

"That's the piece that tied into my cases." I pulled my phone and showed him the picture of bean-bag Bert and Tasha. "Our attacker chokes his victims using his forearm against the back of their necks, applying enough pressure until they pass out."

Chambers flipped through the autopsy report until he found the photo of the victim's back. "Why not just choke her the *normal* way?"

"Our current theory is that he's lacking the hand strength." I walked over to the boxes, setting the top one with the laptop aside, before opening the second box. I dug around until I found the crime scene photos.

"Can I help find something?" Gibson asked.

"I'm looking for the first-on-scene case notes from when the body was found."

"The file you want is toward the back," he said, leaning over to dig through the box. "Here."

He offered me the file but I didn't take it. "Read me the basics."

"Terrance Haines reported his girlfriend didn't come home the night before. He called the police but was told there was nothing they could do. He decided to jog the trail himself and found her body."

"Slow it down. When? What time? Give me the breakdown."

Gibson flipped a sheet over and reread the brief. "The first time Terrance came to the park was around eleven. He claims he yelled a few times, then went home. He called each of her friends, which they later confirmed, before he called the police. Then around midnight, he returns to the park and walks the entire jogging route, but didn't find her. He goes home again. By six a.m. he returns for the third time, but this time brings two of his friends. They found her body at 6:25 a.m. and called it in."

Chambers scratched his chin while he spoke. "Watkin's theory was the boyfriend was both building his alibi and building an explanation for his presence in the park if an eyewitness reported seeing him in the area."

"Which would be smart," I said, finding myself liking the theory, "if Terrance really was the killer. But the events and timeline also support a worried fiancé trying to find his missing girlfriend." I looked back toward the park entrance. "Did she drive here?"

"No. They lived two blocks away," Gibson said. "She liked to run every night after her shift at the hospital. Usually around ten. Terrance was finishing some big presentation for work and didn't notice she hadn't returned until just before eleven."

"What month was this?"

"March."

I looked skyward. "In March, the sun goes near dinnertime. By ten o'clock, the park would be pitch black except the posted lights." I turned to Gibson. "I need another favor."

"Anything."

"I need you to jog the path and figure out why the killer picked this particular spot."

"How will I know? What am I looking for?" Gibson asked as he took off his suit jacket and then removed his tie.

Chambers took off his suit jacket too, piling it on top of Gibson's. "I'll go with him. Two eyes are better than one."

"Appreciate it. I'd go myself but I injured my knee this week." I pulled the first-on-scene photos from the file and showed Chambers. "There's a light post next to every bench. I'm guessing the killer shimmied up the pole and unscrewed the bulb. He planned this location."

"Most criminals break the glass. Why risk getting caught unscrewing the bulb?"

"I don't know. But there's no evidence involving broken glass at the scene and if Terrance really did jog the path trying to find her while it was still dark out, that means the light was out."

"Let's go, Gibson," Chambers said as he started jogging.

After the boys disappeared around the corner, I called Quille.

"You behaving?" he asked.

"Always. You know me, just an innocent little bird."

Quille snorted.

"I need a favor."

"I guessed that the second my phone rang. What now?"

"There's a Detective Chambers in the Belle Aire district who's proven helpful in our double homicide. The way things are shaking out, we might be looking at four bodies."

The Belle Aire district was slang for the rich and entitled neighborhoods in the finer part of Miami. They had their own precinct, with their own detectives who spent a considerable amount of time and energy kissing asses just to survive. Their world tended to have fewer cases involving drug dealers, prostitutes, and liquor store robberies.

"Son of a—" There was a pause in conversation as Quille moved the phone away, but I could still hear him mumbling curse words. When he'd recovered, he asked, "Four bodies? How certain are you?"

"Keep your shit together. I'm working as fast as I can to get this contained, but Chambers is already up to speed on part of the case. I could use his help. Can you reach out and see if we can steal him for a couple days?"

"I'll make it happen. Are you staying safe?"

I looked around, realizing that I was alone on a jogging path bordered by shrubbery so tall and thick that I couldn't see anything except for the grassy knoll at the end of the path. "Yup. Following all the standard precautions and then some."

"I'm going to pretend to believe you." I heard the familiar squeak of his office chair, then the shuffling of paper. "Greg sent a forensic report over to the office. I peeked. Looks like your shirt from the truck stop yielded fifteen different hair samples, including dog hair. DNA is out because none of the hairs except the dog's had root follicles, but he's running chemical trace and other nonsense. He's asking though if you can eliminate some of them by detailing your whereabouts earlier in the day."

"Fifteen seems like a lot."

"I agree. Also says most of the hairs appeared severed evenly at one end. What were you doing on Sunday? Rolling around on the floor in a brothel?"

"Oh, crap. I went to Benny's! I sat in one of the customer chairs."

"Benny's? Please tell me you are *not* referring to *the* Benny—as in Benny The Barber."

"I needed information."

"You just walked right inside and sat down? No swat team or bodyguards? *Are you insane?*"

"It was safe enough. Mickey was there getting a shave."

"Mickey who?"

I laughed as I answered. "Mickey McNabe." I mentally counted down from five, waiting for Quille's temper to explode. When I got to zero and didn't hear anything, I looked at my phone. Quille had disconnected the call.

I slid the phone into my back pocket, tossed the folders back inside their appropriate boxes and carried the top box with the laptop back toward the parking lot. If the boys were willing to jog the mile route looking for evidence, the least I could do was have everything packed and ready to leave when they were done.

On my third walk back to grab the last box, two things happened at the same time. One, I noticed that the lid on the last box was partially off, though I was certain it had been closed. Two, Beast, with a menacing growl, launched into the brush. I could hear his barking moving in the opposite direction at a fast pace.

Gibson and Chambers came running around the corner, Gibson with his gun drawn.

When they looked at me, I held up my hands in an *I-don't-know* gesture before pointing toward the woods.

"I'll go," Chambers said. "Gibson, escort Detective Harrison back to her car."

Chambers disappeared into the greenery.

Gibson holstered his gun and went to lift the box, but I stopped him. "Someone was looking through it. Maybe we'll get lucky and get prints."

He pulled on gloves, then lifted the box from the bottom. I pulled my gun, called in for officer assistance, and hurried with Gibson back to Wild Card's rental. By the time the box was secured in the back of the SUV, two squad cars had arrived and Gibson assigned an officer to wait with me as the rest of them ran toward the back of the park and into the trees.

The officer assigned to watch me looked back at me with a raised eyebrow.

"I know what you're thinking. Why am I babysitting this chick?"

"Just doing my job, ma'am."

I reached into my handbag and pulled my badge.

He laughed. "Okay, now I'm confused."

"You hear about the shooting at the central precinct yesterday?"

"Yeah."

"I'm the target."

He looked at me for a long second before pulling his keys and pressing the button on his keypad to open the trunk of his cruiser. He handed me a bulletproof vest before slipping a second one over his own head. Next, he holstered his handgun and pulled a shotgun from the trunk. He looked over at the hot dog vendor. "Unless you got a death wish, I'd suggest you get the hell out of here."

The vendor rushed to cover everything and release the brake, hurrying along with his cart down the sidewalk in the opposite direction.

"We both know the perp is likely long gone by now. Admit it. It was the smell of sauerkraut, wasn't it?"

When he smiled, a deep dimple formed on his left cheek. "How can people eat that shit in this heat?"

Chapter Thirty-Six

KELSEY
Tuesday, 1:45 p.m.

Upon entering the mansion, my shoulders tensed as I heard Grady and Wild Card yelling. I walked through the foyer, down the side hall, and into the open-layout kitchen where they were faced off, ready to come to blows. The kids were only a few feet away.

"Have you both lost your minds?" I asked while pushing them out of my way to reach the kids and pass them off to Anne and Whiskey.

Bones, who had followed me to the chaos, walked over to Grady and Wild Card. "What the *H-E-double-hockey-sticks* is going on in here?"

"Really, dude?" Tyler asked Bones from the veranda entryway.

"Shut the—" he looked at the kids.

"Front door?" Sara asked.

"Not helping, Sara," Whiskey told her.

I looked at Grady, then Wild Card. "What are you two fighting about now?"

They both looked away. It was against their code to rat on each other.

"Anne? What was the fight about?"

"I don't know. Whiskey and I were out hanging towels when we heard the yelling start. When we got here, Wild Card was telling Grady he had no business ordering Nicholas to do anything."

Aunt Suzanne stood in the kitchen with big eyes and a stunned expression. I raised an eyebrow at her and asked, "What's going on?"

She looked at me but pointed at Grady and Wild Card. "Were they really going to start *hitting* each other over a *sandwich*?"

"What sandwich?" I asked.

"Nicholas' sandwich," she said, waving a hand to the plate on the counter. "He asked if he could have something else to eat."

"Ah," I said, sliding the paper plate across the counter toward me and flipping the top layer of bread off. "Fresh tuna."

"I forgot," Aunt Suzanne said, shrugging her shoulders. "My mistake."

Circling the island counter to the other side, I uncovered the platters and bowls of food. "Nick, do you want turkey, ham, or peanut butter and jelly?"

"Nothing," Nicholas said, tucking his head into Whiskey's shoulder.

"Hey, buddy," Wild Card said, moving away from Grady and taking Nicholas from Whiskey. "This is *not* your fault. This is my fault. And Grady's fault. We shouldn't have yelled like that in front of you."

Nicholas' lower lip trembled as his eyes filled with unshed tears. "I didn't mean to cause any trouble."

"It wasn't *you* who caused the trouble," Aunt Suzanne said. "I did. I'm the one who forgot you only like tuna sandwiches if it's that canned stuff. I should've remembered."

Jackson, Reggie, Bridget, and Wayne entered the kitchen, dumping their stuff on various counters. Jackson handed Ryan two large bakery boxes.

"She didn't," Ryan said, sighing.

"Oh, yes, she did." Jackson took another three steps to reach me, leaning down to kiss my cheek, before walking over to the table. As he sat, he glanced around the room. "Why's everyone hanging out in the kitchen? It's gorgeous outside."

"Oh, just witnessing yet another round of Nicholas being spoiled," Grady growled.

I swear my arm was not connected to my brain when the tuna fillet launched across the room and slapped Grady in the face.

Everyone inhaled in unison as the fillet slid down his cheek and fell to the floor.

Grady raised his head slowly to look at me. His eyes were narrowed, his face flushed. He continued glaring as he stretched his t-shirt sleeve up to reach and wipe his face.

From the corner of my eye, I saw Wild Card pass Nicholas back to Whiskey. Everyone else stood or sat frozen, waiting for Grady's reaction.

"Classy, Kelsey," Grady said as he turned from the room. "Real mature."

Everyone released their breath.

I sighed as I picked up the tuna and carried it, along with the rest of the sandwich, over to the trash. Returning to the counter, I made three sandwiches piled with turkey, lettuce, tomato, and way too much mayo. I added a side of barbeque chips.

"You going to leave some food for the rest of us?" Reggie asked, grinning beside me.

"One's for me, one's for Sara, and one's for Nicholas." I slid two of the paper plates across the island and hands grabbed them from the other side. "Carl? Did you like your sandwich?"

"I made my own. I'm all done now. May I go swim?"

"As long as another adult is with you, then yes."

"You want a cupcake first?" Ryan asked, opening a bakery box as he held it tipped up to show us three dozen cupcakes.

Everyone groaned. Ryan's wife's baking was top notch, but we ate ourselves sick over the tournament weekend, and weeks later, we still hadn't recovered.

"Can I have two?" Carl asked, being the exception to every rule.

"Sure," I said before taking a bite of my sandwich.

"Hey, woman," Wild Card said to me, grinning as he leaned over and stole some chips off Nicholas' plate, "make me a sandwich. I'm hungry."

This time, I knew exactly what I was doing when I sent the cupcake sailing across the room. Wild Card saw it coming and put up a hand to block it. The cupcake blew apart when it hit his hand, though, covering him and Nicholas.

Wild Card stuck first one finger, then another, into his mouth and sucked the blue frosting and chocolate cake chunks off. Then he leaned over and whispered something to Nicholas.

Nick's eyes widened and he shook his head no.

Wild Card whispered again, and Nicholas looked up at me with a spark of mischief.

"I wouldn't," I warned before taking another bite of my sandwich.

Nicholas leaned over and whispered to Sara.

"Yeah, yeah, yeah," she whispered back loud enough for me to hear.

I moved my sandwich to the back counter, next to the refrigerator, before turning back toward the island and shifting the bakery box in front of me.

"That's cheating," Wild Card said as he stood, staring at the bakery box.

"When have I ever fought fair?" I asked before launching a cupcake at Nicholas.

I threw three more before I had to start running. On the second pass around the island, I didn't account for the tile floor being slick with frosting and I went down, accidentally dragging Aunt Suzanne down with me.

Wild Card stood over us and dumped the remaining cupcakes on our heads. The kids pounced, trying to rub the cupcakes into our faces and hair. Somehow, Aunt Suzanne managed to squirm her way from the pile of bodies and stand. She grabbed the large plastic serving bowl of macaroni salad, but as she went to fling the contents our way, Wild Card knocked it the other direction. The bowl went flying toward the other side of the room.

The kids and I watched the bowl disappear from our view. We glanced at each other, before scrambling off the floor to see over the island.

Anne, Whiskey, Bones, Jackson, and Bridget sat at the dining room table, covered in slimy noodles.

Ryan stood off to the side, perfectly clean, and grinning at all of us. I grabbed a dill pickle lying on the counter in front of me and threw it at Ryan. His head snapped my direction as he reached out to catch the pickle, but he was splattered with its juices. Ryan's eyes narrowed.

Wild Card slid the second box of cupcakes in front of us, knocking the lid off. "Arm yourselves!"

The other team started sending missiles of food our way as Wild Card counted down from three and we launched our cupcakes.

The rest was a blur of blue frosting, slimy noodles, and barbeque chips being mashed in my already gooey hair. The bit about the chips was courtesy of Anne, but I deserved it after stuffing a cupcake down her swimsuit and then tackling her to the floor.

Five minutes later, we lay in a pile of arms and legs on the floor, no longer throwing food but laughing. We were a mess. The kitchen was a mess.

"If my wife asks," Ryan started to say, "everyone loved the cupcakes."

"Good thing she's a good baker," I said, looking over at Whiskey and pointing. "Since someone crammed one into my mouth."

Whiskey laughed as he used his hand to knock a pile of noodles off the top of his head.

"What in the world got into you?" Anne asked me. She was half lying across my legs, with an arm wrapped around Sara. "I've never seen you like this before."

"I have," Charlie said from the kitchen entrance, looking down at us with a smile on her face. "Been a while, though."

Alex, Maggie, and a woman in a pantsuit stood next to Charlie.

"The food fight at our wedding reception was way better," Wild Card said as he picked something out of my hair and ate it.

Jackson chuckled. "There was a lot more food to throw and a lot more people to throw it."

"This was pretty good, though," Reggie said, wiping frosting from his left eye.

"Uhh," Alex said, looking around and turning to the woman in the suit. "Let's talk about that deposit," he said, leading her from the room.

"Who was that?" I asked Charlie.

Charlie smirked. "The realtor in charge of the house rental. She stopped in to make sure we had everything we needed. I better go help Alex smooth this over."

I couldn't help but bark a laugh, which made everyone else start laughing again.

"Okay," Wild Card said, crawling out of the pile and standing. His feet slid sideways on the greasy floor. He bent his knees to steady himself. "Half of you stay on the floor and gather the big bits to be tossed into the trash. The other half of you start with the counters, walls and appliances."

"What about the ceiling?" I asked.

Everyone looked up to see blue blobs of frosting stuck to the ceiling.

"Shit," Wild Card said, laughing. "At least our wedding reception was outside."

"Pushups!" Nicholas and Sara said in unison.

"I'll do my pushups when the floor is less slimy," Wild Card said as he helped me, then Anne, then Katie up from the floor.

Everyone except the kids got up from the floor, but Sara and Nicholas didn't care. They were both having fun as they used their bodies to slide piles of food together for Anne and Aunt Suzanne to scoop with paper plates into the trash can. We applied similar methods with the table and counters, Wild Card and I using our arms to slide the mess to one end where trash bags were held to snare it.

Then came the scrubbing, which took a lot longer. By the time we got the worst of it cleaned up, we all went outside to hose off. Afterward, the kids ran toward the pool. The rest of us went to our rooms to shower and change. We regrouped in the kitchen where we found Katie, Tech, Charlie, and Maggie finishing the final wipe down.

"Thanks," Wild Card said to them as he pushed me toward the table. "I ordered pizzas. Jackson went to pick them up."

"Whatever happened to my sandwich?" I asked, looking toward the back counter.

Wild Card laughed. "I ate it. I snuck out of the mix and ate it while I watched the food fight."

"You did not," Anne said. "We would've seen you."

Wild Card flashed his devilish grin at her. "Then how do I know that it was *you* who snuck up behind Bones and dumped the entire bowl of baked beans over his head?"

Anne's eyes widened as she stepped closer to Whiskey.

"It was you?" Bones asked as he pointed at Anne.

Anne giggled into Whiskey's chest. "I'm so dead."

Charlie chuckled as she walked over and sat on the other side of the table. "Not today, you're not. We have too much to do. And I need some help."

Chapter Thirty-Seven

CHARLIE
Tuesday, 3:07 p.m.

Tech ordered Kelsey and me to pause our case discussion until everyone regrouped in the tiki lounge. Not only was it a larger space, but it had a bar which most of us appreciated. Maggie made a pitcher of margaritas while Wild Card made mojitos.

"Aren't you supposed to be catching a flight?" I asked Maggie.

"I called in sick. Between the Marshals hassling you, and Kelsey working a human trafficking case, you guys might need me. Kierson said it was fine. He also asked me to tell you hi."

"Uh, yeah, hi."

Maggie laughed. "Breakups are awkward," she said, watching something across the room.

I looked over to see Grady settling on the couch next to Kelsey. She ignored him, taking a drink of her Pepsi.

"You're the profiler," I said to Maggie. "What do you think about that situation?"

"That situation—" she shook her head "—is beyond my abilities."

My phone dinged that I had a text and I read the message. I walked over to Kelsey. "I invited Spence, Sergeant Quille, a rookie detective assigned to me for research, and a seasoned detective from another precinct. I need you to trust my judgment, and not cause a fuss."

"You trust them?"

I couldn't help but roll my eyes. "Do you think I'd invite them here if I didn't?"

She glanced over at the kids, then back at me. "I'll play nice as long as they stay out of the house."

I shook my head as I turned to walk away. "I'll tell them they have to pee in the bushes," I called over my shoulder.

The security team had already ordered them to remove their guns, likely making them lock them in their vehicles. Spence raised an inquisitive eyebrow. Quille scowled. Detective Chambers looked confused. Gibson looked like he was about to pee himself, watching the guards' every movement.

Tyler jogged up beside me, grasping my elbow. He turned to my guests. "I'm Tyler, head of security. Consider this afternoon a one-day pass to enter the crime-fighting version of Disney. If at any point you are asked to leave, you are to do so immediately. Visitors are not allowed to carry weapons past this point. We also ask you do not discuss this location or anyone here, once you leave. Is that clear?"

"Or what?" Quille asked.

The security guards pulled their guns and stepped forward.

"Okay, okay," Quille said, holding his hands out with palms facing us. "Got it. Keep our mouths shut." Quille turned to Gibson. "One slip up from you, and I'll hand you over to these guys."

Gibson swallowed. "Yes, sir."

Quille turned to me and winked.

"One more hiccup," I said, holding up a finger. "Kelsey doesn't want anyone inside the house. It's a security issue. If you need a bathroom, you'll have to pee on a bush or something."

"Smart in theory," Spence said. "But this is a rental. I'm sure there's enough pictures online to get the general layout. Still doesn't hurt to keep people outside, though."

"Actually," Tyler said, turning to lead us around the house. "The real estate company might be having issues with their website right now."

"Just their website?" Spence asked.

Tyler smirked over his shoulder at Spence. "From what I hear, the problem is affecting all the photos and descriptions online linked to this property. Even the real estate office's files were corrupted, so they can't email pictures either. Sounds like a headache to me."

Spence laughed. "That must've taken hours."

"Took ten minutes and a carton of blue moon ice cream," I said. "We have a guy with mega skills, but a short attention span."

"Can I borrow him?"

Tyler glanced back at Spence. "I'd love to say yes, but he's family, so no."

We entered the tiki lounge and introductions were made as necessary. The boys were offered their beverage of choice and everyone finally settled. Gibson had made several trips with his boxes and laptop and sat on the edge of a chair at a nearby table, practically bouncing with excitement.

Chambers sat down on one side of me and Spence on the other. Quille sat next to Uncle Hank.

Chambers leaned closer to whisper, "What exactly did I walk into? You said this was casual drinks to discuss the case. I get here and find my temporary boss here and a battalion of armed men."

"It is casual. And don't worry about the armed men. They're family."

"And my new work assignment?"

"Ah, yeah. That's my fault. I needed your help. You mad?"

"Not even a little. I was bored in Belle Aire. Just wish I'd made a better first impression," Chambers said as he tugged on his shirt to straighten it.

Chambers was a good decade older than me, had a bit more body fat, and wasn't as snappy of a dresser. He also seemed to be slightly intimidated by his new surroundings, which was odd since he'd been working in the Belle Aire district.

Spence, on the other hand, was leaned back on the couch, one arm stretched across the back, and exchanging jokes with Bones who sat in the lounge chair with Bridget sitting on his lap.

Hearing a rattling noise, I turned to watch Katie push a large whiteboard across the patio and into the lounge.

"It's not fancy," Katie said. "But it should do the trick. I'll take notes."

"Which case are we starting with?" Bones asked.

"Start with the biggest," Tech said. "Is that Kelsey's human trafficking case or Charlie's double homicide?"

"My double homicide might now be four bodies deep, with a possible fifth body in one of those boxes," I said, pointing toward the stack of boxes next to Gibson.

"It's also the case most likely linked to Mr. Tricky," Kelsey said. "I agree, it's the priority at the moment, but the dentist case—"

"Don't," Tech said, interrupting her. "One case at a time, please. Or my head is going to pop."

"Fine," Kelsey said, winking at me. "Give us the rundown, Charlie."

"Wait," Katie said, holding the uncapped marker. "Who's Mr. Tricky?"

"The guy hired to kill me. He deserved a name given his expertise." I stood, but my phone beeped. "Tyler," I said after reading the text. "It appears I have another guest. Can you escort Tasha to the inner realm?"

Tyler looked at Kelsey, Kelsey looked at me, I raised an eyebrow, Kelsey sighed and gave Tyler the nod.

"Wild Card, she's going to want a mojito. She'll ask for it to be extra strong but make it weak. She can't hold her liquor."

Wild Card, still behind the bar, grabbed a glass and started mixing the drink.

A minute later Tasha stomped ahead of Tyler down the path, mumbling complaints. When she saw me, she veered through the decorative tall grass to cut the distance. "Those men out front need to learn some manners. They wanted to frisk me! Can you imagine?"

I pressed my lips together, trying to keep a straight face. "Tasha, you've just entered a black ops site. I'm afraid if you try to leave, you'll be shot."

Tasha looked at me, looked around at all the serious faces, noticed the guns that almost everyone was wearing at their sides, then looked back at me. "I need a drink."

Everyone broke out laughing. Wild Card walked over and handed her a cocktail.

"I was just kidding about the black ops thing. Sit. We're just getting started." I turned to the group. "Tasha is a friend of mine and a top-notch doctor with the medical examiner's office. But she also knew one of the victims, so she has a personal stake in this case."

"Which victim?" Kelsey asked.

"I'm getting to that," I said, pointing to Katie to start writing. "My theory starts two years ago, when Terri Weston, Tasha's friend, was jogging at night in an upscale park. She fought her attacker. But while trying to escape, the perp fell on top of her, stabbing her in the back of the thigh, which severed an artery. Then he climbed on top of her and used his body weight to brace his forearm against the back of her neck."

"Was cause of death asphyxiation or blood loss?" Quille asked.

"Blood loss," Tasha answered. "But she might've been unconscious from the choking while she bled out."

"How's this—" Kelsey started to say but stopped when I held up my hand.

"Detective Chambers," I said, gesturing to him on the couch, "came back from vacation to find his partner had completed a less than stellar investigation, but the DA's office was already too far down the path to stop. Chambers' hands were tied, but he's up to speed on the case."

Detective Chambers looked around the room. "I'll do whatever I can to help. My partner had good intentions, but his work was admittedly sloppy."

"Is he still working cases?" Kelsey asked in a steely voice. Moments like this were when Kelsey could be the most intimidating. It didn't matter what side of the law you were on. If Kelsey deemed you unworthy, she'd take you down. And her confidence to do so emitted a powerful current of energy around her.

Chambers shifted with unease at Kelsey's directness. "He's a researcher now."

She tipped her head in a clipped manner before refocusing on me. Chambers released an audible breath.

I gave Kelsey my *what the hell* expression, but she merely shrugged. Knowing that arguing with her was a lost cause, I turned back to Chambers. "Can you go to the prison tomorrow and re-interview Terrance Haines? I want his statement on the record about that post light being out. Start from the beginning and get a full account. There might be additional details we're missing."

"Sure. I'll leave at dawn."

Quille held up a hand. "What about the guy Beast bit? Was he the killer or this Mr. Tricky?"

"Beast bit someone?" Spence asked, looking at where Beast was lounging under the table. "He's never bitten anyone."

"It was a justified biting," Chambers told Spence. "Someone was in the crop of trees and Beast took off after him. Witnesses say the guy ran out on the other side of the park and got as far as opening his car door before Beast latched onto his calf. The perp kicked Beast a few times with his other foot, finally getting him to release. Then drove away."

Quille leaned forward, placing his elbows on his knees. "Beast brought back a piece of the guy's pants. Greg's running it now."

"But who do we think he was? The killer? Or Mr. Tricky?" Tasha asked.

I thought about it a moment before answering. "It had to have been the killer."

"Why?" Kelsey asked, pulling my attention to her. "How do you know it wasn't Mr. Tricky?"

I shrugged at her. "While Mr. Tricky is good at sneaking up on me, he wouldn't have known the park the way this guy did. This guy knew where we'd be and knew to park his car on the other side of the woods. Mr. Tricky wouldn't have known either."

I thought about the other times Mr. Tricky had attacked me. The time in the alley was after I'd chased him. Then at the truck stop where he could've followed me and waited for an opportunity. The shooting though, that also required some scouting and forethought. I'd have to puzzle about that one later.

"Where did you go?" Maggie asked. "Why do you have that confused look on your face."

I looked up to see everyone studying me. I turned to Kelsey, as if just looking at her would help the pieces in my brain fit together.

Kelsey shook her head. "You're looking at me as if I have the answer, but I don't know the question."

"The shooting," I said. "How did he know where to set up? How did he know which floor of the building was vacant? And why did he suddenly change tactics?"

"About that," Kelsey said, glancing over to where Tyler stood. "Tyler, share your theory."

Tyler, as usual, stood on the outskirts of the conversation, listening while he watched our surroundings, including the kids. "This isn't really my thing. You guys investigate; I just run security."

"I trust your opinion," I said, encouraging him to tell us. "And obviously Kelsey feels it's relevant."

Tyler moved a few feet closer. "Well, seems to me, you've got two different people after you. One wants to kidnap you—that's Mr. Tricky. He's the guy from the truck stop and who kicked your ass in the alley. On both occasions, he could've killed you but chose not to. He wants you alive. And the other guy, well, he shot at you. He might also be the guy from the park today. It's obvious he'd rather you quit breathing."

"This new theory is not making me feel any better," Quille grumbled.

"Me either," Uncle Hank agreed.

I chewed on my lower lip, thinking.

"What are you holding back?" Kelsey asked me.

Maggie read my thoughts before I could answer. "You're not sure the photo Ford found was the shooter. You think your kidnapper was watching you when the shooting occurred. The photo was him deciding to get the hell out of there before we shut down traffic."

"Then, how'd the shooter get past us?" Quille asked, looking between Maggie and me.

"I don't know," I answered. "Maybe he blended in with the employees or hid in a bathroom until the coast was clear. But if Tyler's right—" I paced a few feet to the right before turning to the left "—if the shooter and the kidnapper are two different people, then I need to rethink every interaction. And that includes figuring out which one was the hitman Benny knew about."

"It's time I pay Benny a follow-up visit," Kelsey said. "See if he feels like sharing any additional details."

"I'll go with you," Grady said.

"No," Ryan said, turning hard eyes on Grady. "Not with all the drama between the two of you. The last thing we need is a psycho like Benny reading the body language between you two. Jackson and I will escort her."

Grady scowled, but knew Jackson was right.

"You people just can't help yourselves, can you?" Tech asked, leaning back in his chair away from his computer.

"Can we *please* work *one case* at a time? Terri Weston... What do we know about her?"

I tried to hide my grin. "Sorry. Terri was a nurse at the county hospital. I have a meeting with one of her coworkers later today."

"Take bodyguards," Kelsey ordered.

Bones raised a hand. "Wild Card and I will go."

I ignored them and continued, "I'm still trying to figure out if Terri was chosen or if she was a random victim, but I do think the killer planned the location of the attack. The boyfriend said in his statement that when she didn't come home, he went to the park and jogged her route. He didn't see her."

"I'll confirm his statement tomorrow," Chambers said to me before turning toward the room, "but there was a park lamp not more than a half dozen feet from her body. If the light had been working, the fiancé should've seen her. I called the city recreational department. They're pulling together the park's maintenance records."

"Premeditated," Tasha whispered to herself. She was sitting on the ground in front of the couch with the coffee table in front of her. She lifted her glass, gulping down a third of it.

Chambers leaned forward and placed a comforting hand on Tasha's shoulder. "Gibson and I ran the mile route. The location of the attack was near the end of the trail. The victim would've been both the most tired and relaxed after her jog. The location also offered three escape routes, one of which was through the thick brush where he could easily hide in wait."

Kelsey sat forward. "This information paints a tidy picture, but it's not helping us to find the killer."

I refrained from rolling my eyes. "I went to the hospital and asked about both morphine and any patients who might've had similar bruising on their necks. That led me to the documents Gibson has in one of the other boxes. One of the nurses remembers a DOA—"

"That means dead on arrival," Tasha explained to the group before slurping the rest of her drink through her straw.

I smiled at Tasha as I continued, "A nurse remembered a DOA with a similar bruise. He died of a heart attack about a year ago."

Gibson stood. "I've got all the death certificates but haven't started reviewing them yet."

I smirked at Gibson. "I also heard that a few years back, a kid tried to steal a morphine drip machine from the hospital. He made it as far as the parking lot. Probably just a stoned teenager, but..."

Gibson's face lit up before he grabbed the third box over, lifting it on top of the table. "You had me pull any crimes in the last five years mentioning the word morphine because you won't know what's related, until you read the cases."

I tapped my nose. "You're learning. Yes. But it also means we need help sifting through the data."

"You'll have plenty of volunteers," Maggie said. "But let's discuss the more recent murders."

"I will, but I want to circle back to Terri first."

"Something is bothering you," Kelsey said.

"Yes and no. I want to bounce my theory off you and Maggie. I need you both to tell me if I'm on track or not." I started pacing within a six-foot pattern. "My theory is that the killer intended to stab Terri, but when she fought back then tried to run he fell on top of her, accidentally stabbing her. But in the process of trying to control her, he discovered he could choke someone using his forearm."

Kelsey started to say something but I held up my hand again to stop her.

"If I factor in Tasha's theory that our killer might have diminished use of one or both of his hands, what if the killer also realized he enjoyed the rush of lying on top of his victims while he choked them?"

Everyone was quiet for a long moment.

"*Oh, I brought Bert!*" Tasha exclaimed as she slammed her empty glass onto the coffee table, jumped up, and ran through the tall grass toward the front drive.

"She left someone in her car?" Kelsey asked.

Quille, Chambers, and Uncle Hank were laughing too hard to answer.

I ignored Kelsey and continued with my theory. "So maybe the heart attack guy was the killer's second victim. Whether he was hired to kill the man, or he just wanted to test his new method, I don't know. But if I'm right, there may be more victims, before or after the heart attack guy. And Benny told me the murders in my building were hired hits. So maybe, just maybe, this guy turned professional, but somewhere in the process he turned into a thrill killer."

"Why morphine, though?" Chambers asked.

I shrugged. "Not sure. He somehow has access to it."

Tasha came running back, dragging Bert. She tossed him face down on the tiled floor. "Ready?" she asked me.

I held up a finger for her to wait. "Again, just a theory, but imagine Roseline was at home alone, and she opened her door to her attacker. The killer trips or tackles her, but before pouncing, he gives her space enough to attempt crawling away."

"To get her on her stomach," Chambers said.

"And after she's on her stomach—" I pointed to Tasha and watched her jump on top of Bert, crawling up his body to throw her forearm against his neck, "—then he chokes her until she's unconscious."

"But she was stabbed—" Bones started to say.

"*Pauly shows up*," I said, cutting him off and continuing, "before the killer has injected the morphine. Pauly and the killer fight, shifting the altercation into the dining room. The killer gets Pauly in the same position and chokes him unconscious." I looked around the audience. "Now he's got *two* bodies, but only one syringe of morphine."

"He gives it to Pauly," Maggie said, her face brightening with understanding. "Pauly was the bigger physical threat. The killer had to deal with him first."

"Agreed. But after injecting Pauly, he still has to kill Roseline."

"Wait," Tasha said, jumping up, staggering a bit to the side when she did. "I need a knife for this part of the demonstration."

"You're not getting a knife, Tasha," Chambers said, chuckling as he shook his head. "Here's a straw."

"Fine." Tasha held the straw over Bert's body in a tight grip, ready to pounce. "Okay, Kid, I'm ready."

"You know her wounds better than any of us," I told Tasha. "Go ahead with the demonstration."

"There were two short jabs to the back," Tasha said while demonstrating. "One bounced off the shoulder blade. The other hit a rib." She rolled Bert over. "She was then stabbed a half dozen times in the stomach—about three to four inches deep. But the deeper wounds were on her chest, neck, and face. I'm theorizing that's when the killer doubled his hands on the knife and..." She sat next to the body and turned her hands several directions. "No, this isn't right. I need the report."

I walked over to the table and pulled the file. I opened it to the page where she'd diagramed the body's wounds.

"Oh, no. I don't want to demonstrate anymore." She crawled back to the coffee table. Finding her drink empty, she grabbed my full glass which I'd left on the table.

Kelsey stood and walked over, taking the file to study the diagram. After she reviewed it, she handed it to Maggie, before finishing for Tasha. "The killer then straddled the body, and likely stabbed the victim with full force another fourteen times. In some of the wounds, it appeared the handle of the knife was driven into the body."

"Why?" Anne asked, looking horrified.

"It's called overkill," Maggie said. "Normally it's a sign of intense rage, hatred even."

"But in this case," I said, "I don't think the overkill was hate based. Just like the choking, the killer realized he enjoyed sitting on top of his victim while stabbing them. It's possible he was excited sexually."

"That's sick," Tech said.

"Welcome to my world," I told him.

"What about the blood?" Tasha asked. "How did Pauly get Roseline's blood on his hand and clothes if he died first?"

"It was a small amount of blood compared to how she died. What if she had a nose bleed?"

Maggie dropped the autopsy file on the table and looked over at me. "You're thinking from the forced entry?"

"Yes. Roseline opens the door, expecting to see Pauly, but when she sees the killer, she rushes to close it. The killer then either slams his weight into the door, knocking the door into her, or he punches her after he's inside. By the time Pauly arrives, Roseline is unconscious on the floor. The killer had heard Pauly coming and hid. Pauly rushes to Roseline's aid which would explain the blood trace. Then the killer attacks Pauly."

"If the killer really did enjoy the stabbing," Maggie said as she grabbed her glass, "then we'll have more bloody bodies soon."

Kelsey's face scrunched in disgust. "You could be right. But we still need to figure out who hired him to kill Roseline in the first place. And finding out who wanted her dead could lead us to the killer's identity."

"Maggie," I said, looking her way, "can you con the Marshals into giving you the next of kin contacts for Roseline? I'd like to talk to someone close to her. Figure out what she was really like. What made her tick."

"I'll do better than that. I'll make the call and get the CliffsNotes back to you."

For a split second, I considered arguing with her, but then realized, *who better to make the call than a profiler*? Instead, I turned toward Gibson as I remembered the truck stop manager mentioning leaving phone messages for Roseline. "Was Roseline's cellphone at the apartment? I don't remember seeing it on the evidence log."

Gibson's face paled as he visibly gulped. "I never saw it in the apartment."

"Damn it," Quille complained, pulling his phone out. "I'll get someone to pull the phone records and trace the phone."

Gibson shrank back into his chair.

"Gibson?" Chambers said in a calm voice as he leaned forward to look at him. "You're new. You'll make mistakes. The question is, will you remember next time?"

Gibson gestured a thumbs up. "Find the phone. Got it."

"Cellphone, wallet, shoes," I explained to him, counting them out on my fingers. "Every murder scene, you need to identify the location of those three things. And if the victim is found inside their home, also find their laptop."

Gibson picked up a folder, opening it to review the details. "Her wallet was in her purse which was on top of her bedroom dresser. Her laptop was lying on the bed. There was a pair of shoes next to the dresser. The victim was barefoot when we found her."

"If we're done with the new hire training," Kelsey said, sounding snarky. "What about the last victim? The homeless woman? She was also choked, not stabbed, right?"

"She died of an overdose," Tasha said. "Morphine again. I did the autopsy earlier. There were no stab wounds, but I suspect he injected her before she lost consciousness."

"Which makes sense if you think about it," I said. "Lydia was homeless. She slept beside a dumpster in an alley. I'm guessing the smell caused him to rush the process."

"Or, he wasn't excited by the kill," Maggie said. "Lydia was a witness who needed to disappear—*fast*. He didn't have time to plan her death. It was neither a thrill kill, nor for money. He needed to protect himself. She knew something about him."

Spence had been studying the floor, listening quietly, but his head suddenly snapped my direction. "How did you know about Lydia?"

I was impressed that he seemed to be absorbing every detail. "Pauly introduced us. They were friends. Lydia would sometimes talk to Pauly outside the building. I invited her upstairs for dinner once, but she refused. I saw her on the block often, though, collecting cans."

Quille snapped his fingers. "Lydia might've seen someone watching Pauly or watching the building."

"Maybe," I said. "But let's not forget, Pauly got a gun from Benny The Barber. Someone had spooked Pauly. Lydia was his friend, so he likely shared with her whatever had him acting so jumpy."

"In summary," Maggie said, "we have a serial killer who's killed at least four people—probably more—who could be already preparing to start a slasher spree?"

"That depends," I said, walking over to take my drink from Tasha before she passed out.

"On what?" Tyler asked, not bothering to look our way as he scanned the area.

"Whether he's killing people for money or for the thrill of it. If he's killing for money, if that's his ultimate motivation, he'll wait for the next job. If he's killing for the thrill, then..."

"If money's his motivation, we have time," Chambers said.

"Except for Charlie," Quille said. "He seems determined to stop her from investigating."

Tasha cleared her throat. "I had the victims' clothes rechecked. No sperm was found, but there was a small amount of seminal fluid on Roseline's jeans. Not enough for a DNA match, nor to prove your theory in court, but enough to make me worry your theory is accurate. The killer could be experiencing a sexual thrill during the killing process."

My stomach rolled. "Damn. I was hoping I was wrong." I walked over and opened my bag, taking out the list of erotic asphyxiators Garth had acquired from Baker. Opening the folded sheet for the first time, I saw it wasn't a list of names, but a note instead: *Marilyn Monroe will meet you in The Parlor at seven tonight.*

I turned to look at Kelsey. "It appears I'm meeting with an expert in sexual choking at the club tonight."

"What time?" Kelsey asked.

"Seven." I checked my watch. "I also need to leave soon to meet Terri's friend."

"We need to sort the schedule," Kelsey said. "I also planned an outing at the club tonight. Trigger lifted a wallet from a guy who is associated with the dentist office, a Mr. Owen Flint. Flint's a Tuesday night regular at the club and Evie offered to bait him into a private area—" she looked over at the law enforcement side of the room "—for a little *chat*."

Several of the guys chuckled.

Kelsey looked back at me. "I can speak with your choking expert, if you can babysit the kids."

"Doesn't work," Ryan told Kelsey. "If someone associated with the Remirez family shows up with Owen, your cover is blown. They'll know you're in Miami."

"Wait!" I said, rubbing my forehead. "How does the Remirez family tie into this?"

"Who's the Remirez family?" Spence asked, his head swiveling back and forth between Kelsey and me.

"A Mexican cartel," Wild Card answered. "They came after our family a few weeks back. Miguel and Santiago

Remirez run the cartel. Sebrina Tanner, a dirty DEA agent, and an ex-military smuggler who goes by the name of Shipwreck were working for them."

Kelsey stood, finally caving to the urge to pace. "Miguel knows better than to cross me. And Santiago would be behind bars by now. As for Shipwreck, he's just a pawn. That leaves Sebrina. She might be off her leash right now, but I'm not sure she's crazy enough to declare war on our family. I think she'd target me directly instead."

Half the room glanced at me before looking away. I felt the silent pressure to speak up. "I'm not so sure, cuz."

Kelsey went to ask me why, but noticed everyone was looking anywhere except in her direction. "Why does everyone look so nervous?"

Wild Card stood and started walking toward the bar. "Anyone want another drink?"

"You too?" Kelsey asked him. "What's going on?"

Wild Card looked at me with that devilish grin of his.

I flipped him the finger, *the naughty one*, before facing Kelsey. "Before I left Michigan a few weeks ago, I sort-of shared with the security team my doubts that the Remirez family situation was over."

Kelsey crossed her arms over her chest. She wasn't comfortable with someone challenging her, family or not. "Miguel knows I have the power to destroy him. I proved that. And I gave him the evidence to control his brother."

"You did all that, yes." I walked over and guided her to sit on the couch. I sat on the arm of the couch, trying to act more relaxed than I felt. "And whether Santiago was sent to prison or back to Mexico, Miguel likely has him on a tight leash, which made our family safer." I stalled a moment, not sure how she'd react to the next part. "But I think you underestimated Miguel. I think—" I looked over at Grady "—I think you needed to *feel* like it was over. Before it really was."

Bones moved Bridget to the arm of the chair, before shifting forward and bracing his arms on his knees. "Donovan called his connections and can't get any answers. Maggie asked Tebbs to dig around, but he came up empty handed, too. Wild Card scouted a few known hot spots for them, and nothing. Everyone vanished off the grid."

Kelsey pushed past me to stand again. Without uttering a word, she angrily pointed first at Bones, then Wild Card, and then me. "You *all* knew my family was still in danger—*and didn't tell me!*"

I moved in front of Kelsey, blocking her path so she couldn't storm off. "When was the last time you were wrong?"

Kelsey's face was red, her eyes narrow, and I could practically feel the electrical charge of her anger. She stepped first one direction, then turned the other, seeming trapped by her rage.

"*Did you hear me?*" I asked. "When was the last time you were wrong?"

"What are you babbling about?" Kelsey snapped, throwing her arms out.

"Think about it!" I said, grabbing her forearms. "When, Kelsey? When was the last time you underestimated your opponent?"

Kelsey shook her head, thinking. "I don't know. Probably—" Kelsey looked over at Maggie and her face fell from anger to guilt. She was thinking of when Jonathan took Maggie prisoner.

"*Nope*," Maggie said, walking over to her. "You weren't wrong about Jonathan. You were spot on. That failure was *on me*. On *our security team*. That was *not* your mistake!"

"Maggie's right," I said, rubbing a comforting hand on her forearm. "Jonathan wasn't your fault. And you're not thinking back far enough." I stepped closer, just inches of space between us. Lowering my voice, I watched her closely as I explained. "The last time you were wrong, was years back. Back when you trusted Fiona and Trevor with the information on your trafficking case."

Hearing Fiona and Trevor's names, Kelsey instinctively looked toward the pool, searching for Nicholas. Both kids were tossing a beachball in the shallow end. She turned her head back to me. "What's your point, Kid? What are you trying to say?"

"I'm saying that since the day Nicholas was taken, you haven't stopped looking over your shoulder. You spend all day, *every day*, mentally checking and rechecking every single move, every possible outcome, every possible action or reaction." I tried to blink back the tears that threatened. "You've seen *nothing* but darkness and danger everywhere you've gone for years now." I shook my head, trying to find the words to get my point across to her. "You believed Miguel had been handled because subconsciously, you *needed* a damn break from it all. You needed to pretend, for at least a little while, that everyone you loved was safe."

"No," Kelsey said, shaking her head. "I calculated the odds. I—"

"Sis," Jackson said to her in a low voice, stroking her hair back with a gentle hand. "We had both the Remirez brothers and their top guards in our scopes. You knew what those men were capable of, the crimes they'd committed, but you let them walk."

"I—"

"Hey, hey," Wild Card said, walking over and wrapping his arms around her, tugging her back into his chest. "You didn't do anything wrong. Your plan was worth a shot, and we still don't know if Charlie's right."

"But the family—"

"Was protected," Maggie said matter-of-factly.

"Charlie warned everyone," Tyler said from his sentry position. "We've had double and triple security on the family. We've been operating on red alert. Many of the guys at Aces stayed in Michigan to help with security."

"But I've been so..."

"Normal?" I asked, chuckling. "Feeling a little more like your old self? Acting like the woman who worked hard to put away bad guys but didn't let the work assault her brain 24-7?"

She pointed a finger at me, her hurt feelings once again turning to anger. "*What if your plan had failed? What if someone had died!?*"

I answered without hesitation. "Then I'd own that burden. I'd carry the weight of that decision. Not everything has to be on your shoulders, Kelsey."

"Here, here," Hattie said from the edge of the tiki lounge. Pops was standing next to Hattie with two overnight bags slung over his shoulder and towing two more suitcases by their handles.

"I thought you guys were in Texas," I said.

"We were, dear, but now we're not. Apparently, Ryan called Donovan, and Donovan called Bones, and Bones talked to Jackson, then Jackson told our security team in

Texas to get us on a plane. And then of course, our security team delivered us here."

"You had a security team?" Kelsey asked.

Tyler chuckled, glancing away from the kids long enough to look at her. "Did you miss the part where we explained we had the family covered?"

"Watch it, Tyler," Kelsey warned as she walked over to Hattie and Pops. When she hugged Hattie, a flood of tears broke loose. Pops released their luggage and wrapped his long arms around them.

Spence quietly walked over to me. "I have no idea what's going on, but you're going to be late for your meeting. And I still haven't shown you what I found on that address you gave me."

"What address?" Bones asked, having moved to stand closer.

"Condo address for Evie's ex-boyfriend," I answered Bones without looking away from Spence. "Give me the quick version."

"The condo was purchased with cash, but I traced the property taxes back to a holding company. I then followed the shell companies through the mouse trap back to a parent company in Texas. It's a textile manufacturing plant—"

"Owned by Miguel Remirez," Wild Card said, cutting him off.

"Yeah," Spence said, crossing his arms. "How did you know?"

"We researched his companies and played a little sabotage game with Miguel a few weeks back," Bones explained. "We texted all the employees at the textile plan to take the day off work. It got Miguel's attention."

Wild Card rubbed a hand across his forehead. "Kid, what does this mean?"

I looked over at Tech who was sitting on the couch next to us, openly listening to our conversation. "Tech, email Baker a photo of Miguel and Santiago. Have him show Evie their pictures."

"Can't be Santiago," Ryan said from behind me.

I turned and saw Maggie, Ryan, and Tyler had joined our circle. "Why can't it be Santiago?"

"Evie saw a photo of him this afternoon. Santiago and Sebrina were in The Parlor with Owen Flint, the guy associated with the Dentist office."

"When? When was the picture taken?"

"Six months ago."

"Shit."

"Damn. Baker's efficient," Tech said. "Evie confirmed Miguel as her scary ex-boyfriend."

"Isn't he married?" Ryan asked, seeming surprised.

Wild Card snorted. "Not everyone's as committed as you to their marriage vows."

"Not what I meant," Ryan growled at Wild Card. "I meant..." he turned to face me. "Can we use his infidelity against him? Send pictures to his wife? Disrupt his home life?"

"I'm not willing to put Evie close enough to Miguel for a photo-op." I chewed on my lower lip, thinking.

"Stop doing that," Spence said, tugging my lower lip out. "Think out loud."

I sighed, frustrated. I preferred working alone. "This is too much. How is it that we have Evie, Kelsey's dentist case, Miguel, Santiago, and Sebrina, all mixed in together. It seems unlikely they'd all be related."

"Unless they were always related," Maggie said.

I raised an eyebrow at Maggie.

"We always wondered if Sebrina had really been Santiago's prisoner in Mexico. What if her kidnapping was staged because they found out Kelsey was looking into the dentist office? What if Sebrina was tasked with getting close enough to sabotage the investigation?"

"How was she planning on doing that?" Kelsey asked, making me jump.

I looked around and saw our party had expanded to everyone bunched up in one big badass circle.

I looked at Kelsey. "By killing you."

Her eyes expanded in surprise. "Okay. Assuming that was the plan, what about Evie? How'd she find you? How'd she know we were cousins?"

I thought about it for a long moment, and when the answer popped into my head, I laughed. "She just followed her plan."

Feeling claustrophobic, I slipped out of the circle, walking over to sit on the coffee table. Everyone else separated and moved apart. Spence walked over and sat next to me. Tyler walked back to his post.

I looked back at Kelsey. "Evie came to Miami to hunt down Miguel. She wanted to gather evidence on him. She knew about a dental clinic. Knew prostitutes were involved. And she knew he had business here in Miami. She took a job at an exclusive sex club because Miguel liked anything related to money, power, and probably sex. She was hunting him."

"So..." Kelsey said, thinking out my logic. "The fact that you and I," she pointed between us, "own shares of the club is coincidental?"

"Exactly. Either that, or—"

"No," Spence said, shaking his head. "Evie wasn't sent to spy. She's not undercover. She's been teetering between running and hunting this guy for months. I have hundreds of surveillance pictures to prove it. I've talked to her friends, her family, her coworkers. I've traced her life back to the hospital where she was born. She's not a bad guy."

"For what it's worth," I said, looking at Kelsey. "I agree with Spence. But we should be cautious, just in case."

Ryan shrugged. "Evie offered to play bait to snag Owen. Let's see if she goes through with it."

"But what happens if Miguel shows up with Owen?" Kelsey asked.

Ryan glanced over at Bones, and they both smiled. It was the kind of smile that sent chills down your spine.

Wild Card looked at Kelsey. "We'll take enough guys to protect Evie and handle the Remirez brothers if they show."

Kelsey studied each of them, but didn't say anything. She glanced around, watching everyone, pausing to look at Tyler, then the kids.

"What's wrong?" Grady asked, stepping in front of her and cupping her face with his hands.

She took a half step back, but her eyes never left the pool area. "Nicholas."

I watched as Nicholas dove into the deep end. "What about him?"

"If you're right, if Miguel is coming after us..."

"He'll go after the people you love," I finished for her. "Okay. I know there's plenty of security here, but you'll feel better if one of us is near Nicholas."

"No, Charlie," she said, shaking her head. "Not one of us. I can't lose him again. I can't let this city take him from me again. I need to stay here until I know what Miguel is planning."

"It's a virtual world now, Kel. You *can* be in two places at once." I walked over and grabbed my purse and keys. "Tonight, you can monitor things remotely, and I'll handle both meetings at the club."

"You're sure?"

"Positive. You just keep watch over our boy."

"I also have a job after dark." She glanced at Quille and Chambers. "One that involves Trigger and something illegal."

I'd seen a few of Trigger's jobs on video feed, so my smile was genuine when I looked at her again. "Sounds like my favorite kind of job. You can brief me on the details later."

"If another I.A. file lands on my desk..." Quille warned.

"I'm going to be late if I don't leave," I said to Kelsey, ignoring Quille. "Can you handle all this?" I said, waving an arm at everyone and the stack of boxes.

"The rest of us will split into two teams," Kelsey said, nodding. "One team will plan all of tonight's events. The other team will dig through the boxes and find the information you need for your homicide cases."

"Sounds good. See you later."

"Aren't you forgetting something?" Kelsey asked.

I looked back to see her point at Bones, but then hesitate when she looked at Wild Card. She pointed at Spence instead.

Spence and Bones bumped fists before turning to me.

"Great. More babysitters," I muttered as I followed the path to the driveway.

Chapter Thirty-Eight

CHARLIE
Tuesday, 4:25 p.m.

First stop, Miami County Hospital, where I found Sharon in her closet-sized office. Her office door was open, and I spotted Sharon behind her desk, staring at her computer. I rapped two knuckles on the door, startling her.

She glanced at me, then behind me at Bones and Spence. "Come in. Just you. And close the door."

Bones and Spence wandered down the hall in opposite directions as I entered the office and closed the door.

"Did something happen?" I asked her. "You seem upset."

"After you left, I kept thinking about Terri and remembered something." Sharon glanced back at the door as if expecting it to open any moment.

I pulled the single guest chair out, turning it so I was facing the door, before I sat. "What did you remember?"

"Let me first explain why I didn't remember back then." She sat behind her desk and ran a hand through her short choppy hair. "Terri was one of those rare creatures who never dwelled on bad things. She had the ability to shrug things off, erasing them somehow so they didn't affect her. I think that's how she stayed so cheerful all the time. Others gravitated to her, feeding off her positive energy."

"Got it. Terri was all rainbows and sunshine."

"Exactly," Sharon said, nodding. "Except for a brief moment... the day she died."

Now we're getting somewhere, I thought as I leaned toward Sharon.

"And it really was a brief moment, or I would've remembered sooner."

"What did you remember, Sharon?" I asked, pressing her to get to the point.

"We were here. At the hospital. I walked into the breakroom and found her leaning against the wall. She was shaking. She seemed terrified. I asked her what was wrong, and she waved off my concern, saying she had a bad patient. That was all she said. I tried questioning her, but she never explained. She left the breakroom and about an hour later I saw her laughing with another nurse."

"Any idea what patient could've spooked her?"

"No." She glanced back at her computer monitor, frowning. "Terri was my friend. She was a friend to everyone she met. It's the reason I'm about to do something I've never done during my twenty years on this job." She stood, leaned over, and turned her computer monitor toward me. She looked up at me as she picked up a water bottle. "Detective Harrison, I need to walk to the end of the hallway and fill my water bottle. If you leave before I return, good luck with your investigation."

She walked out, closing the door behind her.

After staring at the door for a beat, I turned my attention to the monitor. "Damn, Sharon," I said, grinning as I saw the list of Terri's patients the day of her murder.

The list contained each patient's full name, social security number, address, and phone numbers. I pulled my phone and took a picture. I was tempted to click around on Sharon's computer and see if I could find the reason for their ER visits, but Sharon was already breaking a few very serious federal laws. I didn't want to press my luck. I turned the monitor back toward Sharon's side of the desk before walking out of the office.

I was passing the cafeteria when both Bones and Spence appeared out of nowhere, flanking me.

"Get anything?" Spence asked.

I clicked the gallery icon on my phone before handing my phone to him.

Spence continued walking as he looked at the image, until he suddenly stopped in the middle of the hallway. "Shit! Is she trying to get arrested?"

I glanced around to make sure no one heard him.

"What is it?" Bones asked, moving next to Spence.

I huddled with them, and whispered, "Sharon told me that one of Terri's patients spooked her the day of her death. Whoever that was, is on that list."

"If we find something, it can't be used as evidence," Spence said.

"I know. But right now, it's all we've got. I'll worry about tying the pieces together for a court case after we catch the bastard."

"Works for me," Bones said.

Spence looked up at the fluorescent ceiling lights and sighed. "Fine. I'll start running the names when we get back to the car. Anything specific I should look for?"

"Criminal records, mental instability, anger issues, and, or, a hand injury."

"Basically, everything and anything then?"

"Pretty much."

~*~*~

I drove. Bones rode shotgun. And Spence click-clacked on his laptop in the back seat. Beast was back at the mansion, swimming with Jager and the kids. After chasing our bad guy in the park, he'd earned himself some playtime.

According to the text I'd received from Kelsey, my next appointment was with Mickey McNabe at Benny's barbershop. I'd considered arguing with her, but I was afraid if I fussed too much, she'd meet with him herself. And she wasn't the only one who felt better with one of us staying behind to keep an eye on the kids. Neither of us would survive something happening to Nicholas again.

I pulled into the parking lot of a Winn-Dixie, the supermarket of the south, on the way to Benny's, telling the boys to wait for me. I jogged inside, finding what I was looking for in aisle four: a chopping knife and a cutting board. Five minutes later, I was back on the road, having tossed my purchases to Bones.

Bones looked inside the bag and smirked. Benny was plugged into all-things crime related in the greater Miami area. He'd know the story of my finger chopping event. I was hoping it'd be enough of a warning to loosen his lips.

Mickey was standing outside the barbershop talking on the phone when we arrived. Bones and I exited the car, walking toward him.

Mickey glanced at us as he finished his call. "Find him. Now."

I glanced at the barbershop door and saw a sign taped to the glass: *Gone Fishing*.

Bones looked at me with a raised eyebrow. "I get the impression Benny doesn't want to talk to you again."

"It happens," I said, sighing.

"He'll turn up," Mickey said, tucking his phone inside his jacket pocket.

I pressed my hands and face to the glass to look inside. The lights were off. No one was in the front room. That didn't mean Benny wasn't hiding in the back, though. I could enter through the back door, picking the lock.

The bells on the front door jingled, and I stepped back to look at the door.

Bones held the glass door open, waiting for me. "What? It was unlocked."

"Like I'm dumb enough to believe that," I muttered as I walked through the door.

Mickey's men rushed past us, heading toward the back rooms. I was okay with them going first. I walked over to Benny's preferred customer chair and dug the cutting board and knife from the bag, setting them in the chair on display. Then I pulled a lipstick from my handbag and wrote on the mirror: *Call me.*

Mickey had been watching me before walking over and grabbing a towel from the shelf. He used the bottle of disinfectant to spray both the knife and cutting board before wiping them down.

"Paranoid much?" I asked him.

"About a decade ago, Benny used another man's knife to take out a target. The guy who owned the knife is serving a life sentence."

"Damn." I looked back at the knife. "Should I pull the file on the guy wrongfully incarcerated?"

Mickey's face turned hard again. "The guy raped two teenage girls."

"Well, in that case, I hope he's having a miserable time."

"All clear, Boss," Mickey's guy said as the pair of thugs returned from the back room.

I looked at Mickey and gestured toward the door. He followed me outside. "I have a question for you. Off the record," I said.

"What's the question?"

"Jameson crew in New Jersey gets their product from someone with a large pipeline. I'm trying to identify that pipeline. They might be the ones who hired someone to take out my neighbor."

"Drugs are a dangerous business. People who buy them, sell them, and transport them, all seem to face either death or imprisonment. Why would you think I'd know anything?"

"I have reason to believe their network has already reached Miami. And we both know you keep a tight grip on all things criminal in southern Florida."

He was about to answer when something over my shoulder caught his attention. The next thing I knew, Mickey threw me to the ground, his arms wrapped around me like a straightjacket, as he rolled us toward his town car. *Gunfire. Glass shattering. A car's tires squealing away.*

With my shoulder bag under our bodies and my arms still pinned by Mickey, I couldn't reach to pull my weapon. "Get off me!" I yelled in Mickey's face.

He glanced down at me, his nose less than an inch from mine. "You could at least thank me," he said without moving.

"Thank *you*? Are you kidding me? *I'm a cop*! If you hadn't pinned me to the ground, maybe I could've caught the bad guys!"

A slow grin formed. "You're sexy when you're pissed. And with your face bright red, the bruises aren't as noticeable."

"Get. Off. Me!"

He chuckled as he rolled to the side and sat upright. I grabbed my bag, swinging it in front of me as I shifted into a sitting position.

Bones ran from the building, along with Mickey's other goon. Spence ran over from the direction of our car. The goons pulled Mickey up from the ground. Once standing, Mickey stepped behind me and lifted me up as well.

I knocked his hands away and looked around. The front of the barbershop was shredded. Both our cars had broken windows and bullet holes.

I looked over at Bones and Spence. "Clear out. I'll stay here and deal with the cops."

"You sure?" Bones asked.

"No reason for all of us to get dragged into this mess."

Bones jogged back inside, returning seconds later with the knife and cutting board. Taking both with him, Bones and Spence took off jogging down the sidewalk.

I turned around and watched Mickey slide into the back seat of his town car. The door closed, before pulling away from the curb and speeding down the street.

I stood alone, surrounded by shattered glass and bullets, as the first squad car barreled down the street toward me. "Well, this is going to be fun explaining," I said to myself.

CHAPTER THIRTY-NINE

CHARLIE
Tuesday, 6:05 p.m.

After wasting an hour repeating over and over to internal affairs that I couldn't possibly be the shooter, I was finally cleared to leave. When questioned about the message written in lipstick on the barbershop mirror, I told them I'd found the door unlocked and I couldn't find a piece of paper to write on. They didn't believe me, but since there was no law against leaving someone a message in lipstick, their hands were tied.

As I watched my car, hitched to a tow truck, disappear down the street, Wild Card pulled up to the curb in my Mustang. The top was down.

From behind the wheel, Wild Card wore dark sunglasses but he flashed me his playful smile. "I heard you might need a lift. Hop in. We have a meeting to get to."

I stepped over the door into the bucket seat before dropping my legs out from under me to flop into a sitting position. Opening the glovebox, I pulled out a pair of sunglasses and slid them on as I settled into the soft leather. "Please tell me we're going someplace where they sell booze."

"We are, actually," he said, chuckling, as he pulled away from the curb. "But first, Kelsey wants us to drive past the dentist office so you know what you're walking into tonight."

"Sounds good."

I closed my eyes behind the sunglasses, enjoying the feel of the sun on my face as Wild Card drove. The sound of traffic faded. Details of the Benny, Mickey, and homicide cases faded, too. And the next thing I knew, Wild Card was shaking my arm. I opened my eyes. I'd fallen asleep. I lifted my head from the headrest to look around.

"The dentist office is the tan two-story at the end of the block," Wild Card said, lifting one finger from the steering wheel to point. "I'll drive by as slow as I can, but you'll only get one pass to check it out. I don't dare make another trip around the block. Your car stands out in this neighborhood."

As Wild Card drove toward the building I turned to face him, leaning closer and placing a hand on his shoulder. I twirled his hair with my fingers, pretending to be a couple, as I studied the building. The main entrance was on the side closest to us. A few construction workers were packing up their tools in the parking lot. The building had a flat-top roof and two windows on each floor on the front and side. The sidewalk adjacent to the building was extra wide. As we drove past the building, I could see on the other side an alley barely wide enough for the wheeled dumpster which was likely rolled to the parking lot on trash pickup day. The alley side also had two large windows on each floor.

The next building over seemed abandoned, but the broken windows made it a likely location for the homeless to hunker down after daylight. I lowered my hand and straightened in my seat.

"You good?" Wild Card asked.

"Yup. Any information on the alarm system?"

"Sounded like Trigger took care of the alarm. He rigged one of the window sensors. Second floor on the alley side."

I laughed. "I like Trigger. He's my kind of crazy."

"He's got style," Wild Card said as he pulled onto the expressway. "What I can't figure out," he shouted over the wind noise, "is why Kelsey hired him. He lacks discipline."

"If you knew the old Kelsey, it would make more sense. Between the two of us, she's always been the serious one. But she also has this crazy-fun side. I think Trigger reminds her of herself, back before..."

"Before Nicholas was taken," Wild Card said, finishing my sentence. "Like the food fight earlier. And the pranks she used to play on me when we were married, putting manure in my bed."

"Exactly. She used to spend as much time and energy enjoying life as she spent tracking down bad guys. She had a good balance. She was the same way when we were younger. She'd take me to the playground or to the lake and we'd goof around all afternoon. Then when we returned home, serious Kelsey would reappear."

"So... Hiring Trigger reminds her of how she used to be?"

"Yes, but I think it's more than that. I think she's trying to find that balance in her life again. It's why she can't sit still. I think it's also why she couldn't commit to Grady, even before he turned out to be an ass."

"Grady's good for her. I don't like to admit it, but they love each other," Wild Card said, looking away. "They'll get back together. She just needs time to forgive him."

"I hope not."

Wild Card glanced over at me, frowning. "You don't like Grady?"

"I adore Grady. And I'll always be grateful to him for helping Kelsey face our childhood shit and for helping us find Nicholas."

"But?" he shouted over the wind noise.

"But I miss the old Kelsey," I shouted back as he exited the expressway. I waited until he stopped at the next intersection to continue. "I miss the woman who challenged me to a hot dog eating contest. I miss the woman who rented a bounce house for my twenty-first birthday, which was an absolute hoot until we puked vodka all over the inside. I miss the woman who dressed up for every Halloween even if it meant cutting up boxes and grocery bags to make our own costumes."

Wild Card smiled a sad smile. "She's in there. I've seen her. But she's been through a lot. She might not be able to make it back to the person you remember."

"That's just it. I adore Grady, but if she stays with him she'll never find her way back. He's too serious. Too much like this newer version of herself."

Wild Card turned into the club's parking garage, pulling the ticket from the machine, and waited for the gate to rise. "Why are you telling me all this?"

I was quiet as he drove to the second level and parked. He shut off the car, but we both sat there.

"Don't give up on her, Cooper. She's different when she's around you. Better."

He didn't face me. His fingers flexed on the steering wheel as he stared at the concrete wall. "After Nola kidnapped her... When she came home, back to Texas I mean... I tried to be there for her. Tried to help her. But it was Grady who got through to her," he said, shaking his head. "Not me, but Grady."

"Grady pulled her out of a very dark place, yes. But you're forgetting that when she escaped Nola, the only place she wanted to be was in Texas. She felt safe at your house. She picked being near you. And you were the one she trusted to watch over her son while she healed."

Wild Card shook his head. "That makes me the protective friend."

"Maybe. But it also makes Grady her shrink, not her soulmate."

"Last I knew, shrinks didn't sleep with their patients."

"I've had three shrinks," I said, opening the car door. "I slept with two of them. Very therapeutic."

He got out and walked with me toward the elevator. "And the third?"

"Female. She's cute, but not cute enough to sway me to the other side."

Wild Card chuckled as we stepped into the elevator. "You're one of a kind, Kid."

"Don't I know it."

"You're going to be late," Baker's voice boomed over the elevator's speaker.

I looked up at the security globe. "You need to chill. It's not even half past six yet."

"Marilyn Monroe is one of our biggest clients. You can't meet her dressed like that."

"Marilyn Monroe died several decades ago," Wild Card said to the camera. "I think she'll look worse."

I laughed. "Buzz us up to the fifth floor. I'll shower and change before the meeting."

The button for level five lit, and the elevator started upward.

"And Baker?" I asked, looking up.

"Yes?" his voice replied.

"Should I be concerned that one of our biggest clients is an expert on sexual asphyxiation?"

"No. You should be concerned that the state laws are changing again. We might need to close the fourth and fifth floors."

"Not everything is about money, Baker."

"Remember that when you're reviewing the first quarter financial statements next year."

The elevator's doors opened and we exited into the hallway.

Garth stood waiting for us. "Mr. Baker is in a mood today."

"Baker's always in a mood." I walked down the hall with Garth flanking me and Wild Card following us. "I need a favor. I need a discreet car for a job tonight. Something reliable, but disposable."

"What time?" Garth asked.

"Around midnight." I dug through my bag for my wallet and pulled my keycard.

"I'll have something parked next to your convertible. Keys will be above the visor."

"You're the best, Garth," I said as I swiped my card in the reader and opened my office door.

Wild Card followed me inside and Garth disappeared down the hall.

I turned to my closet. "Now, let's see. What does one wear to a meeting with a sadist?"

"Black," Wild Card answered, pulling out a one-piece black pantsuit. The suit had an open back and a halter front, which exposed the wearer's skin from the neck to the navel.

"Works for me." I took the outfit, stopped at the dresser for clean underwear, and then carried both into the bathroom with me.

~*~*~

Obnoxious banging on the door from the hallway side alerted me I'd run out of time. Dropping my lipstick onto the dressing table, I turned toward the door. Wild Card opened it, letting me pass in front of him. Baker stood in the hall, eyeing me from the top of my head to my toes. His eyes were all business. He must've approved of my appearance because he turned and led us to the elevators.

"That private investigator, Spencer something—" Baker started to say.

"Russell Spencer. He goes by Spence, though," I said.

"I don't care what his name is," Baker snapped, looking at me. "He's in The Parlor. He informed Garth that you told him to meet you here."

"Yes. He's helping me with Evie's case."

"You trust him?"

"Sure."

"That's not a very confident answer. This is Evie's life you're playing with."

"Geesh. Relax, Baker. I trust him. He's one of the good guys."

Baker scowled at me as we stepped into the elevator. When his phone chirped, he read the text and said, "Marilyn just parked in the garage."

"See? I wasn't late after all."

Baker scowled again.

The elevator doors opened. I was pleasantly surprised to find the room occupied with familiar faces. Bridget and Bones were in a corner booth, both dressed for an evening out. Bridget raised her wine glass to me before taking a drink. Dressed in dark suits, Spence and Trigger sat at the bar sipping from crystal glasses. Jackson, Ryan, Maggie, and Evie were also dressed up and dining at a center table. As Baker escorted me past their food-covered table, my stomach rumbled.

Baker stepped aside to let me slide into the booth. "I'll ask chef Edwin to prepare you something to eat." He didn't wait for a reply before recrossing the room.

Joey, a weekday bartender, delivered a glass of wine. I looked around for Wild Card, but didn't see where he'd ventured off to.

"Strange crowd tonight," Joey said, glancing around the room.

"Maybe, but I'm guessing they'll prove to be good tippers," I said, flashing him a smile.

Joey blushed and tried to hide his own smile. "Mr. Baker ordered the wine. But is there anything else you'd like while you wait for your guest?"

"Not right now, Joey. Thank you."

The elevator doors opened and a tall, dark haired beauty emerged. She paused to speak to Baker, then glanced over to me. She waved off whatever Baker said to her and strutted across the room, sliding fluidly into the booth.

"Good evening," I said, dipping my head in a respectful nod. "Should I call you Marilyn?"

She laughed a full-body laugh before placing her elbows on the table. "Heavens, no." She rolled her eyes. "Baker and his privacy rules. The man is insufferable. Call me, Jackie. It's my name." She held out a hand.

I returned the handshake. "Charlie. Thanks for meeting with me."

"No sweat. Do you mind if I order, though? I'm starving. I've been running around all day and haven't had a chance to eat."

She didn't wait for me to answer. She yelled across the room for Joey to grab menus. He was already halfway to the table with her wine and seemed unsure as to which direction to turn. Wild Card, appearing out of nowhere in a white button-down dress shirt and black slacks, took the wine glass from Joey and carried it, along with menus, to our table.

"Ladies," Wild Card said, bowing slightly as he set the items down.

"Can you recommend something to eat?" Jackie asked as she glanced at the menu. "Something I can pronounce?" she asked, frowning at the one-page selection of items.

"Maybe I can help with that," I said, pulling my phone. I called the kitchen and asked to speak to Edwin, the chef.

"Mr. Baker rang me to tell me you were here. I just started to prepare your dinner."

"Can you make two—"

Wild Card cleared his throat.

"Make that three, dinners? I have a guest tonight, and I'll take the third serving home for lunch tomorrow."

"I'll make enough for you to feast for a week. How's that?"

"Splendid. Thanks, Edwin." I disconnected the phone, dropping it into my purse.

"Well? What are we eating?" Jackie asked.

"No idea," I answered truthfully, picking up the menus and handing them to Wild Card. "But I know it will be sensational." I handed my wine glass to Wild Card as well. "Can you bring me something else? *Anything* else?"

"Me too," Jackie said, handing him her wine glass.

With the menus under his arm, Wild Card carried both wine glasses toward the bar. Since I was the one facing the bar, Jackie didn't see Wild Card drink from my glass. Nor did she see his face pucker as a result.

Turning my attention back to Jackie, I realized she was smiling at me in a way that had me moving my hand closer to my purse and the gun I had tucked inside.

"Baker tells me you needed information about choking orgasms. Are you considering trying sexual asphyxiation?"

I threw my head back in surprise. "Wow. You get right to the point, don't you?" I couldn't help but laugh. Luckily, she was grinning ear to ear.

"Given my preferences toward violent playtime, assertiveness works in my favor."

"I can only imagine. And no, I'm not looking to experiment. I'm working a case. I'm a cop, but this conversation will be completely off the record."

"A cop? Hmm."

"Is that a problem?"

"No. I'm just surprised Baker would arrange for me to speak to a cop."

"I have a business relationship with Baker which has nothing to do with my badge."

"I see. And you think I can help you somehow? With a case?"

"Probably not. But there's a killer out there who seems inclined to choke his victims before killing them with a lethal injection. I'm trying to get in the killer's head. Figure him out."

Jackie straightened in her seat but tilted her head to the side. "I'll need more information. Men, women, or both? Does he choke them with one hand or two? Are they dressed or naked? Does he prefer daytime or night? Indoors or outdoors? Does he cover their eyes? Or bind their hands? Hell, are you sure it's a man? More and more women are stepping out as aggressors in bedroom play."

My jaw might've dropped as I listened to her.

Jackie glanced next to us and when I did as well, I was startled to find Wild Card standing beside the table, holding hurricane glasses.

Jackie took the glasses from him, setting one in front of me. "Oh, what do we have here?" She took a slow sip of her drink. "*Mmm*. It's been ages since I had a good pina colada. This is great, thank you."

Wild Card's eyes swiveled to me before he abruptly spun on his heel and returned to the bar.

"So? Information?" Jackie said, setting her drink down.

"Men *and* women. Clothed. No indication of bondage. And we don't have enough information to know location or time of day preferences, but I'd wager he's more concerned about witnesses than either of those factors."

"And does he use one or two hands to strangle them?"

"Neither." I leaned forward, lowering my voice. "The victims are tackled to the ground and forced on their stomachs. From there, he lies on top of them and uses his forearm across the back of the neck."

Jackie squinted in concentration. "Interesting. You said he injects them? Where exactly?"

"The neck," I answered, raising an eyebrow.

"Ah, yes. That would work. That's his peak moment." She picked up her glass and took another drink, completely unbothered by the conversation we were sharing.

"What do you mean?"

"Imagine old-fashioned ordinary sex. You start off at one pace, kicking it up as the excitement builds, then—*if you're lucky*—you orgasm. Your killer likely is rubbing against the victim, building friction, but I don't think the victim passing out triggers his release. By not using his hands, he's too distanced from the experience. But the injection, that's something he can both see and feel as he presses the needle into the skin and then plunges the contents into their bodies. That's his orgasm trigger."

"He's not sexually excited by the choking itself?"

"I didn't say that," she said, shaking her head. "Controlling his victims is probably enough to make him hard. But it's foreplay. Most people have a preferred sexual position. Some like missionary, some like cowboy or cowgirl, or rear-entry. But your killer always lies on top of the victim's backside. He not only gains control but I'd guess it's also his preferred sexual position." She took another drink of her pina colada. "You really should drink. This is excellent."

I took a long drink through my straw, giving myself time to align my thoughts. "One of the cases involved two people. A man and a woman. My theory is the man interrupted the killer, and then was killed by the injection. The killer then used a knife to kill the woman."

Her face scrunched, imagining the scene. "That's a new ballgame. But if injecting the needle was his orgasm peak..."

"Yeah," I said, nodding. "That's my worry, too. He'll switch out the needle for the knife going forward."

Wild Card brought us two overflowing plates. "It appears Italian is on the menu tonight," he said as he set the plates down. Joey carried over additional plates, containing garlic bread, along with Edwin's promised carryout bag of a weeks' worth of leftovers. Wild Card eyed the bag before glancing at me.

"Can you hold the bag until I leave?" I asked him.

"Of course, ma'am," he said bowing and taking the bag from Joey. "It will be my pleasure."

Wild Card hurried away and Jackie watched him over her shoulder. "He's not really a waiter, is he?"

I laughed. "No. He's my bodyguard." I cut my food before stuffing a huge wad of chicken parmesan and noodles into my mouth.

"And the two guys who just followed him into the back room?"

"Security guards," I mumbled, swallowing my food. "We have a gig later tonight which requires their special skills."

"Hmm. Nice bodies. Think any of them would be interested in a quick *choky*?"

From across the room, Maggie barked out a laugh before throwing her hand over her mouth. I looked around. Everyone was quietly laughing with their heads bowed. They must've bugged our table.

Chapter Forty

CHARLIE
Tuesday, 8:30 p.m.

As the elevator whisked Jackie upstairs to her next adventure, Spence strutted across the room toward me. "We need to talk." He was carrying his laptop which was my clue he'd found something during his background searches. "Preferably someplace without an audience listening." He placed his ear mic on the table.

I slid out of the booth, picking up his earpiece and on our way past Maggie, I handed it to her. With an arm around my waist, Spence steered me toward the elevators.

"This way," I said, turning to the right. "Most of the rooms in the building have surveillance, but Kelsey insisted one was left without cameras."

Entering the employee hallway, I followed the hall to the left, swiping my keycard for the solid metal door labeled: *private*. Inside was one of Kelsey's typical isolation rooms. The room had plain, tiled floors with a floor drain. A metal railing ran along three walls. And, eyebolts were mounted to the floor and each wall in various places.

Spence looked around the room, turning in a slow circle. "Do I even want to know?"

"My cousin is a planner. She likes to be ready for anything."

Spence shook his head, and with a serious face, he opened his laptop, turning the monitor toward me. I waited for him to explain but he remained silent.

I began reading his background notes for the patients Terri Weston saw the day she was murdered. Using the touchpad, I scrolled down to continue reading. And that's when I saw it. Why Spence had requested to speak in private. As I read the details, I felt my knees weaken. "Did you show this to anyone?"

"No. Not even Bones. I figured since we're not even supposed to have access to this list, the less eyes the better."

"He—" I pointed to the screen, "He wasn't a patient. Right? He was with a patient?"

"Right. The patient was being treated for injuries acquired when he resisted arrest. The cop was listed as the arresting officer."

Even though I knew we were in a private room, one with walls crammed full of soundproofing insulation, I still looked around to ensure we were alone. "We need to talk to the prisoner. Find out what happened."

"He's in the state prison. I can drop by for a chat on visiting day."

I shook my head, turning to pace in the small room. "No. Don't do anything. Visitors logs can be monitored."

"Is this really a possibility then? That a cop killed Terri Weston?"

"I don't know. But I'll be damned if I accuse a cop without more information. We should get back. We need to check on the rest of tonight's activities."

I opened the door and spotted Bones and Wild Card leaning casually against the far wall, waiting.

Bones looked over my shoulder and frowned. He stepped over, pushing the door wider and looked around the room. "Kelsey's a nut."

"Maybe," Wild Card said as he also looked inside the room. "But it sure is handy to have one of her holding cells here if we need it later."

Bones smiled at Wild Card. It wasn't a cheerful smile. It held a lot of sinister thinking.

"There's more than one of these rooms?" Spence asked, thumbing toward the room over his shoulder.

"This is the fourth one I know of," Bones answered. "But Kelsey has real estate hidden across the country, so who knows how many cells she's had built."

I laughed as I started down the hallway. "What makes you think she only has real estate in the U.S.?"

~*~*~

Regrouping in Baker's office, Wild Card walked over and kissed my cheek.

"What was that for?" I asked.

"Sharing your dinner. It was insanely good." He patted his stomach.

"I'll be sure to let chef Edwin know." I walked over and sat on the couch near the bar. "Where are we? What's the plan for this evening?"

"Owen Flint won't be here until around ten according to Baker's records," Ryan said, crossing his arms over his chest.

"*Ooh*," Maggie said, rubbing her hands together. "We have time to hit the club downstairs and dance."

Bridget clapped, jumping up and down. "Can we?" she asked me. "Please, please, please."

"In a minute," I said. "First, Maggie, did you talk to Roseline's family?"

"I spoke to her brother." Maggie walked over and sat in a side chair. "According to him, their parents are too distraught to talk, but he gave us enough background to get us started. He described Roseline as quiet, shy even, but intelligent and observant. The family wasn't surprised when she turned in the drug dealers and entered WITSEC. He said she used to volunteer as an advocate for at risk teens and had a habit of fighting for the underdog. And her volunteer work was in addition to working two other jobs. She was a secretary at a large firm during the day and worked nights at a truck stop. She was trying to save up for college. She wanted to be a social worker."

"I'm surprised she was so reserved with me then. She knew I was a cop, yet she gave me the same illegal immigrant BS story she told everyone else."

"She couldn't tell the truth. The rules are very clear: Don't trust anyone. Keep to yourself. Use the same lies every time to help keep them straight."

I thought about the drug dealers. "Had she broken the rules? Had she contacted her family?"

"No. Not according to her brother. The first news they'd received since she'd entered WITSEC was her death notification. They're in shock."

"I bet."

"Charlie..." Maggie glanced at the floor before looking back at me. "Not to pile on your plate, but it's not enough to find the person who killed her."

"I know." I ran a hand through my hair. "We also need to figure out who hired the killer."

"Do you think it was the Jameson crew?" Bones asked.

"Not really. I mean, they're the obvious choice. But Lisa's brother, Phillip, said the Jameson crew doesn't have the reach. He suggested maybe their suppliers, but my conversation with Mickey was cut short when bullets started flying so he didn't have a chance to tell me if he knew of a network in Miami."

"I'll go talk to Mickey," Spence said. "He's more likely to share details with me than you."

"You need backup?" Bones asked him.

"You don't take backup to a meeting with Mickey," Spence said, shaking his head. "He'll read it as an act of war. No, I'm good. I'll be back before ten."

I was staring at the floor, biting my lip. "Spence—" I called out just as he was opening the door. "Ask Mickey about the prisoner from the hospital log. See if he knows anything about the arrest."

Spence dropped his head in a quick nod before walking out.

"What was that about?" Ryan asked.

"I don't know yet. Just a thread that needs to be pulled."

Maggie laughed. "I'll let you keep your secrets, *for now*, if you let us go dancing."

I laughed. "Fine. *Go*. Have fun. But watch the time. I need you guys back in The Parlor before ten."

Bridget started squealing and grabbed Maggie's hand, dragging her toward the door. Bones narrowed his eyes at me before reluctantly following the girls. Ryan sat in the chair that Maggie had vacated. Wild Card sat in one of the guest chairs. Jackson and Trigger looked at each other, then back at me.

"*Go*! I mean it. There's nothing on the agenda until later."

Their faces brightened with smiles as they hurried for the door.

Evie walked over and sat next to me on the couch. "Baker showed me a picture of Xander earlier. Do you know his real name?"

"I do. And it's not good. His real name is Miguel Remirez. He's married, but the bigger problem is that he's the head of a Mexican drug cartel."

Baker muttered an f-bomb as he threw a stapler across the room into one of the monitors, shattering the screen. Garth, who'd been standing guard near the door, shook his head before disappearing down the hall.

We all sat in silence. Several minutes later, Garth returned with a box containing a new monitor. Wild Card walked over to help him.

Baker walked toward me, stopping next to the bar. He stood with his arms crossed, staring at me. "How bad is this situation?"

"*Bad*. I'd wager Miguel's girlfriends don't usually live past the break-up stage. The man is ruthless. We suspect he killed both his uncle and his older brother. His other brother, Santiago, tried to kill Kelsey recently."

Baker's face was hard. Frozen in anger. "What's the plan to protect Evie?"

"For now, she stays here. But no more trips to The Parlor without one of Kelsey's bodyguards."

Garth stopped hooking up the monitor and turned to face me. "Are you questioning my ability to protect her?"

"No. But if the cartel finds out she's here, they'll show up with automatic rifles. They'll shower this place with bullets. You're good, Garth, but you're not bulletproof."

"Well..." He turned back toward the monitor he was installing. "When you put it that way..."

"If I stay here," Evie said, pulling my attention, "I'll be putting everyone in danger."

"Only if they find you. If you stay on the fifth floor, you, and everyone else, will be safe."

"I'm shutting down the private rooms," Baker said, recrossing the room back to his desk. "There are two security doors between this office and the private rooms, but I don't want to take a chance. Owen Flint knows the layout on this floor."

"What about tonight?" Ryan asked me.

I knew what he was asking. He wanted to know if we were still using Evie as bait. "Evie stays upstairs. Maggie or I will bait Owen Flint."

"You sure?" Ryan asked. "Kelsey worried someone new might make Owen suspicious."

"I'm willing to take that chance. One way or another, we'll get him either upstairs or into the holding room on the third floor, but we won't use Evie to do it."

Evie shook her head. "I promised Kelsey."

"It's not your call. It's mine." I smiled over at Ryan. "Besides, Kelsey doesn't scare me. It'll be fine."

Ryan smiled, knowing I was lying.

~*~*~

I needed some thinking time, so I walked out of the office into the hallway. I leaned against the wall, sliding downward to sit on the floor. A sharp pain shot through my bum knee. I carefully stretched out my legs, groaning at all my body aches.

I looked at my hand, but the swelling from being stomped on had receded and there was no bruising. The swelling on my face was also gone, and the bruises, already turning from black to purple, were hidden behind layers of makeup. In a day or two, they'd be a pretty lime green or canary yellow. My knee would heal too, but would require a few days of rest, which wasn't an option right now.

I thought of Roseline and all the clues surrounding her death. Maggie was right. It wasn't enough to find her killer. I had to find the person responsible for hiring the hitman, too. Benny was my best lead to do that, but with him skipping town, that conversation would have to wait.

Baker's office door opened and Wild Card stepped out, tossing me a pad of paper and a pen. "You and Kelsey are a lot alike. Probably more than you know. Create a visual."

I picked up the pen and looked down at the pad of paper. "Yeah, but she gets a whiteboard. I only get paper?"

"Should I go buy you a whiteboard?" Wild Card asked, raising an eyebrow.

"I'd like that," I answered with a grin. "But I'd settle instead for an icepack for my knee."

Wild Card looked behind him. "Garth? Where do I find an icepack in this place?"

"Kitchen. Chef Edwin keeps them in the walk-in freezer."

Wild Card stepped over me and started down the hall toward the elevator. "I'll be back in a minute."

"Since you're going to the kitchen..."

Wild Card paused, glancing over his shoulder.

"Tell Chef Edwin I'll heal faster with one of his desserts."

Wild Card flashed his perfect smile before continuing down the hall.

I stared down at the pad of paper, picking it up to start writing out the details. I drew a circle in the middle of the page with Roseline's name penned inside it. From there, I branched out lines for the Jameson crew,

WITSEC, and Pauly—who also had a second line to Lydia. I wrote under Jameson crew: *supplier* with a question mark. Then under that, I wrote: *Mickey/Spence*.

Returning to Roseline, I wrote a few notes under her name: time of death, cause of death, worked at truck stop, took down drug dealers, fights for underdogs, observant, phone missing...

I paused to text Quille and ask about the phone. He texted back that the tech guys told him the phone was turned off. Roseline's phone records also showed she hadn't received a call since her death.

That was strange, I thought. Even if the calls went to voicemail, her boss's calls should've shown on the phone records. I texted him back, saying as much. He replied with a question mark. I stared at the phone and a good two minutes later, Quille replied he'd recheck.

Knowing Quille, he was at home listening to his wife Miranda screech from across the room that she wasn't a priority. I understood her frustration. And I knew Quille did, too. But the odd hours came with the job and after fifteen years of marriage, she knew a multiple homicide trumped dinner at home with the wife. It was a fact. A fact that every detective knew, and their spouses had to live with.

I looked back at the pad of paper with its odd circles, lines, and even a few stick-figure people along the margins. Then I wrote at the bottom of the pages, something I was avoiding: *Was a cop involved?*

Chapter Forty-One

CHARLIE
Tuesday, 9:38 p.m.

Surprised to realize I'd spent an hour writing notes while sitting on the floor in the hallway, I climbed up from the floor, careful of my knee as I did so. The icepack had left a wet spot on my pant leg. I tucked the pen in my pocket, the pad of paper under my arm, then picked up the icepack and my empty dessert bowl. The bowl had been filled with a hot fudge brownie sundae which I'd devoured in seconds. Carrying my loot into Baker's office, I set the icepack and bowl in the bar's sink, then tore out the used pages in the notepad. I carried the sheets of paper to the shredder, and seconds later, an hour's worth of thinking was split into thin strips, then crosscut into confetti.

"Paranoid, much?" Ryan asked from across the room.

"Best to be safe. Some of my theories are a little controversial." I walked over to the couch. Throwing myself into the soft leather, I leaned my head back. "I need a nap."

"Take one," Wild Card said. "I'll wake you when Owen Flint shows. Maggie's already in position to play bait."

I looked over and saw that an entire section of monitors had been moved. Wild Card sat in a cushioned chair positioned in front of the arranged monitors. They displayed various angles of The Parlor. Maggie was on one screen, sitting with a martini at the bar. Bridget and Bones were on another screen, pushing food around on plates, neither eating. Jackson, Trigger, and Spence sat at a table near the corner, drinking beer.

"Where's Evie?" I asked, looking around.

"She's in my suite," Baker answered without looking up from his paperwork.

"I'm still not happy about the change," Kelsey's voice said from a laptop next to Wild Card.

"I don't care," I said loud enough for the mic to capture my voice. "We're not risking Evie's safety."

"You should've called me so we could discuss it."

"There's nothing to discuss. Let it go, Kelsey." I leaned my head back again. *I really did need another nap*, I thought as my eyes closed.

~*~*~

"Wake up," Spence said, shoving my shoulder.

One eye opened, then the other. I blinked a few times, focusing on my surroundings. "What time is it?"

"Half past eleven," Wild Card answered as he dragged a desk chair over. "Owen never showed."

I sat forward on the couch, tossing the blanket covering me to the floor. I raked both hands through my hair, trying to pull my brain out of the fog. Spence nudged my shoulder again. Looking up, I took the cup of coffee he held out for me and wrapped both hands around the warm mug. I held it under my nose to smell the fresh brew while it cooled enough to drink. "How'd your meeting go?" I asked him.

"Interesting," he answered with a slight smirk. "Mickey's got balls. He called the mysterious suppliers who work with the Jameson crew. They import through Cuba, not Mexico. And they said they weren't connected to the hit on Roseline." Spence sat on the arm of the couch, one foot propped on the edge of the coffee table. "For what it's worth, Mickey believed them. The suppliers said they don't sweat their dealers getting arrested. And if they did feel intervention was necessary, they'd take out the dealers, not a witness."

"That makes sense," Maggie said from the chair next to me. "It's easier to kill the dealers than a federally protected witness. And law enforcement doesn't get as jumpy when the scumbags are knocked off."

"But then where does that leave us?" Wild Card asked. "Who hired the hit, then?"

I looked over at Spence. He continued smirking, but didn't say anything.

"Do we need to talk in private?"

"Not if you can read between the lines." Spence reached down and picked up the blanket, folding it before placing it on the side table. "I asked Mickey about that other thing. His interest was immediately perked. He remembered the arrest. And the reason Mickey remembered it was because of the surprisingly *low* quantity of drugs reported with the arrest. The guy arrested handled restocking the street dealers, so he transported large quantities. But the evidence in his arrest was minimal. A few small baggies of marijuana, two vials of coke, and a few pill bottles."

My brain caught up to what he was saying. "Flying under the radar for trafficking narcotics."

"Exactly. The difference between a five-year sentence and a thirty-year sentence."

I didn't like the direction this case was turning. "I don't know about you, but if I had to choose between keeping my mouth shut or serving an extra twenty-five years in prison, my lips would be glued together so tight you couldn't pry them loose with a crowbar."

"That would be my play."

Maggie stood, crossing her arms over her chest. "At any point in the near future are either of you going to share with the group?"

I shook my head. "Not yet. You'd ask me how I got the lead, and I can't divulge my source." I reached over and grabbed my phone from the coffee table. I had three text messages from Quille and a voicemail from Kelsey.

I read Quille's text messages. Message one: *No other calls were received on the phone number we have for Roseline.* Message two: *My wife is pissed.* Message Three: *Are you going to answer me?*

The fact that no other calls had come in on Roseline's phone could be for two reasons. One, she had another phone we didn't know about. This was a realistic possibility being she was in witness protection. Or reason number two, Sue Dodd, the manager at the truck stop, lied to me. The second reason couldn't be ignored.

I texted back: *Meet me at the mansion at midnight. Have a judge on speed dial and dress for a raid.*

Next, I texted Uncle Hank: *Wake up any cops still at mansion and be ready in 30. Dress in darks and carry your badge.*

Uncle Hank replied seconds later: *We'll be ready.*

I didn't feel like listening to my voicemail, so instead I asked Wild Card, "What does Kelsey want?"

"To ask if you're ready for the B&E tonight," Wild Card answered. "And probably to grill you with a million questions to prove it."

I looked at Garth, who nodded, letting me know the car had been acquired. I looked back at Wild Card. "Change in plans. I'm not going to the B&E."

"Kelsey's going to be pissed," Ryan said with only a hint of a smirk.

"Tough. Kelsey can run the B&E remotely. She's done it a hundred times. Bones, Bridget, and Trigger, you'll take the dentist office job tonight. The car you need is parked on the second floor in the parking ramp. Keys are above the visor. And don't tell Kelsey about the change in plans until you're onsite and ready to roll. I don't want her trying to rush to the scene just because I'm not there." I used my hand to rub my eyes, mentally walking through their job. "You'll need to dump the car after the job, so wear gloves. Garth can show you on a map the best places."

"Got it," Bridget said. "I'll go change."

Trigger followed Garth over to a desk as Baker pulled out a map.

I stood and stretched my arms over my head. "Everyone else—except Maggie—can call it a night. I'll only be taking law enforcement with me."

"You still need a bodyguard," Bones said.

"Anyone who's with me tonight will be officially *on the record*. That means subject to a subpoena to testify if deemed necessary. Anyone really want to take that on?"

Maggie, Bones, Jackson, and Ryan all pointed to Wild Card.

Wild Card shrugged. "Badge or not, you still need someone watching your six. And I don't mind testifying."

"He's actually pretty good at it," Maggie said, giggling. "Entertaining as hell."

"Fine," I said, not having enough energy to argue. "But that's it. No more bodyguards. I'll need to keep a low profile tonight."

"Take Beast, too," Spence said. "He'd be happy to testify if needed. And he's *okay-ish* at keeping a low profile."

An image of Beast sitting in the witness chair flashed in my brain. "And if I don't agree?"

Spence shrugged. "Then expect to see me in your rearview mirror."

Wild Card's head snapped in Spence's direction. "That's a good idea."

"What?" I asked. "Taking Beast?"

"No, *well yes*, taking Beast is a good idea, but that wasn't what I was talking about. Let's have Spence hang back tonight and see if he catches anyone following you."

"Wouldn't work. This guy's trained."

"I've got a bag full of equipment," Trigger said, turning back toward us. "We could put a tracker on your car. Spence can hang back a good mile or two if needed."

"I can drive your truck, instead of mine," Spence said. "He's not likely to know about your Toyota."

"I drove my rental," Ryan said. "I'll take turns with Spence approaching and falling back to see if we spot anyone. It beats heading back to the mansion and being bored."

"And we—" Wild Card pointed between him and me "—can take my rental. It already smells like *ode de la Beast*."

"I'm not ready to call it a night either," Jackson said. "I'll play lookout for the B&E."

"Great. We have a plan," Maggie said, slapping her hands together. "Now, as for clothes. I packed suits, swim suits, and designer wear. I didn't plan on midnight escapades, so what am I going to wear?"

"Definitely not designer wear," I told her. "We'll be creeping around in the dark."

"Maggie's about the same size as Evie," Baker said, walking toward his suite. "I'll ask to borrow some clothes." The way he hurried into the next room, I suspected he'd been waiting for an excuse to check on Evie.

I shook my head. "Those with me, we'll regroup at the mansion. I'm going to change before I leave, so I'll meet you there."

"That's too bad," Spence said, eyeing my body. "I kind of like the romper."

I started for the door, commenting over my shoulder, "If you catch Mr. Tricky for me tonight, maybe I'll reward you by wearing it again sometime."

Chapter Forty-Two

KELSEY
Wednesday, 12:05 a.m.

I fisted my hands as my anger sparked. "What do you mean, Charlie's not coming?" I asked over my mic.

"She had another mission tonight," Bridget answered. "We're good, though. We have a three-man team—Trigger, Bones, and I—to enter the building. And as a bonus, Jackson's parked down the street as lookout."

"Yo," Jackson said over his mic.

"Charlie should've called me so I could plan the job without her. *This wasn't the plan!*"

"Get over it. Plans change," Bones said. "We doing this or what?"

"I can't believe she did this."

"Hey, Boss," Trigger said. "You know something we don't about this job?"

Was there something different? I asked myself. On numerous occasions I'd sent Trigger and Bridget into buildings just like this one. The fact that the building was used to lure women into the world of sex trafficking was the only real difference. And Bones was with them. I trusted him to keep them safe. They were right, we didn't need Charlie. But she'd agreed to do the job, and now she was off doing...

Ah, I thought. *There's the problem*. I don't know what she's doing. She's off my radar.

"Boss?" Trigger said.

"The job's a go. But does anyone know where Charlie went?"

"She's doing cop shit," Bones answered. "She has at least five badges with her, plus Wild Card and Beast."

"Okay. I'll call her later, but you guys have a green light. Tech's tapped into the city's camera system, but none of the cameras are installed on your block. We'll only be able to see cars entering from two blocks north of your location, and about three blocks out on the other three sides. Having Jackson play lookout was a good idea."

Tech reached over and unmuted his headset. "Inventory check. Tasers?"

"Check," Bridget and Trigger responded.

"Zip cuffs?"

"Check."

"Surveillance equipment backpack?"

"Check."

"B&E fanny packs?"

"Check."

"What the hell's a B&E fanny pack?" Bones asked.

Tech ignored him. "Body Cams turned on?"

Two monitors in front of Tech lit up—Bridget and Trigger's cams. The third screen stayed dark.

"Bones," I said, leaning against the post in the tiki lounge. "*Turn your camera on* or you're off this op."

"Told you," Bridget said, giggling.

"How is wearing a body cam for a B&E a good idea?" Bones argued.

"It's a secure connection," Tech said. "No worries, man. The feed is encrypted to ensure I have full control over the data. But it comes in handy for us to be able to see shit on our end."

Bones sighed, but the third monitor lit up.

"Sensor scan," Tech ordered.

"Scan clear," Trigger said, holding the heat scanner in front of his body cam so we could see that there wasn't a significant heat signature coming from inside the building.

"You guys have a body heat scanner?" Bones asked.

Everyone ignored Bones.

"Ready?" I asked

"Ready to roll," Bridget answered.

"Locked, loaded, and amped," Trigger answered.

"This is ridiculous. Can we just go, already?" Bones asked.

"Watch for squatters in the building next door," I said. "They're not likely to call the police, but you never know. Eyes open. Team Kelsey is a go."

Bones' cam jetted up and down as he jogged down the sidewalk and snuck into the alley around the corner.

Bridget giggled as she and Trigger walked casually down the sidewalk before turning into the alley. Bones stood annoyed, with his hands perched on hips, as he waited for them.

Trigger walked over next to the dumpster and interlocked his fingers. Bridget placed her left foot in his hands and with his help, sprang upward, landing on top of the dumpster. By the time Trigger climbed on top, Bridget had the window open and he followed her inside. Bones' body cam showed he was still standing in the alley as Bridget and Trigger's cams split off into different rooms.

"You joining them, Bones?" I asked. "Or are you going to just hang out in the alley?"

"I'm starting to wonder if they even need me."

"They don't. But you standing in a dark alley staring at an open window looks suspicious, don't you think?"

His cam showed him climbing onto the dumpster, then sliding through the window. I pulled a chair over next to Tech and watched all three monitors with him. Tech turned one of the far screens my way and pointed.

"Jackson," I called. "Black and white just entered the neighborhood from the north. We can't tell which direction he'll go."

"Got it. No headlights visible yet. Wait. I see them. Looks like they're working a grid. They're moving east now."

"Tech?"

"On it." Tech slid his chair back to reach for a nearby laptop, which he moved to his lap. After some fast keyboard work, he unmuted his headset, and said, "There's a man with a beard running around my backyard. I think he's *nude*! Can you send a police officer? I live at..."

I stopped listening. I knew from experience, the voice the 911 operator was hearing was being altered by voice alteration software. Tech usually picked the little old lady voice because it tended to get the quickest police response.

"I see blue lights and hear a siren," Jackson said. "Sounds like they're moving out of the area."

"Nice job, Tech," I said. "Bridget and Trigger, am I seeing what I think I'm seeing?"

"Yeah, Boss," Bridget said. "We are several days too early for the party. Everything is still packed up or covered in plastic."

"Do the best you can. We might not get another chance. Bones, you'll need to help them dig through the mess and then restack everything."

"What about the power booster for the waiting room camera?" Bridget asked. "Without the booster, the recorder battery only has a three-day shelf life. If we hook it up now, it'll be dead by the time they're open for business."

"Damn," I said, standing to pace. "Give me a minute."

I turned to pace the other direction, but saw Whiskey standing next to me. He smiled as he sipped his coffee. He was wearing loud Bermuda shorts, a black tank top, and neon green flip flops.

"Were you listening?"

He lifted one shoulder in a half shrug. "You don't need the booster if you hardwire your camera to a direct power source. Want me to walk Bridget through it?"

"How long will it take?"

"Twenty, maybe thirty, minutes."

I walked over and grabbed another earpiece from the coffee table, handing it to Whiskey. "Bridget, Whiskey's going to walk you through hardwiring our power."

"Sweet," Bridget said, giggling. "On the job training."

"Bones," Whiskey said over the mic. "Grab that small desk light in front of you on your right. Cut the cord off for Bridget."

In Bones' camera, we saw him reach out and grab the lamp. He looked over at Trigger's body cam, then down at his own. "This is so weird," Bones said to the camera before he cut the cord on the desk light and handed the remains to Trigger.

"Trigger," I said, getting his attention. "Put the lamp by the exit window. You'll need to take it with you. Best if its owner thinks it was lost during the remodel. Then hurry it up and get the rest of the equipment installed."

"You got it, Boss." Trigger said.

~*~*~

Over the next thirty minutes, I watched all the monitors with Tech, while Whiskey taught Bridget some upgraded electrical skills. Bones and Trigger were putting the last of the furniture and boxes back into the room being used for storage. Tech corrected Bones a few times of where to place a box or stand, ensuring everything was put back in its original location.

Bridget finished wiring the front camera with a secondary mini-cam mounted on top of it. The feed was already routing directly to Tech.

Trigger had tagged about a dozen random items for voice bugging, but we had no idea which rooms the items belonged in, so he also placed bugs under a few built-in counters throughout the building, and one more in a backroom office behind an air vent.

"Pack up and check your equipment," I said over the mic. "Make sure there's no sign of entry. I want you guys out of there."

Tech lifted a pad of paper that was sitting beside him. "Bones, according to my notes, you left a Philip screwdriver on the floor in the hallway, your night vision goggles in the back office, and you forgot to flush the toilet when you peed."

Bones was quiet a moment before he stepped out into the hallway and picked up the screwdriver. "No shit?"

"No shit. Get the goggles and flush the toilet."

Bones walked down the hall toward the office. "I'm changing my mind on these bodycams. We should talk to Donovan."

I laughed. "I mentioned the idea to him, but he told me you guys would never wear them."

Bones snorted. "I can sell it." I heard the toilet flush.

"I'll back him on the sales pitch," Jackson said. "Not that Donovan ever lets us do B&Es, but having a second set of eyes remotely taking screen shots would be super helpful in the protection side of Aces."

Tech looked over his shoulder at me and shook his head. Turning back to the monitors, he reached over and unmuted his mic. "Kelsey already had me order and program the fifty body cams. They're sitting on a shelf in the basement, just waiting to be put to good use."

"When?" Bones asked.

"Two months ago," Tech answered.

"Unknown bogie entering the neighborhood from the south," I said, watching the monitor for the perimeter. "Lights out, boys and girl."

The body cams showed the flashlights being turned off. Trigger and Bridget flipped the switch on their body cams to night vision. I watched Trigger walk over to Bones and switch his body cam over for him. In the green hue on Trigger's cam, I saw Bones raise an eyebrow.

"I've got the bogie in my sights," Jackson said. "He's slowing down." There was a pause. "Damn. He's pulling into the dentist office parking lot."

I looked over at Tech, pointing to his notepad. "Are we clear to leave?"

"Everything's marked off except the drywall dust on the carpet where Bridget worked."

"Bridget," Whiskey said. "Rub your hand back and forth on the carpet to embed the dust."

We watched her give the carpet a good rub down before she sprang upward. She walked blindly through the room, counting out her steps, and then down the hall to where Trigger and Bones were. She had night vision goggles in her backpack, but she never used them. Bridget had partial vision in a pitch-black setting which still boggled my brain cells. She could also memorize the entrances and exits, along with distances and directions. On her way past the boys, she grabbed Trigger's hand and pulled him toward the small stairway. Trigger grabbed Bones' arm and pulled him forward as well.

"I can't see," Bones said. "Stop so I can put my goggles on."

"You don't need to see," Trigger said. "Just listen to Bridget and take Bridget-sized steps."

We watched Bones stumble about before seeing him transition into pacing out his steps to Bridget's counting. Within ten seconds, all three of them were ready and waiting at the upstairs window.

"What's our status, Jackson?"

"Hold. I don't have a clear view. I saw the taillights on the car go off, but whoever it is never walked this way. They could be inside already."

"I would've heard them," Trigger said. "No one's inside yet."

Bridget reached over and covered Trigger's mouth.

"Silent, everyone," Tech said over his mic. "Bridget saw something in the alley."

Bridget released her hand and leaned forward to look out the window again. Because of the angle, we couldn't see on her bodycam whatever she was watching. We did see on Bones' cam when she lifted her hand, and using her fingers, started counting down from five.

"Four, three two, one..." Tech called out for her.

"Got him," Jackson said. "Security guard. He just exited the alley and is walking past the front of the building. Dumbass isn't even bothering to flash a light at the windows. He's on auto-pilot."

We all waited.

"Shit. He just lit a cigarette. He's leaned against the building. Let's hope he's not a chain smoker."

"Jackson, keep your head down. We don't want him spotting you," I said. "The rest of you stay close to the window until we're in the clear."

"Hey, Tech?" Bridget asked in a whisper. "What's the status on the alarm system?" She held the window sensor out. Trigger had rigged it to show a fake connection which had allowed them access.

"It's live. Don't break that connection or it'll get real loud real fast in there."

"No worries." Bridget grabbed Trigger's hand and placed it on the sensor wire, then lifted his hand upward another three inches. Then she pulled super glue from her B&E bag, and while Trigger held the sensor, she glued it to the sidewall. Then she pulled a scalpel out, removing it from its sheath, and used the blade to carefully cut and pry the old sensor receiver off the glass pane. "All set," Bridget said, tapping Trigger's arm to let him know he could let go. She tucked the glue and scalpel back in her bag. "Can we go now?"

"The guard just finished his cigarette," Jackson said. "He's walking back to the parking lot. I'm waiting to see if he's leaving or planning to make another circle."

"Anyone want to swim when we get back to the house?" Bridget asked.

"I could go for a swim," Trigger said. "Hey, Tech, what about you?"

"We'll see. I need to check on Katie. Last time I saw her, she was puking mojitos into a trash can in our room."

"I told her not to mix the mojitos and long island ice teas. Rookie mistake," Bridget said.

"The security guard is leaving," Jackson said. "Pulling out of the parking lot now. Turned north. Exit is clear."

Bridget had Bones and Trigger slip out the window first, then she slid out, closing the window behind her. She pulled a Jimmie stick from her bag, wiggled it between the panes, then jerked her wrist to the side. We heard over the mic the latch snap closed. "Window locked."

She turned and dropped down into Bones' arms.

Bones whispered a chuckle. "You're good at this shit."

"It's so much more fun than working retail," she whispered back, giggling.

Chapter Forty-Three

CHARLIE
Wednesday, 12:37 a.m.

Arriving at the mansion, I parked and shuffled my gear from the Mustang's trunk to Wild Card's rental. Wild Card opened a door on the SUV for Beast, who leapt into the back seat. Doors were closed, and in less than three minutes, we were on our way again with Uncle Hank, Detective Chambers, Gibson, and Quille following us out of the driveway.

Before reaching the truck stop, I pointed for Wild Card to pull into a restaurant parking lot. The lot was empty and the building's interior lights were off. The rest of our gang pulled in behind us. Getting out of our vehicles, we clustered together in the darkest section of the lot.

"What's the plan?" Quille said. "And this better be good. Miranda's livid."

I pulled my phone and texted Miranda: *Will a three-day cruise this weekend get Quille out of the doghouse?*

I watched three dots float back and forth for almost a minute before she finally replied: *Yes.*

I texted Baker to book the trip and sent him Miranda's phone number. "Your wife is happy. But you'll need to take this weekend off."

"How the hell do I justify taking time off with a serial killer running loose in Miami?"

"If we don't catch the killer in the next day or two, it could take us months to close the case. Either way,

Miranda's packing, so if you change the plans on her she really will divorce your ass."

Chambers waved a hand toward our surroundings. "Where are we?"

Gibson pointed across the shaggy brush field that separated the truck stop and the restaurant. "That's the truck stop where Roseline Pageotte worked. But I have no idea why we're here."

"Roseline's boss, Sue Dodd, told me she left several messages for Roseline when she didn't show for her shift."

"Ah, the phone," Quille said, catching up with me. "Did you ask the manager if she called the same number we have on file?"

"No. Either Roseline had another phone or Dodd's lied to me. I'm not willing to tip her off by asking just yet."

"So... This is a stakeout?" Uncle Hank asked.

"Yuppers," I answered.

Everyone except Gibson and Wild Card sighed.

"And there's a fifty-fifty chance we're wasting our time?" Quille asked.

"Yup."

"But you have a hunch," Uncle Hank said as he crossed his arms over his chest and smirked. "Otherwise, you wouldn't have asked for backup. You would've sat on the truck stop alone."

"It's more of a theory than a hunch. And I have no idea if it will play out tonight or a month from now."

Quille sighed and rubbed a hand across his forehead. "Spit it out. I'm not getting any younger."

"When I was here the other night, lots of trucks were coming and going. But as soon as the word cop was uttered, they all turned and fled."

"Truckers keep to themselves," Chambers said. "Why did that surprise you?"

"Truckers avoid cops, yes, but they don't typically flee like rats in a fire. And Dodd said the last time the police were here, it took *days* for the truckers to reappear. Was she exaggerating? Or do the truckers know something we don't about this place and don't want to get caught up in it?"

"What are you thinking?" Quille asked.

"I'm thinking there's something shady going on and Sue Dodd is part of it. And according to Roseline's brother, if there was something shady happening here, Roseline would've picked up on it."

"What are the odds Roseline would be employed at another dirty truck stop?" Uncle Hank asked.

"Statistically, we know that twenty-four-hour businesses tend to have higher crime rates," I answered. "Add in the fact that the truck stop is off the main expressway, has multiple exit routes, and is on the outskirts of most patrol zones..."

"We get it," Quille said, finishing for me. "The perfect real estate for the criminally inclined."

"Not to mention, one side of the building's exterior lights are out," Wild Card said from the outskirts of our circle.

Wild Card stood with his hands on his hips, facing away from us. The field between the truck stop and the restaurant parking lot was mostly flat with a few short scrappy shrubs thrown in. I looked past the field and saw what Wild Card saw. The west side of the building, the side closest to us, had tall post lights on the outskirts of the parking lot, but along the exterior of the building the lights were out, leaving a section of darkness.

"Son of a bitch. How did I miss that?" I whispered to myself more than anyone. "I was just here less than forty-eight hours ago."

"You were pretty busy that night getting your ass kicked," Quille said, letting me off the hook. "But how did *I* miss it?"

"By the time you arrived, there were police lights and spotlights everywhere," I said, letting him off the hook, too.

Uncle Hank turned to look at me. "You've been inside. What's on the west side of the building?"

I thought back to when I was inside the truck stop. I'd parked to the far south, walked north into the building. The cash register was to the west, and the manager's office and employee-only area was behind the register. "Employee only section. Likely a storage room. Definitely an office."

"What's the plan?" Detective Chambers asked.

"You and Gibson take the east parking lot," I said, handing him two earpieces. "I'm limited on cameras, so use your phones if you see anything picture worthy."

"I keep a camera in my trunk," Detective Chambers said. "And before you ask, yes, I'll make sure Gibson turns the flash off."

I smiled at Chambers before turning to Uncle Hank and Quille. "You two can do your good ole' boy routine. Wander inside and buy food your wives would have hissy fits over, then park yourselves at the outdoor tables nearby."

Uncle Hank looked sideways at Quille as he moved his holster from his hip to his back, pulling his shirt out of his pants to conceal it. "Golf vacation? Or business trip?"

"Let's go with business trip since we're both wearing wrinkled button-ups," Quille answered, walking with Hank back to his car. "Insurance sales again?"

"Let's switch it up. How about—" Uncle Hank said before their car doors shut and the rest of the conversation was lost to us.

I turned to Maggie and Wild Card. "The three of us," I paused to look down at Beast, "I meant four of us," I said to Beast before turning back to Maggie and Wild Card, "will set up on the northwest corner of the lot. We can position ourselves in the weeds. We'll have a clear view of the exit."

"No way," Wild Card said, looking at the display on his phone. He turned the display to show a google image of the area. "Let's stay in the field on the west side. There's a canal to the north. I'll guard you against Mr. Tricky, but I draw the line at battling it out with gators."

"That puts us further away from the action," I said.

"Ever hear of a *zoom feature* on your camera?" Wild Card said as he walked over to his rental and started pulling his gear.

I looked over at Maggie. "He's such a baby."

She whispered low enough for Wild Card not to hear, "What are the chances that the gators will be in the field we're about to walk across?"

"Don't know, but I brought both a thermal camera and a rifle with a night-vision thermal scope—just in case." From the back of the SUV, I pulled out my duffle bags, passing out vests and gear.

"When did you pack all this?" Wild Card asked, looking over my shoulder.

"I keep gear in all my vehicles. I transferred everything from my Mustang to your ride when we stopped at the mansion."

Wild Card pulled a utility belt loaded with flash bangs out of one of my bags. "I've been driving your convertible around with explosive toys in the trunk?"

"Yup."

"This is Florida. Doesn't the trunk get hot?" Maggie asked.

"I paid for special insulation to be installed in the trunk. And the bags are also insulated. So, most days it's not an issue. But if we're having a heatwave, Garth moves the gear indoors."

"This is so cool," Wild Card said.

I looked over and saw him playing with the thermal camera. He had it aimed at Beast. You could see Beasts tongue, appearing orange and red on the camera, hanging down about eight inches, dripping red dots. I pulled the strap on my vest and secured the Velcro.

"You want the rifle or the camera?" I asked Wild Card as I closed the back of the SUV with one hand and carried the rifle with the other.

"Camera," he answered, strutting toward the field.

"All right. But watch out for groupings of small lizards."

"Why?" he asked, panning the camera across the field.

"Baby gators. Anything born this year will only be a few inches long, but they'll be grouped together. If they're last year's babies, they'll be around a foot or two in length. Either way, momma gator will be nearby."

"How long will she protect them?" Maggie asked, looking across the field.

"Until they're big enough to protect themselves. Usually four feet or so."

Wild Card looked back at me, offering me the camera as he reached for the rifle. "Just tell me where to shoot."

I laughed and started scanning the field from the road to the furthest distance on the other side. I'd have to keep checking, but for now, it appeared safe enough to cross.

~*~*~

Three hours later, I was about as annoyed as a person could get without screaming. In the earpiece I listened to Gibson babble non-stop about sports. Behind me, Maggie and Wild Card were playing with the thermal equipment. One of them would find a heated image in the field, then they'd guess what the animal was before racing each other to find a match on google using their phones.

At least Uncle Hank and Quille had muted their mics after they'd vacated their patio table and pretended to drive away. I hadn't heard from them since they'd relocated back to the restaurant parking lot, letting me know they were watching the front parking lot via binoculars.

I didn't mind stakeouts. In fact, most of the time, I enjoyed them because I was usually alone. It was quiet. Peaceful. *This* was nowhere near that.

Beast's head swiveled to the right, toward the road. I watched Spence drive past in my Toyota—*again*. Spence and Ryan had set up a loop. One of them passed every twenty minutes. I had no idea what they did the rest of the time, but hoped that Spence had stopped somewhere to put gas in the tank. The short-bed truck was decent on fuel but had a small gas tank.

Beast sat up, leaning his weight into my leg. I reached over to pat him, but realized his head was no longer facing the road. Looking, I followed his stare to the side door of the truck stop. Sue Dodd was opening the door and stepping out to look around. When she didn't see anyone, she flung the doorstop downward to hold the door open. She was on her phone, but I couldn't hear what she was saying.

I turned my mic on, "Stand by. We have activity on the west side of the building."

Wild Card and Maggie turned around in the tall grass, turning off their electronic gadgets.

"What's she doing?" Maggie asked.

I didn't answer. I pulled the camera from my bag, and after checking to ensure the flash was off, I snapped a few photos of Dodd with the zoom feature. I watched her end her call but she stayed by the door, watching the parking lot.

"Got something," Chambers said. "Taking pictures. Sixteen-foot freight truck entered through the back drive off the side road. He's driving behind the truck stop now. His headlights are off."

"Damn it," I whispered. "If he parks in front of the office, I'm going to lose my visual."

"Maggie?" Wild Card whispered. "How long has it been since we scanned the north side of the field?"

"Ten minutes, maybe?" Maggie answered.

"Shit. Okay. Whatever. This is my fault, so I'll fix it." Wild Card grabbed my camera and veered off into the darkness toward the north.

"What's he doing?" I asked Maggie.

"He's the one who made you set up here, so I'm guessing he's moving to where you wanted to be, and he'll take your pictures for you."

I waved a hand at the field. "Idiot. You guys just entertained yourselves for three hours playing *guess the animal*. And now he's sneaking through the same field without the thermal camera?"

"It didn't feel right taking the thermal from you guys," Wild Card whispered back over the mic. "You might need it."

"We have the rifle scope," I said.

"So?" Wild Card said.

"It's also got thermal," Maggie said, giggling.

"Well, shit," Wild Card cursed.

As expected, the truck had pulled alongside the building, blocking my view. I heard the door on the truck open and close. From the gap between the asphalt and the bottom of the truck's freight container, I watched large sized boots walk beside Dodd's to the back of the truck. A man rounded the corner and unlocked the overhead door, rolling it upward. Both he and Dodd grabbed a box before disappearing around the side again.

The boxes were about the size of a case of toilet paper and couldn't weigh much more based on how easily they lifted and carried them. I watched their feet move toward the building door, disappear, then return for more boxes.

"Wild Card, can you tell what's in those boxes?"

"Working on it," he answered.

"Work faster," Quille complained. "I've got a judge on the phone."

"Can you tell how many boxes they have in the truck?" I asked Wild Card.

"Thirty or so. Maybe more. Hang on. They're coming back again. They're arguing, but I can't hear them."

"Just focus on the boxes," Uncle Hank said over the earpiece. "We need to identify what they're moving."

"There's a picture of a man riding a horse on one of the boxes. The truck driver's arm is covering the words, though."

"Cigarettes. Quille, get me a warrant!"

"He's working on it," Uncle Hank said. "Chambers, get ready to drive to the front of the store to cover the front doors."

"We're ready when you are," Chambers said.

"I've got an idea," Maggie said, slipping out of the field and running silently across the parking lot.

"What the fuck, Maggie?" I whispered to her over the earpiece.

She flashed her pearly whites my way as she leaned her back against the cab of the truck on the passenger side.

"Maggie, I'll count out when they step inside," Wild Card said over his mic. "But you'll have only a handful of seconds."

She lifted her hand with a thumbs up in his direction.

"What is she doing?" Uncle Hank asked.

"Just wait and watch, folks," Wild Card said. "This ain't my first rodeo with Maggie. Get ready, girl. Four, three, two, one... now."

Maggie turned, reached up for the handle, opened the truck's door, and jumped up into the seat, closing the door just as fast. I watched her head move around, then duck out of sight.

"Here they come, stay down," Wild Card told her.

"What was the point of that?" I asked.

"When we move in, the driver will go for his truck. Let him. Maggie either pulled the keys or is disabling the electronics. If he had a gun in the cab, she's already confiscated it. He'll be facing the wrong end of a barrel when he tries to flee."

"And I thought Kid was crazy," Quille mumbled. "Judge approved the warrant. Wait for us to move in."

"Chambers," I said over the mic. "You and Gibson come in the front and secure the store. Watch out for the door behind the register. Badges and guns out."

"On it." I could hear Chambers driving, then over his earpiece I heard their car doors opening. A door was slammed shut. "Damn it, Gibson!" Chambers muttered.

Dodd and the truck driver heard the door slam, too. They both froze near the back of the truck. They briefly argued in a whispered tone. Then Dodd held up a finger, the signal for him to wait. She walked back between the truck and the building.

"Move!" I yelled as I launched from the field at a fast run.

Beast ran beside me before jetting past me. By the time the driver turned our way, Beast was barreling toward him at high speed and only a dozen feet away. He jumped onto the tailgate and into the back of the freight truck container. Beast snapped his teeth and growled, but didn't leap inside. Wild Card ran up, jumped on the tailgate, and grabbed the handle on the pulldown door. Hanging his body weight on the handle, the door slammed shut, and Wild Card's feet touched the asphalt again.

I ran past them, between the truck and the building, but didn't catch the building's side door before it was slammed shut. Trying the handle, I confirmed it was locked.

I dropped my shoulder to the side, letting my backpack slide off. Dropping the bag to the ground, I pulled my hammer out of it with my left hand. It wasn't an ordinary hammer. It was a handheld sledge hammer.

"Maggie," Wild Card said. "You can come out of the truck now. The driver is locked in the back."

"I never get to have any fun," Maggie whined, dropping out of the cab as I whacked the door handle with the hammer.

"Give me that," Wild Card said, holstering his gun. Using both hands, he slammed the hammer down, causing the handle to explode in flying pieces.

I pulled the screwdriver from the backpack, used it to fling the throw latch the other direction, and jerked the door open. Taking a quick peek around the corner, I wasn't surprised to see Sue Dodd holding a gun.

"*You come in here, I'll blow your head off!*" Dodd yelled.

"I'm coming inside, whether you like it or not," I yelled from around the corner. "And before you even think of running the other direction, you should know I've got four seasoned cops covering the other door." I glanced over my shoulder to ensure Maggie and Wild Card were standing clear of the doorway before bullets started to fly. "You've got nowhere to go, Dodd. And if you discharge that firearm, I *guarantee you* one of us will shoot you. Your only option is to surrender."

"*I'm not going to prison*," Dodd screamed.

It wasn't the first time I'd heard those words. Far from it. But I'd only heard them said with that level of determination once before. She was prepared to shoot. Either at us, or if necessary, she'd shoot herself. I stepped forward, aimed, and fired.

Dodd's scream pierced the air as Wild Card and Maggie moved into the office behind me.

"Clear!" I yelled loud enough to be heard over the wailing.

Maggie moved around me. "Damn. That's gotta hurt." Maggie kicked Dodd's gun away, then cuffed the wrist on her good arm, looking around for something to attach the cuff to.

Chambers, Gibson, Uncle Hank, and Quille entered from the door on the opposite end of the room.

I pointed to Chambers and Gibson and thumbed over my shoulder. "The driver is in the truck."

They moved past us. Quille continued to stare at Sue Dodd. Maggie gave up trying to figure out what to do with the handcuffs and let go. Dodd used her now free hand to hold together the pieces of her shattered elbow. She wasn't going anywhere but to the hospital.

Quille walked over, whispering in my ear, "I.A. is going to suspend you. You should've let someone else shoot her."

"If we turn the case over to ATF," Maggie said, hearing Quille through her earpiece. "It should buy you about a week before I.A. hears about it. But I can't guarantee the Feds will give your precinct credit for the bust."

Quille's eyes narrowed at me, then Maggie, then back at me.

I shrugged, trying to hide my grin. "You know if I'm suspended before this weekend, your cruise with Miranda will be put on hold. Your choice is divorce court or losing credit on a tobacco smuggling case."

"*Fine*," Quille snapped as he stormed toward the back door. "*Make the call!*"

Chapter Forty-Four

KELSEY
Wednesday, 5:15 a.m.

Sleeping with one ear open, I heard multiple vehicles pull into the driveway. I reached for my phone and waited. Seconds later, I read Tyler's text: *Charlie and crew. All home and safe.*

I sighed, throwing my head back on the pillow. Charlie was going to be the death of me. It didn't matter how old she was, or how good at her job she was, I couldn't stop worrying about her.

Curious as to why they were returning so late, I rolled to the right, off the bed, and stood. Already wearing a sports bra and sweatpants, I pulled a lightweight sweatshirt over my head, added a shoulder holster, and snapped in my gun.

Exiting my assigned bedroom, I paused at the door of the bunkroom, peeking in on the kids. They were sound asleep on their top bunks. Carl was snoring loudly from one of the bottom bunks. Trigger opened one eye and looked at me from the other bottom bunk. He gave a thumbs up. I walked away.

I took my time walking down the three flights of stairs. After only a few hours of sleep, I didn't have the energy to move any faster. At the bottom, I rounded the corner into the kitchen and froze at the chaos.

Hattie and Aunt Suzanne were already up and, it appeared, struggling to find their rightful place in the pecking order of the house. Aunt Suzanne had almost every pan, bowl, and glass dish full of food. Hattie was filling a coffee carafe and snapped at Aunt Suzanne when she stirred Hattie's pan of eggs.

I looked over and saw Charlie standing between the living room and the dining room table. She raised an eyebrow at me as we both walked to the table and sat. Hattie rushed over with a cup of coffee, scrambled eggs, two pieces of bacon, and a bowl of fruit for me. As she returned to the kitchen, Aunt Suzanne rushed to Charlie, setting an overflowing plate of salt, grease, and syrup. I looked over at Whiskey at the other end of the table. He winked at me before taking another bite of his breakfast. Crowded in front of him, he had two plates of breakfast, a bowl of fruit, a cup of coffee, a glass of milk, a glass of orange juice, and a glass of something else that looked disturbingly like tomato juice.

I watched the women as I ate my eggs.

Aunt Suzanne reached for the spatula and Hattie snapped, "*Don't even think about it!*" with a pointy finger aimed at Aunt Suzanne.

"*You're overcooking the eggs,*" Aunt Suzanne argued.

"*I'm cooking them exactly how my family likes them,*" Hattie snapped again as she retrieved a plate and filled it with the eggs. By the time she turned around, Bones had walked into the kitchen and Hattie set the plate and a cup of coffee in front of him.

"Maybe he wanted my pancakes or some fried potatoes," Aunt Suzanne said to Hattie.

"*He doesn't,*" Hattie replied, setting a glass of juice down for Bones.

"I'm a little scared," Bones said to me in a low voice as he watched the women.

"You should do something," Charlie whispered, elbowing me.

"Like what?" I asked. "Call SWAT?"

"I have no idea," Charlie whispered, "but if this goes on much longer, we may need SWAT to separate them."

"If they start throwing punches," Whiskey whispered, "My money's on Hattie."

"I don't know," Charlie said. "That's a tough one. Aunt Suzanne fights dirty. I watched her get mugged once. She beat the snot out of the mugger before calling into the precinct for a black and white to transport him to booking. Then, she said we needed to hurry up or we'd miss our nail appointment. She's scrappy."

"Hattie's old school, though," I said, grinning. "She'd go straight for the biggest fry pan."

"And Hattie wouldn't warn Suzanne first. She'd wait until Suzanne's back was turned," Whiskey added.

"*We can hear you!*" Hattie scolded from the other side of the kitchen island, narrowing her eyes at me.

"*And we're not fighting,*" Aunt Suzanne said with one hand on her hip. "We're merely developing a system in which we can both share such a small space."

We all glanced from one end of the kitchen to the other. It was the largest, longest, kitchen I'd ever seen. There was enough square footage for three professional chefs.

"Sun's coming up," Bones said, grabbing his plate. "I think I'll eat on the veranda."

"Good idea," Charlie said, loading her hands.

"I'm in," I said as I rushed to follow them.

The sun was less than a speck of light on the horizon this early in the morning, but the veranda was well lit.

Uncle Hank sat at a long table with Pops, who was drinking his coffee and reading a paper.

"They still at it?" Pops asked from behind his paper.

"If you mean Hattie and Aunt Suzanne, then yes," I answered, sitting beside him.

"You going to handle it?" Pops asked.

"I think you're more suited to handle this situation."

Pops folded his paper and narrowed his eyes at me. "Baby girl, if you think I'm willing to risk losing the newlywed phase of my marriage with Hattie *over this BS*—you're sorely mistaken."

I looked over at Uncle Hank. "Hell, no," he said, holding up his hands. "I've been married long enough to know better."

I looked sideways at Charlie. "No way," she said, shaking her head. "But if you go back inside, try to steal me a bowl of fruit without Aunt Suzanne seeing."

"*That's too much butter!*" Hattie yelled from inside the house.

"*Mind your own beeswax!*" Aunt Suzanne yelled back.

I forced myself up from my chair, squared my shoulders, and marched back inside. I found Whiskey had left his place at the table and had moved to stand between them. Both women were beyond mad, and ready to do battle.

"All right," I said, holding up my hand. "I love you both, but obviously you two have an issue sharing a kitchen. So... You both have ten minutes to finish cooking breakfast, then you need to walk away. Everyone will eat buffet style and serve themselves."

"But—" Hattie started to say.

"No, buts. As for future meals – Aunt Suzanne, you'll get lunch shift today. Hattie, you'll get dinner. All meals will rotate from there."

"I have a wedding shower to attend this afternoon, so I'd prefer the dinner shift," Aunt Suzanne said.

"Lunch works better for me anyway," Hattie agreed. "Alex is taking me shopping this afternoon. I'm not sure what time we'll get back. Besides," Hattie smirked over at Aunt Suzanne, "that will mean *I* get breakfast tomorrow."

Aunt Suzanne narrowed her eyes at Hattie, but Whiskey raised an arm between them, preventing Aunt Suzanne from reaching her.

"Ten minutes," I reminded them.

They both blinked at me before turning back to their pans and various dishes and rushing around. I looked at Whiskey and he gave me the nod, letting me know he was staying put for the time being.

I returned to the veranda.

"Settled?" Pops asked.

"Doubt it. But Whiskey's playing bouncer." I took a sip of my coffee, but the air had already cooled it. It wasn't worth going to the kitchen for the coffee carafe, though. "Both of them plan to leave the house today. I didn't tell them they'd have to take bodyguards. I'm leaving that up to their husbands to handle."

Pops and Uncle Hank sighed.

I turned to Charlie. "Why were you guys so late getting back? And why didn't you warn me you were skipping the dentist office job."

"I had to prioritize my schedule." She crumpled a slice of bacon into her mouth before continuing. "We set up a stakeout on the truck stop where Roseline had worked. Busted a cigarette smuggling ring."

"How does that fit in with your murder cases?" I asked.

"The manager, Sue Dodd, was the ringleader of the smuggling from what we can tell. She was selling the cigarettes to the truckers on the side. She even had fake state stickers to add to the packs. She's also the one who hired someone to kill Roseline."

"Did she give up a name?" Bones asked.

"She gave up an email address used to contact the hitman, and the location where she dropped the drugs and money. That's the majority of what I squeezed out of her before they had to sedate her."

Pops, Bones, and I looked at each other, then back at Charlie.

Uncle Hank chuckled. "Charlie shot off the woman's elbow."

"Why?" I asked.

"Dodd was ready to shoot her way out of the situation, so I opted to disable her shooting arm," Charlie answered with a shrug. "It was good thing Quille already had an ambulance down the road on standby. The whole room was peppered in blood. Her elbow exploded."

"But everyone was safe on our side?" I asked.

"Yup. Quille went home. Maggie stayed to work with ATF. And everyone else is camped out in the living room. And don't give me any crap about Gibson and Chambers being inside the house. I trust them. Chambers is a solid cop. And Gibson... Well, let's just say he doesn't know enough about *being a cop* to double cross *anyone*."

"Still can't believe Gibson slammed his car door shut," Uncle Hank said, shaking his head. "Stupid rookie move."

"Maybe you should take him under your wing for a while. Show him the ropes," Charlie said to Uncle Hank.

"No thanks. He's all yours. I've got my own rookie issues."

"So now what?" Bones asked, turning the conversation back to the case. "How do you find the hitman?"

"Quille has a team running down the email address and backtracking Dodd's life while the rest of us sleep for a few hours."

"You said drugs and money were left at the drop site. What drugs?" I asked.

"Liquid morphine," Charlie answered while grinning. "The killer made it part of the payment."

"How did Dodd get ahold of liquid morphine?" Bones asked.

"One of the truckers sells pharmaceuticals. According to Dodd, the trucker said his supplier would be happy to sell her more if she needed it. I let Maggie turn the drug side of the case over to the Feds. I have enough already on my plate."

"Are you sure the Remirez cartel isn't the supplier?" I asked.

"Pretty sure," Charlie said. "According to Mickey's contacts, the supply chain runs back and forth from Cuba, which is why I handed that side off to the Feds. How the hitman got the drugs was the only question I needed answered. Smart really. Why risk getting caught buying the drugs yourself if you can get your wanna-be client to do it for you."

"How'd she find the hitman?" I asked.

"Oh, that part pissed me off," Charlie said. "Dodd got the email address from Benny. I'd sure like to have a chat with him when he's back from his fishing trip. He's got some explaining to do."

"Too bad Dodd's fingering him as the middleman isn't enough to lock his ass up," Uncle Hank grumbled.

"A prison sentence is the least of his worries when I catch up to him," Charlie mumbled.

"I'm impressed," Bones said, grinning behind a cup of coffee at Charlie.

"With the hitman? Or Benny?" Charlie asked.

"Neither," Bones answered. "I'm impressed with you. How you put the pieces together."

"I agree," I said. "You're a hell of a detective, Kid."

"I've been telling you that for years. About time you finally get it," Charlie said, winking at me as she stretched her arms over her head. "What about you guys? How did the gig at the dentist office go?"

"We made it work," Bones said. "But it'll be a few days before the dentist office is reopened. Not much to do until then."

"Except track down the whereabouts of Miguel and Santiago Remirez," I said, leaning back in my chair. "I still can't believe the trafficking case is linked to the cartel. It seems too big of a coincidence."

"Maybe," Charlie said, pausing to swallow her food before continuing. "But Maggie's theory of the cartel faking Sebrina's kidnapping to plant her at Aces makes a lot of sense. They were trying to stop your investigation. Tech likely alerted them you were on their trail when he was running background searches. It all fits, when you look at it from that direction."

"I agree," Bones said. "Sebrina knew if word got back to Grady that she was in danger, he'd come running. And from there, she knew she could manipulate Grady into doing just about anything."

"I didn't help the situation by having them drugged and flown to Michigan," I said.

"No," Grady said from the veranda doorway. "That didn't help." He walked over and sat next to me. He seemed calmer than he'd been in weeks. "But that's on me. I should've told you, *or Bones, or Donovan*, that something was off. That Sebrina was playing one of her games. As much as I didn't want to believe it, I knew she'd faked the kidnapping. And until I knew why, I wanted to keep her away from the family."

"So why didn't you at least warn one of us when you got to Michigan?" Bones asked.

"Kelsey and Tech were already monitoring Sebrina. I figured my best option was to go deeper undercover as Sebrina's boy toy. Play along with her game." Grady glanced over at me. "It was a mistake."

"Boy," Charlie said, chuckling. "You really know how to dig yourself a hole."

"Yeah," Grady said, shaking his head and lightly laughing. "Wasn't one of my better plans."

"You seem..." I said started to say but couldn't figure out the words.

"Resolved?" Grady said. "Like I'm done fighting?"

I looked down at the table.

"I haven't given up on fixing this mess between us, but you're right. I did have feelings for Sebrina. I still have feelings for her. I'm not going to keep lying to you or myself about that."

"And what about Wild Card?" Bones asked. "At some point, do you think maybe, you could back off just a smidge?"

Grady's shoulders and facial features tensed. "I'll try. No promises."

Chapter Forty-Five

CHARLIE
Wednesday, 6:30 a.m.

I was in the outdoor lounge, reading the files and notes from the multiple boxes that Gibson had gathered, when Nicholas came over and leaned his head on my shoulder, wrapping his arms around me.

"Morning, champ," I said, dropping the papers to the side table and pulling him onto my lap. "Why so glum this morning?"

"I'm bored," Nick whined.

"It's barely even morning. How can you possibly be bored already?" I asked while tickling him.

His squeals of laughter were enough to finish distracting me from the case as I looked down at him with a smile.

"Okay, so I'm not bored—*yet*," he said, looking up at me. "But I know I will be."

"And how is that even possible? Look at this place. There's an arcade, a pool, an ocean..."

"But you and Mom are always busy. Even Wild Card says he's too busy to play. It's no fun without you guys."

"You're telling me you haven't been having fun swimming?" I asked, cocking an eyebrow.

He smirked, leaning his head against me. "It would be more fun if you and Mom were with me."

"Your mom's here. She's staying here while I do all the running around."

"She's only sort-of here. Like she gets when she's working. She's not really here."

"We should fix that," Kelsey said from a few feet away. Sara was standing next to her, holding her hand. Kelsey unhooked her shoulder holster, handing it to Wild Card who stood behind her. "Come on, Aunt Charlie," Kelsey said to me before grabbing Sara and making a run for the pool. "*The kids want us to go swimming!*"

I cradled Nick close to my body as I jogged after Kelsey. We were both laughing as I struggled to carry his weight. He was a lot heavier than he used to be.

"We're still in our pajamas, Aunt Kelsey!" Sara yelled.

"Too bad!" Kelsey jumped into the pool with Sara.

I followed right after them with Nick, deciding at the last moment to cross my legs under me for a bigger splash. When I surfaced, a wave of water smacked me in the face as Wild Card cannonballed. Bridget and both dogs were next to jump into the pool. By then, a water war had ensued, including so much dunking that I had to swim underwater to escape everyone for a reprieve. I stood in the shallow end, watching the kids and Kelsey play. It was her. The *old* her. The one who morphed from cop into super-fun-mom without warning. For the first time in a long time, I knew Kelsey was going to be okay.

Turning toward the ladder, I spotted Grady standing on the veranda, watching everyone. Grady's expression was sad as he walked inside. I didn't have to look to know what he saw. I could hear it. Laughter. And Wild Card was part of that equation.

"Oh, man," Anne said, handing me a towel when I climbed out. "You really did get your ass kicked." She was studying the bruises on my face.

"Damn. I didn't think about the chlorinated water washing off the makeup. I need to shower and get ready for work, anyway."

"Aren't you going to bed?" Anne asked. "You've been up all night."

"I took a nap at the club last night. I'm good for a few hours. I'm more of a catnap person when I'm working a case."

"You're leaving?" Nicholas pouted from the edge of the pool.

"Sorry, champ," I said, walking over to squat. "I'll do what I can to wrap this case up, though. Promise."

Kelsey swam over and pulled herself out of the pool, but stayed sitting on the edge with her legs in the water. "How about we make a deal?" she asked Nick, but glanced over at me. "I'll stay and hang out with you this morning, if you don't give me crap about working this afternoon. Then Charlie will do the same tomorrow. Deal?"

Nick glanced at her, then at me, waiting to hear my answer first.

"Agreed," I said holding out my hand between us with my palm facing down.

Kelsey laid her hand on mine.

Nicholas looked at our hands and slapped his on top. "Deal."

"Now that that's settled," Kelsey said. "You and Sara better go get ready."

"Ready for what?" Nicholas asked.

"Well, the beach, of course," Kelsey said. "You didn't think we'd come to Florida and not spend at least one morning at the beach, did you?"

"Really?" Nicholas asked.

"Really." She reached over and tousled his hair. "Jackson and Tyler found a secure beach for us. And there's enough bodyguards tagging along that I can focus on beating you in a sandcastle building contest."

Nicholas scrambled up the side of the pool and started yelling for Sara. "Hurry, Sara. Before Mom changes her mind! We're going to the beach!"

After the kids ran toward the house, followed by two sopping wet dogs, I looked at Kelsey. "What's come over you? Two days ago, you were terrified of bringing Nick to Florida. But now you're taking him to the beach?"

"I can't stay frozen anymore, waiting for the moment my world will shatter again. It's not fair to Nick. And it's not what I want my future to look like. I need to live. Really live."

I nodded, rubbing her shoulder. "So... A trip to the beach, then?"

"A trip to the beach," Kelsey said, nodding.

"Sounds about perfect," Wild Card said, pulling himself out of the pool. "Only one problem."

Kelsey looked over at him, smirking. "What's that?"

"I'm going to kick your ass at making sandcastles," he said before shoving her off the concrete and back into the water. Wild Card jumped up and ran toward the house, laughing.

~*~*~

On my way out the door, I woke Chambers and Gibson. Gibson so he could follow me to the precinct. Chambers so he could head out to the prison to visit Terrance Haines. Bones had already loaded the boxes of files into Wild Card's rental for me while I dried off Beast. Between Hattie and Aunt Suzanne, I wasn't sure which one was madder that the dogs and the kids had left puddles of water throughout the house.

As I walked toward the SUV with Beast at my side, Bones opened the driver's door for me. "You sure you don't want me to ride along? Mr. Tricky is still out there somewhere."

"I'm sure. Beast will be with me. Besides, I'll be surrounded by cops most of the day."

"What about Spence?" Bones asked as he opened the back door for Beast to do his leap into the seat.

"He's following me to the station. Then he's off to do his PI thing."

"All right. But call me if you leave the station. We should only be at the beach until around noon. Then both Wild Card and I will be free."

"I'll call if I need you," I said as I climbed into the SUV.

Beast leaned forward with one paw on the center console, panting next to my ear. I raised a hand and shoved him gently backward by the snout. He whined, but then hopped over to the open window, sticking his head out. I pulled out of the driveway, turning left onto the street. Spence pulled out behind me.

Arriving at the precinct, I took the last parking spot on the street side. Spence stopped in the middle of traffic, ignoring the blasting of car horns as he waited for me to jog to the precinct doors. I waved a hand over my shoulder as Beast and I entered.

The desk officer buzzed us through the next set of doors. "Quille wanted me to tell you to check in with him."

"He's here already?" I hadn't expected him to be in the office until at least noon after the late night we'd had.

"He's here. But you might wish he wasn't. He's cranky."

I sighed as Beast and I made our way through the main room to the stairs. Beast paused at the bottom, swinging his head over to look at me. "I'm too tired to race up the stairs today."

"I will," Gibson said, walking over and looking down at Beast. "One," Gibson said, leaning over and positioning himself in a running stance. "Two."

Beast barked.

"Three!"

And they were off. Beast was ahead by three steps before they even reached the corner landing. I felt exhausted just watching them. I walked over and pushed the button for the elevator.

Detective Ford laughed behind me. "This was for Quille," he said, handing me a cup of coffee. "But I think you need it more."

"Have you been upstairs yet?" I asked as we stepped inside the elevator.

"Yeah. Quille gave me the two-minute run down on your tobacco bust last night. Nice job, by the way. Then Quille started barking orders to everyone about getting their paperwork done. He's on a rampage. Everyone's hiding from him."

I grinned as I drank my coffee.

"What? Did you piss him off again?"

I shook my head. "No. But Quille pretends sometimes to be mad so everyone avoids him. Without interruptions he can catch up on his own paperwork. He's going away with Miranda this weekend."

"He's leaving while your double-homicide is still open?" Ford asked as we stepped off the elevator.

Gibson and Beast were waiting for me in the hallway. I patted Beast's head. "I sort-of promised Quille I'd try to solve the case before this weekend. You got time to help?"

"I'll make time. I owe you for helping me with that drive by shooting."

"Splendid. Let's set up in the conference room." I turned to Gibson. "After Gibson unloads the boxes from my car."

Gibson placed fisted hands on his hips. "You could've told me that *before* I ran up the stairs."

I looked at him, tilting my head to the side and narrowing my eyes.

"Uh, never mind." Gibson grabbed the keys out of my hand. "I'd be happy to get the boxes."

Ford laughed as we walked into the main room. "Another week, and you just might have him trained."

"Hardly. He's moved up from lost cause status to barely acceptable."

I stopped at Quille's door, sticking my head inside. "You wanted to see me?"

"At any point in your career do you think I'll manage to get your timesheets without asking for them?"

"Doubt it. Anything else?"

"Whether you need the money or not, HR still requires me to play the payroll game. You've got five minutes to send me your hours."

"Whatever." I turned to walk away.

"Hey!" Quille barked. "Are you drinking my coffee?"

I turned back to grin and take a sip before answering. "Ford thought I needed it more than you."

"One of these days..." he grumbled as I walked away.

At my desk, I leaned over my keyboard long enough to enter my electronic timesheet before I started sorting the stacks of files that had accumulated. Anything related to the double homicide went in boxes to be moved to the conference room. Everything else was either left sitting on top of my desk or doled out to someone else to work. I wasn't ranked any higher than the other detectives, but we functioned on a *I helped you, so now you help me* program. And almost everyone owed me at least one favor.

Two hours into our research, Chambers walked through the conference room doors. I introduced him to Ford as well as two of the homicide researchers, Natalie and Abe.

"Weren't you driving to the prison to interview Terrance Haines?" I asked Chambers as I looked up at the clock.

"Mission complete," Chambers said as he pulled out a chair. "The blond woman at the mansion heard me whining about being too tired to drive that many hours." Chambers smiled a full set of teeth. "She rented me a chopper! Can you believe that?"

"I've never been in a helicopter," Gibson said, sounding jealous.

Ford looked at me and shook his head. Only a handful of the cops knew I was loaded. Katie would've paid for the chopper out of either my account or Kelsey's.

I refrained from asking about the helicopter and inquired about the interview instead. "Did Terrance Haines have anything enlightening to say?"

"Other than confirming that he didn't take a flashlight when he jogged the park that night, nothing new. Said he didn't think of it because the park is so well lit, which was the reason Terri felt safe jogging there at night. And for what it's worth, I believe him. I think he's innocent. Which means if that post light near the bench was really out of order—"

"Already confirmed," Gibson said, holding up a piece of paper. "Recreation department serviced the light two days *after* the murder."

I looked back at Chambers. "Then Terrance couldn't have seen Terri lying in the grass until the next morning." I wondered if Terrance could've saved her if he'd taken a flashlight with him to search. Probably not, based on the autopsy report. "Did you record the conversation with Terrance?" I asked Chambers.

"Yeah. I logged it as evidence already."

I looked down the table. "Where are we at on the death certificates?" I asked Natalie and Abe.

Natalie glanced up from her computer. "We found four possible matches to the DOA the nurse described. I sent the names to the ME's office, requesting they pull the records."

"Good. Gibson, what about other cases involving morphine?"

"Well, out of the fifty-two cases, forty-six are actually cases where a patient, while *high on morphine*, escaped either a hospital or their caregiver. In all forty-six, the police assisted finding and returning them. One guy was so stoned, he drove his car across the beach and straight into the ocean. Another woman went shopping at the mall—nude." Gibson laughed, tossing some files into a box. When he realized the room was quiet, he looked around. "Well, I thought it was funny."

"You better tell Charlie about the other six cases," Abe said. "She not a fan of jokes when she's working a case."

Gibson straightened in his chair and grabbed his notepad. "Right. Well, of the remaining six cases, one was a kid stealing a morphine drip from the hospital, but he didn't get very far. The police got him to admit he was stealing it for his grandfather who was bedridden. Two other cases were hospital workers caught injecting themselves. A fourth was a girl who'd swiped a vial of morphine from a hospice doctor. She was found by police an hour later. Number five was... Let's see here..." Gibson dug through the stack of files. "Ah, yes, number five stole morphine out of a paramedic's hand, but the medic was ex-army and dropped the kid on his ass. By the way, the patient who needed the morphine also lived. And the sixth case was a morphine overdose in an assisted living center."

"*Yoo-hoo...*" Tasha said, barreling through the door and dropping a box at my feet. "Presents. I pulled the four victim files that Natalie requested. Two were marked heart failure, but one of the two had the bruise on the back of his neck. Another one died of an arterial embolism—a blood clot—but he also had the neck bruise. The fourth died of a heart attack, but he had late-stage cancer so realistically his organs were shutting down." Tasha pulled out a chair and sat. "Of the four, we still had two of their blood samples in storage, so I ran a preliminary screening on them. One was clean, though he didn't have the bruise so not surprising. The other was the arterial embolism." She looked at me expectantly, almost giddy.

"And?" I asked, waving my hand for her to get to the point.

"The blood tested positive for coagulant medication! Can you believe that? Heparin to be precise." She bounced in her chair with excitement.

"I don't have a medical license, Tasha. You'll have to dumb it down for me."

"Oh, sorry. Someone with his medical record would never have been prescribed Heparin. In fact, he was on a prescription for blood thinners, so Heparin is a major no-no."

I pulled the files out and found the two with the neck bruises. I handed one to Natalie and the other to Gibson. "Get me everything you can on these victims. I want to know where they worked, their family background, their financial status, everything. And I want it yesterday."

Natalie and Gibson took off out of the conference room with their assigned files.

"Why Heparin?" Chambers asked Tasha. "The morphine was odd enough, but Heparin?"

"I don't know, but I also have these files," Tasha said, handing me three more files that she'd been holding. "Huey and I reviewed the ME office's suspicious death files, looking for the similar bruising. One man died of an Oxi overdose but had no history of drug use. The other two died from hyperglycemia."

"That's low blood sugar, right?" Chambers asked.

"Right. But neither patient was diabetic and insulin levels were through the roof."

"Abe," I said. "Can you search police cases for Heparin and Insulin? See if anything pops?"

Abe didn't answer but click-clacked on his keyboard. "In the last twenty-four months, we've had four cases involving Heparin and twelve relating to insulin. Want me to go back further than that?"

"Take a closer look at the Heparin cases," Quille said from the doorway. "In either case, did we log the Heparin into evidence?"

"How long have you been standing there?" I asked Quille.

"I followed Tasha in," Quille answered, frowning over at me. "I'm not liking that you and I seem to be thinking the same thing about this case."

Ford looked between us, then over at Abe.

Abe studied his screen as he spoke. "We logged the Heparin into evidence for two of the four cases."

Chambers stood. "All right, clue us in. What are you two thinking?"

I looked at Quille but he was just as reluctant to speak as I was. I looked over at Abe. "Can you finish the background check Gibson's running? I need him for another assignment."

"Sure," Abe said, standing and closing his laptop. "Just give me a minute to grab the evidence logs off the printer. I have a feeling you'll be needing them."

Abe was smart, too smart. But he was also good at keeping his mouth shut, so I wasn't worried that he'd figured it out. He returned a few minutes later with six pages of evidence log numbers, in numeric order by box number. Next to each number was the type of drug and the quantity of the drug that was logged.

When Gibson returned, Quille closed the door. "Let me make this crystal clear, what we are about to discuss is only a *theory*." He scowled around the room. "Right now, we have no evidence to support our theory, therefore, we are not required to report our findings to internal affairs—*yet*."

"Internal affairs," Ford said as his eyebrows skyrocketed upward. "You think—"

"A cop?" Gibson said, then looked over his shoulder at the door and lowered his voice. "You think the killer we're hunting could be a cop?"

I looked at each of them, before speaking. "Where is the one place you can find both hospital grade drugs and street drugs?"

Chambers sighed, nodding to the list of evidence logs. "A police evidence vault. Shit." He rubbed a hand over his jaw, thinking. "But wait, the truck stop manager confessed to buying the morphine for the hitman. Weren't we assuming that was how he was getting the drugs for all the victims?"

"Maybe I would've assumed that," I said glancing at Quille. "If the entire precinct hadn't been drug tested three months ago."

All eyes turned to Quille.

Quille scowled at me. "You're too damn observant, Kid." He pulled out a chair and threw himself into it. "This doesn't leave this room, but a few months back, a small amount of Oxi went missing from evidence. We assumed it was taken for recreational purposes. We ran a drug screening, but other than two cops who tested positive for marijuana, we never found anything linking back to the Oxi. We shuffled the staff assigned to the evidence vault, but that's about all we could do."

My hands fisted and thumped the table. "Son-of-a—" I glared over at Quille. "If Internal Affairs spent less energy investigating people *like me*, maybe, *just maybe*, they'd have solved the case—*before two more people died!*"

Ford chuckled. "I think a cop turned hitman is a little out of I.A.'s wheelhouse. Hell, I'm not sure I can get behind this theory, and I've seen a lot of crazy shit."

Chambers looked to Ford. "But if this *is* a cop, he might've lost access when he was reassigned duties. That would explain why he had the truck stop manager supply the drugs for the last hit."

"But it might not have been one of the cops assigned to evidence," Quille said. "The Oxi could've been lifted at any point when the evidence was signed out. Or someone could've grabbed it while they were pulling another box. We never found proof against anyone."

"We need to inventory the evidence room," I said, handing the evidence logs to Quille. "Can you oversee the process while I handle something else?"

Quille looked up from the logs and back at me. "Is this something else *legal*?"

I didn't answer.

Quille's eyes narrowed.

I still didn't answer.

"My office," he said pointing toward the door.

"Wait. Just give me a minute." I stood and paced, trying to think of how much to say. It was moments like this that I hated working on a team. "There's a particular cop I need to check into. I haven't had time to run a background on him. I have a name and address, but that's all."

"And you're just *now* telling us you have a suspect?" Quille asked.

"*He's a COP!*" I said, throwing my hands up into the air. "I don't know about you, but I'm not overly enthusiastic about tarnishing his record without evidence!" I kicked one of the boxes sitting on the floor. It only moved about three feet, but the files spilled out. I crossed my arms and turned back to the group. "So far, the only thing I have on this guy is a suspicious arrest a few years back. The bust sounded legit, but the perp was a middleman drug dealer. According to the rumor mill, the dealer should've had a lot more drugs on him."

"*Name?*" Quille ordered.

I shook my head. "As soon as we run him in our database, red flags will go off. We can't take the chance."

"*Name?*" Quille said again, getting more and more pissed.

My shoulders fell as I looked down at the floor and answered. "Officer Grenway. Stuart Grenway."

"Why does that name sound familiar?" Ford asked.

Quille answered Ford as he walked toward me. "Grenway rolled his cruiser about three years back. He chose riding the desk over disability pay." Quille stood in front of me and leaned into my face. "*He had severe nerve damage in his right hand from the accident.*"

My stomach rolled. I didn't want to be right. I stepped closer to the table, reaching a hand out to balance myself. After a few deep breaths, I picked up my cellphone and called Kierson.

Kierson answered on the first ring. "I miss you."

"I'm sorry, but this is a work thing. I need your help. Or, rather, the FBI's help. And I don't have time to go through Maggie."

"What do you need?" Kierson asked. His voice had shifted from soft and sweet, to all business.

"A background on a Miami cop—without triggering a red flag in our database." I gave him the name and address I had for Grenway.

"Genie's with me now. I'm putting her on speaker."

"Hello, my favorite drinking partner. I hear the gang is in Florida in some fancy mansion. Is it as fabulous as Maggie says?"

"It's ridiculously fabulous. And if you get me the background check I need, I'll send you a plane ticket."

Genie giggled. "Kierson is scowling, so I'd wager me agreeing to the exchange would break some FBI rule, but if a ticket were to magically appear, I wouldn't turn it away."

I could hear Kierson grumbling something in a low tone.

Genie giggled again. "Give me a few minutes to do my thing, and I'll call you back with this background check."

"Thanks. I owe you one."

"You owe me like thirty, but it's all good. I'm happy to help. And if we close our case before this weekend, I'll take you up on the plane ticket."

As Genie disconnected, Abe and Natalie entered.

I focused on them. "Give me the run down."

Natalie gestured for Abe to go first.

"I've got an Allen Franklin. Age forty-eight. Happily married with two kids. He was a volunteer at a teen shelter: The Sunrise Center. Your typical do-gooder."

"My guy is the opposite of Abe's. More of an evil-doer," Natalie said. "Holland Parker. Fifty-six years old. Real estate developer. Net worth in the millions. No kids." She flipped a page on her notepad. "His first wife filed abuse charges two months into the marriage and then split. Wife number two lasted longer, about two years. The official filing in their divorce was irreconcilable differences, but despite a prenup, she received a two-million-dollar settlement. Which makes me think she had some spectacular dirt on him that he didn't want made public. And by the time of his death, Mr. Parker was six months into his third marriage." Natalie flipped another page on her notepad. "He was also investigated a few times, but nothing stuck. Mostly bribery and fraud stuff. White collar crime."

Chambers tapped a pencil on the table as he looked at me. "If our killer was responsible for both victims, then the second guy," he pointed to Natalie's notepad, "would be a prime candidate for a hired hit. Without any kids, the third wife would've raked in *millions* upon his death. But the first guy—" he pointed to the papers in Abe's hands, "was likely killed because he knew the killer. Or he knew something about the killer. Either way, that might be our best lead."

"I can head over to the shelter. Ask around about Allen Franklin," Gibson offered.

I shook my head. "Not yet. Let's wait for Genie."

As if summoned, Genie's face popped up on my phone and it started to ring. I pushed the icon for speaker. "Hey, just a second," I told Genie before looking over at Abe and Natalie and then the door. They both stepped out of the room, shoulders slumped. I fake scowled at Quille, not liking playing the bad cop role, before looking back at my phone. "Go ahead, Genie."

"Do we like this guy? I'm assuming if I'm running a background, then we don't. But I'm having these really conflicting feelings about him."

"What did you find?"

"Grenway was born in Fort Lauderdale. No dad listed on the birth certificate. Mom was a drunk, in and out of rehab. Child services stepped in a few times, but kept sending Stewy back to her when she sobered up. One night she passed out and choked to death on her own vomit. Game over for her. By then, Stewy had suffered fourteen years of alcohol-related abuse. After she died, he bounced around in foster care for three years, but eventually ran away. Six months later he appeared at a teen outreach center. The center helped him arrange independent housing and re-enroll in school."

"Sun..." I took the file from Abe and checked the name. "The Sunset Center?"

"Yup. That's the one. On paper, Stewy sounds like a troubled kid who turned his life around. He joined the police department and all seems normal until about five years ago."

"What happened five years ago?"

"I don't know. But something smells fishy. Stewy traded in his beat-up Camry for a shiny new Corolla. Nothing flashy, but that's when his lifestyle started to exceed his income. After applying all my magic, I didn't find a single loan or credit card that explains how he could afford the car, let alone the three-bedroom house or the cabin cruiser purchased since then. And Uncle Sam wasn't aware of his change in income either."

"Five years? Are you sure?"

"Positive. I'll send you the details. Why is that important?"

"Because I was under the impression he started killing people *three* years ago."

"Oh. Stewy's been bad..."

"You need to stop calling him Stewy. It's creepy."

Genie laughed while asking, "Anything else I can do?"

"Not right now, but thanks. This helped." I ended the call but continued staring at my phone.

"Five years?" Tasha said. "Huey and I looked back seven years, but only found the two cases. We can look again."

"What if..." Gibson started to say. "Never mind."

"What if *what*?" Chambers asked. "If you have a theory, let's hear it."

"What if he changed his MO after the car accident. Remember? He took a knife to the park to kill Terri Weston."

"You're on to something," I said, pointing to Gibson. "I like it. So, before the accident, he was a stabber or slasher. But when he tried to kill Terri, his damaged hand prevented him from killing in his usual manner. He had to improvise. Come up with a new method."

"And now he's improvised again, combining the stabbing with the choking," Chambers said.

"Which is closer to his preferred method," Ford grumbled, throwing his pen onto the table. "This makes me sick. How could a brother in blue be behind this?"

I ignored Ford and opened the door to the conference room. Abe and Natalie were waiting a few feet away. "We need to run a search on unsolved stab victims. But further back. At least a decade."

"We'll get started," Natalie said, moving with Abe toward their cubicles.

I turned back into the room and walked over to Quille. Grabbing the lapels on his suit jacket, I gave them a playful tug like I was straightening them. "Did I ever tell you that you're the best boss ever?"

"What do you want?"

"Can you call your judge friend and get me a warrant?"

"You don't have any evidence. It's all circumstantial."

"Come on. We both know you have mad skills getting warrants." I smirked at him. "*Please*! *Pretty-please*! I gotta bring Grenway in before the rumor mill gets wind of this and he realizes we're on to him."

"Fine!" Quille barked. "I'll get you a warrant, but SWAT goes in first. If anyone ends up shooting this guy, it's sure as hell not going to be you. Not with your I.A. file."

Knowing better than to wait for Quille to change his mind, I grabbed my handbag and keys. Beast had been napping against the wall but bounced to his feet when he heard my keys jingle.

"I'll call when the warrant is signed," Quille said, opening the door for me. "Then I'll get a team together to start inventorying the evidence vault."

Chambers stood. "Gibson and I will help Abe and Natalie run down more victims. We'll do the best we can to put the information together before you get back."

"I'd rather be on the team serving the warrant," Gibson complained.

"Learn what's important and where you're needed," Chambers told him. "Charlie needs that info so she can interrogate Grenway."

"I'll head over to the teen shelter," Ford said, standing and grabbing his suit jacket. "See if I can find anyone who can link some of the pieces."

"Maybe working on a team isn't so bad," I said as I walked out.

Chapter Forty-Six

CHARLIE
Wednesday, 11:27 a.m.

In the movies, the detectives lead the SWAT team into the house, wearing maybe a bullet proof vest, as the SWAT guys fan out around them in full body armor. In the real world, the detectives sit in their car down the block and drink coffee as the specialized team bears down on their target, charging into the home in a synchronized assault. It was fun to watch, but it would be a lot more fun to be part of the *kick the door in* team.

My phone rang and I answered it, knowing it was Crater, lead SWAT officer on the raid. "Talk to me."

"We've got your guy, but he's not going anywhere. You've got a green light to come inside. The house is clear."

I hung up and opened my car door, shutting it after Beast leapt out. I puzzled about what Crater meant as I walked down the sidewalk, then across the yard. At the front door, I motioned for Beast to stay before I stepped inside. The team was huddled together at the entrance to what was likely the living room. "What've we got?"

Crater looked over his shoulder at me. "He's a cop, right?"

"I can't discuss the case."

"Can you assure us that he deserved this at least?" he asked as he and his team stepped back to let me see into the room.

"Damn..." I said as I walked past them. At first, I wasn't sure what I was seeing was real. It was so bizarre. But my brain finally caught up with my vision, and sure enough, Stuart Grenway was duct taped to a chair in his living room, his throat slashed, an oversized red ribbon tied around his waist fashioned into a bow near where his belly button would be. The note taped to his chest simply said: Merry Christmas.

I took a step back, then to the right a few steps, centering myself in front of the body. Taking another step back, I bumped into something. I looked over my shoulder to see a recliner. Glancing back and forth, I realized that if sitting in the recliner, the Grenway's killer could've admired his work.

"I need forensics."

"I already called in for a team," Crater said. "So? Should we be feeling bad for him? Being he was a cop an all?"

I looked up at Crater and his team. "If you ask me, looks like he died too quickly. I would've preferred a few broken fingers or cigarette burns. Even just a *little bit* of torture. Instead, the killer severed his artery. Grenway would've bled out within a minute or two."

"Man," one of the guys I didn't recognize said. "Remind me never to piss you off, lady."

"Watch your tongue, Tailor. Until you know Detective Harrison better, I suggest you shut it," Crater said to the guy before turning back to me. "You good here?"

I glanced around the room, then out the front picture window. Beast was lying in the grass in the front yard, rolling around on his back. I pulled my gun, keeping it held downward. "Yeah. Sure thing. Thanks for the help."

"Uh, we cleared the house," Randol, Crater's second in command, said. "There ain't anybody in here."

"I'm just being careful. I've had a few close calls this week. I'm pretty sure the guy who did this," I nodded toward Grenway's body, "is the same guy who tried to kidnap me."

"Tried to kidnap you?" Crater said, his voice turning cold.

I didn't respond.

"Fan out," Crater ordered his men. "Set up a full perimeter. Two guys inside, the rest outside." The men disappeared in different directions as Crater walked over to me. "Holster your weapon. We've got your back while you work the scene."

"Thanks," I said, nesting my gun back into the holster. "You sure you don't have to be somewhere, though?"

"We get maybe three calls a week. Unless another call comes in, we've got the time. No worries." He nudged my shoulder to get me to look up. "You need more protection after this?"

"No. I've got a security team, but I left them at home. I forgot to call someone when I left the precinct."

"Call them now. Have them meet you over here."

"I will." I studied the look on Grenway's face. He looked almost peaceful for a deranged serial killer.

"Now, Kid. Call your security team."

"Okay. Okay. Geesh." I pulled my phone from my bag and called Bones.

"Yo," Bones answered.

"I've been ordered to call my bodyguards."

Bones chuckled. "Quille?"

"No. Crater." I glanced over my shoulder at Crater. "He's much scarier than Quille. He's team lead for SWAT."

"I'm guessing you left the police station again without backup. Give me your location," Bones said as he continued to chuckle.

I gave him the address and was about to hang up when Crater took my phone from me. "Hey, dumbass, this is Crater," he said into my phone. "What kind of bodyguard lets his clients ditch them?" Crater was quiet for a few minutes as he listened to Bones' reply, then Crater disconnected.

I laughed at the expression on Crater's face. "You're the biggest badass I know in Miami," I said, patting his shoulder. "But Bones, well, he's the biggest badass I've ever met. You might want to make yourself scarce when he gets here."

Crater looked a little nervous. "Is this guy big?"

"Bones is ex-military turned biker who works private contract missions. He does a full cardio, weight lifting and martial arts training every day. He's also a better shooter than me, both with handguns and sniper rifles. Did you think I hired some wanna-be to babysit me?"

"Shit," Crater said, running a hand over his buzz cut. "If he comes asking for me, my name is Fred. Crater left already."

I laughed before turning back to the scene and walking a wide circle around the body. I was careful to stay out of the path of the pool of blood. When I returned to the front, I squatted to look closer at the large red ribbon and note taped to the body.

With the ribbon and note, the staging of the body looked almost playful. Not like mad psycho, but a quirky humor. The kind of humor one gets when they've seen a lot of bloodshed. If this was Mr. Tricky, then it would make sense. After the altercation with him in the ally, and again behind the truck stop, I was pretty certain he'd had some type of military training in his past life. And the death wasn't drawn out like you'd see with someone with mental issues. It was quick. Efficient. Maybe a little too bloody for my taste, but hey, I was never in combat. But the way he left the body, tied up with a makeshift bow on him, suggested he knew I was coming after Grenway. He was playing with me. Having fun while letting me know he was three steps ahead of me. And I had to admit, Mr. Tricky was good. I doubted there would be any DNA left at the scene.

My phone rang at the same time the forensic team arrived. "Hang on a minute, Kelsey," I said before looking at the forensic team. "I need a full sweep of the house for prints. Doors, windows, the works. And I need everything searched, bagged, and tagged. This case will be reviewed by I.A. later, so be thorough."

"You got it," one of the women on the team said.

"Oh, and that recliner," I said, pointing behind me. "I think the killer sat in it. Bag it."

"You want us to bag a lazy boy?" she asked.

"Or whatever the equivalent is, yes," I said before turning my attention back to the phone. "Sorry, Kelsey. What's up?"

"Now who sounds bossy?" Kelsey said.

"Did you need something or are you bored and decided to derail my day?"

"Touchy. Ouch. I called to find out why Wild Card and Bones went running out of here so fast. You in trouble?"

"No. I've got SWAT watching my back until the boys get here. I found my serial killer. We're processing his house right now."

"Great. Case closed. So why do you sound even more stressed out than before?"

"My serial killer is dead."

"Did you shoot him?"

"No! He was dead when I got here."

"Good. Stick to that story. Should I call a lawyer?"

"I didn't kill him! He was taped to a chair and his throat was slit. I think even I.A. would know that's not my style."

"Then who killed him?"

I looked back at the note taped to Grenway's chest. "I'm pretty sure it was Mr. Tricky."

Kelsey was silent on the other end.

I glanced at my phone, but we were still connected. "Hello? Nothing to say?"

"I'm calling Bones. Do not ditch your security team again!"

She hung up as I heard Beast bark. I stood to look out the window. Wild Card leaned over to pet Beast, as Bones pulled his phone from his back pocket, moving it to his ear. I watched him smile, then frown, then his head snapped my way. He pointed at me, then at the ground in front of him. I shook my head no. He snapped his fingers, then pointed again. I shook my head no again. Wild Card watched Bones, then me, and back and forth. He was smiling ear to ear.

"Detective?" one of the forensic techs said. "We found something."

I smirked and waved at Bones before following the tech down the hall. In the bedroom, the tech waved a hand toward a walk-in closet. Inside the closet, multiple guns were mounted to the wall. A small desk sat along the back wall with a laptop and several files. Above the desk were what looked like hundreds of pictures taped to the wall. They were grouped in sets of four or five each, showing several different shots of individuals. I spotted Roseline's picture and studied the grouping. In one, she was at work, behind the checkout counter. In another, she was entering our apartment building. In yet another, she was getting into her car. He'd stalked her. Ran recon on her for at least a few days.

I took a step back, looking at the wall again. "There must be at least fifty victims," I said to myself.

"Detective? Sorry, I couldn't hear what you said," the tech said, standing by the closet door.

"Photograph everything in here before bagging it. And call for extra help. It's gonna be a long day."

"Will do," the tech said, pulling the camera strap off her shoulder to start taking pictures.

I walked down the hall and out the door, calling Quille as I stepped outside.

"I'm still in the evidence room. Do you have Grenway at the station?"

"Not exactly."

"He got away?"

"Not exactly," I said glancing back at the house.

"I'm not in the mood, Kid. Spit it out."

"Grenway's dead. But he's got a shitload of evidence in the house that'll prove he's our hitman. I think it's time to ask Internal Affairs to take over the investigation. Let them sort this shit out."

"Did you shoot Grenway?" Quille asked with a big sigh.

"Why does everyone keep asking if I killed him?"

Wild Card laughed, standing in front of me. Bones was next to him and rolled his eyes.

"Well? Did you?" Quille asked.

"No. His throat was slit."

"Good," Quille said, sighing again. "We all know that's not your style."

"I'm not even going to ask," I muttered, shaking my head. "I.A.?"

"Yeah, I'm good with that. I'll give them a call. They can finish the damn inventory, too. I'm tired of digging through the boxes. We found enough to prove we've had evidence stolen in several cases."

"Send them to the scene and I'll get them started. I'll also give Ford and Chambers a call and tell them to start typing what they have so far and box up the rest."

"You did it," Quille said.

"Did what?"

"Solved the case before the weekend. Miranda's not going to believe this."

"If I don't see you later, enjoy your cruise. I think I might take a few days off myself." I disconnected and tucked the phone into my pocket.

"Which one of these Rambo-wannabees is Crater?" Bones asked, nodding to the SWAT team.

"A-Team," I hollered over to the SWAT team. Everyone except Crater looked over. "I'm all set. Thanks for the extra protection."

"Anytime, Kid," Roland yelled as he slapped Crater on the back and led the team toward their truck.

Crater glanced over at me and dipped his head. "See ya."

"Bye, *Fred*."

Several of the guys chuckled. Bones' head snapped their way, zeroing in on Crater.

Wild Card grabbed Bones' arm before he could move. "We're on duty, remember? Besides, SWAT hung around and did our job for us until we got here. Crater had a right to call us out on letting Kid run the show."

Bones' head snapped my way. "From now on, wherever you go, we go. Got it?"

"No problem. I need to brief I.A. on this case before returning to the precinct to pack some files and write a few half-assed reports. Then, I plan on drinking daiquiris by the pool."

"Nice," Wild Card said, bumping fists with me. "How long will the reports take?"

I called Ford, then Chambers. I told Chambers to have Gibson start writing up the reports. If all went the way I planned, the reports would be ready for me to sign by the time I got there.

CHAPTER FORTY-SEVEN

KELSEY
Wednesday, 4:30 p.m.

"Nice to see you're finally relaxing," I said to Charlie as I sat on the chaise lounge beside her. "Heard you turned the case over to Internal Affairs. What was that about?"

Charlie shrugged as she took a drink of her daiquiri. "Figured between the FBI and ATF, they'd steal the case, anyway. Might as well make them do the rest of the research and paperwork. Besides," she said, glancing over to where Nicholas, Sara and Wild Card were playing a card game, "I want to spend some time with the kids while you guys are here. I feel like I've barely slept, let alone chatted with my favorite guy."

"He'll like that. And it will keep him occupied while I work. It was nice taking the day off, but I also have a case to solve."

"When all this is over, think you guys will come back to visit? Miami, I mean?"

I looked around at everyone. Grady and Bones were grilling food. Pops was barking over their shoulders that they were doing it wrong. Aunt Suzanne and Hattie had finally formed a friendship and were setting side dishes on a patio table as they laughed. Reggie was giving Maggie, Haley, and Bridget facials. Jackson, Ryan, Tech and Alex were drinking beer in the tiki lounge. Others were around, here and there, scattered inside and out. Everyone seemed happy, though. Relaxed. Like they were really on vacation.

"Yeah," I said, nodding. "We'll come back. Maybe not until next year, but I think we should do this more often. I didn't realize how much I missed it. Hell, maybe I should have Alex contact the management company and book a month rental now. Then it'll be on the calendar."

"Or..." Charlie said. "We could buy it."

I looked at her but she just slurped her margarita through a straw as she smirked.

"You're not serious?" I asked, raising an eyebrow.

"Why not? We're rich."

"You'd move into the mansion?"

"Hell, no. I couldn't live in a place this big by myself. I'd never sleep. There's a million places someone could hide and pounce as soon as I let my guard down."

"Then what? Buy it and let it sit vacant most of the year?"

"A place like this—" Charlie said, waving her hand at the grounds and mansion. "Hell, we'll have to hire someone just to sign the keys in and out. Aces guards alone would be begging for jobs in Miami so they could stay here. And we've got employees all over the country we could reward by letting them stay for a week. Then we can also write off the expenses."

I looked around again. I really did like it here. It was like having our own private resort. "Maybe. I'll think about it."

Charlie slurped the last of her drink loudly through the straw before standing. "Better think fast. I put in an outrageous offer. We close on the sale Friday." She hurried away to the bar, giggling.

"Charlie!" I yelled, laughing and shaking my head at her. She was right, though. We could afford it.

"You look happy," Hattie said from beside me, handing me a cocktail. "Mind if I join you?"

"I'd be honored," I said, taking the glass. "I see you and Aunt Suzanne are getting on better. What changed?"

"She took me with her to a wedding this afternoon. It was so much fun. I love a good wedding."

"Better you than me." I took a drink of my mojito.

"How long do you think we'll be in Miami?"

"I'm not sure. Charlie wrapped up her case so we can focus on the Remirez cartel and this dentist office case. I'll be glad when I have it sorted."

"In a hurry to leave?"

"Not at all. I've been having fun. It's been great."

"But?" Hattie asked, looking at me with that mother-knows-best look.

"But... I don't know. I just feel like a storm's brewing. Like the feeling you get before a hurricane moves in, only this doesn't have anything to do with the weather."

"Are you sure it's not just the tension between Grady and Wild Card?" Hattie said.

I glanced at Wild Card who was laughing as he slapped a card down on the table. The kids booed, tossing their cards down. I glanced toward the house, and caught Grady watching me. He glanced away, grabbing a plate to load some of the grilled burgers and hot dogs onto. "Nope. It's not them. But I'm glad to see them staying away from each other right now."

"It won't last, Sunshine. Sooner or later, you'll have to choose."

"But not today," I said, grinning over at her. "How's the construction coming on the new cabin? I haven't heard you talk about it in a while."

"Well, funny you should ask," Hattie said, wringing her hands together. "Seems the contractors quit. That was the third construction company I've hired. They all seem to get spooked a day or two into the job and pack up and leave. Pops keeps telling me not to worry, but for the life of me, I can't figure it out."

"Between us, I don't even want the cabin. I'm not sure I ever did. Doesn't feel right. I can't have a place for Grady and me across the road from Wild Card's home. It just feels wrong. Especially now that I know how he feels about me. Besides, when I'm in Texas I'm perfectly happy bunking down at one of the three ranches."

"Then, you don't want me to hire another company?"

"No. I already had Lisa pay Grady out of my account for the money he gave you. As far as I'm concerned, the land can remain untouched. Maybe someday when Nick is older, he'll build a house for himself there."

"That would be nice," Hattie said, smiling as she imagined it.

"But as I said, all that is between us. As for the instigator who caused the problem..." I stood and walked over to Wild Card, waiting for him to look up at me.

"Did you want to play?" he asked, holding up the deck of cards.

"No, thanks. I'd rather know why you think you have the *right* to interfere in my life and scare off the contractors for the cabin build! Why you think it's okay to stress Hattie out about contractors walking off the job."

He jumped up and stepped backward as I walked toward him. Once upon a time my acting skills were horrendous, but both Charlie and Haley had been practicing with me. As far as Wild Card knew, I was steaming mad. He continued to walk backward, as I continued to advance.

"So, you're pissed I take it?" he asked with a slight smirk. "How pissed?"

"How pissed would you be?" I said, fisting my hands to my hips.

"Well... Since you're already mad. Maybe I should confess something else..."

I had no idea what he was about to confess, but I was pretty sure I wasn't going to like it based on his nervous expression.

"Oh, no," Charlie said, laughing. "You're not going to tell her now, are you?"

I glanced over at Charlie. She was watching Wild Card but she had a hand over her mouth, muffling her laughter.

"She's already pissed!" Wild Card said to Charlie while waving a hand at me.

"*Spit it out*! Confess what?" I ordered.

"We're still married!" Wild Card said, taking another leap backward.

A collective inhale could be heard around me. As for me, I stood staring at Wild Card, trying to process what he'd said. Married? What? I signed the papers... I left them... Shit. I left them for him to file. I never checked to make sure he did. Why didn't I check?

I looked back at Charlie. She stood there grinning at me, unashamed and not hiding it.

"How long have you known?"

"No, no, no." She shook her head at me. "You're not putting this on me. I only found out a couple days ago. With everything going on, I couldn't even tell you what day he told me. But I knew he was going to tell you, so it wasn't my place to say anything."

"We—" I pointed between us "—are family. Family are supposed to be honest with each other."

"By that same reasoning," Charlie said with a smirk, "you and Wild Card are still family, too."

I turned back to Wild Card. He was standing in a defensive stance, waiting for me to attack. I reflected on my emotions, and oddly enough, I didn't feel angry. Embarrassed, maybe. If Wild Card and I were still married, that meant Grady and I...

I turned and looked around, finding Grady standing next to Hattie by the lounge chairs. Pure rage radiated from him. I looked at Hattie and jerked my head to the side, telling her to move away from him. Pops walked over and pulled her back.

Grady's focus was on Wild Card. He didn't see me.

I stepped in front of Wild Card, facing Grady.

His eyes lowered to meet mine.

I stood there, shoulders back, head held high, and I absorbed his anger from a distance. And while doing so, I saw the rage melt into something that could only be described as heartbreak. And I knew that's what it was, because I felt it myself.

The truth was, I was in love with both men. But by standing in front of Wild Card, willing to defend him, Grady had his answer. I saw it streak across his face as if it caused a physical pain. In his eyes, I'd chosen Wild Card. And for the first time, I realized it too. But that didn't mean my heart didn't break right along with Grady's. He'd been by my side for some of the worst times in my life. I owed him more than I could ever repay. Standing against him felt like a betrayal.

Grady turned, walking toward the house in a slow steady pace.

Another piece of my heart cracked.

"I should be happy," Wild Card whispered from behind me. "But he's my friend."

"You should know better than to keep secrets from me," I said before turning and rushing him, surprising him enough that as he retreated backward, he forgot about the pool. I placed both hands on his chest and gave him a rough shove just as he was inches away from the edge. Without waiting for him to surface, I grabbed the kids' hands and led them toward the mansion. "Who's hungry?"

"Me!" Carl answered, hurrying to catch up.

Thank you for reading Hunt and Prey, book eight of the Kelsey's Burden series!

Special thanks to my amazing beta readers: Kathie and Judy. I treasure the feedback you both provide.

Editing services by: Sheryl Lee at BooksGoSocial
Cover Art: *ebooklaunch.com*

Sign up for my newsletter at BooksByKaylie.com to receive new book release announcements!

Next book in series:

Heroes and Hellfire (Book 9)

A drug cartel, a hitman, and a two-sided love triangle?

Kelsey Harrison has experienced the end of her emotional rope on a few occasions. But when Charlie's life is in danger, Kelsey vows to burn down anyone and anything that stands in her way of saving Kid.

Don't miss this explosive wrap to the Remirez backstory!

Kaylie Hunter resides in lower Michigan in the same city she moved to for college. It was the perfect distance from her family–close enough to visit, far enough that it wouldn't become a daily habit.

Feeling uninspired after several semi-successful careers, in 2014 she picked up a pen and an empty notebook and began to write. And while she had dabbled with writing before, starting and stopping multiple novels, this time she was driven to find out if she had what it took. Two years later, she published her first three books in the Kelsey's Burden series and hasn't quit writing since. Her search for what was missing in her life was over.

www.BooksByKaylie.com

Printed by Amazon Italia Logistica S.r.l.
Torrazza Piemonte (TO), Italy